ChangelingPress.com

Cy-Con
Intergalactic Sci-Fi Romance
Jessica Coulter Smith

Cy-Con
Cyber-Punk Women's Action Adventure
Jessica Coulter Smith

All rights reserved.
Copyright ©2023 Jessica Coulter Smith

ISBN: 9781605218779

Publisher:
Changeling Press LLC
315 N. Centre St.
Martinsburg, WV 25404
ChangelingPress.com

Printed in the U.S.A.

Editor: Crystal Esau
Cover Artist: Bryan Keller

The individual stories in this anthology have been previously released in E-Book format.

Table of Contents

Rescued by the Cyborg (Cy-Con 1)
Jessica Coulter Smith

Magnolia Baker has spent most of her life in space with her father. Despite the rowdy crew, she's been sheltered... until pirates board them and kill everyone in sight. She hides, avoiding them at all cost and praying for a miracle. Then more men board the ship. When a sexy cyborg finds her hiding in the cargo hold, she has the strange urge to trust him.

Zelranian cyborg, Lathim, has only ever wanted one thing. A mate. When he boards a stolen ship and finds a frightened human female, his protective urges take over. He's seen human females before, but not once has his body responded to one. Until now. One look at Maggie and all he can think is -- *Mine*.

Chapter One

Lathim sat in the captain's chair and stared out into space. It had been ten years since they'd gained their freedom, such as it was. He thought about that long-ago day and knew they wouldn't have done anything differently, even if it had meant being exiled by their people. The Zelranians had been intolerant and wouldn't listen to reason, so Lathim and many others had taken a stand. It had meant an end to the Cy-Con program, which in his opinion wasn't a bad thing.

"You look deep in thought," Tenz said. "You aren't still upset about that whore screaming her head off when she saw us, are you? We knew it was bound to happen."

"I'm tired of sex bots," Lathim said. "No matter how realistic they make them look, they don't feel the same as a living female."

"If Zelran hadn't labeled us renegades and used the terms 'unstable' and 'dangerous', I'm sure we wouldn't have quite so much trouble. As it is, males want to challenge us and females fear us. If I could kick the Zelranian parliament's collective ass, I would." Tenz snorted. "Not like any of them have been in battle before anyway."

"We're closing in on the ship *Titanium* from Earth," Rorwick reported. "It's been marked as stolen by pirates, with enough goods on board we should be able to do a hefty trade and be set for a few months."

"Shields or other defenses?" Lathim asked.

"It has shields and blasters, but I've locked onto their ship and it seems their shields have been damaged by asteroids. If we hit them just right, we can take out the blasters and damage their engines,"

Rorwick said. "Hit about two meters from the docking port. It will take out the blasters and the heat should kill the engines."

Lathim maneuvered the ship for the best possibly outcome. "Let me know when you've gained control of their systems."

"Done," Rorwick said, having linked with the *Titanium* using his neural transmitters.

Lathim fired three shots at the *Titanium* and waited for the ship to stop. He continued course until they pulled alongside. Blasting open the docking port, they connected to the battered ship and prepared to board. Lathim checked his weapons and waited for his crew to meet at the port. When they were ready, he sent the command for the doors to open, and he and his fellow cyborgs boarded.

They'd expected a crowd of pirates to attack, but the ship was eerily silent. Moving through the cargo hold, they fanned out with two remaining to guard the docking port, and scoured the ship for signs of life. As they neared the crew quarters, they saw what had happened to the original crew. The damn pirates had killed every last one and hadn't bothered to even jettison them out of the airlock. The stench was horrendous as they moved through the ship and drew closer to the captain's quarters.

The captain lay dead on the floor, his chest cavity opened and his heart removed, but the shredded clothing of a female drew Lathim's attention. He knelt and picked it up, noticing it was free of blood. Whoever had worn it might very well still be alive, if she'd fought back and managed to break free. And if there was a human female on board, there might be a chance to save her. And if they saved her, maybe she'd show some gratitude in pleasurable ways. He'd of course seen human females before, but he'd never bedded one that wasn't synthetic and looked forward to the experience.

"Find the woman," Lathim said quietly. "But don't scare her."

Tenz snorted. "She'll take one look at us and scream. The only Zelranians with white hair are those of us from the Cy-Con program. We're hard to mistake for anyone else."

"Just do it," Lathim said tersely.

His men left and he scoured the chamber for any sign that the woman might still be nearby. After he cleared the captain's quarters, he turned to leave, but as he neared the door, a sound stopped him. A slight whimper had come from somewhere in the room. His gaze scanned the area again, stopping on the cabinet across from him. Moving slowly, he eased the doors open, but it was empty. He heard movement behind him and spun, just in time to see a swatch of dark hair and a flash of pink skin disappear around the doorway and down the corridor.

Lathim took off after her, not wanting to scare her, but wanting to make sure she came to no harm in the event pirates were still on board. Whoever she was, she was damn fast, because she'd vanished by the time he entered the corridor. Opening communications with his shipmates, he notified them of the female's presence and continued the search. He backtracked to the cargo hold and examined every corner, looking behind every crate.

The same small whimper drew him again. One of the crates was partially open, containing half a dozen sex bots and one very terrified human female. He lifted his hands to show her he wouldn't hurt her and approached slowly. The female cowered and tried to make herself disappear into a corner of the crate.

"I mean you no harm," Lathim said. "Do you know what I am?"

She nodded slowly.

"I'm not here to hurt you. I want to help."

Her wide eyes said she didn't believe him, and he couldn't blame her, not with the lies Zelran was spreading about his kind. He moved a little closer and watched as she trembled. He noted her lack of clothing, and cursed his body's reaction to her. It had been a long time since he'd had a living female and not a bot, and she was damned tempting with all her sweet curves.

Booted steps came up behind him.

"I see you found her," Rorwick said.

"I'm trying to convince her that she's safe with us," Lathim said.

"We found the pirates," Rorwick said. "They'd locked themselves behind a metal door on the captain's deck. There were only a handful of them, but we handled it. Damn cowards took one look at us and screamed like little girls."

Lathim continued to gaze steadily at the female. "Did you hear that? The pirates are gone and you're safe. My crew won't harm you."

"Not pirates?" she asked, her lips trembling.

"We're cyborgs," Rorwick said with pride. "And the captain is right, we'd never hurt you."

She eased out of the corner.

Lathim broke into a few crates until he found some clothing, and pulled out a long shirt. He helped her into it as she drew near enough to touch. She peered up at him and something about the blue of her eyes and her petite stature pulled at him. He'd not been around many human females and this one seemed smaller than most, barely reaching his shoulder.

"My name is Lathim and this is Rorwick," he told her. "What's your name?"

"Maggie."

Lathim glanced at Rorwick, knowing he was still able to access the *Titanium's* records through the mental link.

"Magnolia Baker," Rorwick said. "Captain Garret Baker's daughter. Her father stole this ship twelve years ago and ran it until the pirates boarded."

Maggie gaped at them. "How do you know that?"

Rorwick winked at her. "Cyborg, remember? I can access the ship's logs, among other things, just by using my mind."

"Will you board our ship with us?" Lathim asked.

"You'll return me to Earth?"

He shared a look with Rorwick before gazing back at Maggie. "We can't go to Earth, Maggie, but we can keep you safe."

"You could come to our world with us," Rorwick said. "We took over an abandoned military base, but it's really nice and we've expanded on it. We have farmland and we've traded for livestock. We even have some of your Earth chickens and get fresh eggs every day."

"Why can't I go home?" she asked.

"It's a little far and too dangerous," Lathim said. "Do you know where you are right now?"

She shook her head.

"In the Galim galaxy, near Ryel. If we were to travel to Earth from here, it would take weeks to reach there, even if we found wormholes and folded space."

Lathim reached for her, but she shied away.

"How long have you been on this ship?" Rorwick asked.

"Since I was a child," she answered.

"She doesn't appear much bigger than one now," Rorwick said softly.

Maggie frowned at him and Lathim tried to get close to her again.

"Maggie, I promise that you will be taken care of," Lathim said. "I give you my word."

Rorwick looked her over. "You know, if we took her home with us, maybe she'd mate with someone."

Lathim felt a burning in his chest at the thought of the scared female pairing off with anyone. Well, anyone but him. He didn't know a damn thing about her, but just looking at her made him want to hold her close and comfort her. He'd never really held a female before. His sexual encounters had been brief when they were with living females and not bots, and even he didn't feel like holding a bot after sex. They were toys to be used and put away.

The female looked frightened at the prospect. "I'm not a whore."

Lathim tried to ease a little closer to her. "No one said you were. A mating is… it's like your marriage on Earth. I think that's the term you use. It's a promise to be together forever. You would only be with one male and he would only be with you."

Some of the fear dimmed in her eyes. "Marriage?"

"Have you been married before?" Lathim asked, the thought of another touching her making intense feelings swell inside of him. Was that what jealousy felt like? "Was your mate on board?"

She shook her head.

He was relieved she hadn't belonged to anyone. He wanted her, but she was so damn scared he couldn't even reach out and touch her. Lathim had no experience with human females and didn't know how to calm her. He wanted her trust, wanted her to hand herself over to his care, but didn't have the first idea how to go about doing that. He'd treat her well if she agreed to mate with him.

"Everything you've heard about cyborgs is a lie," he told her. "We aren't dangerous and we would never harm you."

"You chased me," she said softly.

"I didn't want the pirates to get you. Did they harm you? I saw your clothes were shredded on the floor. Did they…" He couldn't even finish the sentence.

"No. I managed to get away and hide. I've been hiding ever since."

Her stomach rumbled from hunger and she swayed on her feet. Before she collapsed, Lathim lunged forward and wrapped an arm around her waist, hauling her tight against his body. She clung to him and he lifted her into his arms, loving the feel of her pressed against him. *Much better than sex bots.*

Booted steps could be heard drawing near and his brothers came into the cargo hold. They stared, mouths agape, at the female in his arms and Tenz came forward, inching closer and reaching a hand toward her. Lathim stepped back.

"Mine," he said with a growl to his voice. He'd never experienced such possessiveness before and it momentarily stunned him. His grip tightened on the female in his arms and he took another step back.

Tenz dropped his hand and froze. "We had to put down half a dozen pirates and you get a female?"

"Yours?" Maggie asked softly.

"You're the only female amongst a crew of ten males, going to a world with hundreds more."

Her eyes widened and she clung to him tighter, burrowing her face against him. He growled again, wanting to own her in every way possible, even though it was completely irrational. Yes, he'd craved a female for a while, one who would accept him, but he'd known this one a matter of minutes and already he was willing to fight his brothers for her. He assessed his systems and noted his higher heart rate, but everything seemed to be functioning properly. It didn't appear that he needed a medic.

"Someone find her belongings and take them to our ship," Lathim said. "I'm placing her in my quarters."

Zorlok snorted. "Of course you are."

Lathim ignored the remark. "Clear out this cargo hold and load everything onto the *Mystic7*. The sex bots alone should fetch a nice price. Until they're sold, they can entertain the crew."

Lathim walked past his brothers and carried Maggie to the safety of his ship. Her grip on him didn't ease until they reached the captain's quarters and the doors had slid shut behind them. He leaned down to gently place her on the bed and thought she looked damn sexy there. The only thing that would have made it perfect was if she were wearing one of *his* shirts.

Fucking hell. He was so screwed.

Chapter Two

Maggie's hands trembled and she clutched them together in her lap as she watched the cyborg, who seemed content to stare at her. It was almost as if he'd never seen a human before. He tore his gaze from her body and looked around the room before glancing back at her again. There was something about his gaze that left her unsettled. She'd seen lust burning in men's eyes before, but this time her body responded to the call. She should be screaming her head off, demanding to be taken back to Earth, but the truth was that something about the cyborg made her feel safe.

She'd heard of cyborgs, of course, but she'd never met one before. Her father had once warned her the only thing more dangerous than a pirate was a cyborg, but so far Lathim hadn't seemed to want to hurt her. If the hard cock straining against his pants was any indication, he had other plans for her. Maggie knew she should be terrified, but she couldn't deny that the cyborg was rather sexy with his scruffy jaw and long hair, even if it was pure white against his pale lavender skin.

The way he'd touched her in the cargo hold had been gentle and calming. There had been no malice in his touch, no promise of pain. He'd been kind and had kept the others from touching her. She knew it had more to do with the fact he wanted her for himself, but he could have easily passed her along to his crew and allowed them to do whatever they wanted with her. But he hadn't. For some reason, he wanted to claim her for himself.

His leather suit creaked as he walked closer and knelt at her feet. Slowly, he reached for her hands, clasping them gently. While there was lust blazing in his eyes, she saw kindness there too. Maybe the stories of his kind had been exaggerated? Or was he only being nice to her because he wanted her in his bed? Her cheeks warmed as she thought about them being tangled together where she sat.

Being in space most of her life, and never far from her father's watchful eye, she'd never been with a guy before. He'd been overly protective. She'd had a few stolen kisses from some of the younger crew members, but once her father found out, they always found themselves off the ship and far away from Maggie. But her father wasn't here now. Her eyes misted as she thought about the pirates killing him in front of her. Ever since her mother died, it had just been the two of them, and now she had no one.

A tear slipped down her cheek before she could stop it, and the cyborg reached out to wipe it away.

"I'm not going to hurt you," the cyborg said softly, his voice deep and rich.

"They're all dead," she whispered. "My father, his friends… all of them."

"I'm sorry," he said. "The men who killed them have been dealt with and can no longer harm anyone. I would bring your father back if I could."

There was a chime that filled the room and he stood, moving to the door. It slid open and revealed another cyborg on the other side, holding a box. He looked over Lathim's shoulder and raked her with his gaze. Focusing on his captain again, he squared his jaw.

"I'd like to claim the human," the cyborg said.

"No." Lathim took the box from him and stepped back, letting the door close in the cyborg's face. Anger flashed in his eyes when he turned to face her and Maggie hoped it wasn't directed at her. "You're going to be a lot of trouble, aren't you?"

She bit her lip and refrained from commenting. Her father had always called her trouble, said the men flocked to her. It seemed the same was true with cyborgs. She remembered Lathim's words about being the only female on a ship of ten males. Maggie wasn't stupid and knew that if they decided to take her, to force her to submit to them, she would have little choice in the matter. They were bigger, stronger, and far outnumbered her. The only hope she had of escaping such a fate was the man standing in front of her. Her life rested in his hands.

Lathim set the box down and moved a little closer.

"You have a decision to make, Maggie. I could claim you, make you mine in every way possible, without even asking if that's what you want. There are nine other cyborgs on this ship, and right now, they all would like to possess you. A female who can't run from us in terror is an anomaly."

"Why would I run from you?" she asked. Sure, he was large and maybe a little scary with those bulging muscles, but she knew a good man when she saw one. And Lathim was a good man.

"Do you not fear me? Does the fact I'm cyborg not terrify you?"

She hesitated, but realized that was telling enough. Maggie found him attractive, and something told her that she could trust him. It wasn't so much that she was afraid of him, but more afraid of what would happen if she displeased him. If she kept him happy, he'd keep her safe. But what would happen if she made him angry?

He gave a humorless laugh. "As I thought. And yet you're here, in my quarters, with nowhere else to go. I could tie you to my bed and do whatever I wanted to you."

Her thighs clenched together at the thought of the rather sexy cyborg claiming her. She wasn't scared of *him*, but the others… At least he'd said they each wanted to possess her. She hoped that meant they had no plans to pass her around and share her amongst the crew like the pirates had planned to do. She'd known that someday she would get married, but she'd always dreamed a prince would come and spirit her away. Nowhere in any of her fantasies had there been a bearded cyborg with an erection so large it both fascinated and scared her.

His gaze skimmed over her body and a smirk graced his lips. "Or perhaps that scenario doesn't bother you as much as I'd thought it would. Perhaps little Maggie would enjoy being tied to my bed."

Her cheeks warmed but she held his gaze.

He reached for her, pulling her to her feet and pressed her against his chest. "Is that what it is? You want to feel me pound into you while you scream my name?"

She gasped and her hands plastered to his chest, feeling his steady heartbeat beneath her fingers. Did he have a real heart or a mechanical one? And did she really care? There was a glint in his eyes that should have warned her, but nothing could have prepared her for the devastation of his kiss. His lips devoured her, his tongue thrusting into her mouth to bend her to his will. His beard was soft, but he was hard everywhere else.

His walked her back toward the bed that was bolted to the floor. His hands slid from her hips to her ass, giving her a gentle squeeze as he lifted her. Maggie wrapped her legs around his waist and couldn't help but moan at the feel of his hard cock pressing against her. Lathim eased her onto the bed, never breaking contact between them. Her mind screamed that he was a stranger and this was insane, but her body came alive with every touch.

His lips caressed her neck, his teeth lightly grazing her. Maggie's heart pounded out of control as he made her body respond as it never had before, made her crave things she'd never wanted until now. Yes, she'd been curious with other men, wondering what happened behind closed doors, more how it felt than the mechanics, but no one had ever made her want to surrender herself to them before. For the first time, she wondered if those romance books she'd sneaked into her quarters were true. Did the earth really move? Would she see stars? Could the cyborg make her feel complete in a way no one ever had before? Or was it all just fairytales meant to entertain?

A chime sounded again and he growled against her sensitive skin.

"Go away," he barked before continuing his seductive assault on her body.

"Captain, we have a problem," a voice called through the door.

He cursed and pulled away from her, storming over to the door. Before it opened, Maggie pulled her legs up to her chest and made sure the shirt adequately covered her. The doors slid open and another cyborg stood in the doorway, the one who had been with the captain when he'd found her. What was his name? Rorwick?

"What can't possibly wait?" Lathim asked with bite.

"There's a problem with engine two, the men are fighting over the sex bots, and there's a distress call from a life pod a few hours from here." Rorwick hesitated. "The life pod indicates there's a human inside. Could be a female."

Lathim sighed and turned to face Maggie. "I need to take care of a few things. Your belongings are in that box," he said pointing to it. "You're not a prisoner in this room, but if you venture out into the ship be warned the others may try to convince you to mate with them."

The last thing she wanted was to face off against nine cyborgs who wanted her for their own, but she didn't think she could handle being locked in this room with nothing to do either. Not after having hidden for so long from the pirates. She needed something to do. It was doubtful they'd packed any of her books. Being men, they probably hadn't thought of such a thing. She dug through the box and pulled out a blue shirt and black leggings. Her boots were in the bottom of the box. Two sports bras had been thrown in, but she didn't see a single pair of panties.

While she didn't want to wash away Lathim's touch, she did want to get rid of any remembrance of the pirates and quickly moved into the cleansing unit. It was similar to the one on her father's ship and she quickly cleaned up and got dressed. Her hair soaked her shirt and she dug through the box until she found her hairbrush and a package of hair ties. After braiding her hair, she stared at the doors that led to the hall and the rest of the ship. She hadn't paid much attention when Lathim had brought her on board, but how hard could it be to locate him?

She stared at the doors and waited for them to open, but nothing happened. He hadn't given a voice command to open them. There was a panel beside the door and she tried placing her hand over the screen.

The doors still didn't open. Maggie growled in frustration and looked around the room. Maybe if she could pop the panel door off, she could figure out which wires would open the doors. She stared at the panel again and pressed a few buttons to see what would happen.

"Maggie, what are you doing?" Lathim's voice said over an intercom.

"Trying to leave the room. The doors won't open."

A moment later, the doors slid open and his voice filled the room again. "I'm in the command center. Take a right out of the room and when the hallway splits, veer left, then taken another left."

Right. Left. Left. She nodded and set off to find Lathim, her boots clanging on the metal floor of the ship. A few cyborgs gazed at her in curiosity as she passed them, a few giving her a smile, but no one bothered her. She wondered if Lathim had warned them away, or if they were just giving her some space. The cyborg who had come to Lathim's quarters and asked to claim her was walking down the hall and she tensed a little.

His gaze slid over her and the look in his eyes clearly said he wanted her. She made to pass by him, but he stuck his arm across the hall, blocking her way. Maggie took a step back, putting some room between them. He advanced until she backed into a wall.

"Little human, I would treat you very well if you were mine," he said. "We could have a lot of fun in my quarters until we return to my world."

Maggie shook her head. "I just want to find Lathim."

His jaw hardened. "The captain shouldn't claim the first woman we find. He should give you to a crew member instead of being selfish."

"Please let me pass," Maggie said softly. "I don't want to belong to you."

His gaze hardened and he took a step back, allowing her to squeeze by him. She hastened her steps, hurrying to Lathim's side, and hopefully to safety. She didn't think the other cyborg would harm her, but he seemed quite intent to claim her for himself. There was something about him that chilled her and left her wanting to flee his presence. There wasn't laughter and kindness in his eyes, not like Lathim's. The determined cyborg seemed harder, deadlier. If she made him angry, she would fear for her life.

When Maggie burst into the command center, Lathim smiled at her, but the smile slipped from his face and he hurried to her side. His hands gripped her biceps as he stared down at her.

"What's wrong, Maggie?"

"Nothing. I'm fine."

His eyes narrowed. "Don't lie to me. My scan of your body says your heart is racing and your body is in distress. Did someone harm you on your way here?"

She shook her head. "I ran into the cyborg who came to your room wanting to claim me. He didn't want to let me pass."

"Did he threaten you?" Lathim asked softly, his voice far too calm for the tension in his body.

"No, but I don't like the way he looks at me. The others I passed were friendly, but he scares me."

Lathim turned to the cyborg in control of the ship. "Contact the *Wayfarer* and request they meet us at the Alpha9 trading post. I think it's time Haftyr worked on another ship. Request Norkov to be traded to us."

The cyborg gave him a grim look but nodded.

She didn't see or hear him open communications, but a moment later he spoke.

"It's done. They've changed course to head that way."

"Thank you, Zorlok."

Lathim took her hand and led her over to an empty seat. He sprawled in it, pulling her down onto his lap. Maggie felt a little self-conscious with the other cyborgs watching them, but she tried to ignore them and watched out the large window at the chunks of space rock floating past them.

"Sir," Zorlok said. "The life pod has not yet been retrieved. Its location is on the way to Alpha9. Should we still intercept it?"

"Yes. With some luck, there will be a female on board."

"And if it's a male?" Zorlok asked.

"Detain him until we reach Alpha9, then set him free. Make sure the crew knows not to harm him. The last thing we need is someone else spreading rumors that we're vicious killers."

Zorlok nodded.

Maggie curled against Lathim and rested her head on his shoulder. Exhaustion pulled at her, and with his arms cradling her safely against his broad chest, she let her eyes close and her body relax. It had been two or three days since she'd last slept, but her belly cramped from hunger and she couldn't sleep. Her stomach rumbled and Lathim's hands tensed on her.

"When is the last time you ate?" he asked softly.

"Before the pirates boarded us," she said.

He cursed softly and held her tighter. A few minutes later a cyborg came into the command center with a plate of food and a cup of something orange to drink. Maggie sat up and reached for them, but her hands shook. Lathim accepted them from the cyborg and urged her to eat.

"Anything else, Captain?" the cyborg asked.

"That will be all for now, Tenz. Thank you."

Maggie's hands were shaking so badly she could barely get the food into her mouth.

"Easy," Lathim crooned in her ear. "Eat slowly so you don't make yourself sick. There's plenty more. Fill your belly and then rest a while. I'll hold you and make sure no one disturbs you."

Lathim set the cup down next to his seat and picked up a slice of meat, offering it to her. Maggie bit into it and chewed before swallowing and opening her mouth for another bite. He fed her every scrap of food on the plate then helped her drink the sweet juice. When she was finished, someone carried the empty plate and cup away while she curled against Lathim again.

His hand rubbed her back as she settled against him and closed her eyes, and within minutes, she was asleep.

Chapter Three

Lathim worried about the female in his arms. She'd slept for hours as he held her in the command center, and even as he carried her to his quarters, she still didn't stir. The doors slid open and he stepped into the spacious room and gently laid her on the bed. He heard the doors shut behind him as he reached for her boots and removed them, letting them clang against the metal floor. He knew it wouldn't be long before they reached the life pod and he'd be requested in the cargo hold, but until then, he was going to rest with Maggie.

Removing his leather suit proved difficult since it fit like a second skin, but once he'd stripped bare, he crawled beneath the covers with Maggie, wishing it was her skin pressed against him and not her clothes. But after everything she'd been through, he wasn't going to remove her clothing while she slept. He didn't want her to wake up frightened and wondering if he'd done something to her in her sleep.

He connected with the ship's computer and dimmed the lights in his room. Maggie curled against him, her head resting under his chin as her body molded to his. She sighed softly in her sleep, her breath fanning across his bare chest, and Lathim's cock hardened. Closing his eyes, he accessed that part of his systems and commanded his erection to go away. It had always worked before, but with sweet Maggie in his arms, his body didn't listen.

Shifting until he was more comfortable, he stared up at the ceiling and wondered what he was going to do with the woman. He wanted her, and he was almost certain she wanted him. Part of him wanted to tear her clothes from her body, and claim her right now. The other half, the part of him that was still Zelranian, knew that she'd been through a trauma and would need time to adjust. That she would be his was inevitable, unless she chose another cyborg to mate with. Anger burned through him at the thought of another laying their hands on her. He'd found her and he meant to keep her.

Maggie mumbled something in her sleep and he ran his hand through her long hair. She settled again and draped her thigh across his, her knee brushing his balls. Lathim groaned and wondered if maybe she'd been sent to torture him. It didn't seem fair that his crew were able to use the sex bots and get relief, but he had a living female in his arms and his balls were going to turn a dark purple and fall off. All right, maybe nothing that dramatic, but he ached more than he ever had before, and he knew it was because of Maggie. He could use the bots, there was nothing stopping him, but it didn't seem right when he wanted Maggie as his mate.

Lathim had been thirty when he entered the Cy-Con program fifteen years ago, and had been with his share of females. He'd been a high-ranking officer in their military and had considered it an honor to be asked to join the new Cy-Con. If he'd known that when they were finished with him, he would be banished from his world, and all living females would cringe at his touch, he would have told them to fuck off. The fear in the females' eyes angered him, and left him searching for a sex bot instead. At least the synthetic whores didn't care that he was a cyborg.

His chest ached as he thought about all the lonely nights he'd had since Cy-Con had altered him. A metal called Byrilia, native to Zelran, had replaced most of his bones. His lungs had been removed and replaced with mechanical parts that allowed him to go longer periods without breathing. Most believed his kind never aged, but they were wrong. The changes were subtle over the last ten years, but he still got older. He would just live for a really long damn time. His blood had been infused with agents that slowed the aging process, making Zelran's cyber soldiers more cost effective.

Would the female in his arms ever be able to love someone who was part machine? He'd thought he would be content just having a living female to fuck whenever he wanted, but now that he held one in his arms, he found that he wanted more than that. She'd cried over the loss of her father and his crew. If something were to happen to Lathim, would she cry over him too? He wanted her trust, and her affection, and worried that he didn't have a right to either.

Maggie rolled away from him and curled on her side facing the wall. His arms felt empty and he stared at her back, watching her deep, even breaths that assured him she still slept. Knowing he wouldn't sleep, he got out of bed and pulled on a pair of leather pants and a soft shirt, not wanting to put on another leather suit until he had to. Giving her one last glance, he left his room and went back to the command center.

"Captain," Rorwick said in greeting. "The life pod is within our sights. No one else has responded to the distress signal. We should be able to pull it into the cargo hold shortly, and then we can determine if we've rescued a male or female."

"You know if it's a male, he could attempt to fight us."

Rorwick nodded. "And if it's a female, you could have a fight between crew members as they attempt to claim her. She can't wander the ship unattended, and it isn't likely she'll be as understanding as your Maggie. It's probable she'll scream when she sees us."

Lathim sighed. "We'll handle it when it happens. Have Querrill on standby with a sedative so she won't harm herself."

Rorwick nodded and Lathim prowled the command center. When the life pod was close enough, they activated the gravitational laser and pulled it toward the ship, opening the doors to the docking port. Lathim and Rorwick went to investigate, hoping for the best and preparing for the worst. Four cyborgs had gathered around the pod, the glass frosted over from being in space for so long. The pod's signal indicated whoever was inside was still alive, but Lathim searched for a heartbeat and was concerned it was so slow.

"Open it," Lathim commanded.

Pendrik pried open the life pod and Rorwick let out a roar that nearly rattled the ship. The small female inside was pale, almost too pale, and her red hair hung limp. Lathim stared in horror, a cry of his own trapped in his throat, as he looked in anguish at the small lifeless bundle in the female's arms. The pod had sustained the mother's life, but had not calculated correctly to save the child.

Pendrik reached into the pod and removed the lifeless baby, cradling it close to his chest. Life was precious to them, especially that of children, and it was heartbreaking they hadn't reached the pod in time to save them both. Rorwick reached inside and lifted the woman into his arms. There was a look of tenderness on his face that Lathim had never seen before, and he knew the cyborg had decided to claim her as his mate.

"Are there any other life pods in the area?" Lathim asked.

"No, Captain. This was the only one. It came from a cruise liner called *Splendora*, but there is no sign of the ship, nor any debris that suggests it was destroyed." Sanz hesitated. "We could search the area if you think there might be others. This pod was activated a week ago, so it's possible any others have been picked up by now."

"No. Head to Alpha9. Querrill, go with Rorwick and make sure the female will be all right. Please notify me of any changes. I'm going back to my quarters."

Lathim gave the baby one last look and went in search of Maggie. The child couldn't have been more than a year old, and would have been welcome on their world. Children were a gift to be cherished, regardless of their race. They'd all been assured that their cybernetic status wouldn't keep them from having children of their own someday, and as such, they had always been careful when visiting the brothels. Most required their workers to be sterilized, but some of the smaller ones didn't always follow the rules. Would Maggie welcome a child they created together? Or would it be too much to ask of her?

When he entered his quarters, she was rubbing her eyes and seemed to have just woken. He left the doors to slide shut behind him before he fell to his knees at her feet and buried his face against her belly, his arms going around her. She tensed a moment, then relaxed and ran her fingers through his hair.

"What's wrong, Lathim?" she asked.

He took a shuddering breath to get himself under control before looking up at her. "We found the life pod. It was a mother and child, but the baby didn't make it."

She looked stricken by the news. "Is the mother okay?"

"I asked our healer to look her over, but she's unconscious. I don't know if she's aware of her child's passing or not. Rorwick has taken her to his quarters. I think he means to claim her, but I worry she may be too broken. Losing her child… it could have damaged her mind."

"That's heartbreaking. I can't imagine losing a child."

"Do you want children?" Lathim asked.

Maggie's eyebrows lifted. "You can have children?"

"Yes. At least, we were told we still could. None of us have tried. When we were part of the Cy-Con program, it was too dangerous to take a mate because of the missions we were sent on. Then when we were freed, no female would look at us without being filled with terror."

Maggie reached up and ran her fingers through his hair. "Then they're missing out, because there's nothing terrifying about you. I've never met a kinder man than you, Lathim. And to answer your question, yes, I'd like to have children someday. Maybe not right away because I think we need time to get to know one another better, but one day I'd love to have a baby with you."

His heart raced. "Does this mean you accept my mate claim?"

She hesitated a moment before nodding. "As long as you're willing to take things slowly. I've never been with a man before and I've never dated. I don't want to just rush right into having sex."

He sat back on his heels. "But you're up for experimenting a little and doing everything up to that point?"

"Yes." Her cheeks turned pink. "I liked the

kissing earlier, and I loved it when you touched me. I'm just scared of moving too fast and regretting it later. I want our first time together to be perfect. Or is that asking too much?"

"Not at all. I want you, Maggie, more than I've ever wanted anyone, but I'm willing to wait as long as you don't keep me at arm's length. I want to explore your body and bring you pleasure."

The door chime sounded. "Captain, I hate to interrupt, but I have news on the female we found."

Lathim stood and opened the doors. Querrill stood outside, casting a glance at Maggie before focusing on Lathim.

"Will she live?" Lathim asked.

"She was almost dead, captain. There wasn't much I could do for her, but…"

"But what?" Lathim asked.

"I injected her with the serum that was used on us. I've been perfecting it in the event we ever found mates. I also gave her some vitamins and a solution that would strengthen her heart. I think she'll pull through. Physically anyway. I have no idea what her mental state will be when she wakes." Querrill hesitated. "Rorwick has laid claim to her and said he would kill any male who tried to take her away."

"I expected as much. Leave her under his care, but check on her frequently. If she's too damaged by the loss of her child, we'll have to reassess and determine what's to be done with her."

He felt Maggie's hands slide around his waist and she pressed her cheek against his back. It was comforting and he placed his hand over hers. Envy crossed Querrill's features for a moment and then it was gone. He knew the entire crew wanted mates, and he couldn't blame them. It's what he had wanted the past ten years, and now he had Maggie, and it seemed Rorwick had his mystery female.

"Was anyone able to pull more data from the pod and figure out who the female is?" Lathim asked.

"Her name is Jillian Cross. She was a passenger on the *Splendora*, but that's as much as we know right now. Her body was weakened, almost as if it had been ravaged by a virus, but I can't find anything in her system. If she was sick, it's run its course."

"And the child?" Lathim asked.

"The baby has been dead for more than several days. I believe it was either dead or dying when she took it into the life pod with her. I did not do a thorough scan of it, but if you'd like for me to check for signs of a virus I will."

Maggie came around to his side. "Maybe if she knew her child was dying, she will be able to handle the news well. Are you certain there wasn't another pod, maybe one with her husband? If she has a baby, the child obviously had a father."

Lathim frowned. If there was a male out there with a claim already on Jillian, Rorwick wasn't going to take it well. What Maggie said made sense, though.

"See if you can locate another life pod, and failing that, see if you can get a passenger list for the *Splendora* and find out if Jillian was sharing a room with anyone. The *Splendora* is a Star Crossed Lines ship, so hack their systems if you have to." Lathim sighed. "Let's hope there isn't a mate out there looking for her. I'm not sure what Rorwick would do if he found out there's competition for Jillian. As for the baby, there's nothing we can do for it now. Wrap the body and preserve it to be buried on our world."

Querrill nodded. "Enjoy the rest of your night, Captain. I'll ask the crew to leave you alone until your shift tomorrow, unless an emergency pops up."

"Thank you, Querrill."

The doors slid shut and Maggie moved to stand in front of him. "Why don't you take a shower, and then lie down? You look tired."

Exhaustion settled across him like a blanket weighing him down and he nodded his agreement. Moving into the bathroom, he undressed and stepped into the cleansing unit. Lathim leaned his head against the wall and closed his eyes a moment. His cock was hard as steel just from being near Maggie, no matter how exhausted he was. He doubted there would be any mating tonight, so he slicked his hand with soap and stroked his length.

With his eyes closed, he pictured Maggie spread across his bed, her legs open in invitation. His hand moved faster as he thought about entering her, the way her pussy would grip him tight. His hips flexed as he thought about pounding into her and then he bit back a cry as cum erupted over his hand. He rinsed off and stayed in the unit until the water shut off, then he dried and hesitated only a moment before walking back into the room where Maggie waited. If she'd never been with a male before, it stood to reason she probably hadn't seen a naked one.

She was curled on her side in the bed, her eyes wide as he approached. Lathim lifted the covers and slid into bed, drawing the blanket across both of them. Maggie slowly reached for him, her hand sliding across his chest, and then her body pressed against his side. He wrapped an arm around her to hold her close. Feeling her heart beat against him was enough to make his body relax. Lathim dimmed the lights in the room until they were plunged into darkness and then he closed his eyes.

"Lathim?" she said softly.

"Hmm?"

"Will we always live on this ship?"

He smiled in the darkness. "No, after we stop at Alpha9, we'll head home. My crew will want to remain on board, except perhaps Rorwick, but another captain will be assigned for now."

"What's your world like?" she asked.

"Vibrant plant life, two suns, and three moons. Xpashta is beautiful and the weather stays nice year-round. There's never snow or ice, and it never gets too hot to enjoy time outside." His arm tightened around her. "The water on my world is crystal blue and safe for swimming. Our home is an old military base. Most of my fellow cyborgs live in small quarters I believe you would call apartments, but I have a small house there."

"What's it look like from space?" she asked.

"Pink, purple, and teal swirls. It's breathtaking."

"Will it take us long to get there?"

"No. We'll fold space once we're safely away from Alpha9 and it won't take long at all to reach my world. Expect lots of staring when we arrive. Jillian and you will be the only living females there."

"Living females?" she asked.

He felt his cheeks warm and was grateful it was dark. "We have some sex bots that we keep on our world. It's not easy for the males to get to a nearby brothel when they have needs, so it made sense to keep some around. Once more of my people are settled with mates and families, I would imagine the sex bots will be sold."

"Lathim?"

"Yes, Maggie?"

"Thank you for finding me."

He brushed a kiss against her forehead. "I'm the one who is thankful. By agreeing to be my mate, you've given me the one thing I've wanted for a long time. I only hope that I don't disappoint you. I may be part machine, but I'm not perfect."

"You seem pretty perfect to me," she said softly, snuggling closer.

He smiled and held her tight as he finally allowed sleep to claim him. He may not have bedded her, claimed her fully, but she was his and that was enough for now. As long as he had Maggie, he had everything he needed. He only hoped that one day all his fellow cyborgs would know the joy he felt when she was in his arms.

Chapter Four

Maggie looked around nervously and moved a little closer to Lathim. They'd reached Alpha9 an hour ago and were now exploring the trading post. The crew had offloaded some goods and were bartering for items their world needed, while Lathim led Maggie around to the different vendors. They were selling everything from clothing to food to living beings. Seeing the slaves saddened Maggie, and she knew that could have easily been her fate if Lathim hadn't found her before the pirates had. She had no doubt the pirates would have passed her around until they were bored and then would have sold her to the highest bidder.

"Something pretty for your lady?" one of the vendors called out, holding up a handful of jewelry.

Lathim paused and looked over the items available. He lifted a golden armband encrusted with jewels. Maggie's jaw dropped a little as he began to haggle with the merchant over the price. He didn't really intend to purchase something so extravagant for her, did he? When Lathim shook hands with the man, Maggie knew the deal had been made. She stared up at him, wide-eyed, as he reached for her arm and fastened the band around her biceps.

"Lathim, it's too much," she protested.

"I want everyone to know you belong to someone. Perhaps I'll start something new. All of our mates will wear armbands, in the event my world ever gets so many females we need to differentiate between mated females and single ones."

She snorted. "You could just purchase a bunch of slaves and take them to your world."

He paused and looked down at her. "Slaves?"

"It never occurred to you to purchase females?

Plenty of males buy sex slaves."

He growled softly. "We would never do that to a female."

"And yet you purchase their services from brothels. Don't you realize those women were sold to those places? They didn't ask for that kind of life. Visiting a brothel is no different from buying your own personal slave. Except you'd get to have sex regularly." Maggie crossed her arms. "Did you seriously think a woman would sign up to have many sexual partners every day for the rest of her life, until she contracted some sexually transmitted disease and died from it?"

He paled and cursed under his breath, gripping her hand tight. He began tugging her back toward the ship and his crew. She didn't know if she'd overstepped, or if he was anxious to impart her words of wisdom. Had they seriously never considered those women didn't want that type of life? Of course they hadn't. They were men and all men thought about was sex. If they were happy to have it countless times a day with nameless women, then they just assumed the women felt the same way. Idiots.

He stopped where his crew was loading their new items onto the ship.

"No more brothels," he said.

The men stopped and stared at him.

"What do you mean by that?" Tenz asked.

"The living females there aren't there under their own free will. They were sold to those places and don't want that kind of life," Lathim said. "It would be wrong to force them to be with us."

Querrill frowned. "So what do you suggest? That we use sex bots indefinitely?"

"Or find mates," Lathim said. "I know there are hundreds of us on our world, and no females, but maybe we should start purchasing female slaves and freeing them on our world. Surely they would pair off with someone."

Maggie tugged on his sleeve. "Are you guys wealthy?"

"We steal from pirates, that includes any currency they might have," Lathim said. "We just prefer to trade when we're able."

"You could purchase brides," Maggie said.

"Purchase?" Tenz asked. "Wouldn't that be the same as buying a sex slave? Or using the brothels?"

Maggie shook her head. "There's a new program called Galactic Mates, where you can browse a catalog of available females. The women selected are an 80% match to most races for sexual compatibility and come from many different worlds. They have to sign an agreement, and in exchange a large percentage of the money used to purchase them goes to their families. They aren't forced into the program."

Lathim scratched his jaw. "How much do these mates sell for?"

"It depends on race, education, age... lots of different factors. My father once asked if I wanted to join the program since he knew it was doubtful I'd ever find a suitable mate while living on his ship. I think he was also concerned that he'd be raided and I'd be stolen."

"I'll look into it," Querrill said. "We couldn't populate our entire planet that way, but we could perhaps purchase a few brides for those who are more... enhanced than others."

"What does that mean?" Maggie asked.

"When you look at me, can you tell I'm a cyborg? Or my crew members?" Lathim asked.

"There are rumors of cyborgs, with vivid

descriptions. From your appearance, I'd assumed that's what you were, but if I hadn't heard those stories, I'd never have known any part of you was mechanical if you hadn't told me."

He nodded. "Some of our cyborg brothers are not so fortunate. Some of their mechanical parts can be seen on the outside, and the only female companionship they can find are with sex bots. No living female will touch them."

"Captain, everything is loaded. Are we leaving or are we purchasing slaves?" Tenz asked. He looked unsettled by the idea.

"No slaves for now," Lathim said. "We already have two females on board that we need to get home. I think it would be best if we were on Xpashta before Jillian wakes up. I don't know how she'll react, but she could cause problems on the ship if she's unstable."

"I'll set a course for Xpashta," Zorlok said. "We'll be home by the evening meal."

Lathim led Maggie back onto the ship and went to the command center. When he sat, he pulled her onto his lap and looped an arm around her waist. She leaned against him and felt excitement thrum through her. She was going to a new world, her new home. While she was elated that she'd get to see her new home, there was also a bit of trepidation over being on a world with hundreds of males and no females other than herself and Jillian. She hoped it wouldn't cause problems for Lathim.

"Captain, we've messaged ahead to let everyone know about the two females arriving with us, and that they've already been claimed. There may be curiosity, but no one will try to take them from you or Rorwick," Zorlok said. "If anything, they seem excited that females were willing to mate with us."

"It gives them hope they won't be alone forever," Lathim said.

"Captain, with your permission, I'd like to remain with the ship in hopes that there might be other females out there who would mate with our kind," Zorlok said. "Permission to ask your female a question."

"Granted."

Zorlok focused on her. "Maggie, if you had not been running in fear from the pirates, would you have given Lathim a chance to become your mate? Or would the fact he's cyborg have made you too afraid?"

Her brow furrowed. "I've heard the stories about cyborgs and how deadly and fearsome you are. I think I would have been afraid, but all I would have had to do was look into his eyes to know the rumors weren't true. I didn't trust him just as a way to escape the pirates. I saw kindness in his eyes."

"So, you're saying if we treat the females we meet kindly, show them we aren't monsters, then we'll have just as much of a chance as anyone else to claim them?" Zorlok asked.

"Yes. At least, that's how I feel. I can't speak for every woman out there."

Zorlok hesitated a moment. "Do you think that humans like yourself might be more open to accepting us? I've seen reports of your Earth and there are many races living together on your world. Do you think it makes you more tolerant of people who are different?"

Maggie chewed on her lip. "My world is not without its faults. We have prejudices and racism just like other planets. But there are a lot of good people on my world, women who don't care about the color of someone's skin or what world they come from. They won't care you have mechanical parts inside. We have men who come back from war with missing limbs and they're able to find love, so I don't see why a cyborg wouldn't be able to as well."

"Captain, with your permission, after we've offloaded everything and the human females are settled on Xpashta, I'd like permission to use the Mystic7 to find other human females in distress who might be open to mating with us." Zorlok frowned. "I think they might be more open to it than others, and if they are half as lovely as your Maggie and Rorwick's Jillian, then we will be truly blessed."

Maggie felt her cheeks warm at the compliment.

"Permission granted," Lathim said. "Log the orders into the system so the next captain won't put up a fight over it."

Zorlok smiled. "They've assigned Milore. He's been complaining about a lack of mates on our world for a while now. I think he will be open to the new mission."

"I don't believe you'll get complaints from the crew. Rorwick will need to be replaced. Once we know the status of his mate's health and mental state, we can look at reassigning him to a ship, but for now I think he needs to remain on Xpashta."

"Agreed," Zorlok said. "I don't think he'll fight you on it. He's barely left the female's side since he carried her to his quarters. His duties have been assigned to the others for now. Everyone was eager to help out, and we're all hoping the female will be all right."

"Lathim," Maggie said. "I know you want to show me your world, and I want to see it, but do you think I should spend time with Rorwick and Jillian until she wakes up? She might not be as frightened if she sees another human."

Lathim's arms tightened around her. "I don't know if she'll try to attack when she awakens. You're not going anywhere near her until I know it's safe."

"Captain, we're about to fold space. I've notified the crew," Zorlok said.

"Maggie, I want you to take a deep breath, let it out, and close your eyes. Your stomach may flip and you might get lightheaded for a moment," Lathim said. "No matter how disoriented you get, I won't let you fall."

Maggie nodded and did as he said, clutching tight to him as it felt like the ship pitched beneath them. Her stomach flipped and flopped, nausea rose in her throat, and her ears started to ring. She felt like someone had stuck her in a washing machine and put it on spin cycle. The floor rumbled, the vibrations coming through the chair and Lathim to rattle her bones. When it smoothed back out, she gulped in a lungful of air.

"I think I'm going to be sick," she mumbled, burying her face against Lathim.

He rubbed her back and the nausea settled a little. "It won't be long now before we're home, and you won't have to get back on a ship anytime soon."

"You're staying there with me, right?"

"I'll stay for a while. Eventually, I'll be asked to captain the *Mystic7* again, but for now my priority is you. I will probably be assigned duties on Xpashta for the next few months or so. If the idea of me leaving causes you too much stress, I can request to be assigned to Xpashta permanently."

She sighed. "You love being on this ship, don't you?"

"I do, but I like being with you too. If you want me to remain at home, I will."

Maggie didn't say anything else and instead turned her attention to the space surrounding the ship. There were planets in the distance, all varying colors. She looked for a pink and purple one, eager to see her new home. The thought of Lathim leaving her at home to captain a ship again scared her, but only because she didn't know how well she would be received on Xpashta. Zorlok had said the other cyborgs seemed excited that she was mated to Lathim, but she didn't know how comfortable she would feel on a world full of single males.

They passed several planets, and in the clearing ahead she saw it. Xpashta was stunning with the swirls of pink, purple, and teal. There were a few streaks of white here and there. She leaned a little further away from Lathim to get a better look.

"It's beautiful," she said.

"As pretty as your Earth?" he asked.

"Much prettier. How long before we land?"

"About two of your Earth hours," Zorlok answered. "Captain, your presence is requested in the cargo hold. Maggie may stay here if she wishes. I'll keep an eye on her."

Lathim sighed and kissed Maggie's cheek. "I'll return shortly. Zorlok is a wealth of information if you have more questions."

Maggie stood and let Lathim leave the command center. She claimed the seat he'd just vacated and focused on the planet that would be her home from now on. Zorlok turned to look at her.

"I can't read minds," he said.

Maggie laughed. "Do you think I'll be in any danger on your world?"

"From other cyborgs? No. The wildlife on the planet is mostly tame, but there are vicious creatures in the wooded areas. I wouldn't venture far from the military base unless you have a male with you for protection."

"How large is the base?" she asked.

"It comfortably houses several hundred cyborgs, and there is still space for more. We have a market where we trade for things we need. Food is free to everyone. You simply select what you'd wish to eat for the week and carry it back to your home. We never take more than we can use so it's not been an issue."

"Querrill is a doctor?" she asked.

"Yes, he's the ship's medic."

"Are there others on your world? If I get sick, will there be someone there to heal me?"

Zorlok nodded. "Each ship is assigned a medic, and there are more than a dozen who remain on Xpashta. They take turns being assigned to the ships, but once we start settling down with mates, I'm sure things will change."

"Some mates might like travelling in space with you. At least until they have children."

His brow furrowed. "You truly think someone would wish to have children with us? Would you be willing to give Lathim children? It's something we've feared. Even if we found mates, we worried they wouldn't want offspring from us."

"I told Lathim I'm open to the idea, but I want time to get to know him first."

"Then make sure he gets the injection when we reach Xpashta."

"What injection?" she asked.

"When we were part of the Cy-Con program, they created many serums. One of them inhibits production of sperm for up to three months. Instead of relying on our sexual partners to be on birth control, it was decided that we would be injected to ensure no children were created while we were on active duty. It's a temporary thing though, and wears off over the course of about three months. There's no guarantee how long it will work as it varies from cyborg to cyborg. And it's not like it just evaporates from our systems and suddenly we can have children again. It slowly diminishes and the lower the serum level in our system, the better the chance we can get our partner pregnant."

"Is it safe?" Maggie asked. "What if it can't be reversed?"

Zorlok paused. "None of us have had children since entering the Cy-Con program. It's possible that the injections were not reversible. We've continued to get them every few months, for those of us who leave our world. We won't know for certain until either you or Jillian have a baby if the injections wear off like we were told. We've assumed that we're capable of creating life, but perhaps we aren't. We could run tests, but I know after everything we've been through, going to medical isn't our favorite pastime. But if the serum works the way we were told, then Lathim should be able to have children with you when the serum wears off."

"So, there will be pressure put on Lathim and me to have babies?" she asked.

"Perhaps. Our leaders will want to know if it's possible for the two of you to have children. Jillian was damaged and will be allowed more time before they begin asking questions. With you, they will assume you're having sex already."

Maggie's cheeks burned. "How do you know we aren't?"

"The captain wouldn't have come out of his

quarters even if the ship were on fire if you were. He'd have holed up in there and kept you sated for days."

Her cheeks burned brighter. "Sorry I asked."

Zorlok chuckled. "It's nothing to be embarrassed over. You have a cyborg mate, and we have lusty appetites. Especially since it's so seldom we get to be with a living female. The bots have their place, but it isn't the same thing. They're essentially synthetic androids."

"I've heard they're lifelike. The ones on my father's ship certainly looked real."

"To an extent. They are programmed to answer questions pertaining to sex, but you can't really have a conversation with one. They are not sentient beings and cannot learn beyond what they are programmed to do. We could make them more realistic, I suppose, but it still wouldn't be the same as having a mate."

"You know, there are cities on Earth where the women outnumber the men. It's a shame you can't advertise in those areas that you're seeking mail order brides."

He frowned. "Mail order brides?"

"Sending off for a wife, sight unseen, and claiming her as your mate when she arrives to meet you on your world. If only there were shuttles going from my world to yours. I haven't been on Earth since I was a little girl, but I still hear news from there. Have you heard of Terrans?"

"I am not familiar with a race called Terrans."

"They've set up a bride program on my world. Women apply to be mated to them, and once they've been accepted into the program, they're sent to the alien world to select a mate."

Zorlok turned to face her fully. "Do you think these Terrans might agree to extend their program to my world? Are there enough human females on Earth who would agree to such a mating?"

"I think it wouldn't hurt to ask. When you leave Xpashta, see if you can find Earth. Shuttles travel from there to Terran Prime all the time, from what I hear. If your world is too far, maybe one of your ships could meet a shuttle partway and then deliver the women to your world. Just think of how quickly you could find mates then. And I've heard the Terrans are purple like you. I had thought maybe you were related."

"There are many purple races in the galaxies. The closest relation to the Zelranians are Zelthranites. Their ancestors crash landed on Zelran hundreds of years ago and mated with a race of white beings with blue hair who already inhabited the planet. Zelranians today have a lighter color purple flesh than the Zelthranites, and they maintain the blue hair of our ancestors. Those of us in the Cy-Con program have white hair because of all the experimentation. It changed us in many ways."

"Do you still have contact with the Zelthranites?" she asked.

"No, they live many days from our world, much closer to your Earth. We are allies if war breaks out, but we do not communicate often."

"It's a shame. Maybe they know of females who would mate with you."

"After we deliver Jillian and you to Xpashta, I will seek out this Earth and hope we can enter an agreement with the Terrans. Or perhaps they would at least let us consider the females they didn't want."

"You won't know if you don't ask," Maggie said.

Zorlok turned back around and took the controls again. "Brace yourself, Maggie. We'll be entering Xpashta's atmosphere in a moment and it might get bumpy. Not much longer and you'll land on your new home."

Butterflies rioted in her stomach and she forced herself to relax. She wished Lathim was sitting with her, but her mate didn't reappear until after the ship landed on Xpashta. Everyone had filed out of the command center except Zorlok, who waited patiently with her. When Lathim appeared, he looked irritated and she hoped it wasn't bad news.

Chapter Five

The idiocy of his crew astounded him at times. Fighting over sex bots! It wasn't like they didn't already have plenty of them on Xpashta. He'd agreed they could keep two on board, but the rest were to have been traded at Alpha9. Apparently, his crew had disobeyed his orders and kept all of them. He entered the transgression into the captain's log, in hopes Milore would offload the bots somewhere. They didn't need one per crew member, as if they were mates.

Maggie seemed hesitant to come to him, and Lathim realized he must look fierce after dealing with the males on the ship. He smoothed his expression and held out a hand to her. Her fingers were warm against his, and he clasped her hand tight before leading her to the docking port. He'd made arrangements for their belongings to be delivered to his home, but first he wanted to introduce her to the commanders.

She squinted against the bright double suns, but after a moment, she clung even closer to him as she stared at the cyborgs surrounding them.

"They're merely curious about you," Lathim said. "No one will hurt you."

"What if they're like the cyborg on your ship who wanted to claim me even after you said no? What if they take me from you?" Maggie asked.

"We'll ask the commanders to sanction our mating and make it official," Lathim said. "My people won't go against anything the commanders say. If they tell them you're mine, then it will be so."

"Commanders?"

"There are five commanders who govern our people. They help create the laws that keep us safe. A few of them have come to see you. You have nothing to fear."

Maggie didn't look convinced, but followed him through the throng of cyborgs. They entered the military base through a large metal gate, which closed once everyone was inside. The commanders were waiting for them, and Lathim led Maggie straight to them. Pride swelled inside of him as he presented his mate to the rulers of his planet.

"I'd like to present Magnolia Baker, a human female, and my mate. She prefers to be called Maggie." Lathim tugged her forward a little more, but she tightened her grip on his hand.

"Maggie, it's an honor to meet you," Commander Sorus said. "I apologize if so many cyborgs at once frightened you, but our people are most curious about you. No one has ever mated with one of our kind before. My name is Sorus and I'm one of the five commanders who lead the cyborgs."

"I'm Warver," another commander said. "We made sure Lathim's home was stocked with plenty of food and drink for the two of you, and any trinkets we thought you might enjoy were placed within his quarters as well."

"My name is Kiril. Is there anything you need to make your stay here more pleasant?" the third commander asked.

Maggie bit her lip and looked up at Lathim, as if asking permission to speak. He wondered if there was something she wanted that she'd been hesitant to request of him. He should have thought to ask her if she had everything she needed or wanted, and he felt like a bad mate for not doing so. He gave her a nod of encouragement and she faced the commanders again.

"I like to read," she said. "I had a collection of romance books on board my father's ship, but they didn't make it on board the Mystic7. If you have any Earth books, I'd love to have them, or at least some of them."

"Why didn't you say something?" Lathim asked. "I could have found books for you while we were at Alpha9. I want you to be happy, Maggie."

"I am happy," she assured him. "But I know I'll grow bored during the day if I don't have some books to read. I'd read the ones in my quarters many times and always begged for new ones. I always thought that one day when I had my own home, I'd have a library."

"I don't have room in my home for a room just dedicated to books, but we could add some shelves for a small collection," Lathim said.

"Are many females from your world big readers like you?" Warver asked.

"The Earth females I've met over the years all claimed to enjoy reading, but I don't know that it's something all human females necessarily like." Maggie looked up at him again. "If you don't have books here, that's okay. I don't have to have them."

Lathim cupped her cheek. "If you want books, you'll have them, even if I have to put in a request with any ships still out trading."

Kiril cleared his throat. "We do have a room of books on the base. They are from many different worlds and in different languages, but perhaps there are some you would be able to read. Have Lathim show them to you after you've gotten settled into your new home."

Maggie's face glowed with excitement. "Could we go now?"

"If you wish to see them now, I will take you straight there, and then we'll go home," Lathim said. "Our things from the ship should be delivered by then."

Maggie squeezed his hand tight and nodded enthusiastically. He smiled down at her. The commanders moved out of their way as he led her over to a blasen. She looked at it funnily.

"It almost looks like the hover crafts I've seen in sci-fi movies on my planet," she said. "What do you use them for?"

"The base is rather large, so we use them to get from one end to the other. Our home is within walking distance of where we stand now, but the storage rooms are on the opposite end of the base and it would take over an hour to walk there. I thought you might prefer this."

"I don't mind walking, but I think an hour one way is beyond me at this moment. Having lived on a ship most of my life, I haven't had much time to walk about in the open like this. It's something I think I'd like doing often though."

He helped her into the blasen. "We can walk as often as you'd like."

Once she was settled, he pointed the vehicle toward the opposite end of the base and took her to the storage rooms. They were inside the last building on the base. He parked outside, then ushered her into the facility. Each door was labeled in their native language. He pushed open the door for the book room and motioned for her to enter, the lights, being motion activated, turned on once she stepped inside.

A hand lifted to her mouth and she stared at the crates full of books. The room was vast, and every nook and cranny was filled. He wasn't certain they would have anything in her native tongue, but he would help her search. Each crate was marked with a special brand that each world put on their items, so he looked for crates from Earth. When he found one, he opened the lid and stepped back to let her look inside.

Maggie pulled out handfuls of books, biting her lip as she looked at each one.

"There's nothing you like?" he asked.

"I can't read them. The ones I've pulled out so far are in French or German. I need books in English."

Lathim frowned. "There's more than one language on your world? How strange."

"There are many languages on my world, and I only know how to speak and read one of them."

Lathim helped her empty the crate, and then reload it once she determined there was nothing in it that she could read. He scoured the room for another Earth crate and found two others. He let Maggie take her time going through them, and a huge smile lit up her face as she neared the bottom of the third crate. The books were different from the others from her world. They had soft covers and were much smaller than the rest, but she held them to her chest like they were the most beautiful treasures she'd ever seen.

"How many can I take?" she asked.

"As many as you'd like. Make a stack and I can carry them out to the blasen."

She hesitantly looked at the books in her hand and those in the crate.

"Maggie, Jillian and you are the only humans on this world. I'm sure if she wants to read something, you'll let her borrow them. And in the meantime, I'm going to put in a request with some of the other ships still out there and ask them to bring back Earth books in the language you can read." He peered at the ones in her hands. "Are kissing people typical?"

Her cheeks warmed. "I like to read romances, so yes, most have shirtless men or kissing couples on the covers."

He growled a little. "I will be the only male you look at."

"It's just a cover image, Lathim. I'm not looking to run off with the guy who modeled for it. I just like the stories between the pages. I like stories about hope, second chances, and finding love."

Lathim looked at her, scanning her from head to toe. "And is there someone in your past you wish you had a second chance with?"

She rolled her eyes. "That's what you got from that statement? You're such a typical guy."

"Is there?" he asked, a strange feeling building inside of him.

"No." She sighed. "There's no one remarkable in my past, and I told you I'm still a virgin. You've touched me more than anyone else ever has, and I'm yours, Lathim. I agreed to be your mate. I've never agreed to tie my life to someone else's before, so that should tell you something."

The feeling eased a bit, only to change to something warmer. He reached for her, pulling her against his body, her books crushed between them. Maggie tilted her chin up and he leaned down to claim her lips in a kiss. Her hands went around his neck and he knocked the books to the floor, pulling her tight against him. The feel of her soft curves made his cock instantly hard. He wanted her, but not here, not where someone could walk in at any moment. He drew away, leaning down to retrieve her books.

"We'll finish this at home," he said, watching her cheeks pinken again. She didn't protest, even though she'd asked for more time to get to know one another. Maybe she wanted him as badly as he wanted her. And if not, he'd take things as far as she'd allow, and then he'd stop when she told him to. He wanted her trust just as much as he wanted her body.

Lathim loaded her books into the blasen, then helped his mate into the vehicle. He drove it to his home, stopping along the way for her to gawk at everything around her. She didn't seem to mind the other cyborgs staring quite as much when she was trying to take everything in. The base was large, probably over one hundred square Earth miles. While she'd been browsing books, he'd accessed the base's computer and downloaded Earth facts so he could converse with his mate easier. He wanted to know everything about her.

He drove the rest of the way to their home, stopping the blasen outside. Someone would retrieve it if they needed to use it. No one owned a personal blasen, but there were many scattered across the base that were available for anyone to use. They had a community that worked together, helping one another. Those who did well with plant life did most of the farming. Those who had an affinity for animals took care of those chores. He either captained the Mystic7, or he worked on repairs around the base when he was home.

Maggie stepped out and looked around the area and he wondered if there was something she would change. Images of Earth homes had filtered through his brain thanks to his recent download and many had brightly color plants around the houses or hanging from balconies. Would she want something like that? The entire base was nothing but road pavers and stone and metal structures. The only grass was outside of the gates, but if she wanted plants, he'd find a way for her to have them.

The base had been created by Parslips, a race that

had become extinct nearly twenty years ago thanks to their ongoing war with two other races. No one had laid claim to Xpashta, so the cyborgs had taken it over. The homes were made of pale pink and purple stones found on the planet, in caves on the other side of the wooded areas. The glass in the windows was similar to that of his ship and would withstand the elements if there were ever bad storms. It did rain at times, and when it did, there could be a torrential downpour.

Maggie looked around as she approached the front door. He'd have to program his home to respond to her. The sooner she had access to everything the better. Their belongings sat on the front walkway, ready to be carried inside.

"Place your hand on the panel by the door," he said.

She did as he commanded and Lathim linked with his home's computer to grant her access to the house and everything inside. When they got inside, he'd make sure the voice commands would respond to her as well. Once the computer registered a new occupant, the doors slid open and allowed them entry. Lathim carried her books inside and set them down on the table near the front door. As the door slid shut behind them, he led her over to the home's central computer and pushed several buttons.

"Computer, please record new occupant's voice for future commands," he said. "Say something, Maggie."

"Um, hello, computer," she said, giving him a curious look.

"Voice recorded," the computer said.

"Computer, this is Maggie. My mate. You will obey all of her commands."

"Affirmative," the computer said.

"Your home is voice activated like my father's ship?" she asked. "Homes on Earth don't have computers. They're just walls and a roof. Well, the ones I was ever inside of anyway."

"All homes on the base are voice activated and can only be accessed through a palm scan at the front door. The commanders have access to every home on base, and Rorwick has access to my home, as he's my friend. Now that I have a mate, none will enter without permission unless it's an emergency."

"Is that why our things were left outside? They didn't have access to your home?" she asked.

"Our home, and that's correct. I'll go bring them in now. Look around and familiarize yourself with your new home. If you're hungry, I can fix something for us to eat."

He paused in the doorway, watching her for a moment, and then retrieved their belongings, carrying them to his bedroom. No, *their* bedroom. Having a mate was so strange, and yet it was what he'd always wanted. Now that she was here, he was never letting Maggie go. He'd let her put her own things away, in case there was a particular order she preferred. It didn't take him long to put his pants and shirts away, along with his leather suits for future space travel. When he was finished, he found Maggie staring out the windows of the solarium into the enclosed back patio.

"There's no grass," she said. "No plants. Everything is made of some sort of stone."

"I've seen images of your Earth homes and know you have greenery around them. Perhaps there's a way to bring some of the plants here from outside the base walls, I don't know how well they would grow."

"Do you have planters I could use?" she asked.

He frowned, trying to access what a planter was. Linking to his home computer, he requested the image and his neural transmitter showed him a picture of a square box with dirt and plants inside.

"We do not have planters here, but we could perhaps make one. The same substance that's used to hold the pavers together for the roads and the stones together on our home could be used to fuse smaller stones together into a box-like shape. Then we could bring dirt and plants home to fill it from outside the gates. I don't know that they would survive, but I'm willing to try if it will make you happy."

Maggie smiled and nodded, looking out at the stone wall again. "The pinks and purples are pretty, but I've missed seeing plants while I've been in space. It would be nice to have some around the house. Maybe start a garden out there. We could set up a bench where we could enjoy the flowers."

He quickly added a bench to the list of things to procure for her. Shelves for her books, planters for her garden, and a bench for the back patio. He wondered if there was anything else she needed to make the home feel more like hers. Lathim wanted her to be happy here, whatever it took. She turned to face him and slowly approached, her hands coming up to rest on his chest.

"I know you want to take me to the bedroom, and there's a chance I'd let you go farther than I'm comfortable with right now. But can I ask a favor of you first?" she asked.

"I would do anything for you, Maggie."

"Zorlok said there's an injection that would keep you from getting me pregnant for a few months. Would you consider taking it so I don't have to worry about starting a family right away? I'm not saying that

I don't ever want to have children with you, but I think we need the next few months to really get to know one another."

He understood why she wanted to wait, but he couldn't deny that he was heavily disappointed. He'd had an injection before going into space, but it could have worn off by now. Having a mate meant having children, or so he'd thought. Lathim didn't understand why humans felt the need to spend so much time together before creating a family together. She'd agreed to be his mate, and surely understood that children would be part of that. It confused him, her need to wait, but if it meant so much to her, he would agree.

"I'll get it taken care of tonight. If you'd like to put your things away and settle in, I can leave now to get the injection. I already took it a few months ago, so it should just replenish the serum in my system and shouldn't take long to take effect."

She caressed Lathim's cheek. "Thank you."

He nodded and turned to leave, unhappy about his destination, but determined to make his mate content. Now that she was on his world, she would never leave, unless it was by his side. But he didn't want her to be miserable while she was here, and if having a baby right now would upset her, then he would do this, no matter how much he didn't want to. He could have talked to her, made her understand how important it was to him to have a baby with her, but three months wasn't a long time to wait. He'd waited for years to have a family of his own. At least he wasn't alone any longer, which was more than he could say for his fellow cyborgs, except Rorwick.

He wondered if Jillian had woken yet, and how she'd handled seeing Rorwick right away. Most people feared his kind, and now that poor human was on a planet of nothing but cyborgs -- and his Maggie, of course. Perhaps it had been wrong of them to keep Jillian. She'd already lost so much, and now they'd taken her to a world where everything was foreign to her, much like his Maggie.

It sobered him. He'd taken her from everything she'd known. While remaining on board the ship would have never worked, he could have made arrangements for her to return to Earth. It would have been risky, but manageable. While he'd given her a home and planned to shower her with gifts, he was still asking a lot of her. His download from the computer had shown him that humans mated differently from his kind. They went on something called dates and took things very slowly. With Zelranians, the males selected a female, claimed her, and that was the end of it. They were mated immediately, and the female would bear their mate's children. Earth's customs seemed strange, but he would try to learn more about Maggie and give her what she needed. He wanted to be a good mate.

The clinic was quiet and Liroz was on duty.

"I hear you have a mate now," Liroz said.

"Yes, but she has requested more time before we start a family. I believe my last injection has expired and hoped to get another one."

Liroz frowned and motioned him forward. "Let me scan you to make sure the last one is out of your system. If I double dosed you, I'm not sure what the outcome would be."

Lathim held still while Liroz scanned him. "There is a faint dosage left in your body. Come back in a week and I'll check you again. Just be careful with your mate until then. You should bring her to me so I can give her the serum that extends her lifespan. When I heard you were bringing humans here, I downloaded every medical file I could find on them. They do not live for very long. Most die in their eighties or nineties, if not sooner."

Lathim's eyes widened and he rocked back on his heels. "So soon?"

"Do you know how old your mate is?"

Lathim shook his head.

"You should ask and bring her to me tomorrow. I'll scan her to make sure she's healthy and give her the serum. I heard that it had already been given to Rorwick's mate in an effort to save her life. I worry that she will not last many years without constant care."

"Because she was so close to dying?"

Liroz nodded. "I don't know what damage the virus did to her system. I'll feel better after I scan her, but I didn't want to intrude on their first night here. I'm not even certain if she's awakened yet."

"I'm sure we'll know when she is. I doubt she'll be happy to discover she's lost her child and been taken to an alien world."

"True. From what I've learned of humans in the last day, they can be rather loud when they are displeased. I hope for your sake that your mate is quieter. There's still much to learn about them, but I'll work hard to learn all I can so I can treat the new mates when needed."

Lathim didn't care if Maggie started screaming and throwing things, as long as she remained with him. He would put up with near anything to have a mate, especially one as delectable as his Maggie. His groin tightened just thinking about her soft curves pressed against him.

"Go take care of your mate." Liroz hesitated. "I

would not tell her of the injection unless she asks. It might make her leery of being claimed by you until you have more of the serum in your system."

He didn't like the idea of lying to Maggie, but he trusted Liroz, so he nodded and left the clinic to go back home. Many greeted him on his way home, several stopping him to ask questions about his human mate. They were curious about the first females on their world and he couldn't blame them. After he'd bonded more with his mate, he'd meet with the commanders and discuss options for finding more mates for his fellow cyborgs. He wanted everyone to know the joy of having a mate.

Chapter Six

Maggie had put away her things and explored her home some more. Her life had changed so much so fast, but she was trying to adapt. She had to remember that she wasn't following Earth rules anymore. While part of her wanted what she'd have had on Earth -- dates and plenty of time to get to know her mate -- things were different here. Without Lathim, she wouldn't survive on this world. And while he was gaining plenty by taking her as a mate, she was gaining something too.

She felt uneasy being alone, and a little disappointed with herself. It wasn't right that she'd asked Lathim to get the injection to kill his sperm for the next three months. He'd waited so long to have a mate and a family, and now she was trying to take part of that away from him. She'd agreed to be his mate, which was apparently a forever thing to his people, so what did it matter if they knew one another better before having children? Assuming the pregnancy was anything like a regular human pregnancy, there would be plenty of time to become better acquainted before the baby arrived. She felt like a bitch.

She stopped pacing and dug through one of the large crates that must have been left by the commanders. There were Earth items inside, from all around the globe. A Chinese vase in a pretty blue and white pattern, a small replica of the Eiffel Tower that would easily fit on a shelf, a big framed print of Big Ben, and many other wonderful things. She pulled them out one at a time and began placing them around her new home, added color and a touch of hominess to the place. It had seemed so barren when she'd first walked in.

Maggie hoped they had saved some items for Jillian, and decided to leave the other crates untouched in case the other human wanted to look through them. As much as she wanted to surround herself with things from her world, she wouldn't be selfish and claim everything for herself. Jillian had already lost so much. Maggie hoped that a few things from Earth would make things easier for her. She knew that Lathim didn't want her going to visit until he knew Jillian was stable, but she vowed to see the other human as soon as possible. Regardless of what the cyborgs thought, seeing a human face amongst so many aliens might actually be comforting to the other human.

The front door slid open and Lathim stepped inside. He paused, looking around at the changes she made, but didn't seem angry. He stopped and inspected each item, curiosity in his eyes. She'd leaned the framed print against the wall, not knowing how to hang it, or if there even was a way to hang it. She didn't know what types of tools and supplies they had on Xpashta.

Lathim picked up the picture and examined it. "This goes on the wall?"

"Yes. At home, I'd have put a nail in the wall to hang it, but since the walls are stone here... I don't know if it can be hung up or not."

"We have tools that will cut through the stones. I'm sure there's a way to hang it. I'll check on it tomorrow for you. Most of my people are retiring for the night, except those on duty."

"It doesn't even have to be as soon as tomorrow," Maggie said. "I just liked the picture and thought it would be nice to have a few things surrounding me that reminded me of home. You don't mind, do you?"

"Of course not." He smiled. "This is your home now and I want you to be comfortable here. We'll put up as many pictures as you want. There are probably others in the storage rooms."

"You have more items from Earth?" she asked.

Lathim shrugged. "I'm not entirely certain what we have in that building. We take from pirates and they love to board human vessels, although I suspect that has more to do with the humans on board than the goods."

"Why would they want the humans?" Maggie asked, her brow furrowed.

Lathim hesitated. "Human females are highly desired throughout the galaxies. It is rumored that they give the best pleasure and are easier to dominate than some of the other races. Male humans are usually ransomed to your Earth government, or killed outright."

Maggie felt herself pale. "Sex slaves?"

"Yes, but that will never happen to you. I won't let it. I would die to protect you, Maggie. It's not something I say lightly."

"Is that what would have happened to me if the pirates had found me? I suspected they would sell me, but I didn't..." She swallowed hard. "Those female slaves on Alpha9. They were being sold as sex slaves, weren't they?"

"Yes. Although, the more exotic ones might be kept as pets, so at least they would be spared the sexual attentions of their owners. Some males like to collect rare females and put them on display. Others buy them for their own personal harems. Those who are most unfortunate end up on worlds like Vaaden, where there are public harems. I suppose it's like having a brothel on their planet instead of having to go off world to one."

"I knew bad things happened to women in space, knew about the brothels where females were sold to service the customers, but it never really hit me that I could have ended up in such a place."

Lathim took her hands in his, pressing a kiss to her knuckles. "You're safe with me, Maggie."

She moved closer, her arms going around his waist. "You've made me feel safe since you found me in the cargo hold of my father's ship. I'm glad you found me, Lathim. I don't know what made you board my father's ship, but if you hadn't... I don't think I could have hidden from the pirates for much longer, or I might have starved to death."

"I should feed you. It's getting late and you've had a long day."

"Would you... would you kiss me?" she asked, her cheeks warming.

"I will gladly kiss you anytime you'd like." He smiled as he lowered his head to hers, his lips brushing across hers in a gentle caress.

She reached up to thread her fingers through his hair, loving the tingles that shot through her. She'd been ready to surrender to him on his ship, before they were interrupted, and since then he'd kept his hands to himself. She'd asked for time and he was giving it to her. But she wanted his kiss, his touch. It scared her, thinking of letting him claim her completely, but her body warmed at the thought as well. He'd been so patient with her, so tender. No one had ever treated her as well as Lathim did.

Maggie didn't know how to put her thoughts into words. She didn't want a relationship just based on sex, and she worried if she slept with him too soon that's what would happen. But she tried to remind herself that Lathim was an alien and a cyborg. The rules were different than if she were marrying a human man. Lathim didn't think the same way as a human, and she doubted that he thought about a mating the same way. Yes, he'd said it was forever, but that didn't mean he had to remain faithful. Did it? She'd seen the married members of her father's crew cheat on their wives, screwing anything in a skirt. Part of her worried that if Lathim went back on the Mystic7, leaving her behind, that he would be tempted by another female while he was gone. She didn't think she'd survive the betrayal.

Lathim pulled away, his gaze concerned as he stroked her cheek. "Something is bothering you. You ask for my kiss and yet you seem far away."

"Just silly human thoughts."

"Your thoughts and feelings aren't silly. Not to me. Is something bothering you?" Lathim asked. "You can tell me anything. Do my... do my kisses not make you want to mate with me?"

Her cheeks warmed. "It's not that. I do want to mate with you, but I'm scared. I've never done this before, never had a relationship, but I've seen so many of them destroyed because their wives weren't enough for them. What if I'm not enough for you?"

A smile teased the corners of his lips. "How could you not be enough for me? You're my heart, Maggie. You're everything I've ever wanted, a precious gift that I shall cherish always. Don't you know this?"

"N-not really." She licked her lips. "I know you wanted a mate, but I was just convenient. You'd have accepted any woman you'd found on that ship."

His arm tightened around her waist. "Is that what you think? That any female would do?"

"Isn't it true?"

He released her and took a step back. "Perhaps you're correct that we need more time to get to know one another. If you believe that I would accept any female, then there is much you don't know about me."

The hurt and anger in his eyes made her miserable. She hadn't meant to upset him, and he'd said she could tell him anything. Maybe if she explained how things worked with her people he would understand. They didn't just have the different races barrier, he was also part machine and she didn't know how much that changed his thought process, or the way he felt about things or people.

"Lathim, I didn't mean to hurt you," she said. "Where I come from, it's not uncommon for the men to cheat on their mates. They also abuse them and treat them like property. I don't know anything about you or your people. I don't know how you're similar to human men or how you're different. Do you understand?"

He seemed to consider her words.

"Humans take time to get to know one another and we fall in love. That person becomes the most important thing in our lives and we would do anything for them. But my people don't instantly fall in love with someone, not usually anyway. I've heard stories about love at first sight, but I don't know if it's true." She held out a hand to him. "I didn't mean to offend you."

He placed a hand on his chest. "When I saw you cowering in that box, how frightened you were, and how brave for avoiding the pirates, something shifted in here." He patted his chest. "I wanted to protect you, to care for you. I decided that you were mine."

Maggie decided they were having a language

gap because she still didn't understand. Was she like a puppy? Property? How could he just decide that she was going to be his? He couldn't have known if they'd get along. What if they'd kissed and there hadn't been a spark? Would he have claimed her as his mate anyway just because he'd decided that's what would happen?

Lathim looked frustrated at her silence. "Do you not desire me then? Do you not wish to spend your life with me?"

Maggie bit her lip before responding. "No one has ever made me feel the way you do, and it scares me a little. I want to be with you, Lathim, I just worried that it meant something else to you. I didn't know if you would be like the human men on my father's ship and find pleasure elsewhere when you go on missions."

He looked physically ill at the thought and reached for her, lightly touching her hair. "You're mine, and I'm yours. We're mates, Maggie, and mates are forever. It means there will be no other females in my bed but you. I don't want anyone else."

"I think… I think we're saying we want the same thing. You won't cheat on me and I'll only be with you."

He nodded.

"And you picked me because you felt something?" she asked uncertainly.

"Yes. I knew you were meant to be mine."

Maggie wasn't sure that she completely understood, but it seemed they were on the same page, and that was good enough. They'd learn to communicate better over time. Even though everyone who left Earth was equipped with a translator, some things probably didn't translate well from his language to hers. She'd once told an alien that his clothes were cool and he'd looked perplexed and told her they didn't lower his body temperature.

Her stomach rumbled and he placed a hand there. "I'll prepare something to eat. Billok steaks with clarion root. It will be filling."

She didn't have any idea what a billok steak or a clarion root was, but she was starving and she'd try anything. Living on her father's ship, she'd tried many alien cuisines over the years, but her father had always tried to purchase Earth rations when he could. They'd been hard to come by depending on the galaxy they were in, and were always pricey. Her planet was still primitive when it came to space travel, compared to the alien races in the surrounding galaxies.

Maggie followed Lathim to the kitchen and watched as he prepared their food. His kitchen was similar to the kitchen she remembered on Earth, with a stove of sorts that looked more like a large griddle and lots of counter space and cabinets. There was a stone block that she decided was like a refrigerator when she saw Lathim open it and pull out two large, blue steaks. She'd never had blue meat before, but he didn't seem concerned by the color.

Lathim reached for some jars on the kitchen counter and gathered a few. He removed the lids and sprinkled seasonings on the meat. He boiled water in a pot and added what she assumed were the clarion roots. They were strange looking, misshapen things with a pinkish tinge to them. While he cooked, Lathim talked.

"We've only been on this planet for about ten years. That's when the Cy-Con program was closed and we needed a new home."

"You couldn't remain on your world?" she

asked.

"We were exiled. It worked out in the end. We're relatively happy here, if a bit lonely. Bringing females to Xpashta will ease that loneliness. Maybe if they see that we make good mates, they'll be content to settle here."

"I'm sure they would be lucky to be claimed by your friends. If they're half as nice as you, then I can't imagine them being discontent. I like being with you, Lathim. Even just talking while you make dinner is nice, and maybe one day, you can tell me how to cook the food available on your world and I'll be able to help."

He nodded. "I don't mind cooking for you while you settle into life here on my world, and even after. If you decide you don't like cooking, I won't ask you to do it. I've had to cook for myself for a long time, even before the Cy-Con program, so I don't mind."

"What exactly was the Cy-Con program?" she asked.

"They wanted a line of super soldiers. Hundreds of us either volunteered or were asked to join the program. They injected us with many things, and for a while we remained in a type of stasis while they operated. My bones were replaced with a dense metal, and some of my organs were replaced. They put transmitters in my head that allow me to communicate with any technology around me, amongst other things."

"Didn't it hurt, having all that done to you?" she asked.

"By the time we were awakened, our bodies had healed. It felt strange, being different from before. It took a year from the time I entered the program until I was considered active. I worked for the Zelranian parliament, going anywhere they ordered, for four years. Then their requests began to bother some of us. They no longer cared if women and children were hurt on our missions, and we decided we no longer wished to obey."

"So you tried to overthrow your government?"

He seemed to think about it a moment before answering. "We gave them an ultimatum. In the end, we lost and were exiled from our world. They began to spread lies about us, making it impossible for us to find shelter on any nearby worlds, so we took the offered ships and went in search of our own planet to call home. There were rumors about an abandoned military base and we decided to claim it for ourselves."

"An ultimatum?"

"We demanded to be freed from the program if they were going to force us to slaughter innocents. I suppose in a way we did win because we're free from the Cy-Con program, but we were not allowed to return to our friends and families. We were exiled from the planet and left homeless. Some of us left mates behind, mothers, fathers. Those who were mated were first forced to have their mating revoked by the parliament before we were escorted to the ships that would take us from our loved ones for the final time."

"So they gave you ships to use but wouldn't let you say goodbye to your families or take the mates with you?" A horrifying thought occurred to her. "Did you leave a mate and children behind?"

"No. I was never mated. Even before the Cy-Con program I was a soldier, and while my role on Zelran was essential, I was not from what I believe you would call a good family, and not a desirable male for mating."

"Why wasn't your family considered good?" she

asked.

"My father was imprisoned for crimes against the parliament and the citizens of Zelran. My mother took her life to avoid the shame. The females of my world worried that I would pass those genes on to our children." He plated their food and studied her a moment. "Is this a concern of yours as well?"

"No. You're a good male, Lathim, anyone can see that. And I know you'll pass those qualities on to your children. I don't know what crime your father committed, but I don't believe you're capable of doing something bad."

He nodded and handed her the plate of food and a glass of juice. She followed him to a small ledge along the far wall with four stools. Lathim claimed the stool on the end and set his plate and glass on the ledge, and Maggie realized it was a bar for eating, much like the island she remembered in the kitchen of her childhood home. She took a tentative bite of the meat and was pleasantly surprised. It tasted like a cross between a deer and a cow. He'd mashed the roots and they tasted a little like cauliflower, but he'd seasoned them with something that gave the food a bit of bite.

"It's really good," she said, smiling.

"I'll make different dishes over the next few days to see what you like and don't like. Never hesitate to tell me if something is unappetizing. I want you to like the food here. We have some of your Earth chickens here if you'd like eggs tomorrow."

She nodded and ate another bite of her dinner.

When they were finished, Lathim carried their dishes into the kitchen and placed them in a machine that Maggie assumed was a dishwasher. He pushed a button and then walked away. He hesitated only a moment before taking her hand and leading her back to their bedroom. The lights came on when they stepped inside, but Maggie noticed they were dimmer than the other rooms. She didn't know if Lathim had programmed them that way or if all the homes were like that.

Maggie stood uncertainly near the doorway, even after the door slid shut. Lathim began removing his clothes and she wondered if he was going to strip completely bare like he had the other times they'd shared a bed. Was wearing pajamas only a human thing? He certainly didn't seem shy about baring his body to her. When Maggie had unpacked, she'd noticed that she didn't have pajamas. Did he expect her to sleep naked too?

He paused in his undressing and studied her. "Are you not ready to go to bed? I thought you might be tired."

"Is there something I can sleep in?" she asked.

His brow furrowed and he looked at the bed.

"No, I mean something I can wear to bed," she said.

"Humans wear clothing to sleep? Why?"

Her cheeks warmed. "We're a little shy about showing our bodies to people. I know we're mated, but we're still strangers to each other. It's awkward to be naked in front of you."

Lathim approached, shirtless and with his pants undone, his feet bare. He stopped near enough that she felt the heat from his body. Maggie fidgeted, not knowing what to expect from him. His hands reached for her, skimming her curves and she shuddered at his touch, a bolt of longing surging through her. His caress was light, despite the possessive glint in his eyes.

"You're beautiful, Maggie. If you'll remember,

I've already seen you bare, and I couldn't take my eyes off you. I won't take things farther than you'll allow, but I want to hold you, to feel your skin pressed against mine."

She felt her resolve weakening as his hands slid around her back and pulled her tight against his body. Her head tipped back and his lips descended, making her body heat from the inside out as her hands gripped his biceps. Lathim was strong, stronger than anyone she'd met before, and yet his touch was gentle every time he reached for her. His hands teased the hem of her shirt and she didn't protest as he lifted it, his palms sliding against her skin.

"Let me pleasure you," he said softly. "If that's all you want, then we'll stop there. I want to taste you, Maggie, everywhere."

Her legs trembled and she worried they wouldn't hold her as she hesitantly nodded her consent. He gave a soft growl as he stripped her shirt over her head, making her gasp. She held still, her eyes wide, as she waited to see what he would do next. Lathim reached for her sports bra tugging the material until her breasts were freed. He tossed the garment aside.

"I don't like that thing," he muttered.

She smiled and reached for her pants, shimmying out of them. When she was bare, she didn't feel as self-conscious as she'd thought she would. His heated gaze caressed every dip and curve of her body before he reached for her again, lifting her into his arms and carrying her to the bed. He laid her down then stood back, admiring her, as if he could stare at her forever.

"Have you been with a human before?" she asked, remembering that he'd used brothels in the past.

"No, but I downloaded information pertaining to human anatomy and clips of humans of having sex so I'll know how to please you." He frowned. "Do human females really like it when males shove their cocks down their throats and yell at them to take it all?"

She bit back a laugh, realizing he must have found some porn clips. "No. Those videos are for entertainment purposes only. Most human females don't really enjoy that, although I'm sure there are those who do."

"And you prefer my cock only in your pussy and not in your other hole?"

Her cheeks flamed. "I've obviously never tried that, but for now, let's just stick with doing things the regular way."

He nodded and ran his hands up and down her legs before kneeling at the foot of the bed. Lathim watched her as he spread her thighs and lowered his face toward her. Her breath hitched in her throat and she moaned as he buried his nose against her and his tongue flicked out to taste her. He lapped at her slit before spreading her wide and sucking lightly on her clit. Maggie nearly came off the bed at the contact and her heart hammered in her chest.

"Did I do that wrong?" Lathim asked, looking up at her in concern.

"No. So very, very right."

He chuckled and went back to his task. His lips were firm and his tongue hot and wet as he teased and tormented her. Lathim flicked his tongue against her clit in a quick rhythm that had her screaming his name as she shattered, stars bursting behind her closed eyelids and panting for breath. Her world felt like it had been turned upside down, but in the best of ways.

Despite her body throbbing from her force of her release, she still ached and felt empty.

"Maggie, we can stop now, or we can keep going," he said, rising to his feet.

She stared at him through heavy-lidded eyes, her gaze caressing him, and she knew what she wanted. "Keep going."

He nodded and reached for his pants, sliding them down his thighs and kicking them out of the way. Maggie's eyes widened as she took in the length and width of his cock. She'd never seen one before, but she didn't think he looked like a human male. The shaft was ribbed and there were three slits at the top. He looked from her to his cock and back to her again.

"There's nothing to fear, Maggie. I won't hurt you."

"I've heard it always hurts the first time."

His brows dipped and a fearsome expression crossed his face. "I won't hurt you."

"Lathim, I just meant that if you do, it can't be helped. It's my first time and I've heard there will be pain and blood."

His face paled a little. "I'll make you bleed if I mate with you?"

Maggie crawled onto her knees and inched down the bed toward him. He backed up a step, putting more space between them, looking horrified that he could hurt her during sex. It showed her that he did care for her at least a little.

"Lathim, it's fine. I knew it would happen whenever I finally had sex. It's normal for human women on their first time."

He shook his head and held up a hand. "Get under the covers. I'm going to talk to one of the medics. There has to be something that can be done to take away the pain. I refuse to harm you."

"But…"

Before she could utter another word, he stormed into the next room, a determined look on his face. Maggie sighed and crawled under the covers and waited. Sooner or later he'd have to return, right? After all, he'd left the room naked so she didn't think he was going very far. As the minutes ticked by, she began to worry, but not enough to get out of bed naked. What if there was someone else in the house? Burrowing further under the blankets, she decided to wait and see what happened.

Chapter Seven

Lathim paced the front of his home, not caring that he was naked. Liroz handed a vial to him. Lathim eyed it, wondering what the purple goo was. He'd never seen anything like it before, and he'd been to medical plenty of times since becoming part of Zelran's military.

"You'll have to rub it inside of her, where your cock goes," Liroz said. "It will help lessen the pain and ease your entry. She should only feel a pinch. There's nothing I can do about the possible bleeding though. From what I've studied of human anatomy, it is common for their females when they are with a male for the first time."

"And this is safe to use on her?" Lathim asked, staring at the goo.

Liroz nodded. "It obviously hasn't been tested on human females before, but my studies tell me that it will be fine. If there's a reaction, please notify me and I'll come right away."

Liroz left and Lathim carried the vial to the bedroom, where Maggie peeked at him over the edge of the blankets. She'd covered herself completely, and he was glad she'd wanted to hide her body from their guest. He tugged the blankets from her and showed her the vial. "The medic says this will ease the pain. Will you let me use it on you?" Lathim asked.

"Do I drink it?" she asked, her nose wrinkling.

"No, it goes inside you."

Her lips formed an O and she stared wide-eyed a moment. "All right. I'll give it a try."

She still looked slick and wet from her orgasm and he coated his fingers with the purple goo before sliding them inside of her tight channel. She gripped his fingers so snugly, he worried he would rip her in half when he entered her. Were human males so much smaller than him? He'd never seen one naked before, not in person, but he supposed they must have inferior cocks to be able to go somewhere so small without causing damage. He worried again that he would hurt her, despite Liroz assuring him otherwise.

"It tingles," Maggie said. "And it's a little cool."

Lathim coated his fingers again and added more, wanting to make sure she was well lubricated with the goo, in hopes it would ease his entry and be less painful for her. He'd never bedded a virgin before. Maggie wiggled on the bed and gave a little moan as he thrust his fingers in and out of her several times.

"Are you ready for me, my mate?" he asked.

Maggie bit her lip in that enticing way she often did and nodded. Lathim crawled onto the bed, settling between her splayed thighs. His heart thundered in his chest as his cock brushed against the damp curls covering her pussy. He groaned, aching to be inside of her. Maggie's hands slid up his arms and her fingers curled around his biceps. She gazed up at him trustingly and gave him a smile of encouragement.

Slowly, he sank into her, pausing to give her time to adjust to his size. Sweat coated his skin and it felt like it took hours to enter her fully, but once he'd managed to fill her completely, he felt a sense of rightness settle in his chest. She was his now, and would always be his. There was no hint of pain in her eyes, no pinched look on her face. Her foot rubbed his calf and he drew back, only to slowly ease into her again.

Maggie's lips parted and she whimpered a little. "More."

Lathim set up a steady thrust and retreat until he

thought he would go mad. Maggie clawed at his shoulders, her legs hooking around his waist, as if to urge him on. His strokes came faster, harder, until she was crying out her pleasure, her head tossing from side to side. A scream erupted from her throat as her pussy clenched him tight and spasmed along his length, her release coating him.

Unable to hold back a moment longer, he pounded into her sweet body, taking what he needed, what he craved. When he came inside of her, he groaned with his release, his body trembling from the force of his orgasm. As the last spurt of cum slicked her channel, he rested his head in the crook of her shoulder to catch his breath. He could hear her heart beating just as hard as his and he smiled against her soft skin. Her hands caressed him gently and he rolled to the side, pulling her into his arms, against his body.

"I never imagined it would feel like that," Maggie murmured.

"I didn't hurt you?" he asked.

"No, it felt wonderful."

He smiled and kissed the top of her head. "Good. It was better than anything I've ever experienced and I'm glad you enjoyed it too. I was worried about harming you because of our size difference."

She snuggled closer, her breath fanning his chest. Lathim was more content than he'd ever been before. Even though he'd held Maggie while she slept, this was different. Now that they'd joined, they were one, truly mated. She was everything he'd ever wanted, and now she'd never leave. He should have told her about the injection, let her know it was possible in the next week or two he could get her pregnant, but he'd worried she'd hold him at arm's length. He knew it was wrong of him, but he never wanted anything as much as he wanted Maggie.

As she cuddled closer to him, he felt her breathing even out and knew that she slept, but sleep wouldn't come for him anytime soon. He wanted her again, his cock already hardening. But he'd let her rest. She'd had a hard day and he didn't know what tomorrow would bring.

He must have dozed off at some point because the next time Lathim opened his eyes, sunlight streamed through the windows. Maggie was still curled up in his arms, pressed tight against him, her breath fanning across him. She was warm and soft, and he wished he could stay in bed and hold her forever. While he hadn't been assigned any duties yet, he knew it was only a matter of time. They wouldn't let him hole up in his house for long. Until then, he'd enjoy his time with Maggie.

Rolling out of bed, he checked out the things she'd tucked away in drawers. She didn't seem to have much. Aside from what she'd worn yesterday, she had two pair of pants, another of those things that went across her breasts, and two more shirts. His mate needed more clothes. Connecting with the communications center, he put in a request for more human clothes and gave them Maggie's measurements. He didn't know how long it would take for more things to arrive for her, and placed an order for books as well, stressing that they needed to be in the human language called English and that she liked books with kissing people on the covers. He knew he'd get harassed about that later, but as long as his mate was happy, that was all that mattered.

Lathim showered and pulled on a fresh pair of leather pants and a light blue shirt. Since he didn't intend to leave the house just yet, he remained barefoot. His mate would be hungry when she woke, so he went to the kitchen to make something for her. He remembered that she wanted eggs from her Earth chickens and connected to the farming center to request some be delivered to his home. Another day, Maggie might enjoy going to collect them herself.

She'd enjoyed the billok steak, so maybe she'd like porshwine links with her eggs. He pulled some flat bread from the cabinet and placed it on the side of the plate before adding the rest of the food. He didn't know what humans ate with their morning meal, but he hoped she would like the offerings of his world. There was a mash he could make too, but he decided to save that for another day.

Lathim set their plates out on the counter and went to wake his sleepy mate. When he stepped back into the bedroom, she was sitting up in bed, rubbing her eyes. Her hair tumbled around her, making her look soft and sweet. She smiled when she saw him watching her.

"Morning," she said. "Did I sleep too long?"

"Morning. I have the morning meal ready, if you're hungry."

She nodded and slipped out of bed, her cheeks turning pink. "I'll just borrow this," she said, grabbing his shirt off the floor and pulling it over her head.

The sight of her in his clothes was enough to set his heart racing. He took her hand and led her over to the counter where he'd left their food and helped her onto one of the stools. She smiled when she saw the offering.

"Eggs and sausage?" she asked, picking up one of the large links with her fingers.

"Porshwine links," he said. "I hope you like them."

She took a bite and her face lit up. "It's really good."

So far, she'd liked everything he'd prepared for her. Maybe it wouldn't be hard for her to adjust to the food on his world, and he could always request the ships to find Earth food for her. They finished their meal and his mate yawned widely, stretching her arms over her head. The movement lifted her luscious breasts and made his mouth water. Lathim wanted to taste her again, lick her from head to toe, before sinking deep into her tight channel. But he worried she might be sore from the previous night.

An incoming link made him pause.

"I'm worried about my mate," Rowrick said.

"So call the medic. What do I know about human females?"

"You have one," Rorwick responded. "Bring her to see my Jillian. Something is wrong with her."

"I'm not risking Maggie."

He ended the communication and noticed his mate was staring at him intently. His eyebrows lifted as he waited to see what she would say or do. She looked around the room then back at him again.

"I didn't hear anything, but it looked like you were talking to someone. With your mind," she said.

"Rorwick linked to me."

"How is Jillian?" Maggie asked.

Lathim shrugged, not wanting to tell her what Rorwick said for fear she may want to see the other woman, and he wasn't certain it was safe. Her eyes narrowed at him and her lips pursed. Lathim braced himself for whatever was about to come out of her mouth, but she just stared at him a moment then shrugged and went back to the bedroom. Either she wasn't going to put up a fight, or she was going to get him later when he least expected it. He was still learning about his mate and didn't know when she would strike or how. Or if she would at all.

He heard the water running a moment later and knew she was showering. He cleaned up their breakfast plates and cleaned the kitchen. When he was finished, she was striding back into the room with a wet braid down her back and dressed in another of her stretchy pants and tops. He wouldn't have minded if she'd stayed in his shirt all day, but the gleam in her eye told him that she didn't intend to stay home.

"Show me my new home?" she asked.

"You want to explore the base?"

She nodded. "For now. I'd like to see what's outside of the walls too. You mentioned water that was safe for swimming, and a farm area. I want to see it all."

Lathim went and put on his boots then reached for Maggie's hand. "Are you sure you don't want to stay home today?"

"I'm curious about this place I'm going to call home," she said. "What if you have to leave and I don't know where everything is or who anyone else is except Rorwick and the few commanders I met yesterday?"

She had a good point. He wanted her to know many people so she would be safe and looked after whenever he had to go on another mission. Unless he took her with me, but if she was expecting, that would be impossible. Lathim would never make her give birth on a ship when she would be much safer here. He still hadn't confessed that he hadn't gotten the injection yesterday, but maybe it wouldn't come up. He hated lying to her, but he didn't want her to push him away either. His conscience pricked. It was wrong to deceive her.

"Maggie, there's something I need to tell you," he said.

"About our outing?"

"No, it's about…"

She held up a hand. "Anything not pertaining to our outing can wait. Now, where should we go first?"

"Would you like to see the market? It's where we select out food and if a ship has landed recently, there may also be goods to look over. It's much like your shopping on Earth, except we don't use currency. Everyone has a job and helps out, and any money that we get comes from plundering pirate ships, and is then used to better our society by purchasing goods at trading posts that we can't get here."

She nodded. "Either you or Zorlok mentioned that yesterday. If everyone has a purpose here, does that mean I'll get a job assigned to me too?"

He hoped he didn't look as horrified as he felt. "It's my job to take care of you. The position I have pays for both of us and any children we may have. It's not necessary for you to work, and there aren't really any jobs to be had."

"So, I'm just to sit at home all day every day?" she asked with a frown.

Lathim hesitated. She didn't sound happy about staying home. Did she really want a job? He'd thought she was just asking because she didn't understand how their society worked, but if she was worried about sitting home all day every day… he didn't know what he'd come up with, but there had to be something she could do.

"You said I could put a garden out back, right? If we can get anything to grow in planters?"

He nodded.

"Then what if I helped other people do the same

thing? Maybe they'll like our garden so much they'll want one of their own. If everyone is busy working, they won't have time to set up a garden. But I could do it for them, as long as the plants and dirt were provided for me."

She looked so hopeful he didn't want to tell her no right away. But the decision wasn't really his to make. It would be up to the commanders if she would be allowed to have a job, and what that job would be. Setting up gardens for people seemed like a simple enough task, if their garden worked out. If the plants couldn't survive out of the ground, though, it would be a wasted effort, as the areas around their homes had little grass and were mostly rock.

"We need to see if our garden thrives before you ask if anyone else wants one," Lathim said. "In a few weeks, we should know if the plants will make it. If they do, we can present your idea to the commanders."

"You'll request the planters I need? And the plants?" she asked.

"I'll request both."

She smiled and let him lead her out of the house and toward the market. Many of his people waved as they walked past, but none asked for an introduction. By now, they all knew who Maggie was, even if she didn't know their names. He wanted her to be comfortable in her new home, but if he introduced her to every cyborg they passed, they would never reach the market.

Telfir stopped them, waving at them with a huge smile. "Lathim, this is your enchanting mate?"

"Telfir, this is Maggie. Maggie, Telfir is one of my best friends. If I'm not around and you need something, look for Telfir."

She smiled and waved at Telfir shyly. "Hi."

"Many have wondered if you would show her around today. They were placing bets on how long you would keep her locked in your bedroom," Telfir said with a good-natured laugh.

Maggie's cheeks flushed and Lathim held her closer.

"Maggie wished to explore her new home. She asked about the market so I thought we'd go there today," Lathim said.

"I believe that Balize and Skronle were setting some items aside for your mate, in case she wanted them for your home." Telfir smiled. "I'd enjoy sharing a meal with the two of you sometime. After Maggie is more settled."

"It was nice meeting you," Maggie said softly.

"It was a pleasure to meet you as well, Maggie," Telfir said.

Lathim guided his mate toward the market, curious what his fellow cyborgs had set aside for her. He liked that everyone was trying to make her feel more at home, and he hoped she appreciated their efforts. The marketplace was bustling when they reached the center of the base. There were tables set up with food, some set with goods, and a third table that was nearly overflowing with miscellaneous items that looked like they mostly came from Earth.

Balize smiled in greeting. "We've been putting things aside for your mate. Others have helped. We thought she might like first choice of anything from Earth. We were going to offer Rorwick's mate the same, but she isn't awake yet. The medics are treating her now."

"Jillian hasn't woken?" Maggie asked, her brow furrowed. "Shouldn't she have woken up by now? Was she sicker than you thought?"

Balize shrugged. "The medics will determine what's to be done. I'm sure they will take very good care of her. Rorwick called them in first thing this morning. Although, I worry how Rorwick will handle it if she never wakes up. It's possible she was too far gone when you rescued her."

Balize motioned to the table of human items. "Please pick whatever you want, Maggie. And if there are things you like on the other tables, you may select from those too. We want you to be happy here."

Maggie smiled at him and began browsing the items. She selected a few small things from her world and then a Kesphan blanket and an Urian wrap. She fingered the tunics from Kalibras but moved past them. When she'd finished making her selection, Lathim picked up a few fruits to keep at the house in case she wanted a snack. Then he arranged to have the items delivered to his home. He carried the fruits with him in a canvas sack Balize provided.

Lathim pointed out a few other buildings before they went back home, but Maggie seemed restless. When they entered their home, she sat down and stared out at the garden, or where her garden would go. There was a viewing screen across from her, but she hadn't asked for entertainment. When he'd mentioned he was bringing home a human, he'd been informed they would download as many videos from her world as possible, to help her feel more at home.

"Would you like to watch something?" Lathim asked. "We have videos from your world."

Her gaze was curious as she looked at him. "Like what?"

He connected to the viewing screen and pulled up something called a movie. From what he understood, they were meant to entertain humans, like the sex videos they'd discovered. Except they'd thought they were for instructional use. He was glad that Maggie had told him otherwise before his fellow cyborgs used those tactics on other humans as a way to lure them to their beds. He'd passed the word along, especially to those leaving on missions.

Her eyes lit up when she saw the movie on the screen. There were others, but he didn't know anything about them. This one seemed to be magical children and weird beasts. Maggie was delighted with the selection and curled up amongst the pillows. Lathim eased down next to her to watch it. While he didn't understand most of what was happening, he found it entertaining just the same.

"Do you have others?" she asked when it went off.

"Many others. The computer can control the viewing screen, so if you wish to see something and I'm not home, simply request a movie to play." He frowned. "I don't know that they're all in your Earth English though. Being a world of many languages, it's possible some you wouldn't understand."

Maggie nodded.

"Are you hungry?" he asked. "I have fruit, or I could make the afternoon meal for us."

"I don't think I'm ready for lunch yet. I'm still pretty full from breakfast."

"Another movie then?"

"What do you do when you're here alone?" she asked.

"I mostly work, even when I'm on my home planet."

"I meant here in the house," Maggie said.

He felt his cheeks warm. "I used to pleasure myself instead of using the sex bots. I got tired of them."

Maggie bit her lip but it looked like she was trying not to smile. He didn't understand why that would amuse her. Maggie moved closer to him, placing her hand on his thigh. His cock jumped at the contact, and he wished they didn't have clothes separating them. Was she trying to tell him that she was ready to go back to bed? Was she not tender from last night?

Maggie slowly unfastened his pants before reaching inside to stroke his cock. He hissed in a breath at the contact of her small, soft hand against his hard shaft. Lathim wanted to reach for her, to strip her bare and lavish attention on her, but he held back, not knowing what she wanted from him. Her hand on his cock gave him an idea, but what if she was just playing and didn't intend to follow through? She was bound to be curious, and he would let her explore his body as much as she wanted.

Maggie pulled at his pants until he lifted his hips and helped her slide them down. They pooled around his boots, not letting him spread his legs very far. He tugged his shirt over his head and tossed it aside, giving her as much access to his body as possible without stripping completely bare. Her hands were warm and soft as they coasted over his skin. His cock pulsed in time with his heartbeat, a bit of pre-cum beading on the tip.

She reached for him again, but hesitated.

"You can touch me wherever you want," Lathim said.

Her cheeks warmed as her hand closed around his cock again, giving it a slow stroke. Maggie licked her lips and with her gaze fastened on his, she leaned forward and flicked her tongue against the head of his cock. He fought to remain still as she explored his length with her lips and tongue, teasing him.

Her lips closed around him, sliding down his shaft, as her tongue flicked along the underside of his cock. Lathim groaned and fisted his hands at his sides to keep from reaching for her. He let Maggie taste and explore as much as she wanted, his need growing with every suck, and every sweep of her tongue. His transmitters willed his cock into submission, but the harder she sucked, the closer he was to exploding in her sweet mouth, his body ignoring his commands.

"Maggie, if you don't stop, I'm going to come," he warned. "I can't hold on much longer."

Her cheeks hollowed as she sucked him harder than before and with a cry, his hips bucked and he came, filling her mouth with his cum. Maggie drank it down and then licked her lips as she stared at him. His breaths came out ragged and harsh as he reached for her, smoothing her cheek with his fingertips. No one had ever done that for him before, except the sex bots, and he didn't count those. He reached for Maggie, pulling her down onto his lap and kissing her fiercely. Already, his cock was hardening again, eager to be inside of her, if she'd allow it. She might be his mate, but he would never force himself on her. If she accepted him into her body, it would be because she wanted him as much as he wanted her, and never because he'd forced her to take him.

"I want you, Maggie, but tell me and this stops right now."

"I want you too," she said softly before pressing her lips to his once more.

Lathim kicked off his boots and pants, then rose, lifting Maggie into his arms. He carried her through their home and to their bedroom, where he eased her down on the soft bedding. She had on too many damn clothes and it took him only minutes to strip her bare, tossing her boots and clothes onto the floor. The curls between her legs were already damp with desire, and he groaned, needing to feel her wet heat wrapped around him.

"I want to go slow, to make it wonderful for you," he said, as he leaned down to kiss her again.

"I don't want slow," she said.

"Maggie… you don't know what you're asking for. You should tell me to be careful with you, to take my time. You should remind me that you're fragile."

She snorted. "I'm not fragile, Lathim. I managed to escape the pirates on my dad's ship. If I were some delicate flower, I'd have been screaming for help while they did whatever the hell they wanted to me. Instead, I fought back and I got away."

"And I'm grateful for that," Lathim said. "But compared to my people, compared to the sex bots I've been using, you are fragile. I love that you fought back against the pirates, and I'm glad you remained safe until I found you, but you deserve to be treated with the utmost care."

"Lathim?"

"What is it, my precious mate?"

She wrapped her hand around the back of his neck and pulled him down. "If you don't fuck me right now, I'm going to take care of myself."

His eyes widened at her coarse language and the image of her pleasuring herself. It was something he wouldn't mind seeing in the future, but not right now. No, right now he wanted inside of her, desperately. Her hips cradled his as his body settled over her and with one sure thrust, he entered her. Maggie gasped and her nails bit into his shoulders. Lathim groaned from the sheer pleasure of being inside of her.

"Let me know if I hurt you," Lathim said.

Maggie nodded, looking up at him with complete trust. The way she so easily placed herself in his care humbled him, and made him even more grateful that she was his. He'd always dreamed of a mate, and now he had the perfect one. Lathim drew back and slammed his hips forward, entering her hard and deep. Maggie cried out, but her eyes were glazed with pleasure and not pain.

He took her hard and fast, their bodies slapping together. He surged inside of her, only to pull back and slam home again. His grip on his control was slipping, his release getting closer and closer. Maggie gripped him tight, her channel pulsing around his shaft. She cried out as the wet heat of her orgasm slicked his cock even more. Lathim growled and let loose of his control, snarling as he powered into her, driving every bit of his cum as deep as it would go. Despite Maggie's talk of waiting for babies, he couldn't wait to see her round with their child.

He thrust deep one last time and pressed tight against her. Maggie lay panting for breath under him, her skin dewy with sweat. Her hands absently stroked his arms, almost as if she were petting him. Lathim pressed a kiss to her lips before rolling and taking her with him. Their bodies still joined, he wrapped his arms around her and just held her close. As much as he didn't want to tell her the truth, he couldn't keep it from her any longer. She needed to know they might have created a baby. It wasn't right for him to keep something like from her, no matter how much he wanted her.

"Maggie, I need to tell you something," he said.

She cuddled closer. "Is it bad news?"

He hesitated.

"You paused which means it could be bad news," she said. "I don't want to ruin the mood."

"But it's important," he said. "I should have told you before now."

Maggie sighed and looked up at him. "Then tell me now and get it out of the way."

"Remember when I said I was going to get the injection that prohibits sperm production?" he asked.

She bolted upright. "You lied to me?"

"Not exactly. I did go to get the injection, but the medic wouldn't give it to me. He said there was still some serum in my system and he didn't want to double dose me. There's a slight chance I could get your pregnant anytime between now and when my next injection is due."

"You had to have known that before we had sex for the first time," she said.

"I did. I'm sorry I didn't tell you. It was wrong of me, and…"

Her hand cracked across his cheek. Lathim worked his jaw to make sure she hadn't broken anything, then reached for her hand to make sure she hadn't injured herself. Her palm was red and her fingers looked a little puffy. She tried to pull away from him.

"Maggie, stop. My bones are made of metal and you could have broken your hand."

She stilled and let him examine her hand, but she glared at him the entire time. When he finished examining her fingers, she ripped her hand out of his and stormed into the bathroom. He heard the water turn on a minute later and he sighed, realizing he'd screwed up. He should have told her from the beginning that he couldn't get the injection, but he hadn't and now he'd have to pay the price. He only hoped she wasn't mad enough to renounce their mating and find another bed to warm.

Despite their short amount of time together, he truly did care for her. He just hadn't been thinking when he'd kept the truth from her. He'd known it was wrong and yet he'd done it anyway. It wasn't a logical thing to do and he had to wonder if maybe his circuits were malfunctioning. He did a quick assessment of his systems and determined that everything seemed to be in proper working order. It had been a very illogical, male response to mate with her and not tell her there could be consequences, because he'd known she would probably tell him to wait. And he hadn't wanted to. Perhaps if Liroz hadn't told him to lie... No, he couldn't completely blame Liroz. He'd gone along with it.

What was that human term he'd heard before? Asshole. Yeah, he was an asshole, and he needed to make it up to her somehow. Lathim pulled on his clothes and hesitated only a moment before leaving. It was obvious his mate didn't want to speak to him right now, and he didn't blame her. He linked to the base's main computer to access the human files that had been downloaded once he'd notified them two human women were coming to Xpashta. He scanned through them, hoping to find something about how to soothe his mate's hurt feelings, and came up empty.

He changed course and went to Rorwick's home, hoping that perhaps Jillian had woken and might be of some help. He rang the chime outside Rorwick's home and waited for his friend to answer. The scowl on Rorwick's face told him that he'd come at a bad time, but he was desperate to win his mate's affection once more. He'd thought they were growing close, before he'd gone and ruined it.

"Is Jillian awake?" Lathim asked.

Rorwick snorted. "She's awake. If your mate wants to visit, now might not be a good time."

"I was actually hoping that Jillian could help me with something. I made a mistake with Maggie and I don't know how to fix it. None of the files we've downloaded were any help."

Rorwick stepped back. "You can see if she'll talk to you. So far, she just likes throwing things at my head."

Maybe it was a good thing he hadn't brought Maggie to visit. She may have decided to follow Jillian's example and thrown things at him when he made her mad today. As it was, her angry glares were bad enough. Rorwick motioned for Lathim to follow him and he led him straight to Jillian.

"You're back?" a sharp voice said. "If you're hoping I'm out of things to throw, guess again."

Something shattered against the wall and Rorwick winced. "I brought company. Remember that I told you one of your kind mated one of my kind? He's come to talk to you about his human mate."

Jillian snorted. "Like I want to help any of you assholes."

Lathim stepped into the room and noticed how pale Jillian was. She might be well enough to throw things, but it was obvious she was not at full strength yet. He decided to keep his visit short so he wouldn't tax her any more than necessary. She eyed him with a hostile gaze and he settled on the stool across from her.

"My name is Lathim, and I'm afraid I've done something very wrong and I don't know how to fix it."

"So, your mate's pissed at you too?" Jillian asked. "Good. Serves you assholes right for kidnapping human women."

"I didn't kidnap Maggie."

"No? So, you offered to take her back to Earth?"

"Well, no."

"Then you kidnapped her. What else did you do to make her mad if that wasn't enough to send you scurrying for cover? Does she at least have good aim? I can't hit the big lummox over there no matter how many things I throw."

"Maggie has never thrown anything at me. She did strike me tonight though, which isn't like her. She's normally very sweet and quiet."

Jillian nodded. "If you pissed off one of the quiet ones, then I'm surprised all she did was hit you. Did it at least hurt?"

"No, and I worried she might have broken her hand. Now she isn't speaking to me."

"Well, if kidnapping her didn't piss her off, what did you do to make her so mad?" Jillian asked. "I have to know what's going on before I can try to help you. And honestly, I don't know that I should. Maybe your Maggie and I should ask for housing where we can bunk together and leave you two dumbasses out in the cold."

He didn't understand everything she said, but he caught the gist of it. "I kept something from her, something important. She thought that she couldn't get pregnant if we mated, but there's a slight chance that she can."

Jillian's jaw dropped and her gaze swung to Rorwick. "You can get us pregnant?"

She screamed in outrage and searched for something else to throw, but it seemed she was out of ammunition. It made Lathim wonder just what she and Rorwick had been up to for that bit of news to upset her so much. Had the two already mated? She'd been so sick, he thought it was doubtful, but that didn't mean Rorwick hadn't made his intentions clear.

"How do I fix things with my mate?" Lathim asked.

"You don't. She needs time to process that you lied to her. If she's giving you the silent treatment, be glad that's all the punishment you're getting. If it were me, I'd have threatened to cut off your balls."

He winced and placed a hand over his cock, in case she was feeling bloodthirsty and decided practice on him before going after Rorwick. He pitied his friend if this was the mate he'd chosen. She was nothing like his sweet Maggie, although, it seemed even his mate had a temper when she was angered. He never should have listened to Liroz when the medic suggested that he not tell Maggie about the injection. He'd lost her trust and he didn't know how to get it back.

"Will she ever forgive me?" Lathim asked.

Jillian shrugged. "I don't know her so I can't really answer that. If it were me, I'd want you to be scarce for a while. Is there a hunting party you could join for a few days? Or maybe get back on whatever ship brought us here and disappear for a while."

The thought of leaving his mate made him sad, but if that's what she needed in order to heal, in order to forgive him, then he would do it. He'd make sure someone checked on her often, in hopes that it was only him that she was angry with. Going back on a ship seemed like the best option. The Sphinx would be going on a short run. He just needed to make sure he was on board before it left. He wouldn't be gone more than one of her Earth weeks, and maybe that would give her time for her temper to cool.

"Thank you, Jillian," he said, rising to his feet. He

motioned for Rorwick to follow him.

"Are you going to take her advice?" Rorwick asked.

"I think I will," Lathim said. "But I need someone to provide meals for Maggie three times a day, and keep an eye on her."

"Consider it done. If I need help watching over her, I'll ask Sorus. I'm sure he would consider it an honor to help guard your Maggie."

Lathim hurried home. He quickly packed and sought Maggie. He found her in the solarium and he paused inside the door, not certain if his presence would be welcome. But whether she wanted to talk to him or not, she needed to know that he would be gone for a little while. He was sure she'd welcome the chance to be away from him, if she was still as angry as she'd been before.

"Maggie," he said softly. "I know you're mad at me, but I need to talk to you."

She folded her arms across her chest. "What is it, Lathim?"

"I'm going on a short trip on the *Sphinx*. I'll be gone about one of your Earth weeks. Rorwick will provide meals for you while I'm gone, and you can go visit Jillian if you wish. If you need something, don't hesitate to ask someone."

"So that's it? We argue and you take off?"

"I thought you might like some space. I'm sorry that I lied to you, and I'm even sorrier that you're mad at me. I thought if I took a short trip, maybe it would give you some time to calm down. Just know that I would never do anything that would hurt you, Maggie."

"You took away my free will, Lathim. You could have gotten me pregnant, knowing that I didn't want a baby right now. That's a pretty big betrayal. It's not something I'm just going to get over."

He nodded. "I'll return soon and we can talk. Until then, know that I'll be thinking of you every second that I'm gone."

She snorted and turned away from him, presenting her back.

Lathim's heart ached but he gave her the space she seemed to want. He left quietly and hurried to the *Sphinx*, joining their crew for the short jaunt to the Riley Space Station. He didn't know what they were going after and he didn't care. With some luck, they'd run into some pirates and he'd get to fight out his frustration. Anything would be better than the pain he felt at knowing he'd harmed his mate.

Chapter Eight

Maggie had spent the first three days holed up in the house, not wanting to talk to anyone. Even poor Rorwick got the silent treatment when he brought her meals, but on the fourth day, she realized it wasn't very fair to be mad at the entire planet just because her mate was an asshole. When Rorwick came to check on her, she tried to be more pleasant.

"You claimed the human that was found in the life pod, didn't you? That's what the others said. Her name is Jillian, right?" Maggie asked.

He nodded. "Jillian is my mate. Why do you ask?"

"I was hoping I could go visit with her for a little bit. I haven't had anyone to talk to for days, and it would be nice to talk to another human woman. I never really had a chance to interact with females much on my dad's ship. It would be nice to have a friend right now," Maggie said.

"You may come with me. Stay for the evening meal and then I'll return you so you may rest. Be warned, my Jillian can be prickly."

She smiled. "I take it you pissed her off like Lathim pissed me off?"

"If that means I made her angry, then yes."

"You cyborgs just can't help yourselves, can you?"

Rorwick didn't answer but motioned for her to follow him. His home wasn't very far away and the walk was short. When they entered his home, Maggie could hear a movie playing on his viewing screen. A redhead was munching on a piece of fruit as she watched a romantic comedy, but when Maggie walked into the room, Jillian smiled and patted the spot next to her.

"You must be Maggie."

Maggie nodded. "I thought maybe we could visit for a little while. Rorwick offered to let me stay for dinner."

"He's probably hoping I won't throw food at him if we have a guest."

Maggie's jaw dropped. "You throw food at him?"

"And anything else I can get my hands on. He's insufferable. Did he tell you that he kidnapped me so I can make babies with him? I didn't even know about the baby part until your mate stopped by the other day."

"So, your mate lied to you too?" Maggie asked.

"Yeah, it would seem so. Rorwick made it clear that he'd taken me as his mate and expected sex, but he'd left out the part where he could knock me up. Maybe he was hoping if I was already pregnant, I wouldn't be as angry."

Was that what Lathim had thought?

Rorwick leaned against the doorway. "I didn't lie to you. It just never came up."

"Well, it came up with Lathim and he still lied to me," Maggie said.

"Do you know the one thing we want just as much as mates?" Rorwick asked. "We want families. Children. For ten years, women have run in fear of us. We'd thought we'd never have a chance to have a baby with someone, and now that Lathim has you, Maggie, he wants it all. I know how pleased he is that you're his mate, how much he cares about you already, but he wants more. When you told him you don't want children right now, did you stop to think that maybe it was something he's wanted for a long time and you were asking him to put off his dreams?"

Maggie squirmed in her seat. "Well, no. Maybe. All right, so we'd discussed it a bit and I knew he wanted them, but if he wanted children so badly, why didn't he just say so? Why did he try to trick me into getting pregnant?"

"Because he worried you would say no, and I'm guessing that he was right. If you'd known there was a chance for you to get pregnant, would you have pushed him away that night? Everyone on board the *Mystic7* knew you hadn't consummated your mating. Claiming you meant that he got to keep you."

Maggie looked from Rorwick to Jillian and back again. "Are you trying to say that someone would have taken me from Lathim if we didn't have sex?"

Rorwick shrugged. "It's doubtful, as long as you chose to remain with him. But he likely thought you would leave him if he didn't claim you. Lathim wanted you tied to him so you could never leave. You have no idea how lonely it is to know that no one wants you. For ten years, we've lived solitary lives with only each other for company, or the paid company of a whore, and even some of those wanted nothing to do with us."

Maggie suddenly didn't feel quite so angry with Lathim. If anything, she felt kind of bad. Yes, he'd lied to her and it was wrong on so many levels. He'd done something he knew she didn't want. But she understood him a little better now. It wasn't that he'd been trying to take something from her, it was that he was trying to hold onto something for him. She wished he would have just told her how he felt instead of telling what she wanted to hear. If he'd wanted children that badly, they could have talked about it. It took two people to be in a relationship, and she'd only been thinking of herself.

"You're going to forgive him, aren't you?" Jillian asked.

"Yeah, I think I am. I just wish he would have talked to me instead of making the decision on his own. If I'd known he wanted a baby that badly, I wouldn't have just said no right away."

"You really are one of the sweet, quiet ones, aren't you?" Jillian asked.

"Maybe you could take notes from her," Rorwick said before turning and walking away.

Jillian rolled her eyes. "I guess I haven't been thinking of anyone other than me since I woke up in this strange place with a man who claimed to be my mate. I was so angry that I hadn't been returned to Earth, that I was claimed like a piece of luggage, that I never stopped to ask why he'd do that."

"I'm sorry about your baby," Maggie said. "I'm sure with you mourning your child, that Rorwick won't ask you to have another one right away. He seems nice."

"The baby wasn't mine," Jillian said.

"Then, why did you have it in the life pod with you?" Maggie asked, brow furrowed.

"Because the guy I was being sold to was going to have the baby as a delicacy. I decided that taking a chance on the life pod supporting both of us was better than me being a slave and that baby being eaten. Who's to say I wouldn't have ended up on the menu too at some point?"

Maggie's jaw dropped. "Who would eat a baby?"

"A Morvik. Nasty looking creatures. Although, to be honest, being on the menu would have been preferable to ending up in that thing's bed." Jillian shivered.

Rorwick came back into the room, a fierce look

on his face clearly stating he'd heard everything. "Why was slave trading happening on a luxury liner?"

Jillian's eyebrows rose. "If that thing started as a luxury liner, it wasn't by the time I got on it. There were rooms of slaves being traded and sold. I was lucky to get to a life pod, and even luckier they didn't come after me. Maybe they decided I was more trouble than I was worth and decided to cut their losses."

"A Morvik was purchasing you?" Rorwick asked. "You're certain?"

Jillian nodded. "I saw him, and felt his slimy tentacles grab my ass. Not to mention the noxious smell coming off that thing. Any fate was better than being sold to him. I don't know why he wanted me, but if it was for sex, I'm doubly glad I got out of there."

"You can't begin to know how lucky you are," Rorwick said. "Morviks mate with their slaves, and then pass them around to their friends. When the female's mind snaps, they serve her for dinner."

Jillian paled. "Good to know."

"And you balk at having a baby with me?" Rorwick looked pissed. "Have I not treated you kindly? Have I not given you many of your Earth things to make you more comfortable here?"

Jillian held up a hand. "Now isn't the time. Right now, let's focus on Maggie, all right?"

He nodded and leaned against the wall.

"Is there a way to get Lathim home sooner?" Maggie asked.

"No," Rorwick said. "The ship was going straight to the Riley Space Station and returning home. They were only docking there for a matter of hours. There's not a way to get him here sooner."

"All right. Then I guess I have a lot of waiting to do. It's been four days, so I have another three to go."

Maggie sighed. "Do you think he'll forgive me? I struck him before he left."

Rorwick grinned. "Puny female, you couldn't hurt him if you tried, not physically. You wounded his heart more than his jaw. I'm surprised you didn't break your hand."

"Lathim was worried about that, but looked it over and I guess it was fine. I wasn't really in a frame of mind to listen to him right then. And now I wish that I had, maybe he'd have opened up and talked to me if I hadn't been so angry."

"I'm going to make the evening meal," Rorwick said. "And after that, I'll take you home, Maggie."

When he left, there was a strange look on Jillian's face. Almost a look of longing. Was it possible that she actually liked the big cyborg and just didn't know how to react to him? Maybe coming today had solved two issues. Her fight with Lathim, and whatever problem Jillian had with Rorwick. Maybe Rorwick explaining more about their lives and their desires had opened Jillian's eyes as well.

"So, I wonder when you'll find out if you're pregnant," Jillian said. "With the creepy way they have of checking our vital signs and stuff, I wonder if they could hear a baby inside of you. Does it even have a heartbeat this soon?"

"I have no idea. I think their medics have special scanning capabilities that the others don't, so it's possible one of them could tell me. Do you think I should see one just in case?" Maggie asked.

"Wouldn't hurt. You could ask Rorwick to take you before he takes you home tonight. Although, if you're pregnant, I doubt that you'll be allowed to stay in the house by yourself. If you fell or had an accident, there wouldn't be anyone there to hear you."

"Good point," Maggie said. "So, I lose what little independence I have and find out if there's a baby on board, or I wait until Lathim gets home and take a chance on something happening."

"You're going to the medic, aren't you?" Jillian asked.

Maggie nodded. "I think it would be the best option. I don't think Lathim would ever forgive me if something happened to the baby because I was too stubborn to get checked out. I'll be lucky if he's speaking to me when he gets home as it is. I must have really hurt his feelings with the way I was acting."

Jillian smiled a little. "They're massive, and can be a bit arrogant, but I think deep down they're like teddy bears. Except with metal parts."

"Mechanical teddy bears?" Maggie asked.

"Yeah, something like that. Just don't tell Rorwick I compared him to a stuffed animal. I don't think his macho male pride could take the hit. It's bad enough I've been throwing shit at him since I woke up and he refused to take me home. I guess I've been a bit of a bitch."

"You woke up to a strange man on a strange world. I don't think anyone faults you for reacting the way you did."

"Maybe not," Jillian said. "But I think I took it too far. Ever since I opened my eyes, all he's wanted to do is help me. He feeds me, clothes me, brought me all kinds of trinkets he thought I might like. And to repay him, I've broken nearly everything in his home that wasn't nailed down. Yeah. I'm a bitch."

"Then maybe you can make it up to him, now that you know why he's refused to take you back to Earth." Maggie put her arm around Jillian. "It's never too late to start over. And I have a feeling that Rorwick would be very receptive to whatever form of apology you offered. Especially if you used your tongue."

Jillian cracked up and hugged Maggie back. "I think I'm going to like you. A lot."

Rorwick called them to dinner. No one said much as they ate, and the tension between Jillian and Rorwick was palpable. Maggie wondered how long her new friend would hold out before welcoming the big cyborg into her bed. She didn't miss the covert glances Jillian sent his way, or the perturbed expression on his face at every snippy comment that came out of Jillian's mouth. She almost felt sorry for the cyborg because he'd definitely met his match.

Rorwick cleared the table after their meal then waited by the front door for her. Maggie hugged Jillian and promised to come see her again soon. When she reached Rorwick's side, she placed her hand on his arm.

"Can I ask a favor?" Maggie asked.

"Is there something you need for your home?" Rorwick asked.

"No, I was hoping you would take me to the see the medic."

His eyes widened and he looked her over from head to toe. "Did my fierce mate wound you when I wasn't looking?"

"No, nothing like that. I'm not hurt. But I hoped that one of your medics could tell me if I'm pregnant."

"How long has it been? Four days?" Rorwick asked.

"Technically five since the first time."

"They might be able to tell you. I'm not sure how much the cybernetics have changed us in regards to reproduction. A Zelranian pregnancy can usually be determined within seven days. It may be too soon.

Then again, I don't know anyone of my race who has mated a human before."

"So you'll take me?" she asked.

Rorwick nodded and motioned for her to exit his home. He led the way through the base to the medical clinic, where two cyborgs were on duty. They went on instant alert when she stepped into the room, rushing toward her.

"Did the human get injured?" one of them asked.

"Maggie, this is Wrylack and the other medic is Liroz. There are several others on our world and some on board the ships that are currently off world," Rorwick said.

"It's nice to meet you both," Maggie said.

"If she's not injured, why did you bring her here?" Liroz asked.

"Maggie wishes to know if she might be pregnant," Rorwick said. "Lathim is currently off world so I brought her."

Liroz smiled. "We'd be happy to check and see if you're carrying."

Wrylack's eyes began to glow an intense blue. He scanned her from head to toe, then came back to rest on her belly. The lights in his eyes dimmed and returned to normal, although now she could see he didn't have gray eyes, but metal ones. He must have been one of the cyborgs Lathim had mentioned that had parts on the outside that made them different and harder to match with someone.

"I detect two life forms in your womb," Wrylack said. "I hope this is happy news. I know the commanders will be overjoyed to hear that there's been a successful mating. It will give the rest of us hope."

Maggie placed a hand over her stomach and fought down the momentary panic. She'd never been around children and didn't know the first thing about taking care of a baby, much less two. She took a few deep breaths until she didn't feel quite so much like she might pass out. Her hand shook as she smoothed it over her belly and she wished that Lathim were with her. He'd know exactly what to say to calm her down.

"This isn't good news?" Wrylack asked, looking concerned. "You don't seem pleased."

"I wasn't trying to get pregnant," Maggie said. "I think I'm just in shock. I mean, you said there are two of them and I don't even know what to do with one baby. I've never even held a baby before."

"How old are you?" Wrylack asked. "If that isn't too rude to ask."

"I'm twenty-two," Maggie said. "But I've spent most of my life on my father's ship and I was the only female on board. Even when we docked places, it wasn't often he let me leave the ship and if I did I always had guards with me. I always thought he was just being overprotective. I mean, I'd heard about women being sold to brothels, I just never thought something like that could happen to me."

Wrylack's eyes widened. "The females in brothels have been sold? They aren't there willingly?"

"There may be a few who choose that life, but most women aren't into doing multiple guys of multiple species every day of their life. A lot of those women have been stolen and sold and are given no choice in the matter."

Wrylack paled. "I'll not be using brothels anymore then. I'm sure if you told Lathim about this, then he's shared it with our Commanders and that information will be shared with all. I didn't realize the females were being abused like that. It's the same as force and it makes me sick to think I participated in something like that."

It sometimes surprised Maggie just how sheltered the cyborgs were. How could they have possibly thought the women chose that life? It just showed that all men, regardless of their race, thought with their little heads and not the one above their shoulders. If they'd stopped for two seconds to think about something other than getting laid, maybe they'd have realized most women wouldn't want to live a life like that. She wasn't sure if she wanted to bash them over their heads for being idiots or feel sorry for them since she'd ruined their fantasy with reality. It was almost like she'd just taken their favorite toy away from them. Even Liroz looked a little sickened by the thought of bedding unwilling women.

The cyborgs might have their faults, but Maggie could admit that they treated their women well. They were misguided at times, like when Lathim lied to her, but their hearts were in the right place. They were so desperate for love and affection, for a chance at a family, that they were blinded to anything that might stand in their way and just bulldozed over it. She should probably still be angry with Lathim, but she understood why he did it. She didn't agree with it by any means, but she understood.

"Since you're expecting, your body is going to need more nutrients. Will you allow me to administer some injections?" Wrylack asked.

"Just vitamins?"

"You should give her the serum to extend her life. It will crush Lathim if something happens to her," Rorwick said.

"What kind of serum?" Maggie asked, leery of what they might be injecting her with.

Wrylack hesitated a moment. "It's a complex

compound that has nanobytes that will repair tissue damage and keep you from aging as quickly. You'll still be human, but just a little extra as well."

"Just how long do you guys live?" Maggie asked.

"An unenhanced Zelranian can live nearly two hundred years. With our cybernetics, we will live much longer. We also age slower because of what was done to us," Wrylack said.

"So how old is Lathim?" Maggie asked. "He doesn't look much older than me, but if you guys live so long..."

Rorwick's eyebrows rose. "He's forty."

"F-forty? But... That's how old my dad was!"

Rorwick chuckled and even the medics looked amused. She was mated to someone her dad's age? Not that Lathim looked forty. Her father had been going gray at his temples and there were fine lines around his eyes. She'd thought Lathim was maybe twenty-eight. They'd warned her that they aged differently, but she hadn't realized how much. Did that mean in ten years she'd look older than her mate? Would he still want her when he looked young and she had gray hair?

"You said the nano-whatevers would make me live longer. Will they make me age slower too?" she asked.

"To my knowledge, Jillian and you will be the first humans to use the serum. It's hard to say how it will react with your system for certain. Jillian has already been dosed and there were no adverse effects, so it appears to be safe to use on you."

Maggie's hands clenched into fists. "What about the babies? Will it harm the babies?"

Wrylack hesitated. "Uncertain."

"Then don't give it to me until after I give birth. I can survive nine months without it." She narrowed her eyes. "You aren't going to tell me your people are pregnant for like three years or something, are you?"

"Actually, Zelranian females give birth at seven months. I'm not sure how long your pregnancy will last. We will monitor the situation and check on growth and development as the months progress. Within four months, we should have an idea of how long you'll carry them." Wrylack smiled. "Lathim is going to be thrilled when he hears the news."

"If you're done with Maggie for now, I'll return her to her home," Rorwick said.

"We should give her vitamins to boost her immune system and make her stronger," Liroz said.

"Why don't we wait for Lathim to get back?" Rorwick suggested. "I think any treatments should be discussed with him first. It would be one thing if her life were in danger, but she seems perfectly healthy."

Wrylack nodded. "My scan of her systems did indicate that she is in good health. A pregnancy will wear on her body, but the vitamins can wait a few days. It's understandable that you'd prefer to wait for Lathim's return. As her mate, he will have final say over her treatment."

Maggie folded her arms over her chest. "Excuse me, but as it's my body, I get final say over my treatment."

Wrylack tipped his head in acknowledgement.

"Thank you for telling me about the babies," Maggie said. "I'll come back after I've talked to Lathim."

Rorwick escorted her back across the base to her home. The house seemed cold and lonely with no one to talk to. Lathim couldn't get home fast enough. He was likely to find her skeleton on the couch, her final resting place from having died of boredom.

Chapter Nine

Lathim felt like he'd been gone forever. Guilt ate at him for the entire trip, and worry. He should have stayed and talked to Maggie, even if she was angry with him. Her temper would have cooled eventually. He knew that he'd done a bad thing, but he wasn't sorry for it. Well, maybe a little sorry. He was sorry that he'd hurt Maggie, but he wouldn't take back the memories of their time together for anything. She meant everything to him, and he hoped that she would see that. All he'd wanted to do was claim her and make her his in every way that mattered.

It was unfortunate that he'd broken her trust by doing things his way. But if she'd come to trust him once, she could do it again, right? He just needed to get back home so he could tell her how much she meant to him. He didn't care if they ever had children; as long as he had Maggie, that would be enough. Having a family had seemed like the most important thing in the world to him, until he'd worried that he'd lost his mate. It had made him realize that what he wanted most was her. Just her.

"You look like a lovesick fool," Ralkir said.

"I'm missing my mate."

"We already broke through the atmosphere. We'll be setting down any minute. Try to refrain from running all the way to your home."

Lathim snorted.

"Did you have someone notify her of your return?" Ralkir asked.

"No. When I left, we weren't on good terms. She was angry with me, and she had a right to be. I'm hoping that she's calmed enough that we can talk now. I need to apologize to her."

Ralkir shook his head. "If this is what happens to a male when he takes a mate, I just may stay single indefinitely. Love makes you weak."

"No, having Maggie in my life is the best thing that ever happened to me. When you fall in love, you'll see."

"So you love her?" Ralkir asked.

Lathim froze. He hadn't meant to utter those words, but they'd slipped out. And he realized, they were true. He really did love Maggie. She was his entire world, his everything. If she left him, if she decided she could never forgive him, he would live a long and miserable life because there would never be another female for him. She was it.

The ship shuddered as it touched down and Lathim braced his feet. When the vibrations faded, he briskly walked to his quarters and retrieved his belongings. He ground his teeth in frustration as everyone bottlenecked trying to leave the ship, and they were all moving incredibly slow. When his feet touched the ground, he picked up the pace, not stopping to talk to anyone. He hated to be rude to his friends, but Maggie was his top priority. It had been a week since he'd last seen her, but it had felt like an eternity.

As he neared his home, he felt a rush of excitement over seeing his mate again. Even if she was still angry with him, he'd take her hurtful words. Anything was better than the ache he'd felt being apart from her. The door opened and he set his things down. He could hear the viewing screen and hurried in that direction, hoping his mate was nearby. Maggie lay curled amongst the cushions, tears dampening her cheeks. His heart lurched at the sight and he rushed to her side.

"What's wrong? Are you hurt? Where is the pain?" he asked quickly, reaching for her.

"Lathim? You're home." She gave him a tremulous smile and wrapped her arms around him. "I'm not hurt. It's just a sad movie."

His hand smoothed down her back and held her close, breathing in her scent. Peace settled over him now that she was back in his arms. Feeling her soft skin, hearing her sweet voice, it made everything right in his world again.

"I'm sorry, Maggie. I'm so damn sorry."

She drew back. "Sorry for what?"

"For hurting you, lying to you. It was wrong of me. I should have given you a say. You had every reason to be mad at me."

Her hand smoothed over his cheek. "I'm not mad. I was for days after you left, but then Rorwick explained a few things to me and I realized you hadn't done it maliciously."

"What did Rorwick say?"

"He explained about how precious a mate was to you and that you'd wanted to claim me so I couldn't leave. Although, just to be clear, having sex does *not* mean I can't walk out the door. Even pregnant I could leave if I chose to do so. You're my mate, my other half, but you aren't my boss. I know mating is forever here, but it's different where I come from. I'm still adjusting to all this."

He nodded. "I understand. And will you be leaving?"

His heart hammered in his chest as he waited for her answer.

"No, I want to stay here, with you. Besides" -- she took his hand and placed it over her belly --"your children are going to need their father to teach them the ways of this world."

"Children?" Stars danced in his vision and he swayed. There was more than one baby? His knees buckled and his breath left him in a *whoosh* as he collapsed onto the floor, staring at the ceiling a little dazed.

"Lathim!"

Maggie knelt at his side.

"I'm fine," he assured her. "Babies? There's more than one?"

"Two. According to Wrylack anyway."

"What else did he say? Are you able to carry two? What if it's too much strain for your body?" Lathim asked.

"He said I'm perfectly healthy but recommended some vitamin injections to give me a little boost. I decided to wait and get them after I'd talked it over with you."

"Do you need anything?" Lathim asked. "Are there any foods you want more than others? Should we start preparing a room for the babies? Did Wrylack say how long the pregnancy would last?"

Maggie giggled. "Slow down, daddy. The babies will probably be born in seven to nine months, but he said we won't know for sure until I'm further along. He wants to monitor their development and it will give him a better idea of my due date. So I think we have plenty of time to prepare a room for the babies. Although, if this is a world of only males, I'm curious what exactly you have lying around that would work for a baby's room."

His eyes widened and he realized she was right. They'd never had children on this world. Babies needed special beds, didn't they? And diapers. There was much to plan, but if they truly had seven months or more, then there was time. For now, he'd enjoy being in his mate's company again.

"I love you," he said, gazing up at her.

Maggie looked pleasantly surprised. "Did you just discover that? You seem awfully certain."

"I was on board the *Sphinx* when it hit me. But I wanted to tell you. I wanted you to know how much you mean to me, that you're my everything. Even if we'd never had children, my life would still be blessed because you're in it."

Her eyes misted with tears and she leaned down to press her lips to his. "I love you too. And I'm sorry I was so bitchy before and didn't give you time to explain yourself. I promise in the future if I'm ever angry with you that I will give you time to explain why you did or said whatever set me off."

"I hope to never make you angry again."

Maggie smiled. "That's not likely because I think we're going to have a long life together. But right now, if you're no longer unable to stand, there's something important you need to do."

"Anything you want."

She laughed. "What if I wanted you to do something painful?"

"You'd never cause me harm on purpose."

The smile slipped from her face. "No, I wouldn't. I want you to take me back to bed, where our argument started, because I want to replace that bad memory with a good one. And being in your arms is always good."

Lathim rose to his feet and lifted Maggie into his arms, being extra careful with her. He had everything he'd ever wanted. A mate and children. His heart was full, and he couldn't imagine ever wanting something more than what he held in his arms. He'd fought in wars, been to hell and back, and travelled across the galaxies in search of treasures. But the greatest treasure he would ever find was right here, in his heart and in his home. Maggie was his everything, and he would gladly spend the rest of his life making her and their children happy. He didn't care if he never left the surface of Xpashta ever again because even the stars in the sky couldn't compare to his sweet mate.

He only hoped that in the days to come his fellow cyborgs would find the happiness he had with Maggie. He hoped to one day see his planet populated with happy mates and even happier children. That the loneliness etched in every cyborg's heart would be erased with love, because if Maggie had shown him anything, it was that all things were possible, even when you'd given up hope.

Offered to the Cyborg (Cy-Con 2)
Jessica Coulter Smith

When the Zelranian cyborg's ship *The Sphinx* is attacked by a reptilian race called the Meori, Wrylack is the only cyborg left standing. Forced onto the Meori vessel, his skills as a medic are demanded in exchange for his life. But any plans Wrylack may have had to escape died the moment he laid eyes on Shaylee, the human female slave in the Meori med bay. Even injured, she's the most beautiful thing he's ever seen. And when the Meori realize they can use her to control Wrylack, they are only too pleased to give her to him.

Shaylee has only known pain and suffering all her life. First on Earth, passed around the foster care system, and later as a slave to one alien after another. No one has ever touched her with kindness, has ever cared what happened to her. When the sexy purple cyborg with the strange eyes and gentle touch says she's his, Shaylee is almost scared to hope that her life is changing. But the big male isn't interested in owning her as a slave. He wants a mate!

Chapter One

A blast rocked *The Sphinx*, making the floor tilt under Wrylack's feet and sending him careening into a wall. Two Meori ships had cornered them. One was firing while the other had docked. Locked in the med bay, Wrylack cursed the captain for giving him orders to stay put. He might be a medic, but he was a damn good fighter too. As it was, he was stuck in medical with no weapons. According to the onboard computer, there were now thirty lifeforms aboard *The Sphinx* instead of their crew of ten. Wrylack understood that the captain wanted him safe, so he could heal any who were injured, but this was ridiculous. He should be out there kicking ass with everyone else.

Behind his sealed door, he could hear the sounds of fighting down the corridor and knew it was drawing closer. A scream of pain echoed down the hall, and he hoped it wasn't one of his brothers. If the Meori had gotten near medical, which was in the heart of the ship, it must mean his fellow cyborgs were having a hard time fighting them off. Had there been casualties? He didn't want to link to anyone and put them in danger.

His hands clenched at his sides as he scanned the room for anything he might use as a weapon. There was an old-fashioned scalpel he still used on occasion, but it wouldn't do much against laser weapons or ion blasters. His hand closed around the scalpel and he held it at his side, hoping that his crew would be all right. He'd unsuccessfully tried to open the medical doors three times, wanting to help the others, but the captain had recoded it so that the portal would only open from the outside. That would only keep Wrylack safe if the cyborgs won the battle, but his captain apparently hadn't thought of that.

Wrylack tried to connect to the system with his neural transmitters, but access was locked. He had to admit the captain was smart and had thought of everything, even if he was foolish enough to leave Wrylack out of the fight. He'd trained alongside the others on Zelran and could fight as well as anyone. If anything, his cybernetic eyes, an anomaly even amongst his kind, would give him an edge in fighting. He could see the weak points on any opponent, including internal ones. Frustrated, he slammed his fist against the wall, denting the metal of the ship.

The ship grew quiet, and Wrylack tried to communicate with his fellow cyborgs, but no one was responding. He feared they'd all been killed, which meant the Meori would come for him next, once they realized he was on board. He could hear the clang of boots coming down the corridor and braced himself. When the doors to the med bay slid open, he stared at the green and gold aliens, with their serpent-like eyes and tongues.

They looked him over, laughing when they saw the scalpel clutched in his hand. Two held ion blasters pointed at him, and he knew there was no way he was taking them out. Not on his own and only armed with the scalpel.

The three Meori in front hardly had a scratch on them, but the ones in back were pooling blood on the floor. Wrylack tried not to smile at the sight. It seemed his brothers had fought hard, even if they hadn't been victorious. Would they kill him now too?

"The healer thinks to fight us," the larger one up front said.

Little did they know he could kick their asses, if it weren't for the unfair advantage of the blasters in their hands. He might be enhanced, but he wasn't indestructible. Going into a blaster fight with nothing more than a scalpel would get him killed.

"Where's my crew?" Wrylack asked.

The alien shrugged. "Alive, but incapacitated."

Why hadn't they killed everyone? What was it they wanted?

"And your plan for us?" Wrylack asked.

The alien smiled, his pointed teeth showing. "The others will be dropped at Alpha9, for a fee of course, and we're commandeering this ship. You, however… " The alien looked him over again. "We need a medic. Ours died and since your cyborg brothers did some damage, my crew will need to be tended. Serve us well and you will be rewarded."

Wrylack could read between the lines. Service would be required regardless, if he wanted to live. He would imagine the reward would be his freedom. What they didn't know was that the moment he'd laid eyes on them, he'd hacked into the telecommunications system and had the computer send a message to the commanders on Xpashta, with their present location and information on who had taken command of the ship. It wouldn't be long before the cyborgs' other ships were on their way to lend aid. He only hoped it wouldn't be too late.

One of the Meori gripped his arm tight, making the nerves in his arm go numb, and the scalpel fell from his hand, clattering to the floor. Wrylack allowed himself to be dragged through the ship and taken aboard the Meori vessel. He wasn't stupid enough to think he could take on two ships himself, which meant he had to follow orders and stay alive until backup arrived. The ship was much larger than *The Sphinx* and had probably once been a luxury liner, judging by the artwork on the walls and the dense carpet under his feet. Slave females of all races shuffled down the hallways and gathered in open rooms. Some were dressed in transparent tunics, and he knew they were breeding stock. The thought made him ill.

When they reached medical, Wrylack was shoved inside, and he froze at the sight before him. Two human females lay dead, the sheets covering them stained with blood, with a third huddled in the corner, her eyes wide in fright. Blood dripped down her arm, and her clothes were torn. Anger welled inside him, and he turned to snarl at the Meori who had dragged him on board.

"You attacked innocent females?"

The Meori shrugged. "When we purchased them, we didn't realize they wouldn't be sexually compatible. Their master was raving about how good it felt to fuck them. We stopped a male from mounting the third when the first two died."

Wrylack was horrified and sickened. Moving slowly, he approached the female in the corner. He knelt in front of her and used his cybernetic eyes to scan her. Aside from some bruising and the bite mark on her shoulder, she seemed to be healthy. All of her organs were in good working order, and he was thankful to note she wasn't pregnant. Judging by the scarring in her womb, even if the Meori hadn't been able to breed with her, someone had been successful at some point. The haunted look in her eyes spoke of someone who had lived this life for a while. His heart ached for her, imagining the horrors she'd probably faced as a slave.

Wrylack pulled aside her slave tunic and studied the bite. It was deep and the tissue around it was badly bruised. The Meori who had tried to mount her had likely bitten her to hold her in place. Wrylack hoped she'd fought like hell. No one deserved the fate of being a breeder, especially to the Meori. He stood quickly and rummaged through the cabinets until he found what he needed. With a tube of livron gel in his hand, he sank to his haunches in front of her again. Wrylack squeezed the gel onto his fingers and spread it over her wound. She flinched at his touch, but didn't lash out at him. He knew the gel would cool the angry wound first, then numb it within minutes. If applied regularly, the wound would seal in a few days.

"My name's Wrylack, and I'm a medic," he told her. "I'm going to help you."

"She's useless," the Meori said. "No sense in treating her. We're just going to toss her out an airlock. I can't take the chance that she would sell right away when we reach Alpha9, and I don't intend to stay there long. She's a waste of space."

Wrylack growled and glared at the Meori. "You're not tossing her out an airlock."

The Meori rocked back on his heels. "You seem rather fond of her."

"She's a helpless female." Wrylack wasn't about to admit that he thought she was the most beautiful female he'd ever seen. Looking into her eyes, he wanted to be her hero. But he was just as much a captive right now as she was. But then, if they'd met under other circumstances, how likely was it that she'd have let a cyborg get anywhere near her? Especially him with his strange-looking eyes.

"And females are precious to your people, aren't they?" the Meori asked slyly. Wrylack wasn't certain he liked the look on the Meori's face. "Do what we say, and you can keep her. Consider her your reward for good behavior."

Keep her? Wrylack hesitated and glanced down

at the female. Her hair was black as pitch and hung in long curls down to her ass. The elfin face that peered up at him had beautiful lavender eyes, a color he'd never seen on a human before. The female's skin was pale as ivory and had felt soft when he'd administered the gel to her wound. He lowered himself in front of her again, bracing his fist on the floor, and leaning in close. She didn't shrink away or seem afraid of him.

Her gaze met his. When he reached for her, smoothing her hair back from her face, she didn't so much as flinch. "Do you know what I am?" he asked.

"No," she said softly.

"I'm a Zelranian cyborg."

"Is that why your eyes are so different?" she asked. "They're beautiful when they glow. Why do they only glow sometimes?"

Her voice was soft and mesmerizing, much like her. "My eyes are cybernetic, along with my lungs and heart. My eyes glow when I'm doing a scan to check for injuries. I'm different, even from my people. Does that frighten you?" he asked.

Her gaze strayed to the Meori in the doorway before returning to him. There was a question in her eyes that she didn't seem to want to voice. The Meori had mentioned her previous owner had used her for sex, and the Meori had intended the same. It stood to reason she would wonder if he would hurt her if they were intimate.

"I won't harm you," Wrylack assured her. "Unlike the Meori, Zelranians are compatible with humans."

Her cheeks flushed, but she held his gaze.

"If they throw you out the airlock, you'll die," Wrylack said. "Space is cold, and your organs will begin to freeze, assuming you don't die from asphyxiation first. I won't force you to be mine, but it's the only way I can save you."

It hadn't occurred to him until that moment that maybe she would prefer death. It saddened him to think she might feel that way, but there was something in her eyes that said she was a fighter.

"I'm Shaylee." She smiled softly, seeming to accept that she was his now.

"Shaylee." Wrylack reached for her again, smoothing his fingers down her cheek. "I will treat you well, this I promise."

The Meori moved closer. "If you try anything, she dies. And it will be a painful death. We'll make you watch as she's mounted many times, and you see what happened to the others with just one Meori."

Wrylack's jaw tensed, and he rose to his full height of well over six feet. He glared at the Meori and fought not to punch the alien. Wrylack's bones had been replaced with metal after he'd been accepted into the Cy-Con program. In hand-to-hand combat, he had no doubt he would win. Bones easily shattered from the impact of his fist. But he also didn't know how many Meori were on board, and knew that Shaylee would be harmed if he retaliated. That was the only thing that kept him in check right then. To even think of something so horrible happening to her, that the alien would even threaten such brutality, infuriated him.

"I'll do as you say. For now," Wrylack said.

"Then I'll show you to your quarters. Bring your female with you."

Shaylee stood on legs that trembled, and Wrylack swung her up into his arms, carrying her down the corridors as he followed the Meori. Shaylee clung to him, her arms around his neck and her face pressed against him. While it had always been his duty to treat those who were injured, he'd never been responsible for a living being before. The soft female in his arms was a surprise, but a welcome one. Even if it did mean he had to serve the Meori until his fellow cyborgs could locate and rescue him. That had been his intention, but had it just been him, he might have tried escaping if the opportunity presented itself. With Shaylee, that wouldn't be possible. He would never risk her life, not even to save his own.

Little did the Meori know that all cyborgs were equipped with tracking devices, attached to their skeletal systems and completely undetectable by most technology. He supposed he should thank the Zelranian parliament for that, since it had been at their insistence that the trackers were installed. It meant that the parliament could locate them anytime they wished, but it wasn't like the cyborgs were hiding. They lived their life in the open, and had lived in peace, as long as they never returned to Zelran.

Once the other cyborgs realized *The Sphinx* was gone from its last location and that Wrylack was not among those left on Alpha9, they would activate his tracker and come for him. Somehow, he needed to discover how many Meori were on board this vessel, and how many others were nearby, and get that information to the commanders. He only had to keep Shaylee safe from the Meori until then. Once they were picked up, he'd request time on Xpashta to get better acquainted with his mate.

Mate. It didn't seem possible that someone like him, with his strange eyes, would be holding such a delectable female, and that she was his. She was only with him as a way to live, but he knew in time he could win her affection. Wrylack would give her everything she'd ever wanted or needed. As of now, she was his top priority.

The Meori stopped in front of a door on the second level of the ship. He placed his palm against the control panel and the door slid open. Wrylack stepped into the room, noting the large bed, bank of windows, small table and chairs, and a door he assumed led to the bathroom. It was a spacious room, compared to most ships, but probably one of the smaller ones on board. The suites of a luxury liner could be vast, but this seemed more like a common room. He crossed to the bed and eased Shaylee down onto the soft bedding, then turned to face the Meori.

"If anyone harms her, you'll find out exactly what I'm capable of," Wrylack said.

"I'm Vrek, captain of this ship. You have my word no one will touch your female. Now that they know she isn't compatible with them, she will hold no interest for them. As long as you obey my commands."

"We'll need clothing," Wrylack said.

Vrek nodded. "I will see if there's anything in the cargo hold that will fit you. With your build, we may not have anything, but there are still crates down there from when we took over the vessel."

"My female needs clothing too, and not another slave garment."

"Very well. She's not to leave these quarters unless you're with her. You're free to roam the ship as long as you don't attempt to leave. Break your word to serve as our medic and she dies. While the human's screams are unpleasing to my ears, I will listen to it in order to prove a point."

Wrylack ground his teeth together. "I won't try to escape."

"Once your female is settled, I expect you back in

the med bay. I have wounded who need attending."

Vrek grunted and stepped out of the room, letting the door close behind him. Shaylee stayed on the bed, her knees drawn up to her chest, as Wrylack walked over to the windows. He stared out at space, wondering how far they were from Alpha9. The sooner his fellow cyborgs were located at the trading post, the sooner everyone would know to search for him. Once he was more familiar with this ship and how the Meori ran things, he could take a chance on using the ship's computer to contact his fellow cyborgs. Until he was certain it was safe, he wouldn't risk Shaylee.

The door chime sounded a moment before it opened. Another Meori stepped inside, his arms laden with clothes. Wrylack crossed the room and took the garments from him. The Meori stared at him a moment, glanced at the female, then left. The doors slid shut, and Wrylack set the clothing down to see what they'd been given. There were three tunic style dresses for Shaylee, all of them a thicker material you couldn't see through and much longer than what she wore now, along with a few pairs of leather pants for him. Apparently, they hadn't been able to find any shirts in his size, not that he was surprised. He was rather broad across the chest and shoulders.

"Would you like to bathe and change?" Wrylack asked.

Shaylee hesitated a moment and reached for one of the dresses, a deep rose colored one that would leave one shoulder exposed. She skirted around Wrylack and disappeared into the bathroom, the door closing behind her. He heard the cleansing unit turn on and wished she'd asked him to join her. He didn't expect her to fall right into his arms, but he'd hoped that by helping her he might have gained her trust.

Humans were strange creatures. If a Zelranian female had been given to him, she would have wanted him to take care of her. There was no denying that he wanted her, but he wouldn't press for more than she was willing to give. It had probably been a long time since a male had asked her what she wanted.

"Shaylee," he called through the door. "I'm going to medical to treat the wounded. Don't leave this room."

"I won't," came her muffled response.

Wrylack exited the room and wound his way through the ship back to the med bay. There were several Meori waiting to be tended. He went through them as quickly as possible, giving them the medical care they needed, but not exactly using a gentle touch. It went against his training to cause pain to those in his care, but he made an exception after the way they'd threatened Shaylee. By the time the last Meori was patched and sent on his way, Wrylack was worried about his new mate. He didn't know when she'd last slept or ate. He felt like a bad mate, leaving her the way he had. But if he didn't keep the Meori happy, he would lose her.

She was staring out the window when he returned to their quarters. She turned slowly to face him. The tunic she'd donned hugged her curves perfectly and accented her ample breasts and hips. He felt his cock harden and hoped she didn't notice. The last thing he wanted to do was scare her. After the abuse she'd suffered, he would imagine a gentle touch would be needed when it came to his mate.

"When is the last time you ate or slept?" he asked.

"I don't know," she said. "Time passes differently here. As a slave, I was kept in a windowless room with other women. Sometimes it felt like forever between meals. The men mostly came when they needed us for other things."

He didn't want to think about what those other things were. The thought of someone touching her angered him, especially knowing what she'd recently suffered.

"Are you hungry?" he asked.

She hesitantly nodded.

"Let me get cleaned up, and we'll go find something to eat. I don't want to touch you until I'm certain I don't have any Meori blood on me."

Wrylack grabbed a pair of the leather pants, hoping they would fit decently enough, and stepped into the bathroom. He peeled his leather suit off and let it drop to the floor before entering the cleansing unit. He washed quickly, ignoring his hard cock. As much as he'd love to take the edge off his arousal, now wasn't the time. He stepped out of the unit and pressed the button for the automatic dryer. It evaporated the water on his skin and dried out his hair. Wrylack pulled on the leather pants, which fit better than expected, and picked up his suit, tossing it into the corner of the bedroom to be cleaned later.

Shaylee's eyes were wide as she stared at him. She trembled on the bed, her gaze glued to his bare chest. Wrylack wished he had the words to soothe her, but he didn't yet know what exactly she'd been through. It was obvious they'd traumatized her, but were the Meori the first to harm her? From the look in her eyes, he would say no. He'd seen that expression before, on slaves who had been sold time and again, and often to unkind masters. He wanted to learn everything about his new mate, but he knew it would take time. Until then, he would try to go slowly.

He moved closer and held out a hand to her. She hesitated only a moment before standing and sliding her palm against his. His lack of clothing seemed to distract her, and he noted her elevated pulse. It was just unclear if her reaction was one of a female who desired him, or more out of fear and uncertainty. He hoped it was desire because the thought of frightening her made him ill. He didn't want her to fear him.

Shaylee seemed nervous as they exited their quarters, and he kept a tight hold on her hand. It didn't take long to find the galley. If the ship had a designated cook, he wasn't nearby. Wrylack rummaged through cabinets and the cold locker until he'd gathered a large platter of meats, bread, and fruit. He could tell Shaylee didn't like being out in the open, so he carried their food back to their quarters and sat on the bed, placing the large plate between them. He could have used the table across the room, but this felt more intimate, and he wanted to be closer to her.

Shaylee stared at the food, her lips trembling. And yet, she didn't reach for a single thing on the platter. Wrylack picked up a chunk of meat and offered it to her, holding it up to her mouth. Her gaze clashed with his and she opened, accepting the bite of food. He waited until she'd chewed and swallowed, then offered her another bite. It wasn't until she waved him off a few minutes later, placing a hand over her belly, that he allowed himself to eat anything. She watched him quietly, and he wished that she'd talk to him.

The empty plate was placed in the corridor, and then Wrylack didn't know what the hell to do. Shaylee seemed unsure around him, as if she didn't yet know her place. He knew the best thing to do would be to open up to her, but he worried he'd make her more nervous. He didn't yet know what would or would not upset her, and the last thing he wanted to do was traumatize her further. Wrylack eased onto the bed.

"Are you tired?" he asked, noting the shadows under her eyes.

Shaylee looked longingly at the bed before returning her gaze to his.

"Shaylee, I would never hurt you. I want to take care of you."

"I'm yours. They gave me to you," she said, licking her lips. "I'm your slave now."

"No!" he said harshly, making her flinch. He slowly reached for her, cupping her cheek with his palm. "Mine, but not my slave."

"Not a slave?" she asked.

Wrylack shook his head.

"But yours," she said.

"Mine. Only mine."

Confusion clouded her eyes, and Wrylack leaned closer, giving her time to pull away. His lips brushed against hers, softly, slowly. He knew he shouldn't have made such a move so soon, but he'd wanted to taste her. Shaylee didn't push him away, but she wasn't exactly throwing herself into his arms either. Wrylack slid his hand down to her waist and lifted her onto his lap. Her breath caught and she tensed a moment, but he continued kissing her gently, hoping she would realize she had nothing to fear from him. It wasn't long before she relaxed against him, her hand pressing against his chest.

Wrylack drew back and stared down at her. "Mine."

Shaylee curled against him, and he wrapped her in his arms. Wrylack was content to hold her, even though he wanted more. The taste of her lips was sweet, and he wondered if she was as sweet everywhere. He wasn't foolish enough to think she'd let him claim her anytime soon, even if he was hopeful. It was almost cruel to finally have a mate and not be able to savor every inch of her.

"We should sleep," Wrylack said. He stood and set Shaylee on her feet before turning down the bed. He motioned for her to crawl in.

She seemed to freeze when he reached for the fastenings on his pants, but he knew from experience that sleeping in leather wasn't a good idea, and the sooner she became familiar with his body, the better. Wrylack stripped out of the pants. Reaching for her, he pulled the tunic over her head and let it fall to the floor. She gasped and her cheeks flushed, but she didn't try to cover herself.

Wrylack held back a groan at how fucking beautiful she was. His hands itched to trace every inch of her, and his lips wanted to taste her. He got into the bed and pulled her down beside him.

"We're just going to sleep," he told her. "I meant what I said. I will never hurt you."

He held his arms open, and Shaylee settled against him. He breathed in her scent and felt more content than he had in a long time, which was ridiculous since they were being held hostage by the Meori. There was no sense in doing anything but accepting his fate at this point, unless he wanted to risk Shaylee, and he'd never do that. He'd play by the Meori's rules until his fellow cyborgs arrived. However long that would take.

She shifted in his arms, and Wrylack smoothed a hand down her back, pressing her closer. Shaylee sighed and fidgeted some more. His cock was harder than it had ever been before, and he felt pre-cum gathering on the tip. He knew she had to notice.

"What's wrong?" he asked.

"What's going to happen to me?" she asked softly.

"One day I'll take you to my world. Xpashta. It's beautiful there. Very peaceful."

"Because I'm yours," she said.

"Yes. Mine."

She was quiet for a moment. "What does that mean? You say I'm yours and yet say I'm not a slave. Then what am I?"

Wrylack tightened his arms around her. "You're my mate, Shaylee. The Meori gifted you to me, and I plan to keep you. I'll have the commanders make it official when we get to my planet, but with or without their blessing, you will always be mine."

"Mate. Like a pair? A breeding pair?" she asked.

He growled. "You're more than that to me. A mate is… I believe your Earth term is husband and wife."

Her gaze jerked to his. "Wife? I'm your wife?"

"Is that acceptable to you? I swear that you will never be a slave again. You're mine, and I will protect you with my life. No male shall ever touch you except me."

She stared at him, as if she were trying to see into his soul, and eventually she nodded. If she'd balked, or had seemed frightened, Wrylack didn't know what he would have done. He didn't want to force her to be with him, but he didn't want to let her go either. Soon she would see that he would be good to her, treat her gently, and give her anything she wanted. Even though he'd never had a woman in his life before, he knew he could be a good mate.

Shaylee settled against him again, and after a few

minutes, her breathing evened out. While she slept, Wrylack held her tight and vowed to keep her safe at all costs. He'd been given an incredible gift, and he would do anything to keep her alive and in his arms. Even if it meant finding a way to kill every Meori on board the ship. If only he knew how to do that without risking Shaylee.

Chapter Two

Shaylee woke pressed against a hard body. For a moment, she panicked, and then she remembered it was Wrylack who held her. He'd kissed her, but hadn't pushed for more, even though he'd stripped them both naked. She'd thought for sure he was going to force himself on her. He'd said she was his wife now, but she didn't quite understand. There hadn't been a ceremony or anything. Maybe the official thing he'd mentioned when they reached his world was a wedding ceremony? The Meori had given her to him, like passing along a slave. She'd been a slave for so long, Shaylee wasn't certain she knew how to be anything else. What exactly would he expect of her?

Her cheeks flushed when she felt the hard length of Wrylack's cock against her belly. It seemed her new mate was aroused, even in sleep. Part of Shaylee wanted to pull away from him, put some much needed distance between them. But he'd been so kind to her, so tender, that she was a little curious. All she'd ever known from men was roughness, but the alien sleeping with her was different. He claimed to be a cyborg, but she didn't know if that meant he was more machine than man. He'd mentioned mechanical parts other than his eyes. Did he have feelings like other people?

His arms tightened around her, and Shaylee tried to relax in his embrace. He hadn't done anything to make her worry that he would be cruel to her, but experience told her that men didn't know how to be any other way. Even on Earth, she had never known the soft touch of a man. She'd spent her life in the foster care system, until she'd been abducted by aliens when she was seventeen. She'd spent the last five years as a slave. Somehow, she'd hung onto her humanity, but there were days she thought she'd break.

She felt lips brush the top of her head, and she looked up to find Wrylack watching her.

"Morning," he said.

"How can you tell? With all that dark space out the window, it feels like endless night."

He smiled a little. "My systems tell me it's day. On my world, the suns would be rising by now. Did you sleep well?"

Shaylee thought about it a moment before nodding. It was odd, but she really had slept well. Even with him holding her, or perhaps because he'd been holding her, she'd had the best night of sleep since her nightmare first began. While she still wasn't completely certain about him, she felt oddly safe and comforted when his arms were around her.

Wrylack hesitated a moment before lowering his head to hers. His lips were soft as he kissed her slowly. One of his hands fisted her long hair, but it didn't frighten her. The strong arms wrapped around her made her feel protected and not scared. He didn't want a sex slave; he wanted a wife. And that made him different from any male she'd ever met. Shaylee was almost afraid to trust that things were changing for her, that perhaps the horror was finally over. There were things she should tell him, if he really was claiming her as his mate.

Wrylack drew away, reluctantly, as if he wanted to kiss her for a while longer. Shaylee didn't think she would have minded. His kisses were nice, better than anything she'd ever experienced. Her lips tingled where they'd touched his and there was a warmth spreading through her that she didn't understand. Wrylack's grip on her hair eased, and his hand smoothed down her back to rest against the curve of her ass.

Shaylee's heart thundered in her chest, wondering how far he was going to take things. She'd never been with a male without force being involved, but if Wrylack wanted her in that way, she wouldn't fight him. It was the least she could do to repay the kindness he'd shown her. And if it hurt, like it always did, she would try to hold her tears at bay.

"I can feel your heart beating faster and the quickness of your breathing," Wrylack said. "But I don't know what you're thinking right now. Do I frighten you?"

"No," she said softly. "If you were going to hurt me, I think you would have by now." At least, if he were going to intentionally hurt her. She knew that when he claimed her body it would hurt whether he meant for it to or not. It always had.

Wrylack sat up on his knees and pulled the blankets away from her. She lay still, not knowing what was going to happen. His eyes glowed as he scanned her from head to toe, and she remembered he'd said something about his special eyes doing that during an exam. When those glowing eyes came back to her abdomen, he stopped. Wrylack's hand slowly reached for her, splaying across her lower belly.

"You've been pregnant before," he said. "I noticed during my scan of you in medical. You have scarring on your womb."

"A few times."

"Where are your children?"

"I don't know," she said softly. "Some didn't live long enough to be born. Only two had successful deliveries, but I don't know if they live still. They were taken from me immediately. I never even got to hold them, or find out if I had a boy or girl."

She'd never admit how much that had hurt. Yes, they were the product of rape, but she'd carried them in her womb, had felt them kick and roll inside her. They were a part of her, and even if their fathers had been monsters, she couldn't have hated her children. She'd loved them, had wanted to see their little faces when they were born, but they'd been ripped away from her before she ever laid eyes on them. She didn't know if they had been killed, sold into slavery like her, or if their fathers had kept them.

His gaze was sad as he stared down at her. He reached for her face, his fingers grazing her cheek. "I'm sorry for all that you've suffered. I will protect you with my life, Shaylee. As long as there is breath in my body, I won't allow anyone to harm you again."

Tears gathered in her eyes at his sweet words, and when he lay beside her again, she willingly went into his arms. "I know you say I'm your mate, but what if I can't have children anymore? Don't you want children?"

"As long as I have you, that's all that matters. But I don't detect anything wrong with your reproductive organs. Even with the scarring, you should be able to have a successful delivery. Do you know why you miscarried the other babies?"

"No. I was never told anything."

"The babies who lived long enough to be delivered, do you remember who owned you at the time? Perhaps we could track down your children."

"You would… you would allow another male's children into your home?" she asked. "What if their fathers are your enemies?"

"They are first and foremost the children of my mate. Since you are mine, they are mine as well. I will raise them as if they were my flesh and blood."

Shaylee felt something foreign blooming inside her. It was... hope. She didn't know if her children could ever be located, if they even still lived, or if they would want anything to do with her. Even though she'd carried them and given birth to them, they'd never seen her. She would be a complete stranger to them. But to see them, even once, to hold them in her arms... a tear slid down her cheek. He was offering her a gift far greater than anything she'd ever dreamed of.

"I want to find my babies," she said.

"When we get off this ship, I want you to tell me the names of the fathers and anything else you remember. There are cyborgs where I live who specialize in finding lost items or people. They were used on special missions by the Zelranian parliament before the Cy-Con program ended. I will have them find your children and bring them home to you."

"Thank you, Wrylack."

"You don't have to thank me, Shaylee. They're my family now too."

"Do you really think the Meori will ever let us go?" she asked. "What if they hold us here forever? Or... what if you get hurt? Will they make me a slave again?"

"I don't think they're going to have a choice but to free us. When my fellow cyborgs realize I'm not among those left at Alpha9, they will come for me. And I'm not leaving this ship without you."

"But there's so many of them. Aren't you worried the Meori will wipe out your people if they're attacked?"

Wrylack rolled to his back and stared at the ceiling. "It's a concern. They disabled my crew easily enough, as much as I hate to admit it. Granted, they outnumbered my crew, but there are no guarantees the cyborgs coming for me will have high enough numbers to extract us. I'm permitted to move around the ship, so I'll study the Meori and search for weaknesses. I'll also try to get a sense of how many are on board and whether the other ship is still nearby."

"What if there aren't any?"

"Everyone has a weakness, Shaylee. It's just a matter of finding it."

"What's yours?" she asked.

He rolled back to his side and traced the contours of her face. "You."

Shaylee's breath froze in her lungs. No one had ever considered her important before, except for the money they thought they could get for her, or the sexual satisfaction they'd get when they forced themselves on her. But Wrylack was different. When he said that she was his weakness, she knew he meant it. For whatever reason, she was important to the handsome cyborg. Not as a commodity, but as a person.

"I want to know more about you," Wrylack said. "But I don't want to bring up painful memories."

"I'm afraid I don't really have any happy ones. Even before I was abducted from my world, things never seemed to go my way. My parents gave me up when I was a baby, and I went into the foster care system, bounced from one home to another. Some weren't so horrible, but others… let's just say I was thirteen the first time I realized just how rotten men are."

"How old are you now?" he asked.

"Twenty-one. I think. Maybe twenty-two? It's hard to keep track of time, but I believe around five years have passed since I was taken from Earth. I was seventeen at the time and on the run from yet another bad foster family."

"So young," he murmured.

"What about you? You don't look very old."

"The Cy-Con program changed us in many ways. Our aging process was slowed down, and our lives were extended. I was twenty-five when I entered the program. I'm thirty-five now. Does our age difference bother you? I'm fourteen years older than you."

"No. You've treated me kindly, something no one has ever done before. That's far more important to me than how old you are. Besides, thirty-five isn't all that old."

"And my eyes. They don't bother you?" he asked.

"They're different, but not in an unpleasant way. They're a pretty color, and they're beautiful when they glow. It's a little unsettling that you can see my internal organs whenever you wish, but as a medic I can understand why you were given that ability." She paused. "It is just my organs, right? You can't like look through my clothes and see me naked?"

Wrylack chuckled softly. "No, I can't do anything like that. In order for me to see you naked, you'd have to not only be undressed but couldn't be covering up with the bedding either. When my eyes glow, I'm accessing a type of x-ray vision that allows me to scan your bones and organs. The rest of the time, I just see like anyone else does."

"You asked if it bothers me about your age and your eyes, but does my past bother you? Knowing that I've been owned by so many. I lost count of how many owners I've had. I've been pregnant five times, by five different men, and have been with many more than that. Some owners liked to pass me around to their friends, and they didn't always take turns. I'm tainted, Wrylack. Dirty. For all I know, I'm diseased. Why would you ever want to claim someone like me as something as sacred as your mate?"

Wrylack swallowed audibly and smoothed her hair back from her face. "If I could take away everything that was done to you, I would. You were a victim, Shaylee. Nothing that happened to you is in any way your fault. Those males hurt you, abused you, and I would gladly tear them apart with my bare hands if I could. Your past doesn't define who you are. From the moment the Meori gave you to me, you were no longer a slave. You became mine, my mate. And you are far more precious to me than anything else in all the galaxies. If it would make you feel better, I could draw some blood and run some tests, but if you were diseased, it would have affected your organs, and everything is working perfectly. I don't see a taint in your bloodstream."

"I don't want you to get sick from being with me. You probably shouldn't have even kissed me."

"I'll get dressed, and we'll go to medical. I don't want you to worry for another moment. Afterward, I'll find something for us to eat."

"Will you still like me when I'm fat?" she asked.

He gave her a startled look. "Why would you think you're going to get fat?"

"I haven't had regular meals, pretty much ever. What if eating all the time makes me fat?"

"Shaylee, I don't care if you're skinny or fat. You're mine, and I will cherish you regardless. If you gain weight, there will just be more of you to hold. That doesn't sound like a bad thing to me."

The ship vibrated, and Shaylee tensed. Wrylack rolled out of bed and strolled over to the windows. Her cheeks flushed as she took in his naked body, noticing that even though his cock wasn't hard anymore, it was no less impressive. While his chest was hairless, the area around his cock and his balls contained a light dusting of short, white hair. He turned and found her blatantly staring at him. His lips curved in a smile as he returned to the bed, caging her between his arms.

"If you keep looking at me like that, we'll never make it out of this room."

Shaylee bit her lip and cast her eyes downward, but he tipped up her chin.

"There's nothing to be embarrassed about. You're welcome to look at me anytime you wish. You can touch me if you want. When I said you were mine, I also meant that I'm yours."

"Mine?" she asked.

"Yes." He kissed her softly. "Yours. You belong to me, and I belong to you."

She lifted a hand, pausing a few inches from his chest. Her gaze held steady with his, uncertain if he meant what he said. When he didn't stop her, Shaylee pressed her hand to his hot lavender skin. His muscles were firm under her fingertips, and she traced his pectorals and down his abdomen. She gasped when his cock stirred with interest.

"Perhaps if you're going to touch me, we should get those tests out of the way first, since you seem concerned you'll give me a disease if we're intimate."

Shaylee withdrew her hand and nodded.

"We're at Alpha9," Wrylack said. "I'm sure most of the crew will disembark. There are slaves for sale here, among other things, and they'll need to leave my crew with someone. As quiet as it's been, I'm going to assume they've kept them sedated."

"You could escape now," she said. "If there

aren't many on board, you could slip away."

"I'm not leaving you, and I won't risk your life in an attempt to run from the Meori."

"Then… what if we fought back? With so few on board, could you overtake them?"

"If I'm caught, they will do horrible things to you before ending your life," Wrylack said.

"Some things are worth the risk," she said. "I've never known true freedom. First I was a captive of the foster care system, and later a slave to aliens. You said you wanted to take me to your world. I would have freedom there, wouldn't I?"

"Yes, Shaylee. You would be free there."

"Then I want to fight. I don't want to live in fear anymore of what tomorrow will bring. And if they catch us, if I die, at least I will have known kindness once in my life. Whatever they do to me won't be anything I haven't been through before. I know if they try to mate with me, it will kill me, but sometimes I think death is preferable to the life I've led."

"Shaylee, you're breaking my heart."

"Please, Wrylack. I don't want to be the reason you lose more of your people. If your cyborgs come for us like you claim they will, they could die trying to save us. I would rather you lose me than lose so many more. There will be other mates."

"No," he said harshly.

"Wrylack, I… "

He silenced her with a kiss. It was deep, and rough, and Shaylee's toes curled. A warmth suffused her and an ache built between her legs, something she'd never felt before. She didn't understand what was happening to her, why she was growing damp between her legs, but the longer he kissed her, the more she wanted to feel his hands on her body.

Whatever this feeling was, she somehow knew that only Wrylack could make the ache go away. No one's touch had ever caused this desire to build inside her before.

"I need you, Shaylee. I don't care about the damn tests. I need to feel you wrapped around me."

She understood. He wanted to claim her, and she gave him a cautious nod, even though she knew pain was soon coming. If he wanted her, she wasn't going to deny him.

Wrylack groaned, and his hand trembled as he reached for her breast, cupping the mound with a gentle touch. It felt... strange. Her body seemed to yearn for something. Wrylack stroked her nipple and pleasure shot through her. Shaylee gasped and pressed her breast tighter against his hand. Whatever that was, she wanted more of it.

"You're so damn responsive," he said, his voice a near growl.

Wrylack lowered his head and took her nipple into his mouth. His teeth lightly grazed it as his tongue flicked against the tip. Shaylee whimpered and fisted her hands at her sides, not knowing what to do.

"You can touch me," he said, before taking her nipple between his lips again.

Shaylee sifted her fingers through his hair, holding him closer to her. Wrylack's other hand skimmed down her side to the curve of her hip, before sliding across her belly and down between her legs. She tensed a moment, but the stroke of his fingers against her wet lips was pleasant. As his fingers teased her bare skin, she found herself wanting to get closer to him, to feel even more of the incredible sensations. No one had ever given her pleasure before, and she wanted the moment to last forever.

Wrylack plunged a finger inside her, thrusting it in and out. He switched from one breast to the other, giving the second nipple just as much attention as the first. His fingers stroked deeper, and his thumb pressed against her clit. Sparks shot through her as Shaylee cried out. She could feel herself getting wetter, and her thighs trembled. Without conscious thought, she began riding his fingers, wanting more. Wrylack kissed her again, deep and hungry, as an intense wave of pleasure rolled over her. She clung to his shoulders as her hips thrust against his hand. Stars burst behind her eyelids as her legs gave out, and she collapsed against the bed.

Through heavy-lidded eyes, she watched as Wrylack sucked the juices from his fingers. If anything, it just made her ache even more.

"What just happened to me?" she asked softly.

"Have you never had an orgasm before?" he asked.

She shook her head, her gaze fastened on him.

"My poor, sweet mate. I promise there is much more where that came from."

"Will you claim me now?" she asked.

Wrylack growled and lowered himself over her body, lying hip to hip. She could feel his hard cock pressing against her slick pussy.

"Yes, I'm going to claim you now," he said. "And I promise you're going to like it just as much as you loved having my fingers inside you. Maybe even more."

Shaylee doubted that, but she didn't say as much. As beautiful as Wrylack's cock was, she knew they caused pain. He would hurt her, even if he didn't mean to. She widened her legs to accept him into her body, giving herself to him completely.

Wrylack kissed her hungrily as his cock slowly eased inside her. Shaylee tensed, waiting for the pain, but as he stretched her wide and filled her deep, the ache he'd just quelled began to build inside her again. Wrylack stroked in and out of her. He took his time, his thrusts slow as he filled her completely again and again. When he drew back, his gaze steady on hers, he took her harder, faster. With every plunge of his cock, he'd grind against her before retreating and filling her once more. The ache intensified until her hips were lifting to meet his.

There was no pain, only intense pleasure that left her gasping and wanting more. While she felt impossibly full with his cock buried inside her, it only seemed to make her wetter. Her body had never reacted this way with anyone before, and while it frightened her a little, she trusted Wrylack. If something were wrong, he'd have said so. Was this what it was supposed to be like when a man and woman were intimate?

Wrylack reached for her hand and slid it between their bodies until her fingers met her wet pussy. "Stroke yourself. Make yourself come."

Shaylee had never touched herself before, had never once been curious after experiencing the pain of sex, but she did as he commanded. Her fingers pressed and rubbed against her clit until the sensations rolling through her became so intense she didn't think she could take another moment of it. Wrylack pounded into her, driving her hips into the mattress. Her body tensed, and her climax nearly took her breath away as she came long and hard, his cock never slowing as he took her fiercely.

As the world came back into focus, she stared up at Wrylack. His jaw clenched, and he growled out his release, pumping his hips several more times until he stilled inside her. She felt the warmth of his cum and wondered if they'd made a baby together.

"Mine," he said fiercely before kissing her hard and deep. "Whatever thoughts you have of escaping, of risking your life, I will fuck them out of you if I have to. We will remain in this bed, my cock buried in your sweet pussy, until I'm called upon. And then when I return, I will crawl right back between your thighs. Do you understand, Shaylee? You're too precious for me to do anything that would risk your life."

"I understand," she said. "But what if the Meori don't keep their word?"

"What do you mean?"

"They gave me to you. What if they take me away?"

"Then I will kill every last fucking being on this ship until you're in my arms again."

She felt his cock harden inside her. With his gaze fastened on hers, Wrylack began stroking in and out of her again. This time he didn't hold back even a little. It wasn't slow, it wasn't sweet. It was a thorough claiming as he took her as fiercely as a warrior returning from battle, and when he was finished, she knew that she would never be the same again. Wrylack had touched a part of her she hadn't even known existed. He kept his word and remained in bed with her for hours, taking her again and again, her pleasure going higher every time until she was breathless. And as she fell asleep in his arms, she realized that she had finally found home.

Chapter Three

Wrylack had kept a close eye on the Meori the last few days. He'd studied their numbers, their physical weaknesses, and had determined the second ship was no longer with them. There were thirty Meori on board, with only a handful still suffering from injuries. While it was impossible for him to take them all out alone, he'd discovered something that gave him hope things would work out. The ship's systems were a few years out-of-date, and from what he'd seen of the Meori, they weren't very technologically advanced. Wrylack had been able to hack into the systems with his neurotransmitters to send a communication to the commanders on Xpashta, which he hoped they would relay to whatever crew was coming for him. He'd given them coordinates, numbers, and anything else he thought might help.

He hadn't said anything to Shaylee, thinking it was better to keep her in the dark. If the Meori were to question her, she would honestly be able to tell them she didn't know anything, and it was better that way. He didn't want to do anything that could put her in danger. Well, more danger than they already faced. He hadn't missed the way they looked at her, some of their gazes calculating. He had a feeling they were waiting for something, but he didn't know what. What if Shaylee had been right? It unsettled him that they might take her away from him, and he knew if that happened, he would fight them to the death. What was the point of living if he had to do it without his mate?

There was another thought that concerned him. He ran a check on his systems every morning, and the serum that prevented him from having children had run out. As often as he was intimate with his mate, it was only a matter of time before she conceived, and he really didn't want to be on this ship when that happened. It was dangerous enough for his mate to be around the Meori, but protecting her while pregnant was not something he looked forward to. He hoped his fellow cyborgs reached them before that time, because as much as he didn't want to get her pregnant while they were held captive, he knew he couldn't keep his hands off her.

She'd surrendered to him so sweetly the first time they were together, and had seemed surprised when she enjoyed what happened between them. Discovering that his precious mate had been so ill-used she'd never experienced an orgasm before, Wrylack had done his best to make sure she had several a day. It wasn't like he didn't enjoy the experience. Even when he only used his mouth to bring her pleasure, he loved feeling her come apart, the cries that filled their room when she found her release were music to his ears. He wanted to make her happy.

His world only had two other mates, both of them human, and from what he'd heard, both women had wanted to return to their world. Not once had Shaylee asked if he could take her home. She'd told him a little of her time on Earth, and it sounded almost as bad as the slavery she'd endured the past five years. She'd been so young when she was taken, was still young. It hardly seemed fair her life had been so hard. Not that cyborgs had it easy. The Cy-Con program had been brutal, but at least they'd led normal lives up to that point. Shaylee hadn't known kindness or love in all her life, and it broke his heart. He tried to show her as often as possible how much she meant to him, but he didn't know if it was enough. There was only so much he could do while they were trapped on this ship.

Wrylack was on his way back to his quarters from the med bay when Vrax intercepted him in the hall with two other Meori. They grabbed onto his arms and slammed him against the wall. Vrax looked pissed, his forked tongue flicking in and out rapidly. Before he could question them, Wrylack heard Shaylee cry out. His head jerked in the direction of their quarters and watched in horror as two more Meori dragged her from the room. They brought her closer, her skin turning red where they gripped her tight. She was terrified, and he struggled against his captors, wanting to comfort his mate.

"You were warned," Vrax said.

"I didn't do anything," Wrylack protested. "I've healed your people as you've asked."

Vrax hissed at him. "Then why are there two cyborg ships closing in fast? They could not have found us if you hadn't disclosed our location. You were told what would happen if you tried to escape."

Shaylee's eyes were wide and filling with tears as she stared in horror at Vrax.

"Shaylee," he called to her. When her gaze focused on him, he gave her a smile. "It's going to be okay."

"You think I'm kidding?" Vrax said. He turned to the aliens holding Shaylee. "Take her to the common room and strip her, then gather everyone. The cyborg is going to learn what happens when the Meori are defied."

A rage built inside Wrylack as Shaylee struggled to break free. He used the ship's systems to connect to his brother cyborgs, urging them to hurry. When his gaze focused on Vrax again, he knew he had no choice but to fight. He wouldn't let them kill his mate. He'd held back before, not wanting to endanger her, but with the immediate threat hanging over her head, he had nothing to lose.

Shaylee struggled and slowed them down. Wrylack hoped he could get to her in time. The fate they had planned for her was horrific. While his people could be brutal when necessary, they would never think to defile a female. Vrax didn't yet realize it, but he'd just sealed his fate.

Vrax gave him a sinister grin, his sharp teeth flashing. "My crew will have fun with your punishment. Every last Meori on board. There will be nothing left when we're done with her."

Wrylack looked at his mate and tried to convey to her that everything would be fine, that he would save her. She dug her feet into the carpeting and pulled against her captors, but they merely laughed and dragged her along.

He scanned the Meori who were holding him, noting that the one on the right had a fractured rib. He focused on Vrax, watching the captain, but the Meori's attention was on Shaylee. Wrylack knew it was now or never. He jerked downward on his right arm, loosening the Meori's grip, then jammed his elbow right into the fractured rib. While that one was doubled over, he twisted toward the one on his left, sending an uppercut to the alien's jaw. After two more well-placed blows, one of them cracking the Meori's sternum, he turned his attention to Vrax.

The captain's serpent-like eyes had narrowed, and he reached for the ion blaster at his hip. Wrylack had anticipated the move and kicked out at Vrax's hand. With his metal skeletal system, and the force he'd put behind the kick, the bones in the Meori's hand had shattered. Vrax let out a scream that halted

Shaylee's captors. Wrylack didn't tear his gaze away from Vrax, though. Not yet. The captain hissed, his tongue flicking in and out, and Wrylack went for the kill. Forming a fist, he punched straight through the Meori's stomach, where his heart lay. Wrylack put all of his substantial weight behind the hit, tearing through the soft tissue and ripping the still-beating heart from the captain.

Vrax fell to the floor, a gaping hole in his body that poured blood onto the carpet. Turning back to the two Meori he'd already dropped, he swiftly ended their lives, ensuring they would never come between him and his mate again. The two Meori holding Shaylee dropped her arms and ran. Even if they got the others to aid them, it was too late. The vibrations under his feet told him that the cyborg ships had already docked. It wouldn't be long before Meori blood soaked the walls and floors of the vessel, and every last one was taken out. Wrylack would settle for nothing less, not after what they'd done to Shaylee and those other two poor human females.

His sweet mate staggered down the hall in his direction, but he held up a hand.

"Don't touch me until I've cleaned up."

Wrylack turned and felt her fingers tuck into the waistband of his pants. With her trailing behind him, he went to the med bay. He washed his hands and cleaned the blood spatter from his chest and abdomen, while he opened communications with his fellow cyborgs. With the captain dead, the Meori would falter and be easier to take down.

The sound of fighting reached his ears, and Shaylee pressed closer to him. Wrylack dried himself and took her into his arms, holding her against his chest. She looked up at him with wide eyes, and he kissed her gently.

"My people have come for us," he said. "I don't want you to get caught in the middle so we'll wait here."

"What if the fighting comes this way?" she asked.

"Then I'll take care of any Meori who pose a threat to you, just like the ones in the corridor."

She blinked up at him. "I thought you were a medic. That's like a doctor, a healer."

"I am."

She glanced at the hall and back to him. "But you took them out. You killed three of them by yourself when they had you pinned to the wall. You didn't even have a weapon."

Wrylack smiled. "I trained alongside the warriors on my world. I may choose to heal people, but I'm able to protect you, Shaylee. I let them take me from my ship because the odds weren't in my favor. And I'm glad I did because it brought you into my life. But I'm not as helpless as you seem to think."

She cuddled closer, pressing her cheek against him. Wrylack kept an eye on the med bay doors, ready to defend his mate if necessary. He didn't try to contact the other cyborgs again, knowing they needed to focus. When he saw Lathim and Zorlok, the tension in his body eased. His friends smiled and studied the female in his arms with curiosity.

"Nice to see you in one piece," Lathim said. "I'm assuming the bodies in the hall were your doing."

"Your mate actually let you leave the house?" Wrylack asked.

Lathim chuckled. "Only after I promised to seriously hunt for more human females to bring home with me. She likes talking to Jillian, but I think they want more friends. And we could certainly use more mates."

Shaylee looked up at him. "What will happen to the other slaves on board?"

Wrylack saw Lathim and Zorlok tense.

"She's a slave?" Zorlok asked, looking disgusted by the thought. Not that Shaylee disgusted the male, but the thought of her being owned by someone did.

"No. She's my mate," Wrylack said.

Lathim looked her over, then nodded. "Where are the other females she mentioned?"

"Lower level," Shaylee said softly. "There may be some in the common room as well. If they heard the fighting break out, they may have hidden somewhere on the ship."

The look on Zorlok's face said he knew exactly why they would be in the common room, and he wasn't pleased.

Wrylack had to agree that the thought of using females the way the Meori had was sickening. Not all of them would be compatible with his kind, if any, but those who were would be a nice addition to Xpashta.

"This ship is secure," Lathim said. "If you'll take your female to the *Mystic7*, we have a room set aside for you. It will be smaller than those on this luxury liner, but I don't think she wants to stay here. There's a bit of a mess."

Which meant the Meori had not only been killed, but it had been a bloody battle. Wrylack couldn't feel any remorse for them, not after the suffering the females had endured at the Meori's hands. He knew it was likely any slaves who had been compatible with the Meori would not be possible mates for his people, but they could at least free them.

He lifted Shaylee into his arms.

"Hide your face against me," he told her.

Shaylee turned her face and closed her eyes, her arms tightening around his neck. Wrylack carried her through the ship, stepping over dead bodies along the way. When they reached the Mystic7, he still held her, not ready to let her go. Those on board looked at the female in his arms with envy. It was no secret the greatest wish of every cyborg was to have a mate. He'd gotten lucky.

"The captain put you in the room next to his," Tenz said. He slowly reached for Shaylee's hair, then drew his hand away at the last moment. "Are there others? Like her?"

Shaylee opened her eyes and looked at Tenz. "I didn't see other humans, except the two they killed."

Tenz nodded, though he looked sad. Ever since Lathim had claimed Maggie as his mate, every cyborg had wanted a human female of their own. Anyone walking by Lathim's house could hear Maggie's cries of passion, and it made them all envious.

Now that he'd experienced it firsthand, Wrylack could understand why human females were sought after. Not all females enjoyed the intimacies of the bedroom, and he doubted any felt as incredible as his mate.

He carried Shaylee through the interior of the ship until he reached the corridor where the captain stayed, then opened the door to the room next to Lathim's. It was tiny, with only room for a bed and a little walking space, but his mate was safe and that was all that mattered.

He eased her down onto the bed and smoothed her hair back from her face. Shaylee smiled up at him, and he couldn't resist tasting her sweet lips.

"You're free," he told her. "We are safe with my

people, and no one will ever hurt you again."

"What will happen to the others?" she asked.

"If they are compatible with my people, they will be taken to Xpashta. There are currently only two females on my world. Two mates. You make three. There are hundreds of cyborgs, and they're lonely."

"And those who aren't compatible? Will they be sold?"

His gut tightened. "No. Arrangements will be made for them to return to their people. If they wish to return home, that is. Some may be like you and have nothing on their home world to return to. They will be taken wherever they want to go, and they will be kept safe."

Shaylee nodded.

"Now, my sweet mate, you're going to tell me about your children. The male I mentioned before, who has skill at tracking down those who are lost, is likely on this ship. I want to get the information to him as quickly as possible," Wrylack said. "And I promise that Norkov will not stop until your babies are returned to you."

Tears gathered in Shaylee's eyes, and Wrylack caressed her cheek.

"I don't know the name of my first child's father. I was passed around so often, it could have been anyone, but my owner was a Mardian by the name of Grunshner. My child would be around three years old now, I think. Like I mentioned before, I don't really know how much time has passed. The days all blur into one another when you're a slave."

Wrylack knelt in front of her, using his neurotransmitters to reach out to Norkov. As he'd suspected, the male was on board, and Wrylack relayed the information. He felt a spark of Norkov's fury over what had been done to Shaylee and her missing children, and knew that he'd made the right decision to ask the cyborg for help.

"My second child's father was a Vrotu by the name of Kinlor. He wasn't overly cruel to me, but he hadn't been pleased I was pregnant. I don't know what he did with my baby." Tears slipped down her cheeks. "For all I know, my children are dead now or sold into slavery."

"If they live, Norkov will find them," Wrylack promised her. "He won't stop until he either brings them home or finds out what happened to them. If they've been harmed, he will seek vengeance for them."

"Do you really think there's any chance they're still alive?" she asked. "What if they don't want to be with me? For all I know, they're content where they are."

"Your second child will know who you are without any doubt," Wrylack said. "The Vrotu are very aware of things, even in the womb. They have a sense of knowing that can be downright eerie at times. Your child will remember your voice, and if they ever saw you, even for a moment as an infant, they will remember your face."

"Really?" she asked, hope shining in her eyes.

"Really."

She smiled softly, and Wrylack relayed the rest of the information to Norkov. He knew that if her children weren't found, or had been killed, it would devastate his mate. It might have been wrong of him to give her hope, but he wanted to reunite mother and children, and give her a life she'd never thought she'd have.

He didn't care that the babies weren't his by

blood. They belonged to his mate, and that made them part of his family. And Wrylack was going to make damn sure his family was complete -- his mate happy and his kids safe.

Chapter Four

Shaylee felt safe, truly safe, for the first time in her life. Wrylack had kept her by his side, and even though the other cyborgs eyed her in curiosity, none made a threatening move toward her. They seemed a little in awe that he'd managed to get a mate. There were comments about his freakish eyes, and there was mention of a mail-order bride. Had her mate intended to order a bride from somewhere? Shaylee looked up at her handsome cyborg and didn't understand why everyone thought his unusual eyes were such a big deal. She thought they were rather amazing. They allowed him to see things others couldn't and made him an even better healer.

Wrylack smiled down at her and squeezed her waist. He'd been touching her in one way or another since he'd brought her on board. She didn't know if he was trying to keep her calm or letting the others know she was taken. It still amazed her that someone like Wrylack would want a woman like her. He was so kind and incredibly sweet. And the way he'd taken out those Meori on his own... She'd never seen something so brave before. It seemed to her that any woman would be lucky to have him as a mate. She didn't know why he'd settled for a slave who had been ill-used for so many years. Her past seemed to make him angry, but he never looked at her as if he thought she was less for the things she'd endured.

Norkov studied her from across the room, his arms folded over his chest. Wrylack had introduced them and explained that Norkov would be the one searching for her children. He'd been staring at her for the last few minutes, though, his gaze scanning her from head to toe, and she was starting to feel nervous.

Did he think she wasn't good enough for Wrylack?

Wrylack noticed her unease and glared at his friend. "You're scaring her."

Norkov's gaze slid to Wrylack. "Just making sure I remember what she looks like. There's a chance her children may resemble her."

"Try again," Wrylack said. "You had every detail of her memorized the moment you met her."

Norkov's eyebrows rose. "Perhaps I just like the way she looks."

"Get your own mate," Wrylack muttered.

"The males who may still have your children, did they have other human slaves?" Norkov asked.

"Yes," Shaylee said. "You'd be surprised how many human women I've seen in captivity since being captured all those years ago. Some don't make it, couldn't survive what their owners did to them. Others slowly go insane."

"But you didn't, which means there may be others who withstood everything they've been through and remained strong." Norkov pushed away from the wall and approached her. "The males who owned you, if offered the right amount, would they part with any human females they have?"

Shaylee shrugged. "It's possible. It's not like they're in love with them, so if you offered enough for them to replace those women, I don't see why they would turn you down. Slavery is a business to them, and a way to slake their lusts whether sexual or otherwise. But why do you want them? I thought cyborgs didn't own slaves."

"We don't," Wrylack assured her.

"I thought of purchasing them and bringing them to Xpashta. You seem content being Wrylack's mate. It stands to reason the others might be receptive to a cyborg mate as well." Norkov studied her again. "Are all human females small and pretty like you and the ones already on our world? All three of you are so tiny."

"Humans come in all shapes, sizes, and colors. Some are thinner than others, or taller... I've seen women on my world as tall as you. We have many races, so humans aren't all one color. We also speak many languages," Shaylee said.

"The two mates already on Xpashta speak your Earth English, but since you can understand us, you were fitted with a translator at some point," Wrylack said. "I noticed the small implant behind your ear when I did my scan of you in the med bay that first time."

"It was likely done so she would understand the orders given to her," Norkov said with a grimace.

Shaylee didn't care why it was done. She was thankful for the implant if it meant she could understand Wrylack. No one had ever been as kind to her as he had been. The moment she'd been given to him was the best in her entire life, even if she hadn't realized it at the time. She only hoped any females Norkov tried to bring back to Xpashta would realize that he was going to help them. She hated that they might be afraid of the large cyborg.

"Are we near Xpashta?" she asked.

"We're a few days from home," Wrylack said. "I know this ship is smaller than the one the Meori had, but you're free to wander. No one on board will bother you, even if they are extremely curious. You may get asked some questions, but they know you're mine."

"I'd rather stay with you, if that's all right?"

Wrylack nodded and brushed a kiss against her lips. "I want you to be happy, Shaylee. If you're happier when you're with me, then stay by my side. I want you to enjoy your freedom."

"Why are there only two other mates on your world?" she asked.

"Females are scared of cyborgs," Norkov said. "The other two were found during a recent mission. Lathim rescued his mate from pirates, and Rorwick claimed a woman rescued from a life pod."

Wrylack snorted. "Except Rorwick's mate hasn't been happy with her situation. She wishes to return to her world and has been very vocal about it. Anyone passing their house can hear her screaming at him. I don't know why he wants to keep her."

"Maybe she's just scared," Shaylee said. "If she had a good life on Earth, it must have been hard for her to lose her friends and family. And now she's on a strange world with only one other human."

Norkov nodded. "I supposed none of us have thought of it that way. Rorwick would give her a good life, if she'd allow him to. Hopefully I can find human females like you and Lathim's mate. You both seem… quieter."

"It's easier to accept something new when what you've left behind is so horrible," Shaylee said. "No one has ever treated me as well as Wrylack does. Perhaps Lathim's mate feels the same about him."

Norkov nodded.

"My Maggie loves me," Lathim said as he strolled into the room, a big smile on his face.

"Do I need to remind you of her reaction when you got her pregnant against her wishes?" Wrylack asked.

Lathim's cheeks flushed a dark purple. "I thought I was doing the right thing. She forgave me, and now she's thrilled about the baby."

"Thank you for leaving your mate and daughter in order to come find me," Wrylack said. "I didn't want to chance an escape with Shaylee's life in the balance. They threatened to rape and kill her if I didn't do as they said."

Lathim's gaze darkened. "I wish we could kill them all over again."

"Anyone who threatens violence against a female should be taken out," Norkov said.

Shaylee had never known men like these existed, and she only wished she had met them sooner. What if Wrylack had found her when she'd first been taken? They could have had so many good years together. He tipped her chin up and looked concerned as he gazed into her eyes.

"You're sad," he said.

"Only wishing I could have met you sooner."

"You would have been so young then. You wouldn't have wanted anything to do with me. You were still a child when you were taken."

"Seriously?" Norkov asked incredulously. "They're stealing children as slaves?"

"I was seventeen. Hardly a child," Shaylee said. "In some places on my world, that's old enough to get married and start a family."

"Were all of the human slaves as young as you?" Norkov asked.

"Some were younger," Shaylee said. "There was a girl who was barely fourteen. She was a favorite of one of my owners."

Norkov looked sick, and as Shaylee looked around the room, she saw the others felt the same. She'd never met anyone like them before. Even the men she'd known on Earth had thought they could take what they wanted, regardless of how old she was.

"If there are young ones when you go," Lathim said to Norkov, "bring them home anyway. They will grow and will eventually be old enough to mate with someone. Don't leave them in that hellish situation. We'll find a place for them to live, or assign them to someone."

"Assign them to someone?" Shaylee asked. Maybe she'd been wrong. They were going to enslave them?

"A male who would watch over them and protect them. Nothing sexual would happen between them. My people would never harm a child," Lathim said.

Shaylee nodded.

"We would give our lives to protect a female or child," Norkov said.

"Enough talk of dark subjects," Wrylack said. "My mate has suffered enough without thinking of those still in captivity. Do what you can to find her children."

"I won't stop until I find them," Norkov said, then looked at Shaylee. "You have my word. If they're still out there, I will bring them home to you."

"Thank you," she said softly.

"You should rest," Wrylack said, leading her away from the others and back to their room. "I don't want their words to upset you. They shouldn't have had such a discussion in front of you."

"It's all right, Wrylack. I lived it. I know how bad slavery can be, especially for a woman or child. If I can tell them anything that could save someone else, I want to help. If Norkov really thinks he can free more women or save those girls, then it will be worth it."

Wrylack caressed her cheek. "You have such a tender heart, even after everything you've suffered. If you wish to help them, you may. I don't want to hold you back from anything, Shaylee, but I *will* protect you at all costs. If I think for one moment that anything you tell them could endanger you, I will remove you from the discussion immediately."

"What could I possibly tell them that could put me in danger? I'm going to your world. I'm safe there, right?" Unless he'd lied.

He nodded. "I suppose you're right. I just worry. I don't want to lose you now that I've found you."

Shaylee wrapped her arms around his waist and snuggled close. "I'm not going anywhere. I like being with you, Wrylack."

And she did. She loved being in his arms, loved his kiss and his touch. Being with him was the best thing that had ever happened to her, and perhaps because of that, part of her feared this new life would be ripped away from her.

"Not even if you were allowed to return to your world?" he asked.

Shaylee looked up at him. "Not even then. I'm happier with you than I've ever been in my life. You've given me something no one else ever did."

"And what's that?" he asked softly, his thumb lightly rubbing her cheek.

"Kindness. I could lose my heart so easily to you, Wrylack, and that should scare me. But it doesn't." Not in the strictest sense. Although, she did worry that he would never love her in return.

"Why doesn't that frighten you?" he asked.

"Because I know that you will always keep me safe. Even my heart. If I give it to you, then I know you will treat it just as gently as you do me." And he did treat her gently, as if she were spun glass. He was protective of her, and made her want things she shouldn't. She knew that he would never harm her on purpose, but he could destroy her so easily without even trying, without meaning to.

"You saw me rip out a male's heart with my bare hand. I worried that you would be scared of me after that."

"I could never be scared of you, Wrylack. You saved me, in every way possible. I used to hope that I would meet someone like you, before I became so hardened and broken that I decided people like you didn't exist."

"You're not broken."

"Until I met you, I'd put up a wall around my heart. I'd tried so hard to make sure nothing would hurt me anymore. It only took one touch from you before that wall started to crumble." What she didn't say was how much that scared her. Yes, Wrylack was a gentle giant, and the cyborgs seemed different from the men she'd known in the past. But it was still hard to believe that things were really different for her now.

He hesitated only a moment before his lips brushed against hers. He kissed her softly, his arm banding around her waist to pull her tight against his body. She felt the thickness of his cock and knew he wanted her, and yet he took his time. The others had never been soft with her, had never cared if she enjoyed what happened between them. They'd found pleasure in her body while creating pain and humiliating her every chance they had. But not Wrylack. Her cyborg was tender and caring.

Tears slid down her cheeks, and he drew away. His brow furrowed as his fingers wiped the moisture away.

"I didn't mean to upset you," he said.

"You didn't. I'm crying because I'm happy."

Wrylack didn't look convinced. "Females cry when they are upset or in pain."

"And sometimes we cry when we're really, really happy. And you make me happy," she said. And perhaps that was the worst part of all. She'd experienced true joy with him, and it terrified her that she could lose it, could lose him.

His thumb caressed her cheek. "You should rest. It's been a difficult day."

"Will you stay with me?" she asked softly.

He glanced at the bed that was much smaller than the one they'd shared previously, but nodded. Wrylack pulled her dress over her head and tossed it aside before removing his clothes. He nodded toward the bed.

"Lie down while I get cleaned up. I rinsed off in the med bay, but I want to make sure no blood remains on me."

Shaylee crawled under the covers and pressed her back to the wall, leaving enough room for Wrylack to join her when he was finished. He left the bathroom door open, and she admired the hard lines of his body. When he stepped into the cleansing unit, he disappeared from her sight. She still didn't quite understand what was between her and Wrylack. He wanted her, that was no secret, and he treated her really well. But she wondered if he'd ever be able to love her. She didn't know anything about cyborgs, didn't know if they were capable of such a thing as love.

Even if he couldn't love her, she knew her life was far better since meeting him. He'd make her happy -- already did for that matter. And she knew that he would make a wonderful father. She hadn't seen him interact with children, but anyone as kind as Wrylack would never be cruel to a child. He'd promised to treat her children as if they were his own, if they could be found. There was a pang in her heart as she thought of the babies she'd carried. Those who had been born and taken from her, and those who had never lived to draw breath.

Could she have a child with Wrylack? He'd said her body was still capable of bearing children, but what if she got pregnant and couldn't carry to term? What if she had another miscarriage? Would Wrylack see her as defective? Would he come to resent the fact he'd claimed her?

He said he wanted her, that she was his. But she'd belonged to so many over the years, and they'd eventually tired of her. He seemed so different from the others, but what would she do if Wrylack ever tired of her? He said they didn't own slaves on his world, but that didn't mean he had to keep her. She didn't think he'd ever be so cruel as to abandon her, but if her children were too much of a burden, if she couldn't give him a child of his own, what would happen to her?

Wrylack returned and stared down at her, his expression concerned. He slid into bed and drew her into his arms, holding her against his chest. His hand smoothed down her hair, and he pressed a kiss to the top of her head. Shaylee tried not to think of what could happen in the future, and reminded herself that Wrylack had saved her. Yes, she was afraid, terrified of the unknown even after all this time. But he was a good man, and he'd given her no reason to doubt him. Her past was best left where it belonged, and she'd try not to let it ruin her future.

"My sweet mate," he murmured, his arms tightening around her. "We'll be home soon, and you'll be safe. Nothing will ever harm you again. I won't let it."

Shaylee breathed in his scent and closed her eyes. If Wrylack said he would protect her, then she would believe him. He'd killed for her. He'd asked someone to find her children so she would be happy. Despite what her past had taught her, she was going to have to believe in him. If he said she was safe, then she was.

Her words came back to her. She'd told him that she trusted him, that she knew he would never hurt her, even said she would give her heart to him. And then her past had scared her into thinking the worst about her mate. She felt horrible for letting those doubts creep in for even a moment, and vowed to never let it happen again. Wrylack was good to her, and was nothing like the men in her past.

She curled tighter against him, her hands pressed against his hot skin.

"What's wrong?" Wrylack asked. "I can tell something is bothering you."

"I'm being stupid. It's nothing."

He eased away enough to tip up her chin so she was forced to look at him. "If it's something that has you worried, then it's not nothing. You can tell me anything, Shaylee."

She knew better than to voice the thoughts in her head, knew it would only bring trouble. But the look in his eyes said he wouldn't relent until she told him something.

"I'm scared," she admitted.

"The Meori are gone, and we'll be home soon."

"It's not that." She bit her lip, ashamed of her doubts. She couldn't voice them, couldn't see the look in his eyes when he heard the turn her thoughts had taken.

"Tell me," he said. His words were soft, but she heard the demand, and years as a slave had taught her to obey, even if she knew there would be consequences. She only hoped she could pay the price without breaking.

"I'm scared of what will happen if you decide you don't want me one day. That my children will be too much for you, or that I won't be able to give you one of your own. I'm scared that I'm going to fall in love with you, and you'll decide I'm too much trouble to keep around," she confessed, the words falling from her lips. "That you'll realize you can do so much better than someone like me. The way they've used me... I'm no better than garbage."

He was still and silent. When she looked into his eyes, she saw the hurt there, the betrayal. Her heart shattered as she felt him withdraw, could feel him pulling away even if it wasn't physical.

"You think I'm like the others, the other males who have laid claim to you," he said. "That I will make my demands of your body and then throw you away. You think I wish to own you, to use you? You believe that I could ever degrade you the way they did?"

She bit back her sob as her tears flowed freely.

"Answer me," he said.

"No, I... " Shaylee reached up and cupped his cheek. Wrylack flinched but didn't pull away. "I didn't want to tell you because I knew it would hurt you, and I never wanted to do that. I'm trying, Wrylack, I'm trying to trust that my life is different now. But it's hard. My past... I want to forget it, to move on. I want a new life, with you."

He stared at her, his lips thinned, and he remained silent.

"The way you touched me, the way you kissed

me. It gave me hope that things could be different, and I want that so much. But I'm afraid that when I least expect it, everything will come crashing down, and I'll be left even more broken than before." Her fingers caressed his cheek. "Because you have that much power over me. No one could ever destroy me the way you can, and I know you won't mean to. You could never be cruel on purpose. You're a good man, Wrylack, and I know that. But I don't feel worthy of you. If you knew… "

She cried harder and withdrew her hand, curling in on herself as the memories assaulted her. All the faceless men, all those hands touching and inflicting pain. The degrading things she'd been forced to do. If he knew, he would never touch her. She'd told him a little, glossed over what had happened to her. But the worst of it she could never voice. No matter how many times she scrubbed herself, she'd never be clean. Not ever again. And she'd learned to live with it, had accepted her fate, until he'd come into her life. Now she wanted something she'd never have, something she didn't deserve, and it was far worse than anything she'd been through.

Time passed and still she cried. Arms came around her, pulling her closer, and she stifled a gasp and looked up at him. Wrylack pulled her against his chest and tried to soothe her, even though she was the one who had inflicted pain. It had been her words that caused a rift between them, her words that had hurt *him*. And yet he held her, comforted her. It just made Shaylee cry harder and feel even worse. He was so good, so kind… and she was less than nothing. How could something ever work between them? How could he ever come to love someone like her?

Chapter Five

Her words had infuriated him, made him angry enough to put his fist through a wall. Wrylack had given her no reason to doubt him, had killed to protect her. He'd claimed her as his mate. And yet she thought he would toss her away like some unwanted *thing*? He tried to remain calm, not to do anything rash, but he wanted to lash out.

The way she'd curled in on herself, the sobs wracking her small body, made him realize that she was hurting far worse than he was. Her words had hurt, but her tears said her pain was greater than his. He didn't understand what had happened to her to make her feel so unworthy of him. She'd told him about the men, sometimes more than one, had told him about the pregnancies. He knew she'd been a sex slave, had been with countless males before him. And he'd accepted her, even knowing those things. While he was sorry for all she'd been through, none of that mattered to him. She was sweet and beautiful, and she was *his*. But she'd said *if he knew...* knew what? Did she think there was anything she could tell him that would make him walk away from her?

Did she not understand that being his mate made her the most precious thing in his life? Her tears soaked his skin, but they began to slow, and she took a shuddering breath. He thought he'd explained about mates, thought she knew what she meant to him. But the way she'd fallen apart, the doubts that had clouded her mind, proved otherwise. He knew from the things Lathim's mate had said that humans didn't mate in the way cyborgs did, it didn't always mean forever with humans. He wanted to be angry with her, but he couldn't. It wasn't her fault. She'd been used and ill-treated for so long, had confessed she'd never known kindness until him, not even from her own people. It would take time for her to learn that he wasn't going anywhere, that her new life wouldn't vanish before her eyes. And he'd need to be patient with her.

Wrylack tipped her face up and wiped the tears from her cheeks. She stared up at him, uncertain and scared. The fear in her eyes made his gut clench. He'd put that fear there, his harsh words had caused this. In that respect, he was no better than the others she'd known, and it made him sick. He'd never harmed a female before, not even verbally, and to have done it now… and to his mate. He was so ashamed.

"Forgive me," he said softly.

"F-forgive you?" she stammered. "For what?"

"My words hurt you, and I never wish to cause you pain."

"I hurt you first."

"It doesn't excuse my behavior. I should have controlled my emotions better, have been more careful with my words. It was obvious you were hurting, and I made it worse." He smoothed her hair back from her face. "I never want to cause you pain, of any kind."

"Are we okay?" she asked. "Are you mad at me? Do you… do you want me to leave?"

His arms tightened around her. "I don't want you to leave."

"There will be other women coming to your world. Some who might not be as damaged as me."

"You're my mate, Shaylee. I don't want anyone else. I'm sorry for the things you suffered. I wish I could take those memories away from you, but I'm not sorry I found you on the Meori ship. I'm not sorry they gave you to me. You're mine, and I'm never giving you up."

"What if my children are horrible, and you don't like them?" she asked.

He smiled a little. "They're yours and could never be bad. They may be traumatized depending on what they've been through, but we'll deal with it. I have no doubt that Norkov will find them and bring them home. And I will welcome them with open arms."

"What if they're gone?" she asked, her voice a near whisper. "What if something horrific happened to them? What if... what if Norkov is too late?"

"Then you will mourn them, and when you're ready, we'll start a new family."

"When I'm ready?"

He nodded. "There is a shot I can take on my world that will inhibit my sperm for short periods of time. I don't have any left in my system now, so if you don't want another baby, then I can't touch you until we reach Xpashta."

"You're sure I'm not pregnant already?"

Wrylack shook his head. "I've scanned you every morning. Your womb is empty."

Her eyes clouded, and he hesitated a moment.

"This makes you sad?" he asked.

"I want to give you a son or daughter, someone who is blood to you, and at the same time I'm worried I'll miscarry again."

"Shaylee, I won't lie. I want children with you, as many as you're willing to have. But if something happens, if you can't give me a child, it won't lessen your worth in my eyes. I will be content having my mate safe in my arms every night."

"I want to try. I want to try having a baby with you. And not just for you... Even if my children are found, I've missed so much of their lives. I want to experience everything, from the first moment my baby draws breath. And I want to experience that with you."

"It doesn't have to be now, Shaylee. We can wait. I'm not going anywhere, and neither are you. We have more than enough time to start a family."

She slowly nodded and snuggled closer again.

Wrylack smoothed his hand down her hair and breathed in her scent. He would have to remember that she wasn't like Lathim's Maggie. She hadn't escaped the males who took her, had not been spared the horrors of being a slave. And while she was strong, in many ways she was still very fragile. He'd have to be careful with her, and remind her often that she was important to him.

There was a chime at the door, and Wrylack reluctantly pulled himself away from his mate. He pulled on a pair of leather pants and made sure Shaylee was covered before opening the door. Norkov nodded for him to step into the hall. Wrylack glanced at Shaylee before leaving the room and letting the door shut behind him. Whatever the cyborg had to say, it must not be meant for his mate's ears.

"I used the ship's main computer to contact a few people and begin my search for your mate's children." Norkov's expression was grim.

"Are they dead?" Wrylack asked.

"I haven't found anything that leads me to believe they're dead, but... did she say anything else about the first child's father? Any suspicion who it might have been? Maybe someone who... resembled us?" Norkov asked.

"No. She said the male who owned her passed her around."

"There is talk of a half-human female, the age Shaylee's child would be today. The male who owned her sold the child, but getting her back won't be easy."

"Why? Who would buy a baby?" Wrylack asked.

"Wrylack... her daughter is half-Zelranian. Mishka is her name, and she was sold to the father's family," Norkov said softly. "It's Bekvir."

Wrylack felt like his knees were going to buckle. The general over the Cy-Con project? There was no one crueler that Wrylack had ever met. The male was ice-cold and laid death and destruction everywhere he went.

"He raped her?" Wrylack asked, his voice a near whisper. He was horrified that one of his people would do something so horrible. "He harmed my mate? She said no one had ever been kind to her before, that she'd only known pain. He made her suffer, and now he has her child?"

Wrylack leaned against the wall, no longer certain he could remain upright. It sickened him that a male he had once followed into battle could do something so cruel to anyone, especially a delicate female like Shaylee. He closed his eyes as pain pierced his heart. If Mishka was on Zelran, there was no hope for retrieving her. The moment any of his kind set foot on their old world, they would be destroyed and the peace they'd maintained would be gone.

"I'm sorry," Norkov said. "Truly."

"Is she well? The child... do you know if she's taken care of?" Wrylack asked.

"I don't know, but I don't think they would have bought her if they didn't intend to keep her. Perhaps they are raising her as Bekvir's daughter. It's possible she's treated well and will integrate into the society there with little trouble."

"I can't leave her there. Not with him." Wrylack opened his eyes and stared at Norkov. "I want her. I want Mishka, whatever it takes."

"I'll see what I can do."

"And the other baby? The half-Vrotu?" Wrylack asked.

"Nothing yet."

"I can't tell her about Mishka. If I tell her I know where her child is and that I cannot retrieve her, then Shaylee will not understand. She will be angry and perhaps distrust me more than she already does. I don't wish to keep things from her, but perhaps this one time it would be better," Wrylack said.

"I haven't mentioned the child to anyone else, and I won't unless I think it's necessary. I still have some contacts from some of our Cy-Con missions. I make no promises, but maybe one of them can help. There are a few I would trust to bring the child to her mother, without trying to sell her elsewhere."

"Thank you." Wrylack looked at his friend. "How do I go back in there knowing that one of our people abused her so horribly? You know Bekvir. He's always been cruel and a monster. He wouldn't have just used her for sexual release and let her go, even if she hadn't belonged to him. He would have inflicted as much pain as possible on her small body, and probably laughed the entire time. Even pain wouldn't have been enough for him. He probably degraded her in every way possible."

"Your mate has been through a lot, Wrylack. She may not have told you everything, and I'm sure she has her reasons, but she told you enough. Knowing Bekvir got his hands on her, maybe that's something you struggle to accept. It's understandable. But she needs you. And you need her."

"You saw what Bekvir did during the Cy-Con missions. He's a large part of why we refused to fight anymore. The things he would do to the females he captured… " Wrylack's stomach nearly revolted. "Every time I close my eyes, I'll see him doing those things to Shaylee."

"She was a slave," Norkov said softly. "Even if we were to lodge a complaint with the Zelranian parliament, she had no rights at the time those things were done to her. She's your mate now, but back then she was just property. If her owner gave her to Bekvir for his entertainment, then there's nothing we can do about it."

Wrylack closed his eyes, and a tear slipped down his cheek. He hated to look weak in front of anyone, especially his fellow cyborgs, but now he partially understood what Shaylee meant when she said *if only you knew*. And he wished he didn't know. How she could still smile, could still be so sweet… how she wasn't completely broken in both body and mind, he would never know. But he was thankful that she was with him, that he could hold her every night, and that he could give her a better life than she'd had before.

"I want vengeance," he told Norkov. His eyes opened, and he stared at the cyborg. "Bekvir must pay for what he's done. I don't know when, or how, but he will suffer for the harm he caused my mate and for taking her child."

Norkov's jaw tightened. "I'll make it happen."

"Good." Wrylack pushed away from the wall. "My mate needs me. If you find out anything else, let me know."

He re-entered the quarters he shared with Shaylee, letting the door close behind him. She slept, her chest rising and falling evenly. He watched her a moment, thankful she was part of his life. Wrylack removed his pants and slid into the bed next to her, gathering her against his chest. He'd never know how she survived all these years, and he'd never ask her about her past, but he vowed that she would be safe for the rest of her life. And she would be avenged. He tightened his arms around her.

And she would be loved.

He'd never experienced love before, but the intensity of his feelings for her suggested that he more than just cared about Shaylee. She was his entire world, and if anything happened to her, he would be devastated. Now that he'd held her in his arms, had tasted her sweet kiss, he couldn't imagine a world without her in it.

Shaylee murmured in her sleep and cuddled closer, her fingers tangling in the strands of his hair. Wrylack pressed a kiss to her brow and hoped her dreams were sweet. He linked to Lathim.

Can you ask the commanders to have my things moved to a house? The small quarters I have now aren't fit for a mate.

He felt Lathim's agreement. There were plenty of empty homes on the base they'd claimed. Most cyborgs preferred the close quarters of the smaller units in the large buildings. But with a mate, Wrylack knew he would want more space, especially when her children were brought home. Only a handful of cyborgs had taken a house prior to having a mate. If everyone had a mate one day, they would have to expand the walls and build more homes. But for now, there were sadly only three mates on their world, or there would be three once Shaylee was safe inside his home. Three mates and hundreds of cyborgs. It hardly seemed fair.

"You're thinking too hard," his mate said softly, her eyes still closed.

"I'm happier than I've ever been," Wrylack

confessed. "But it seems wrong when so many others are still without mates. I'm one of the cyborgs who had been considered undesirable and the least likely to find someone."

"Why?" she asked, her eyes opening.

"Because of my eyes," he said. "Cyborgs who don't have mechanical parts showing already scare people, mostly because of our reputation, but with my eyes... " He shrugged.

"They're beautiful," she said.

"There are others on Xpashta who are like me, with cybernetic parts on the outside. It's been a concern that perhaps a mate will have to be purchased for them. We've recently learned of a program that provides brides or mates, at a cost of course. But I don't know that it's any better than purchasing a slave at auction."

"Wrylack, have you learned nothing?"

His brow furrowed. "What do you mean?"

"There are some out there who might be afraid of them, but if those cyborgs are half as sweet as you, half as kind, then they have nothing to worry about. That's what most human women want... to be treated right, especially if they've been abused in some way. Maybe instead of focusing on purchasing mates, you should try rescuing some."

"Like the slaves Norkov plans to bring with him from your old master?" Wrylack asked.

"Yes," she said softly. "Either send those cyborgs with him, or make sure they're the ones who help the women when they get to Xpashta. A gentle touch will go a long way with a woman who's been a slave. Every owner I had took what he wanted. I was never asked if I wanted something, my physical comfort or well-being was never considered. And I would imagine most slaves you rescue would be the same way."

"Lathim's mate suggested that we have a meeting with some race called Terrans. It seems they have a program in place on Earth to provide brides to their people. So far, we haven't been able to discover any world where a race called Terrans exist, although it does seem to be a common way to refer to humans. But that doesn't make any sense. If the bride program was for humans to mate with humans, why would they be sent off-world?"

Shaylee frowned. "I remember seeing some of them on the news when I lived on Earth. They actually look a bit like you. Their skin is a darker hue of purple, and their hair is pitch-black. But their general build and features are the same."

Wrylack stared at her. "Dark purple eyes?"

She nodded.

"They aren't Terrans. They're Zelthranites and are related to my people. Some Zelthranites landed on my old world a long time ago and mated with the people who already claimed the planet as their home. My people, the Zelranians, are descended from a mix of the two races."

"Why don't you live there anymore?" she asked.

"The Zelranian parliament designed a program for… I guess you would call us super soldiers. Cyborgs. The program, Cy-Con, took active and retired military and altered us. In some cases, males were selected who had never joined the military but had skills our government thought would be useful. When we revolted, we were exiled."

"What did they do to you when you joined the program?" she asked.

"Our bones were replaced with a dense metal, some of our organs were replaced with cybernetic ones. In my case, they gave me cybernetic eyes with X-ray vision, thinking to enhance my medical abilities. As I told you before, they also replaced my lungs and heart. I was one of the top medics in the military when I joined the program. I guess they were trying to improve me."

"And no one else has eyes like yours?"

"No. The doctor presiding over the procedure told them it was too traumatic to try it again. I apparently died twice while they were enhancing my body. Once when they replaced my heart, and again when they removed my eyes."

"And the others who have cybernetic parts on the outside… what are they like?" she asked.

"One has a cybernetic arm from shoulder to fingertips. It looks well enough like a regular arm, but it's made of special metal. Indestructible. Another has legs made of the same material."

"Are there others like the three of you?" she asked.

He hesitated. There had been others, but not anymore. Those memories were best left in the past, though, and he didn't need to burden Shaylee with them.

"No. It was decided that it was better to keep our cybernetic parts hidden, so all other cyborgs look… normal I guess is a good-enough word." Not an entire lie. Out of the current living cyborgs it was true anyway. Some of the Cy-Con experiments had ended up more machine, and the results had been disastrous.

"What's going to happen when we reach your planet?" she asked.

"My current quarters were not suitable for a mate, so I've requested a house for us. My things are being moved." He frowned. "I'll have to arrange for more clothing for you. I didn't think to grab the ones the Meori gave you."

"I'd just as soon not have anything they've touched," she said.

"There are store rooms on the base where we live that may have clothing that fits you. We can look through the crates and see what we find. If there's nothing that will work, the next ship leaving Xpashta can pick up some things for you at Alpha9 or another trading post," Wrylack said.

"What if the other mates don't like me?" Shaylee said softly.

"They're going to love you," Wrylack assured her. "How can they not? My mate is sweet, and her smile lights up the darkest room."

Shaylee's cheeks flushed.

"Rest," Wrylack said.

Shaylee didn't argue and closed her eyes, curling against him. With his arms around her, Wrylack kept watch. Even though they were safe for now, the Meori had proven that cyborgs were not invincible. Until they reached Xpashta, he would stay vigilant. No one would take his mate from him, not as long as he drew breath.

Chapter Six

Shaylee stared wide-eyed as a large group of cyborgs gathered around her. She'd known she was coming to a world with only two other humans -- only two other females for that matter -- but this... she'd never seen so many men at one time, especially ones built like these. Was there such a thing as a skinny, puny cyborg? It was like being surrounded by a race of massive warriors, and she supposed that was essentially what they were, thanks to the Cy-Con program Wrylack had mentioned. The Shaylee who had been mistreated all her life would have been terrified to be surrounded by such men, but after spending so much time with Wrylack, things were different. She was still damaged, but she was learning that not everyone would harm her.

"They won't hurt you," he whispered in her ear and nudged her forward a little, as if reading her thoughts.

They all watched, curiosity blazing in some of their eyes, and sadness in others. From what Wrylack had told her, they were lonely and wanted mates. It was a little heartbreaking that there so many males here on Xpashta who would treat a female kindly, and yet they were alone. And then there were slavers out there, taking whoever they wanted when they wanted, and hurting innocent women. It didn't seem fair.

"What is it?" Wrylack asked.

"I want to help them," she said.

"Help them?"

She nodded. "There are women out there, like me, who could benefit from being the mate of a cyborg. As long as... the cyborgs weren't picky."

"Picky?" Wrylack asked.

"I'm talking about women who may be damaged mentally, physically, and emotionally. They will need someone to care for them, to show them not all men are monsters. If your fellow cyborgs are anything like you, then I think those women would be lucky to have one as a mate."

"You still want us to rescue slaves and claim them?" Wrylack asked.

"It would benefit you and the women."

"She wants us to take slaves?" a cyborg asked, horror etched on his face.

Shaylee felt the blood drain from her face, and she pressed tighter to Wrylack. If they were so opposed to women who had been slaves, they would never accept her. Had Wrylack lied when he said his people would welcome her? A murmur went through the crowd and accusing glances were cast her way.

"What does she mean, Wrylack?" a deep voice asked.

"Remember when Maggie mentioned that we could purchase slaves and free them here on Xpashta?" Wrylack asked. "My mate is suggesting we track down women who have been kept as slaves and bring them here... as mates. I assure you, Sorus, she didn't mean that we should keep slaves."

Sorus gazed down at her from his imposing height, even taller than Wrylack. "And how do you suggest we do that? Visit every outpost in the galaxy and purchase slave women?"

"I don't know," Shaylee said. "I just thought... "

"You thought what?" Sorus asked.

"You want mates, more than anything, and there are a lot of human women who are being kept as slaves, probably far more than Earth even realizes. If you could save those women and give them a better life, it would benefit not only your cyborgs but those women as well. They would get rescued from a hell you can't imagine, and your men would have families."

A cyborg stepped forward. "If we commandeered a few more ships, it would be possible to have two crews of ten each out searching for mates on a regular basis. Her idea isn't a bad one, Sorus."

"Very well, Jaksil. Get a crew together and see what you can do about procuring more ships for us. We'll go from there," Sorus said. He turned his gaze back to Shaylee. "And you... you were pleased to be mated to someone like us? You're not afraid?"

"My life has been very hard since I was a small child, even on Earth I was never shown affection, unless it was the wrong kind. Wrylack is wonderful to me. It doesn't bother me that some of his parts are mechanical," Shaylee said.

Sorus nodded. "Very well. With two mates suggesting we rescue human female slaves, perhaps it's something we should seriously pursue. We were intrigued by the idea when Maggie brought it up, but have not actively pursued it yet. Welcome to Xpashta, Shaylee. I hope you like your new home."

She shyly smiled up at him, and then Wrylack was tugging her through the crowd again. He stopped in front of a large cyborg with a metal arm.

"Tark, this is my mate, Shaylee," Wrylack said, pulling her forward a little.

"It's nice to meet you," Shaylee said.

Tark gazed at her in curiosity before looking at Wrylack. "You had to force her to be your mate?"

"No," Wrylack said.

"He saved me," Shaylee said. "I'm with him because I want to be."

Tark looked at her again. "And his eyes don't bother you?"

She shook her head. "They're beautiful."

He gazed at her another moment before looking at Wrylack again. "Your home is ready. You were given one between Lathim and Rorwick, so your mate would be equal distance to both of the other human females."

"Thank you," Wrylack said.

"I'll take you there," Tark said, glancing at Shaylee once more before turning and heading off away from the crowd.

It was quite a walk to their new home, but Shaylee took everything in. Her new home was… interesting. She hadn't known what to expect when Wrylack had said he was taking her to a planet of cyborgs. The house in front of her appeared to be made of some sort of stone, but there was glass in the windows. Wrylack opened the door and ushered her inside. It was sparsely furnished, but seemed to have the essentials. Shaylee wandered through the rooms, noting there were five bedrooms.

"It's rather big," she commented.

Tark had followed them inside. "It was mentioned that your children might be joining you, and since Wrylack will likely want more children, you were given one of the larger homes. The commanders wanted to make sure you had plenty of space."

Shaylee tried not to think about what would happen if her children weren't found, or were already dead. Wrylack seemed convinced they were alive and would be returned to her, but she had her doubts. Today was a day for happiness, though, so she pushed aside the sad thoughts plaguing her.

"Food has been stocked for you," Tark said. "If

your mate would like to select some items from the storage rooms, the commanders said she had permission to do so. I believe most of the books from Earth have been picked over by Maggie, but I'm sure she would share."

"I can't read," Shaylee said.

Wrylack looked at her in surprise. "You can't?"

She shook her head.

"Why were you not taught to read?" Wrylack asked. "Isn't that a common thing for humans to learn?"

"I didn't go to very good schools and no one cared if I learned or not. Most of the schools I attended were in bad parts of town, and most of the kids were passed whether they earned the grades or not." She shrugged. "I had other things to worry about."

Like surviving.

Both cyborgs blinked at her, like they didn't know what to make of her statement. She hoped Wrylack didn't think less of her. She wasn't book smart, but she had street smarts. That had to count for something, didn't it? Shaylee didn't think she was stupid, but no one had ever cared if she learned how to do something. Ever since she'd gotten old enough to gain a few curves, all anyone had cared about was whether she got them off. Even those who were supposed to protect her.

She hadn't lied when she told Wrylack she was trash, and he could do so much better than her. But he hadn't listened. She wondered if now he was regretting that decision. Just because his people were desperate for mates didn't mean they had to take just anyone. As a medic, he could have been more selective. He had to be smart, probably smarter than the average warrior wandering around this place, and now he was stuck with a mate who couldn't do something as simple as read.

"I need to visit medical," Wrylack said. "You'll be safe here."

"Or I could go with you," she said.

"It's a long walk and you're tired, Shaylee. Stay here and rest, and I'll return soon. Explore your new home and think of some items you want or need." Wrylack reached out and cupped her cheek. "I want you to be happy here."

"I will be," she assured him.

"Medical?" Tark asked. "Were you injured?"

"No, but I would like to give Shaylee more time before we start a family," Wrylack said.

Tark turned an accusing gaze her way. "You would keep him from starting a family when it's all he's ever wanted? What kind of mate doesn't want children with the male she's chosen?"

Wrylack wrapped a hand around Tark's arm. "It's not her fault. She's agreeable to having children with me. It's my decision to do this."

"I asked him not to," Shaylee said. "If he wants to start a family now, I'm all right with that."

Wrylack focused on her. "And I told you that we would wait until your children were found and returned. I'm not an unreasonable male, Shaylee. I can't ask you to have a baby when the two you already gave birth to are out there somewhere."

Tark scanned her from head to toe. "She doesn't look old enough to have two children."

"Shaylee was captured on her Earth when she was only seventeen and then sold into slavery. Her children were born while she was owned by two different males. Norkov is tracking them down," Wrylack said.

Tark paled. "You were taken when you were so young?"

"Still a child on her world," Wrylack said. "And she said there are others, even younger, who have been captured and sold. I asked Norkov to bring them here if he's able to locate any."

"What are we going to do with children?" Tark asked.

"Protect them," Wrylack said. "I'm going to speak to the commanders about willing cyborgs who will take those young females into their homes and guard them. They will have been abused and some may have never known a soft touch or kind word. They need us."

Tark nodded. "Very well."

Wrylack pulled Shaylee into his arms and kissed her softly. "I won't be long."

"Please don't go," she said, holding onto him. "I know you think it's best if we wait, but I don't care. Babies are meant to be miracles, Wrylack. Who's to say we have one right away if you don't get the shot? It could still take a while."

"I'm not taking a chance, Shaylee. You'll thank me later. You need time to adjust to life here, to freedom. Take time to enjoy your life. When your children are brought home, you're going to have your hands full. It's not wise to add a baby to the mix."

She sighed and nodded. She had to admit that he made good points. Shaylee watched Wrylack and Tark walk out the door, closing it behind them, then she wandered her new home. There wasn't much to explore since the only personal items delivered were Wrylack's clothing and grooming supplies. There wasn't a single picture on any of the walls, no items that he'd taken a liking to and kept... nothing. Just bare walls, plain furniture, and his belongings.

She did notice a large screen on one wall, but didn't have a clue how to make it work. Did cyborgs have movies? Or was it a communication device of some sort? She studied it a moment and then turned her gaze to two large doors that led out into a courtyard of sorts. Really, it was a stone patio surrounded by tall, rock-like walls. There was no grass, no plants... nowhere to sit. She found it curious and wondered why they had them if they obviously didn't go out to enjoy the area. Maybe Wrylack could find her a bench so she could sit out there when she wanted fresh air but didn't want to be gawked at by all the cyborgs.

There was a knock at the front door and she approached it cautiously, then scoffed at herself. A planet full of cyborgs and two humans... who did she think was out there? It wasn't like she was getting abducted again. At least, she didn't think that would happen here. Wrylack had assured her she was safe on his planet.

"Who's there?" she called out.

"My name's Maggie. I'm Lathim's mate," a feminine voice called back.

Shaylee stared at the door and after several tries, realized that she had no idea how to open it. "I don't know how to let you in."

She heard Maggie sigh. "I guess they haven't programmed the house to respond to you yet. I'm going to leave some things on your doorstep. Wrylack can bring them inside when he returns. My mate mentioned you were alone right now, and I'd thought to come keep you company. I brought a few gifts."

Gifts? Someone had brought her gifts? Shaylee couldn't remember ever receiving a gift from someone before.

"Thank you," Shaylee said. "I'm sorry I can't let you in."

Maggie laughed. "It's all right. We'll meet another time. Wrylack knows where we live. You can come visit anytime."

She heard the woman walk away and slammed her hand against the stupid door. What good was freedom if she was trapped in the house? She hoped Wrylack returned soon. Maggie had said something about programming the house to respond to her. Did that mean there was a computer in the house like on the ship? She didn't know anything about this world and felt a little lost.

She banged on the door once more and let out a startled gasp as it slid open, revealing a rather imposing cyborg on the other side. His gaze scanned her from head to toe before settling on her face.

"So, you're the human female Wrylack claimed as his mate," the cyborg said.

He stepped across the threshold, pressing her backward into the house.

"Who are you?" she asked, wondering if perhaps she was in danger. How was it this cyborg had access to her house, but Maggie couldn't come in?

"My name is Kiril. I'm one of the cyborg commanders."

"Does that mean you're in charge?"

He smiled slightly. "Something like that."

"Wrylack isn't home," she said.

"I know. I came to see you."

"Me?" For some reason, she didn't think that meant anything good.

"Wrylack is... different from the rest of us. I know that circumstances put the two of you together, but now that you've seen how many cyborgs are without mates, I wanted to make sure you wanted to remain with him."

Shaylee's brow furrowed. "I don't understand."

"If you wanted a different mate, someone more... normal... then I could make that happen," Kiril said.

More normal? What was he...? Shaylee gasped, and fury ignited inside her.

"There is nothing wrong with Wrylack! Why does everyone act like he's some sort of freak or something?" she demanded.

"His eyes are unusual and most females have found them unsettling."

"Females?" She swallowed hard. "What other females?"

"Before we learned that the females at the floating brothels weren't there of their own accord, we used those facilities regularly. Now we only use sex bots."

Wrylack, her sweet Wrylack, had been with whores? But that meant... The room spun a little. If those women weren't there willingly, then it was the same as him relieving himself with a slave. Those women didn't ask for his attention and had likely felt forced.

"I think I'm going to be sick," she said a moment before she ran to the bathroom and threw up.

Kiril followed, a frown on his face. "What's wrong?"

"Wrylack did that? He used those women without any care about... " She couldn't even finish the sentence. "That makes him, makes all of you, no better than those who have owned me."

"What are you telling my mate?" Wrylack asked

harshly from behind Kiril. "You've upset her."

Shaylee looked up at him with tears in her eyes. "You used them. You didn't even care that they didn't want to be with you. Willing or not, you took what you wanted from them."

Wrylack froze. "What are you talking about, Shaylee?"

"The women at the brothels."

His face paled and he sank to his knees in front of her. "I never knew, Shaylee. Until Lathim's mate told us those women were sold to those places, we thought they were there willingly. I never would force myself on a female."

"But you did," she said brokenly.

"Shaylee," he said softly, reaching for her. She drew away, and his hand fell to his side. "The moment I found out those women were forced to be with whoever purchased their services, I stopped using the floating brothels. I don't even use the sex bots there anymore. I could never knowingly harm a female. It goes against everything I believe in."

She kept her distance, wanting his words to be true, but after everything she'd been through, how could she trust him?

Wrylack growled and stood, facing the other cyborg. "Why did you come here and tell her those things?"

"I wanted to make sure she was with you because she wanted to be and not because she felt like she had no choice. You know you're different from most of us, with your strange eyes. I was merely explaining that all other females had been scared of you. I didn't realize she'd fall apart," Kiril said.

"You tried to take my mate from me?" Wrylack asked.

"I wanted to make sure she understood she had options. It's my job to ensure everyone's happiness, Wrylack, not just yours. If she felt coerced into being with you, she needed to know that she could leave."

Wrylack slammed a fist into the wall. "Leave."

Kiril nodded and turned. He paused at the doorway and looked back at Shaylee. "If you wish to leave him, let me know. We'll find you a better mate."

Shaylee didn't give him an answer. Wrylack had been wonderful to her, the perfect mate, until she'd found out about the whores. But if what he said was true, if he hadn't realized what he was doing was wrong, could she really hold it against him? After the other cyborg left, Wrylack turned and knelt in front of her again, a look of anguish on his face.

"You hate me now," he said.

"I don't hate you," Shaylee said.

"I truly didn't know about those females," he said. "If I had thought for one minute they really didn't want to be with me, I'd have never touched them."

"Kiril said they were afraid of you."

"Some were," he said. "I left those alone. I've only been with two living females aside from you, Shaylee. Both were at a brothel, before I knew they didn't really want to be there. The rest of the time I've used sex bots. It was easier than dealing with a hysterical female when she saw my eyes. While I did stop going to the brothels, we have some sex bots on Xpashta as well."

"How could you not tell?" she asked.

"On my home world, casual sex isn't a thing. If you have sex with a female, you take her as your mate. Other than the experience I had with the two females at the brothel and with sex bots, I didn't have anything to compare it with. They didn't tell me to stop, didn't push me away." Wrylack reached for her again, brushing her hair off her face. "If I had known that one day I would have a mate like you, I would have never touched them. I'm sorry that I used them, I'm sorry that they touched me without wanting to, but mostly I'm sorry that the knowledge of those two encounters hurts you. I would do anything for you, Shaylee. You're my entire world."

Shaylee rolled to her knees and flung herself into Wrylack's arms. "I'm sorry I reacted the way I did."

"You had every reason to be upset," Wrylack said. "It happened long before I met you, Shaylee. And if I had known that you would be in my arms right now, I'd have waited. I would have preferred my first time with a living female to have been with you."

"I should have trusted you," she said. "You've given me no reason not to."

"I'm not upset with you, Shaylee. I'm furious with Kiril, though." He drew in a deep breath. "Do you wish for another mate? I would understand if you did."

Shaylee reached up and cupped his cheek. "I don't want anyone but you."

He nuzzled her nose with his. "I want you, Shaylee. Only you, for as long as I live."

His lips brushed against hers, and Shaylee curled her fingers around the long strands of his hair. She loved it when he kissed her, loved feeling his arms around her. Being with Wrylack was unlike anything she'd ever experienced before, and she wondered if she'd ever get enough of him. He stood, taking her with him, and carried her out of the bathroom and into the room they would share.

Wrylack eased her down his body and reached for the hem of her dress. She didn't stop him as he lifted it over her head and let it fall to the floor. Wrylack caressed the curves of her body before drawing her close and kissing her deeply again.

"Mine," he murmured against her lips.

"Yours," she said.

Wrylack pulled away and began removing his clothes. When he stood before her completely bare, Shaylee reached for him. Her fingers glided across his muscles; Shaylee wanted to memorize every inch of him. The contrast of his light lavender skin and her milky white hand was beautiful, and she wondered what their children would look like. When he lifted her and laid her down on the bed, she went without protest. Since leaving the Meori ship, he hadn't touched her intimately, and her body ached for him.

He stood, watching her, his gaze tracing her from head to toe. Wrylack reached for her, wrapping his hand around her ankle and dragging her to the edge of the bed. His hands gripped her thighs and spread them wide. She let him look his fill and shivered in anticipation.

Wrylack fell to his knees in front of her. "I learned a few things about pleasuring a human female while I was in medical. If this doesn't feel good, tell me to stop and I will."

Her heart hammered in her chest as he leaned forward, his fingers opening her wide. The first lick of his tongue against her slick folds made Shaylee gasp. Wrylack licked her again, his tongue flicking against her clit. Shaylee didn't care where he'd learned to do that, as long as he didn't stop. Wrylack feasted on her, his tongue plunging into her tight channel before circling her clit again.

"Wrylack," she said, her voice filled with need.

His lips closed around the bundle of nerves, and

he sucked on it until she was screaming his name, her hips bucking against him. He gently lapped at her until the last of the tremors subsided, then he rose over her body. Her thighs gripped him as his cock brushed against her.

"My sweet, Shaylee. My perfect mate," he said.

Before she could respond, he thrust hard and deep, entering her fully. Shaylee's nails bit into his shoulders and her eyes closed a moment. She loved feeling Wrylack inside her. He took her slowly, the slide of his cock igniting every nerve. He took his time, being gentle and loving. A tidal wave of bliss carried Shaylee away, and one orgasm turned into two.

"Harder," she begged.

He growled a little and drove into her. With her cries begging him for more, Wrylack took her like a male possessed. She felt his release spill into her, and he groaned in her ear, her body clutched against him. His heart pounded in his chest, and she kissed him, everywhere she could reach.

"My Shaylee," he murmured before claiming her lips. "I would stay in bed with you for days if I could."

"Why can't you?" she asked as he eased out of her.

She looked at his cock, glistening with their mingled release, and felt some trickle out of her. If he hadn't gone to get that shot, then right now, she could possibly be pregnant with his child. She hoped he didn't come to regret that decision.

"There's something I need to do. It's going to require me to leave for a short while, but I think you'll be pleased when I return. I'll make sure the house is set to respond to you before I go. I don't want you to feel trapped here."

"You're leaving? But we just got here!"

"Norkov has a lead on one of your children. I'm going with him," Wrylack said.

"Then take me with you."

Wrylack shook his head. "It's not safe. I won't put your life in jeopardy."

"If it's dangerous, you shouldn't go either."

He cupped her jaw and pressed a kiss to her lips. "I'm going after our child. I promise to return to you safely. Nothing will keep me from your side."

"Be careful, Wrylack. I only just found you. I don't think I could handle losing you."

Wrylack kissed her deeply, then helped her clean up and get dressed. Shaylee listened carefully as he explained how everything in their new home worked, and had the computer read her voice and scan her handprint so she would have access to everything. When they were finished, he showed her the Earth items Maggie had brought to her. And while she felt joy over the items, her heart was sad that Wrylack was leaving so soon.

He said not to worry, but she couldn't do anything except worry. Until he was beside her once more, she would pray daily that he stayed safe. It had been a long time since she'd prayed, having felt that God had forsaken her long ago. But being with Wrylack made her realize that she still could live a long, happy life. As much as she hated her years as a slave, if she hadn't been abducted, she never would have met Wrylack. Shaylee wouldn't have wished those horrifying years on anyone, and would likely have nightmares the rest of her life, but all of that pain and suffering had brought her to the sweet cyborg who took such good care of her, the male who showed her that kindness and love weren't just a myth.

"Wrylack," she said, drawing his attention her

way. "I love you."

A wide smile stretched across his face and he gathered her close. "I love you too, my sweet mate."

It would be enough for now. She could tell that he was determined to bring her child home to her, and knew that nothing she said or did would dissuade him. But knowing that he loved her, that he wanted her in his life, would help her through the lonely days ahead. And when he returned, she hoped it would be for good.

She spent the rest of the night in Wrylack's arms, his body claiming hers until the sun streamed through their bedroom windows. And with one last lingering kiss, he dressed and walked out the door. Shaylee stared after him, hoping it wouldn't be the last time she saw her mate. Something told her that Wrylack was walking into something bad. A feeling in her gut screamed that he should remain with her.

"Please let me be wrong," she whispered. "Bring him home to me."

Chapter Seven

Wrylack stood on board the Mystic7 with Norkov, Milore, Tenz, Zorlok, and a handful of other cyborgs. Each had volunteered for the mission, despite how dangerous it was, and their crew was fuller than usual. The Mystic7 usually ran with a crew of ten, but over a dozen males had volunteered.

"You're sure the male you spoke with is going to retrieve Mishka and bring her to us?" Wrylack asked.

"You're going to have to make a choice, Wrylack," Norkov said. "I have a male in place to bring Mishka to us, and another in place for Bekvir. You need to decide which is more important. Revenge for your mate, or getting your daughter home safely."

Wrylack growled. "Why can't I do both?"

"The sooner we get Mishka home, the better," Norkov said. "The male retrieving Bekvir has a certain set of skills. He's waiting for instructions."

"I need to take care of Bekvir, or at least look him in the eye and tell him why he's going to die," Wrylack said.

"We can cloak the Mystic7," Zorlok said. "It would give Wrylack enough time to satisfy the urge to protect his mate, and keep his daughter safe too."

"Are we landing on Zelran?" Wrylack asked.

"No, we're meeting both males at the Garva outpost. I asked them to make certain Mishka didn't see Bekvir at any time. We don't want to upset her more than she already will be," Norkov said. "I can only imagine how terrified she'll be."

"I'll see Mishka first," Wrylack said. "Zorlok, while I attend to Bekvir, will you watch my daughter?"

"I would be honored," Zorlok said.

Time seemed to pass slowly for Wrylack as they

neared Garva. When they landed, he followed Norkov with Zorlok right behind them. People watched them pass, but no one stopped them along the way. Wrylack wondered if he looked as fierce as he felt, wanting both to know that Mishka was safe and that Bekvir would die a horrible death.

"I should warn you, the male who has your daughter is… a bit brutal," Norkov said. "He would never harm a child, but his appearance tends to scare people."

Wrylack didn't say anything, but his gut clenched. He hoped Mishka was all right. He hoped the child wouldn't be terrified, taken from her home and what was possibly the only family she'd ever known. If it had been anyone but Bekvir who had her, he might have convinced Shaylee her daughter was safe and well taken care of. But there was no way he'd leave the child with that monster.

They entered a small building in the center of the Garva outpost and Wrylack's eyes adjusted to the dim lighting. A scarred Skuriu warrior held Mishka close to his body, his stance protective. The male's black hair hung long down his back with two braids over his shoulders. But it was his eyes that nearly made Wrylack halt. They were black as obsidian and so cold. The eyes of a killer.

"Norkov, you will keep your promise?" the warrior asked.

"Yes, Herok. You may join my crew when we search for the other slaves, and claim one as your mate. It is a small price to pay for the service you have done for us," Norkov said.

Wrylack slowly approached and knelt in front of the small child. She was only three, and already she was stunning. She had the blue eyes so common with

Zelranians, and while her skin wasn't the pale ivory of Shaylee, it wasn't quite the color of a Zelranian either, but somewhere in between. Her hair was black with teal highlights, and he knew she would be a heartbreaker when she was older. Her facial features resembled his Shaylee, and he was thankful she'd inherited little from her birth father. As far as Wrylack was concerned, that monster was no more than a sperm donor. This was Shaylee's daughter, and therefore *his* daughter.

"My name is Wrylack," he told her softly. "And your mother is my mate."

She stuck her thumb in her mouth and studied him.

"Your mother's name is Shaylee. She's a human," Wrylack said. "Did you know that you're part human and part Zelranian?"

Herok covered her ears with his hands and spoke low. "I found her locked in a room with no windows and a narrow bed. It looked like they fed her on the floor like an animal. You can't tell in this lighting, but she has bruises. They were not kind to her."

Wrylack pulled the male's hands away from Mishka's ears. "You don't remember your mother because you were taken from her the moment you were born, Mishka, but she loves you and misses you very much."

The little girl blinked up at him and kept sucking on her thumb.

"I love your mother, and since you're part of her, that means I love you too. I want to take you home with me, to my mate, where we'll be a family. Do you understand, Mishka? Do you know what a family is?"

She hesitantly moved away from Herok and came closer to him. Her little hand reached up and touched his face, then his hair, before she curled herself against his chest. Wrylack wrapped an arm around her and closed his eyes.

"I promise you will be safe, Mishka. I have claimed your mother as my mate, and I now claim you as my daughter."

Wrylack stood, holding her against him. Zorlok was standing nearby and Wrylack passed his daughter to his friend. Mishka tensed and stared at him with wide eyes.

"There's something I have to do," he told her. "I'll return to you shortly."

Wrylack touched her cheek, then leaned forward and kissed her forehead.

Zorlok walked off with Mishka in his arms, the little girl staring over his shoulder in confusion as she was carried away, and Wrylack focused on Norkov. "Where's Bekvir?"

"In an abandoned building at the edge of the outpost," Norkov said. "We thought it best he was away from everyone... so the screams wouldn't raise any alarm among the people here."

"Is that the man who took her?" Herok asked. "The one who has abused that sweet girl?"

"Yes," Norkov answered. "Her birth father. He raped her mother, then took the baby when she was born."

Herok's eyes flashed gold a moment. "I'm coming with you."

They followed Norkov to the edge of the outpost and a building that looked like it might collapse at any moment. Screams came from within, and Wrylack pushed through the doors and came to a stop just inside. Bekvir had been strapped to a metal table and blood pooled underneath. His eyes were wild as he begged for his life. The once ice-cold general he'd followed into battle didn't look so fearsome right now. The way he begged for his life was pathetic, and Wrylack was fairly certain over the stench of blood he could detect urine. What sort of warrior pissed himself? It just proved that the male was a coward who picked on those weaker than him.

Wrylack approached the table and looked down at the male in disgust. "Do you know why you're here, Bekvir?"

The Zelranian's eyes went even wider. "Wrylack?"

"You made a fatal error," Wrylack said.

"Whatever you want, it's yours," Bekvir said. "Just free me."

"I have what I want. I have my mate, and now I have her daughter."

Wrylack knew the moment Bekvir realized who he meant. The male paled and began breathing harder. There was a wildness to his eyes as he comprehended no one was coming to save him. He was going to die this day, and it would be a horrible death. Wrylack couldn't think of anyone more deserving of such a fate, except perhaps the male who had given Shaylee to this monster.

"She was a slave. Just a slave. She meant nothing," Bekvir said.

Wrylack growled and leaned close. Drawing a blade from the belt wrapped around his waist, he pressed the metal against Bekvir's arm, drawing more blood.

"That slave, that female you think meant nothing, is my mate. You terrorized her, raped her, then stole her daughter. I might have been more lenient if you had been kind to Mishka, but it's obvious she's been abused. I will do anything to make sure my females are safe," Wrylack said.

He dug the blade deeper, not stopping until he hit bone.

"Shaylee is mine, and now Mishka is mine. And the male who took you will make sure they never have to be afraid of you again. As much as I want to end your life myself, my daughter needs me," Wrylack said. "Mishka and Shaylee are more important than my need for vengeance. Especially when there are others as disgusted with you as I am, who are more than willing to get the job done."

He jerked the blade from Bekvir's arm, the male screaming out once more. Wrylack sheathed the blade and stared at the Drelthene across the table. The male flashed his fangs in a cruel smile, and Wrylack knew that he would make sure Bekvir didn't go easy. The Drelthenes were a bloodthirsty lot to begin with, but when it came to those who harmed females and children, they were even more fearsome.

"Make him suffer," Wrylack said. "Draw it out as long as you can, then end him. You can have whatever you want in payment."

"I already made a deal with Norkov. It will be my pleasure to take care of such a male as this one. Females should be cherished, not brutalized. Go to your child and your mate," the male said.

"Thank you," Wrylack said, then turned and walked out of the building. Norkov followed, and they returned to the Mystic7. He didn't know what deal Norkov had made with the Drelthene, but it wouldn't surprise him if it was the same as Herok's deal. Both Drelthenes and Skurius were in need of mates. While the Drelthenes did have some females on their world, they had a tendency to breed more males, making their population uneven. Wrylack couldn't fault either male for wanting to rescue a slave to take home as a mate. And if what Shaylee said was true, those females would be lucky to have those males. Assuming the females weren't terrified of them.

Wrylack entered the Mystic7 and stopped long enough to clean his blade and make sure he didn't have any of Bekvir's blood on him, then he went in search of his daughter. He found her in the galley with Zorlok, a piece of fruit in her small hands. She hadn't yet taken a bite and stared at the fruit, almost as if she were afraid she'd get into trouble for eating. It infuriated him that she'd been treated so poorly. Children were innocent, and yet Bekvir and his family had abused his own flesh and blood.

"Her stomach was growling," Zorlok said.

Wrylack gently picked up Mishka and cradled her against his chest. "We're going home, to see your mother. She'll be so happy to see you."

"We're making a stop on the way," Zorlok said. "I arranged for us to go to Alpha9. I thought you might want some clothing and toys for her, since she didn't come with anything other than what she's wearing, and what better place to find them than the trading post?"

"Thank you," Wrylack said. "I'm afraid I hadn't thought of that, and since we don't have children on Xpashta yet, it's doubtful we have anything there for her. As anxious as I am to return to Shaylee, I want to make sure Mishka is properly cared for as well."

"I sent a message to the commanders. They're going to let your mate know that you're safe and will be returning soon." Zorlok clapped him on the back. "Your daughter is a beauty. Guard her well."

Wrylack carried Mishka to the room he'd been

assigned. They'd placed an extra cot in there, and he eased her down onto it. She finally bit into her piece of fruit, finishing it quickly, and curled up on the bed. He wondered when she'd last eaten, and anger surged inside him again. Wrylack drew a blanket over her, then sat on his own bed and watched her. She stared back at him, but she didn't seem afraid. For some reason, she seemed to trust him, as if she understood he was going to protect her. Now that she was under better lighting, he saw the bruises marring her arms and legs. It infuriated him that someone could harm a defenseless child.

"No one will ever hurt you again, Mishka. I will bring death to anyone who dares to harm you," he promised.

He didn't know how much of his words she understood. It had been a long time since he'd been around someone so young, but she seemed to find comfort from the sound of his voice if nothing else, and closed her eyes. It wasn't long before she was resting peacefully. He felt the Mystic7 lift off and couldn't wait to see his mate once more. He only hoped that Norkov would have good news about the second child, but for now, they would focus on Mishka. She was here, safe, and he would do anything to make sure that didn't change.

Garva was several days journey from Xpashta. Even though he'd slept little since leaving his planet, Wrylack spent most of his time watching over Mishka and introducing her to the other cyborgs on board. He'd wiped her off with a cloth, but hadn't had any clean clothing for her. She seemed hesitant around everyone, clinging to him like she was afraid he'd pass her off to someone else and never return. When they reached Alpah9, he carried her through the marketplace. Mishka kept her face buried against his chest most of the time, but Zorlok helped him select clothes and a few toys for her.

"Children grow quickly," one merchant said. "You should purchase a few things in a larger size so your daughter can grow into them."

Wrylack thought it was sound advice and picked up four more outfits, so Mishka wouldn't go without when she grew a little more. As long as she had a few things to get her by, he could always travel to Alpha9 for more later. It was only a day's journey from Xpashta. The rest of the crew picked up some things they either needed or wanted, and then they loaded everything back onto the Mystic7 and began the journey home.

Zorlok followed Wrylack back to his room, setting Mishka's new things down on the bed. His daughter hadn't bathed or been changed in days, and while it seemed she knew how to go to the bathroom on her own, she still needed to be clean before she saw her mother. He supposed the male who rescued her hadn't bathed her, fearing it was inappropriate. If the warrior was like Wrylack, he likely hadn't been certain of the proper protocol for taking care of a female child. The bruises were fading on her arms and legs, and Wrylack had done a scan of her small body, thankful not to find any lasting damage from her time with Bekvir.

"Mishka, have you ever used a cleansing unit before?" he asked.

She stared at him and didn't say anything. In fact, she had yet to utter a single word, and he started to worry that perhaps she didn't know how to speak. Wrylack led her by the hand into the bathroom and started the cleansing unit. She stared at it wide-eyed, and didn't protest when he removed her small clothes and nudged her under the water. The bottom of the unit turned brown from the dirty water running down his small daughter, and he knew she needed some soap, but he wasn't about to touch her in any way that might make her uncomfortable. Instead, he tried to show her how to do it herself. She didn't do a perfect job of getting clean, but was much improved.

"We'll let your mother work more with you on that," Wrylack said. "I'm not certain of the rules about daddies bathing their daughters."

The unit shut off, and Wrylack turned on the dryer. Her hair gleamed under the lights now that she was clean. Unfortunately, her bruises were more pronounced now that her skin was even paler than before. He knew Shaylee was not going to be pleased that her daughter had come to harm. Wrylack helped Mishka get dressed in her new clothes and showed her the toys he'd purchased for her. While she played, he observed her and did another scan of her body, focusing on her bones and then her head.

He couldn't detect any brain damage that would keep her from speaking and decided she'd either never been taught, or chose to be silent for whatever reason. He pointed to different things around the room, telling her what each item was.

She watched, and seemed to be paying attention, but she still didn't utter a sound. There had to be something he was missing. With her head tilted back as she studied the ceiling, he did yet another scan, this time focusing on her throat. He adjusted his gaze to study the soft tissue more than the bones in her neck. It was so faint he wasn't surprised he'd missed it before. Fury engulfed him at the horrors this small girl had been through.

Wrylack slowly reached for Mishka and pulled her onto his lap. Turning her head sideways, he ran a finger down the column of her neck, pushing her hair aside. There was a faint pin prick, large enough for a small rod to have been pushed through, and he found a match on the opposite side. While her vocal cords hadn't been completely severed, there was just enough damage that it probably made speaking uncomfortable for her, or perhaps she didn't like the sound of her voice. It looked like the rest of her throat had healed well enough not to hinder her from drinking or eating. Tears gathered in his eyes as he held her tightly.

"I'm so sorry, sweet girl," he murmured. "I will do whatever I can to make it better."

There were options, but he didn't know if Shaylee would approve. Mishka was too young right now, but as she grew, cybernetics would be a possibility to correct the issue. It was possible that surgery could help, even though it wouldn't correct the problem completely, but that seemed rather harsh for someone so young.

In the meantime, they would need to find a way for Mishka to communicate with them. He rocked her in his arms until she fell asleep curled against his chest. Wrylack knew he should prepare Shaylee, get word to her before they landed, but he didn't want her more stressed than she already was.

"We'll get you home to your mother, and then we'll figure things out. You're safe, Mishka. That's the important thing."

He continued to hold her as she slept. Even though she was not of his blood, he already felt as if she were his. Perhaps, over time, she would forget the trauma she'd suffered at the hands of Bekvir. She was still so young. He hoped she would be able to live a full and happy life without darkness clouding her future.

"I love you," he whispered to the girl sleeping in his arms, and vowed to tell her that every day for the rest of his life.

Chapter Eight

Shaylee paced the house, more than a little nervous. The commanders had sent word that Wrylack was returning today. They'd assured her that Wrylack was fine and hadn't been injured during his trip, but she still felt like something was horribly wrong. The feeling wouldn't ease no matter what she did. When the front door opened, Shaylee froze and stared.

Wrylack stepped through, a small girl in his arms. Her skin was such a light lavender that she was nearly as pale as Shaylee. Her black-and-blue-streaked hair was mesmerizing, and her eyes... her eyes looked like that of every cyborg she'd met since coming here. Wrylack set the little girl down, and Shaylee tried to understand what she was seeing.

"She could be your daughter," Shaylee said. "A mix of both of us, except for the blue in her hair."

"The blue is a throwback to the original people of my home world." His gaze was assessing. "This is Mishka. She's half human... and half Zelranian."

Shaylee's heart nearly stopped. "What? But that's... you're Zelranian."

He nodded.

Shaylee stared at her daughter and knelt, holding her arms open. The little girl clung to Wrylack's leg for a moment before cautiously moving forward. As Shaylee studied her, she saw the slight bruising and wondered what her poor baby had been through. Mishka stopped in front of Shaylee and reached for her hair, playing with the long, black strands.

"I'm your momma," Shaylee said. "You're home now, Mishka."

"She can't talk. Or won't," Wrylack said. "There's some damage to her vocal cords. I haven't heard her make a single sound yet, not a cry, a whimper… nothing. I'm uncertain if the damage was bad enough she's unable to make noises, or if she's refusing for some reason."

Shaylee lifted her eyes to her mate, fighting back tears. "What did they do to her?"

"Her birth father had her. He's one of my kind. I've always loathed Bekvir and everything he stood for. He's a cruel male, and it seems he had no problem harming his own child. He's been dealt with."

"Bekvir," she whispered, digging through her memories. She gasped when she recalled the male similar in coloring to Wrylack who had done so much damage to her. All of the faces of her past tended to blur together, but his didn't. He'd been worse than the others, more vicious, and had thrilled in her pain and humiliation. Tears slipped down her cheeks as she held her daughter tight.

Wrylack let the door close and came toward them, wrapping them in his arms. "He won't hurt either of you ever again. I was assured he wouldn't remain breathing for much longer, and that was days ago. By now, he's gone."

"I hope he suffered," Shaylee said.

Wrylack tightened his arms around them.

"Are you both hungry?" Shaylee asked. "Maggie's been by the last few days to show me how to make some different dishes. I could cook something for us."

Mishka tugged on her.

"What is it, sweetheart?" she asked her daughter. "Do you want to eat?"

Mishka blinked up at her.

"Can you talk, Mishka?" Shaylee asked. "Can you tell me what you want?"

Fear crossed the girl's features, and Shaylee's gut clenched. She knew that look, had seen it on other slaves. Whatever had been done to her daughter, she feared speaking.

"It's all right to talk here," Shaylee said. "You won't get in trouble if you make noise. I want you to make noise! Make all the noise you want. Scream, laugh, bang things."

The little girl's eyes widened, and she looked from Shaylee to Wrylack, as if seeking assurance.

"Your mother is correct, Mishka. It's all right to speak or make any sounds you wish. You won't be punished."

"Hungry," the little girl said, her voice a raspy whisper.

"You're hungry?" Shaylee asked. "You can talk louder if you want."

Mishka stuck her thumb in her mouth.

Shaylee took Mishka's other hand and began leading her to the kitchen. She set her daughter at the counter. Wrylack placed his hand at Mishka's back and rubbed gently. After a moment, the little girl pulled her thumb from her mouth. Mishka watched Shaylee's every move, and Wrylack watched their daughter.

Lathim had provided several fish for Shaylee to cook, and she prepared them for her family. They'd already been cleaned and deboned. She seasoned them, and while they cooked, she made some vegetables on the side. It didn't take long for the meal to be ready, and she plated everything, then joined her family at the little bar.

Mishka looked at the fish and poked it with her finger.

"It's fish," Shaylee told her. "Have you ever had fish before?"

Mishka shook her head.

"I couldn't get her to eat meat on the ship," Wrylack said.

"Mishka," Shaylee said softly. "Were you allowed to eat meat at the other place?"

"No," Mishka said in that same raspy whisper.

"You can have as much as you want," Shaylee said. "This is your home now. Do you understand? You're going to live here with us from now on. No one will hurt you ever again."

"Bad man," Mishka said.

"The bad man is gone," Wrylack said. "He's not going to come for you. You're safe here, Mishka."

Mishka slowly reached for the fish. When no reprimand came, she started stuffing her face until the plate had been cleaned. It hurt Shaylee's heart to know her daughter had suffered. But she knew the little girl would be well-loved now, not only by her but by Wrylack as well. A chime sounded at the front door, and Wrylack went to answer while she cleaned the kitchen. He returned a moment later, his arms full of clothes and toys.

"Mishka's things were delivered. Do you have a particular room set up for her?" Wrylack asked.

"I put her next to us. I found a blanket in the market that I put on the bed. It's a soft green, and I thought the color might be soothing. The commanders assured me that anything we need they can find for us."

Wrylack nodded and carried their daughter's belongings to her new room.

"Do you want to see your bedroom?" Shaylee asked.

Her daughter whimpered and turned stiff as stone.

Jessica Coulter Smith   Cy-Con

"Mishka? What's wrong?" Shaylee smoothed the little girl's hair.

"Dark," she said.

"No, honey. It's not dark in there. You have a window where you can look out, and there's a light for when it's nighttime." Shaylee reached for Mishka's hand. "Come on. I'll go with you and you'll see it's a pretty room. We can decorate it however you want."

Mishka followed her, but the little girl's steps were hesitant. Shaylee stepped into the bedroom and gently tugged Mishka in behind her. Light spilled through the window, and the green blanket made the room look a little cheery. Wrylack had placed a stuffed bear on the bed, and the rest of the toys were lined up along the wall. Her clothes were already put away.

Mishka ventured a little farther into the room, looking at everything.

"Come here," Wrylack said, waving her over.

She went straight to him without any hesitation, and he lifted her into his arms. They walked over to the door, and he pointed to the area around it.

"This door doesn't lock. Not from either side. If you want to leave, press your hand to the door and it will open. Why don't you try it?" He set her down, and Shaylee stepped away from the door so it would close. Mishka whimpered, then pressed her chubby little hand to the panel and it slid open.

"See? It will never lock," Wrylack said.

Mishka smiled up at him and hugged her arms around his leg.

"Do you want to stay in here and play?" Shaylee asked. "This is your room, your own space. You can play in here or sleep. The other door is the bathroom."

Mishka looked at the other door in curiosity. It was an open doorway, and when she stepped into the

- 220 -

bathroom, the light came on. She explored a moment, then went back to the bedroom and started playing with her toys. She paused as Shaylee and Wrylack were leaving, looking at them with a trembling lower lip.

"Safe?" Mishka whispered.

"Yes, baby. You're safe," Shaylee said.

That seemed to be enough for Mishka, and she started playing, ignoring her parents. Wrylack led Shaylee out of the room and into their own space next door. When the door closed behind them, he pulled her into his arms and kissed her deeply.

"I missed you," he said.

"I missed you too. Wrylack, what happened to her?"

"It looks like they inserted rods into her throat and damaged her vocal cords. The wounds look old so I think they were done when she was a baby. Maybe she cried too much. Bekvir is a monster, and it wouldn't have taken much to set him off. Or he was. She was covered in bruises when I picked her up, but they've mostly faded now. I can't say for certain what all she's been through the last three years, but they found her in a dark room with no windows. She'd been fed on the floor like a pet." He paused. "When she's older, it's possible that surgery or cybernetics could help her, but for now the damage is irreversible. She's too young to chance it. She can communicate with us, and she's safe. That's the important thing."

Shaylee wrapped her arms around his waist and buried her face against his chest. She cried silently, for all that her daughter had suffered. How could anyone have harmed a child? She was innocent! And from what little Shaylee had seen, so very sweet. But then, the man she remembered as Bekvir wouldn't have cared how innocent or sweet a child was. He would have done anything in his power to destroy her, and Shaylee was thankful that her daughter lived at all.

"Thank you for bringing her home," Shaylee said.

"She's my daughter as much as yours," Wrylack said. "Once I knew who had her, there was no question about bringing her home. I wanted to give your children back to you, no matter what it took, but I just didn't know how we were going to pull it off. We've been exiled from Zelran and would have been put to death if we'd landed on the planet."

"How did you get her?"

"Norkov made a deal with some males. He arranged for one to get Mishka and the other to get Bekvir. We met them at the Garva outpost."

"And my other child?" she asked.

"Nothing yet, but Norkov is working on it."

"If he hasn't found my baby, then it means the father didn't keep it. The Vrotu was the least cruel of my owners. Not to say he was a kind man, because he took what he wanted and demanded obedience in all things, but at least he didn't share me with others. I'd hoped maybe he'd kept our child."

"Norkov won't stop until the baby is found. He's trying to go through your previous owner's transactions to see if the child was sold. There hasn't been a lead yet, but it doesn't mean there's no hope," Wrylack said.

"What about death records?" Shaylee asked. "Did he check those?"

Wrylack held her close. "Norkov will leave no stone unturned. He will not stop searching until we find out what happened to your baby, Shaylee. This I promise."

"Should we check on Mishka?" she asked.

"Soon." His fingers trailed over her cheek. "There's something I need to do first."

Before she could ask what he meant, his lips lowered to hers, and he kissed her with a passion that took her breath away. Wrylack's hands caressed her curves and slowly pulled up the hem of her dress. His palms gripped the cheeks of her ass and lifted her until her legs went around his waist. She could feel the hard ridge of his arousal through his pants and knew what he wanted.

Wrylack walked her toward the bed and dropped her onto the soft bedding. As he pulled off his clothes, Shaylee removed her dress and let it fall to the floor. His cock was already hard, and the tip glistened with pre-cum. He stroked his shaft a few times, his hand going up and down the length.

"Spread your legs, sweet mate," Wrylack said, his voice having a hint of growl to it.

Shaylee's thighs parted, and he groaned as he stared at her, his gaze fastened on her pussy. She felt herself grow wet, just watching him and knowing what was to come. Wrylack reached for her, his fingers sliding down her wet lips before plunging inside her. She gave a soft cry, trying to stifle her sounds of pleasure so they wouldn't upset Mishka.

Wrylack pumped his fingers in and out of her tight channel, his thumb brushing against her clit. Shaylee moaned and thrust against his hand, wanting more. It had been a week since Wrylack had left, and she ached for him. He continued to stroke his shaft as he pleasured her with his fingers.

"Come for me, Shaylee. I want you nice and wet when I enter you."

She whimpered as her body tightened and

strained for release. He stroked her faster with his fingers, and the hand on his shaft did the same. She watched, her passion rising, as his cock seemed to harden even more. She came with a soft cry, biting her bottom lip, and as the last tremor left her breathless, Wrylack thrust his cock inside her.

He groaned and grasped her hips with both hands, slamming his cock into her over and over, driving into her deep and hard. The fierceness etched on his face left no doubt that he was claiming her all over again. She was his, and it seemed Wrylack wanted to make sure she knew it. Sweat glistened on his skin as he pounded into her, and soon she was coming, harder than ever before. She bit down on her lip to keep from making too much noise as Wrylack came inside her. With every jerk of his hips, she felt another splash of cum bathe her channel, until he finally stilled.

"I'm sorry that didn't last longer," he said, then leaned down to kiss her. "But I promise next time I'm going to make you come and come again, until you're begging me to stop."

Her toes curled at his words, and she gave him a soft smile.

"You're mine," Wrylack said. "My mate. The mother of my children. My heart. There is nothing I wouldn't do for you."

"As long as you love me, that's all I need," she said.

"I will love you until I take my last breath," he promised. "You're everything to me, Shaylee."

He withdrew from her body and helped her stand. The room spun, and Shaylee fell against his chest. Wrylack's arms tightened around her a moment. She closed her eyes and focused on breathing, and slowly, she got her legs back under her.

"What's wrong?" he asked. "Was I too rough?"

"No. Just dizzy."

Wrylack frowned and held her at arm's length. His eyes began to glow, and she knew he was scanning her. When he stopped on her stomach and his gaze seemed frozen, she panicked.

"What do you see?"

The glow in his eyes faded, and he looked at her, stunned. "You're pregnant."

"But... you said you went and got that shot, the one that prevents you from getting me pregnant."

"I did. I never assessed my systems to make sure it was working."

Shaylee studied him and could tell he was doing that very thing. "And?"

"There's not even a hint of the serum in my body, but that's impossible. I watched Liroz dose me."

"Could he have mixed up the serums?" she asked.

"No, I... " Wrylack frowned. "Another cyborg was there at the same time, getting an injection of vitamins."

"It sounds like Liroz accidentally switched them," she said softly.

"I'm sorry, Shaylee. It's my fault for not being more careful."

She reached up and cupped his cheek. "Wrylack, I'm not sorry we're having a baby. I told you before that I wanted to have children with you. You're the one who insisted on the shot. Do you... do you think you could be happy about us having a baby?"

Wrylack kissed her softly. "I can't think of anything I'd love more than to watch you grow round with my child. I just wanted to give you more time."

"I don't need time, Wrylack. I just need you. And

Mishka. We're a family, and we're growing. That's what families do."

"Go get cleaned up. I'll join you in a moment. I need to connect with Liroz and let him know what happened. If that other cyborg already had the serum in his system and got double dosed, it could have bad side-effects."

Shaylee nodded, kissed his cheek, then went into the bathroom. She stared at her reflection in the mirror, her hand splayed over her belly. A baby had never been something to celebrate for her, but this time would be different. She had the love of Wrylack and could already tell he was a good father. He was so gentle with Mishka, and she knew he'd be the same with this baby.

Her new little family would be perfect... if only they could find her other child.

Chapter Nine

A month had passed and while Mishka grew more confident every day, Wrylack knew that his mate was still worried about her other child. Norkov had left two weeks ago to find the Vrotu and ask him directly about the child, as no amount of digging had produced any results. The commanders had given him access to enough funds to purchase the child if necessary, assuming the Vrotu even still had the baby. Wrylack hadn't mentioned the trip to Shaylee in case things didn't end well. The other cyborg was due back any time, and Wrylack hoped it was with good news.

He stood in front of the glass doors that looked out over the back of the house. A courtyard, Shaylee had called it. His mate had asked for a bench to be added to the space, and Wrylack had provided one for her. In addition, Maggie had helped set up some planters with various flowers along one wall so there was a splash of color out there. Shaylee took Mishka out back every day and let her run around in the fresh air for a while, carrying out a handful of toys with them.

Something made Wrylack turn from the touching scene in front of him and go to the front door. He pulled it open and saw two commanders on his doorstep. Norkov stood behind them, a resigned expression on his face. The males stared at him and Wrylack stepped back, allowing them entry into his home. If Norkov had returned without the child, the news couldn't be good. He hoped Shaylee remained outside until he'd heard what they had to say.

"Your trip went well?" Wrylack asked Norkov.

"I found some disturbing things while I was there," the cyborg said. "You're certain Shaylee said he was the least brutal of her owners? The male was clearly unstable."

"She said he wasn't exactly kind, but he didn't pass her around."

Norkov shook his head. "I won't tell you the things I witnessed while I was there. You'd never sleep again."

"And the baby?" Wrylack asked.

"The Vrotu's mate claim it died within minutes of being born," Norkov said.

"Mate? He's mated and keeps slaves?" Wrylack asked.

"She's Perigen and can only mate once per month, is only fertile once per year, so she allows him to keep one slave... as long as no children are born between them. And Shaylee had a child," Norkov said.

"So she was sold because of that," Wrylack surmised.

"The mate forced the Vrotu to get rid of her, but even though I have no doubt he abused Shaylee, I think in some twisted sense he cared for her. You should have seen his face when I mentioned her," Norkov said.

"So the child is dead," Wrylack said.

The commanders looked at one another. Then Warver focused on him. "The child is in medical. We thought you should be the one to run any necessary tests."

"Why would tests be necessary?" Wrylack asked, a feeling of unease settling in the pit of his stomach.

"The Vrotu kept the child hidden from his mate. He made sure the baby ate, and it had clothing. I suppose he took care of it the best he could under the circumstances," Norkov said. "But there's something not right. A Vrotu-human pairing shouldn't have produced a child that looks like this one. We need to know what the baby's genetics are before you bring it home to your mate."

"Why do you keep saying it and baby?" Wrylack asked. "Is it a female or male?"

"We don't know," Kiril said.

Wrylack stared at them. "You don't know? Has it been so long since you've been with a female you've forgotten the differences between us?"

Kiril snorted. "No. The baby won't let anyone near it."

Wrylack opened his mouth to question them, and then decided to just go see for himself. They left and walked to medical on the other side of the facility. All was quiet when they entered the room, and Liroz was staring intently at a bundle on the table. It lay still, and Wrylack didn't understand what they meant when they said the baby wouldn't let anyone near it. How could a swaddled baby keep full-grown cyborgs at bay?

"Show him," Kiril demanded.

Liroz winced and slowly approached the child. When he was within arm's reach, the cyborg grabbed his head as if in severe pain and dropped to his knees. Wrylack stared in shock and looked from his fellow medic to the child on the table. Approaching, he paused partway across the room. How had they managed to rescue a child who had that kind of power?

"Does the baby have a name?" Wrylack asked.

"Lycon," Norkov answered.

Wrylack watched the baby, unable to see so much as a hint of what lay under the blankets. The name sounded male to him, but what did he know?

"Lycon, my name is Wrylack. I'm mated to your

mother, Shaylee. Do you remember your mother?"

He felt ridiculous talking to a baby who couldn't be more than a year old, but if he was part Vrotu, then he would understand. Perhaps that's how the baby had been rescued? Had they reasoned with the child? The blankets shifted, and a small head poked out. The first thing he noticed was the silvery hair and the pale icy blue skin. A set of violet eyes peered over at him as the baby sat up completely.

No, this child wasn't just a mix of human and Vrotu. There was definitely something else in there. The silvery hair came from the Vrotu genes, and the baby's sense of knowing. The eyes came from Shaylee. But that ice-blue skin... and the ability to cripple a full-grown male with some sort of psychic ability. There was only one race like that, and Wrylack could hardly believe what he was seeing. The Kristos were supposed to be extinct, and yet this child clearly had Kristos genes.

"Lycon, I need to make sure you're healthy, and then I'll take you to your mother. Some of the tests might hurt a little, but I would never willingly cause you pain," Wrylack reasoned with the child who had the power to knock him on his ass.

The baby stared at him, and Wrylack took that as a sign of acceptance. He retrieved a needle and a few vials so he could take blood samples. Getting the painful part out of the way first, he kept a steady eye on the child. Lycon merely watched him. When he'd gathered the samples he needed, he handed them to Liroz and then scanned the child.

"He's perfectly healthy," Wrylack said. He looked over at Liroz who was testing the blood samples. "Anything?"

"It's fascinating, and I don't understand it at all,"

Liroz said. "He's not just a mix of Vrotu and human. There's Kristos in there, which shouldn't be remotely possible, and even some Keshpan."

"Shaylee is just a human," Wrylack said. "Are you certain the father is Vrotu?"

"He looked Vrotu," Norkov said.

Wrylack reached for the child, hesitating only a moment, before lifting the baby boy into his arms. The child was an anomaly, and something of a miracle. But Wrylack didn't understand how this baby's genetic makeup was even possible. Lycon reached a chubby hand toward Wrylack's face and placed his palm against Wrylack's forehead. Images burst into his mind that left him reeling.

"How do you know that?" Wrylack asked the child.

Lycon gave him a grin with two teeth showing and then more images burst into his mind.

"What's going on, Wrylack?" Warver asked.

"I need to talk to Shaylee before I discuss it with anyone else," Wrylack said. "I'm going to take my son home. Please have his belongings delivered."

The commanders stepped aside as Wrylack carried Lycon back to his home, and his waiting family. During the mental link with the Wrylac, Lycon had seen images of his mother and sister, and now the child seemed to buzz with excitement. The moment Wrylack stepped through the door, Shaylee and Mishka came toward him. Shaylee's gaze was fastened on the child in his arms.

The baby reached for her, and Shaylee cuddled him close.

"His name is Lycon," Wrylack said. "And he's different from what we expected."

Lycon placed his hand on Shaylee's temple, and

she gasped, her eyes going wide. Wrylack didn't know what the child was showing his mother. He gathered Mishka in his arms, and they waited until the mental link was broken.

"I don't understand," Shaylee said softly. "How is that even possible? Kinlor was Vrotu. I saw plenty of them while he owned me, and he looked just like them."

"It seems he's hiding something from his people. Without testing Kinlor's blood, I can't say for certain, but it seems he's a hybrid of three races. During my medical studies, I was required to study many races. The Vrotu were one of them. Their females are... unique. Their bodies are designed to take more than one male at a time. If I had to guess, Kinlor's mother was Vrotu, and he has two fathers. A Kristos and a Keshpan. I know such a thing isn't common on your Earth, but there are races where such a thing is possible."

Shaylee stared at the child in her arms. "And my baby looks different because of those genetics?"

"Yes. I tested Lycon's blood. It shows a mix of human, Vrotu, Keshpan, and Kristos DNA. He shouldn't exist, but he does."

"Why shouldn't he exist?" Shaylee asked. "If Kinlor's mother had two mates, then it seems logical to me."

"Kristos are thought to be extinct. No one has seen them in several of your Earth centuries. Their race was supposedly wiped out because of their abilities. People feared them." Wrylack came closer and smoothed his hand over Lycon's silvery hair. "He'll need to remain on Xpashta until he's old enough to seek a mate. There are those out there who would hurt him, want him dead just because he exists."

"How did you get Lycon?" Shaylee asked. "Kinlor wouldn't have just handed him over, not if it would expose who he really is. If he's kept that part of himself hidden all this time, he wouldn't risk it now."

Lycon snuggled against her shoulder and grabbed a handful of her hair. Wrylack wouldn't tell her the other images the baby had shared with him. Not in detail. Shaylee had had enough violence in her life and didn't need more. She especially didn't need to know what the baby was capable of, not just yet. The feelings Lycon had shared through the mental link assured Wrylack that his family was safe with the child. Anyone the boy deemed a threat was another matter. His psychic abilities were stronger than anything Wrylack had witnessed before, and a little frightening.

He felt Warver linking with him.

The child poses a problem, Warver said.

He's my son. Shaylee's son. If you didn't intend him to live with us, you wouldn't have brought him here.

Norkov told me what happened. Your son psychically killed his own flesh and blood, making his head explode, when the male refused to let Norkov take Lycon. What happens when your mate tells him he can't have something? Warver asked. The male brought up a good point, but he didn't think Lycon would ever harm his mother. The link he'd shared with her had not only projected images into her mind, but if he had the abilities Wrylack believed he possessed, then he'd been able to read her memories. The boy knew what his mother had been through, even if he didn't quite understand everything. Or maybe he did. The way the boy looked at Wrylack made him seem ancient. There was something in his eyes that spoke of a being far older than any Wrylack had met, and yet the child was only a year old. He didn't understand it. But after what he'd witnessed in medical, he had no doubt the boy understood far more than he should. As long as he understood he was safe here, that no one on this world was a threat to him, then everything should be fine.

I don't think he would ever harm Shaylee, Wrylack said.

If he kills anyone on Xpashta, you know what will need to be done, Warver said. *He may look like a baby, but he's not. He's something more, something dangerous.*

Shaylee gave him a worried look. "What's wrong?"

"The commanders are worried," he said, his gaze going to Lycon. "Our son is rather powerful, and they are concerned about the safety of those on Xpashta."

The baby lifted his head and looked at Wrylack, reaching for him. Wrylack didn't hesitate to pull the child into his arms. Despite what the commander said, Lycon was a baby, his mate's son and therefore his son. The child needed love and encouragement, just as Mishka had, not fear. Lycon placed his hand against Wrylack's head again, and a sense of calm infused him. Images played in his mind, an older Lycon and Mishka, and other children who looked like a mix of Wrylack and Shaylee. A happy family. More images spilled into his mind, Lycon much older and ready to become a warrior, telling his family goodbye before boarding a ship.

Through Lycon's gaze, Wrylack saw his family as they would be in years to come. Mishka with one of the younger cyborgs by her side and a baby in her arms. Three other children at various ages, and an older Wrylack and Shaylee. "You see all of that?" Wrylack asked the boy as Lycon removed his hand.

Lycon grinned at him, showing those two teeth

again.

"What did you see?" Shaylee asked.

"Our future." Wrylack smiled at her. "And let me just say that in twenty years or so, you are every bit as beautiful as you are now."

Her cheeks flushed. "He can really see the future?"

Wrylack nodded. "It's his Kristos genetics."

"And what else did this future show?" she asked, reaching for her son again.

"That our family will be truly blessed, not only by these two, but our other children as well. We're going to have a long, happy life together, Shaylee." He looked at Lycon, now sleeping against her shoulder. "The commanders and other cyborgs will learn in time they have nothing to fear from our son. He's going to grow up to be a strong male, a good warrior, and I have no doubt he will be an asset to our people."

Mishka rubbed her eyes, and Wrylack picked her up. "What do you think of your baby brother?"

Mishka reached for the boy, her fingers softly stroking his arm, then she grinned at Wrylack. They carried the children into Mishka's room and laid them both in the bed for a nap. Mishka curled protectively around her baby brother, and Lycon snuggled against her. Wrylack paused in the doorway, just watching his children for a moment. It hardly seemed possible that he, a cyborg thought least likely to find a mate, would have a woman as delectable as his Shaylee, and would one day have a large family.

Shaylee pulled him away from the children's room and dragged him into their bedroom. She cupped his cheek and pressed a soft kiss to his lips before wrapping her arms around his waist. Wrylack held her, stroking her long hair, and feeling her heartbeat's steady thump against him.

"You are my everything, Shaylee. The day the Meori gave you to me was the best in my life. You've brought two wonderful children with you, unique in their own way, and the gift of a child we've created together."

She smiled up at him. "I love you, Wrylack. And I love that you've accepted my children as your own, despite how they were conceived. There's not another male out there with as much heart, as much compassion, as you have. The day you entered my life my entire world changed for the better."

His hands framed her face as he kissed her slowly, softly. He didn't want to just tell her with words that he loved her, adored her. He wanted to show her what she meant to him. And as their children slept peacefully in the next room, he worshipped every inch of her body, taking his time and giving her so much pleasure she was soon begging him for his cock.

Wrylack joined their bodies together, his lips tasting hers. "My mate. My love."

"My gentle cyborg," she said softly, her hand going to his cheek.

Their gazes held as he made love to her gently. In her eyes, he saw such passion, such love, that it made his heart nearly burst from the emotional connection they shared. Wrylack knew that no matter how many times he drove his cock into Shaylee, no matter how many times they kissed, touched, or just held each other all night… he would always crave more.

She was the light in his world, the air he breathed, and every beat of his heart was now dedicated to her and their children.

And he couldn't have been happier.

Saved by the Cyborg (Cy-Con 3)
Jessica Coulter Smith

Intimidating. Damaged. Unlovable.

Tark wanted a mate even before he joined the Cy-Con program. His sheer size made females fear him, and now that he's been turned into a cybernetic freak they avoid him even more. When he finds a female being held in a brothel against her will, he knows that he can't leave without her.

Tark means to take Suki home to his world, a place where she can heal and start a new life. He never realized she'd want to start that life with him, or that she'd insist on leaving the safety of Xpashta in an effort to rescue others like herself.

Brave. Fearless. Pregnant?

Tark saved the alluring human female once. When she's captured during a dangerous mission, he knows he'll have to do it again, and this time, he's not letting her out of his sight -- especially when he finds out she's pregnant with his child.

Chapter One

Tark wandered the space station, clinging to the shadows in an effort to not draw attention to himself. Not that someone his size ever went unnoticed, especially since one of his arms was entirely made of Byrilia. He was large even for one of his people, towering over those around him. Tark had always been broad as well, his shoulders barely clearing most doorways.

Before the Cy-Con program, the females of his world had been too wary of him to accept a mating for fear he would crush them with his brute strength. And back then he'd been fully Zelranian, with not a single mechanical part in sight. He'd been part of his world's elite military, but even that hadn't gained him a mate. If anything, word of his exploits in battle made people even more fearful.

When he'd been asked to join the Cy-Con program, Tark had thought maybe things were turning around, that such an honor would help him gain the affection of a female. He'd signed up enthusiastically, not caring about the danger involved or the possibility he could die during transition. He'd been so wrong.

Tark had thought about purchasing a slave, thinking it might be his only option, and that was why he was now heading toward the trading post at the edge of the space station. The things bought and sold there weren't always legal, but Tark could look the other way if it meant he might finally have a companion. As much as he found slavery distasteful, it wasn't against the law.

If he could just find a mate, any mate, then he would count himself lucky. He knew the Commanders had spoken of purchasing slaves and bringing them back to Xpashta in hopes they would agree to pair with the cyborgs who called his world home. So far, only two males had successfully found mates.

A third… Tark winced when he thought about poor Rorwick. He'd claimed a human female, Jillian, but the female refused to accept the mating. It had already been nearly a year, and all they seemed to do was argue. Jillian had broken nearly everything in Rorwick's home by launching items at his head. If the male didn't look so tortured, it might have been funny. Tark wasn't certain what would happen between them, but he thought the Commanders might have to step in at some point.

Tark neared the trading post and began scouting the area for the slavers. Even through the busy marketplace, the sound of his boots could be heard over the din of voices and clinking of coins as he passed various booths, domes, and glass buildings. The scents weren't overly pleasant in this part of the trading post, and he shut down his olfactory senses.

The sound of someone retching made Tark halt. Some illnesses could spread rapidly, taking out entire populations. Cyborgs were immune to such things, thankfully, and because of that they often helped those in need when they were able.

"Worthless," a male muttered. "Useless piece of trash. I should have dumped you out an airlock on the way here. I can't have you throwing up on the customers. Lie there and rot for all I care."

The male stomped off in another direction, and Tark waited a moment to make sure he was gone. The last thing he needed to do was get into a fight with someone. He'd likely end up killing the male, and that would cause more of a headache than he wanted to deal with tonight. Tark didn't think he would be able to contain his anger, especially if a female was involved.

The retching continued and Tark moved a little closer. Customers? He looked around and noticed the sign at the front of the porta-dome. *Exotic Females. 2000 nuroks per turn.*

A brothel? The large porta-dome contained a brothel? Tark felt his cock harden at the thought of being with a female, even if the services were paid for, but then he remembered that even whores wouldn't accept him into their beds.

A whimper drew his attention to the shadowed area behind the temporary structure. His hand gripped his weapon. The soft sound came again, and he scanned the darkness. He didn't sense danger, but even a male such as him could never be too careful. Tark silently approached the figure huddled on the ground. The body was small, and as he drew nearer, he could make out the naked form of a female. An Earth female. His heart pounded in his chest and he froze for a moment. The slaver had an Earth female as part of his brothel? Were there others? He knew males kept Earth females as slaves, but he'd never run across one in a brothel before.

"I can't," a voice said softly. "Please don't."

Tark looked around. He didn't see anyone else, other than the small human. Was she speaking to him? Did she think he would harm her? As pitiful as she sounded, it was possible she'd already been harmed.

Tark stepped closer to the huddled form and knelt at her side.

"I can't," she said again, whimpering once more.

Tark reached for her, surprised that her skin was icy and yet slick with sweat. He gently shifted her onto her back, looking for signs of injury. A trickle of blue goo leaked from the corner of her mouth, and bile rose in his throat when he realized it wasn't goo. The female was dying, and had to be in horrible pain.

"He made you service a Barkwanie male?" Tark asked. His gaze scanned the rest of her and what he found sickened him. Not just the Barkwanie, but others too. Her skin was orange and green in other spots, a sure sign of poisoning from the bodily fluids of males who should have never touched her.

Tark carefully lifted her into his arms and strode from the trading post. The female shivered against him, and he wished that he had a blanket to wrap around her. Soon enough, he'd have her at a med clinic. He only hoped he hadn't found her too late and she could be healed.

* * *

Tark moved swiftly as he carried the small weight in his arms, not stopping until he reached the safety of the med clinic. Some stopped to stare at him, but Tark didn't care. Let them think what they wanted. The door shut behind him and the bright lights nearly blinded him. Tark eased the female into a med bay unit. She didn't look good, and as her eyes opened, he saw they were dilated. Tark listened carefully, searching for her heartbeat. When he found it, he feared that she wouldn't last the night. It was so slow, it had nearly stopped already. He could only imagine the agony she must feel.

The lid closed and he watched as the unit scanned her slight form. An android med tech came over to read the coding on the lid, then tapped a few buttons until it was in a language Tark could read. Despite the words on the screen, he didn't know how to heal her, or at least make her more comfortable. She'd not only been heavily poisoned, but she'd contracted space pox and another nasty disease called verilia. She had also been sterilized at some point.

The readings changed, and he knew that she was about to die. He felt helpless, not having any medical training. The lid lifted and Tark moved closer as she stared up at him.

"I'm sorry," he said, reaching out to smooth back her dark hair. She was human, and yet looked completely different from the Earth females on his planet. "There's nothing we can do for you."

"Sister," she murmured. "Save Suki."

"Suki? Suki is your sister?" Tark asked, wanting to make sure he understood her.

The female slowly nodded. "Tell her... Yoko... sent you. Tell her... sorry."

The female, Yoko, took a shuddering breath, and as she exhaled, Tark watched the life leave her body. His heart broke for her. At least her suffering was at an end. He only hoped that her sister didn't face the same fate.

"She's gone," he said.

"Authorities have been notified," the android said. "Your DNA is not a match to the males who harmed her."

"She worked in a brothel," Tark said.

Two males in uniform strode into the med clinic. One sneered at him and pulled out a set of restraints. Tark braced himself, but the android moved between him and the officials.

"The male did no harm. The female was a prostitute," the android said.

"What race was the female?" one of the officials asked.

"Human," the android said. "Not illegal to own, sell, or trade. The cyborg is innocent of any wrongdoing pertaining to her death."

The officials dismissed him and Tark didn't hesitate to leave the premises. He knew the med clinic would properly dispose of Yoko's body. She hadn't deserved a fate like this, no one did, but there was little he could do about it. Except find the Suki she mentioned.

Was Suki another female at the brothel? He retraced his steps through the trading post and stopped outside the brothel. Were all the females as badly cared for as Yoko had been? Were they all dying? He didn't know if he could handle seeing a tent full of females without killing the slaver responsible for their care. Not when the males on his world would give anything to have them as mates, would treat them as if they were the most precious things in all the galaxies. It didn't matter if they'd been whores. A cyborg would never look down on a female for any reason except treachery.

He pushed open the door covering and stepped inside. The slaver slithered his way, greed burning in his eyes as he scanned Tark. A Kronkite, he was reptilian in appearance and small in stature. Breakable, in Tark's opinion. Before the creature could reach him, he scanned his surroundings. Several females of various races were servicing customers out in the open. None seemed to be in distress, and none were human. He checked the interior again, looking for a female similar to Yoko. The slaver moved closer and Tark eyed him, having no idea how he kept the slaves in line with such a weak appearance.

Then again... Tark looked around once more. The females who weren't servicing customers were lounging on cots, most staring at the roof of the structure. The few whose eyes he could see had a blank stare, as if they weren't present. Drugged. It was the only explanation. Or perhaps so badly beaten that they had no fight left in them. Even those currently in service didn't appear aware of their surroundings.

"I have females available. How many do you wish? A male of your size could easily handle two or three, I would think," the slaver said.

"I want the female called Suki," Tark said. "Human."

The slaver got a gleam in his eye. "That one is special. One such as you would likely break her. Her services are reserved for those of a higher rank. Princes. Ministers. Kings."

Tark took a step toward the slaver, then another, until he saw a flash of fear in the male's eyes. The slaver backed up, and for every step he took, Tark took another. Soon, the disgusting male was pressed against a wall and had nowhere left to go. His skin camouflaged until he matched the color of the structure, but Tark could still see him clearly.

"I. Want. Suki," Tark said.

The slaver waved a trembling hand toward the back of the porta-dome. Tark growled at him and the scent of piss filled the air as the slaver soiled himself. The cyborg smirked as he made his way to the back, scanning the females for a human.

In the corner, her knees drawn up to the chest, he finally found her. Her long, dark hair was matted and there were bruises on her arms and thighs, as if she'd been forcefully held down. Rage filled him at the sight and he turned to face the slaver again. The male had enough sense to put a lot of space between them.

"You want her? No charge. Use her all night," the slaver said, his voice quivering. "You tell your friends that Porie is the best in the business and offers many beautiful females."

"Mine," Tark said, his voice deeper than before as he snarled at the slaver. "Mine to keep."

The slaver narrowed his eyes and shook his head. "Too valuable."

"I said. She's. Mine," Tark growled.

The Kronkite flexed his fingers and claws popped out. They appeared harmless and he laughed at the creature, but it had only been a distraction. Energy bolts hit the center of his chest and he glared at the shiny weapon in the Kronkite's hand. Tark advanced on him, receiving three more blasts, but the little reptile had miscalculated. Tark was no longer just Zelranian. He was cyborg, and the energy blasts only served to increase the power to the receptors in his brain.

Tark lashed out, his fist slamming into the Kronkite's jaw. The creature flew half the distance of the dome and landed in a tangle of limbs. One foot was bent at an awkward angle, but Tark didn't care. He advanced on the slaver, landing blow after blow, almost hoping he killed the nasty being.

The male began dragging himself backward, looking around as if seeking help, but none of his customers were paying him any attention. Panic blazed in his eyes as he moved even further away. The stench coming off him suggested he'd done more than just piss himself. *Weakling*.

"Whatever you wish," the slaver said. "There are other females, if you'd prefer someone more exotic?"

"Her," Tark said, pointing at Suki. "And only her. You will never touch her again, and neither will anyone else."

Suki trembled as Tark lifted her into his arms. Her eyes were dark, filled with terror, and he wished that he could soothe her, but this wasn't the place or the time. For whatever reason, she didn't appear to be drugged like the others. He needed to get her far from here.

He went straight to the med clinic. If Suki was sick, like her sister had been, he wanted to know. Maybe if they caught it soon enough, she could be cured. Tark didn't understand why she was considered a prize possession while her sister had been given to the lowest of the low and then left to die. But he did know that he needed to protect her, at any cost.

The med clinic was nearly deserted and he went straight to an empty bay and set Suki inside the scanner. As she stretched out on the padded surface, the lid began to close. Her gaze met his, her fear even stronger than before. Perhaps he should have explained what was happening, that she was in no danger. Had she never been treated before? Every space station was equipped with a med clinic similar to this one, but maybe this was her first time at a place like this.

One of the android med techs, a different one from before, rolled over to them and began pressing buttons on the bay lid.

"Welcome back, cyborg," the android said.

Tark gave him a nod of acknowledgement. The machine then scanned Suki from head to toe, multiple times to provide a reading of any injuries she may have sustained. Tark waited impatiently, watching Suki and wishing she didn't look so frightened. When the med bay beeped and a readout appeared on the lid, Tark tried to make sense of what he was seeing. All of her blood levels seemed fine, and there was no sign of disease.

"She has been sterilized?" he asked, not overly

surprised since her sister had been as well. Perhaps it was common for whores.

The android med tech set the bay to a healing frequency to remove the bruises on Suki's fair skin. As Tark stared through the clear lid, he could see her healing, watched as the marks began to fade. When the bay had finished, the android waited for more instructions.

Tark opened the med bay and Suki bolted upright. He could see her pulse fluttering in her throat and he hated that she was terrified.

"My name is Tark, and your sister sent me."

Her lips parted. "Yoko?"

He nodded. "I'm sorry, Suki, but Yoko couldn't be healed. The med bay was able to heal your injuries, except for one. It seems you've been sterilized. Was it by choice?"

"I can't have children?"

"No, I'm afraid not. Do you want a family in the future?" Tark asked. "It's possible for the procedure to be reversed, if that's your wish."

She stared at him and didn't say anything. Tark waited, giving her time to process what he'd told her. She hadn't reacted to her sister's passing quite the way he'd expected. Didn't females cry when given that sort of news?

"I can choose?" she asked quietly. "Choose to have children?"

"Yes. You can choose."

Her gaze roamed over him and he felt a little self-conscious, wondering if she pictured those children with him. And did the idea frighten her? They hadn't spoken until now, and she had to be confused. He could tell she was scared, and he didn't blame her. He was a complete stranger, and a brute of a male compared to most. He'd be concerned if she weren't afraid of him.

"You're safe now, Suki," he said. "Did you understand what I said about Yoko?"

Suki's eyes filled with tears. Her lower lip trembled and he heard her heart rate increase. She might not have reacted before, but she definitely was now. She placed her hand over her mouth as she sobbed. Her body shook and Tark wanted to comfort her, his hands flexing at his sides. He didn't dare reach for her.

"She asked me to find you, Suki. I want to take care of you, if you'll let me. I promise that no harm will come to you. I will protect you with my life."

She took a shuddering breath. It took her a moment to get her emotions under control, but the tears slowed. After another few minutes, she could breathe easier and no longer seemed to be as distressed.

"I'm safe?" she asked.

"Yes, Suki. You're safe."

"With you," she said. "I belong to you now?"

Tark rocked back on his heels. This wasn't going as planned. Perhaps he hadn't explained things well?

"I'm not your owner, Suki. No one will ever own you again. You're free. I want to take you to my world, where you can find a mate. He would be like me, a Zelranian cyborg but you could have a family if that's what you want."

What he really wanted was to keep her, but he wasn't about to take away her right to select her mate, not after everything she'd obviously suffered.

"Family," she murmured, her gaze dropping to her lap.

Tark tried hard not to stare at her naked body. It

had been so long since he'd been this close to a female, much less one without clothes. Yoko may have been naked as well, but she'd been so far gone he'd barely spared her a glance, and only seen someone damaged and dying. While there were three human females on his world now, he always kept a safe distance from them, worried his size would scare them. He wanted to touch Suki, to hold her. But as terrified as she was, after everything she'd been through, he didn't know if she would welcome his touch.

She looked up at him again, once more tracing over his body with her gaze. If his size intimidated her, she didn't show it this time. She seemed to be assessing him, but for what reason he didn't know. Mere curiosity? Or something more? She focused on his metallic arm before meeting his gaze again.

"What are you?" she asked. "What's a Zelranian cyborg?"

"Cyborg means I'm part machine, and Zelranian is my race. My arm is the only non-organic part you can see, but some of my organs are mechanical as well. My heart. Lungs. The bones in my body are made of metal. I have transmitters in my brain."

"You can have children?" she asked.

"Yes. Aside from my cyborg status, I'm very much like the males of your world."

She smiled faintly. "No one on my world looks like you. I've never seen anyone as big as you."

"Is that a bad thing?" he asked.

"No. You're strong. You can protect me."

"Yes, I can protect you, and I will. But there are others like me, cyborgs, who would treat you well. My world is full of males who want mates. There are three human females there now, but it's my hope that one day every male will have a female."

She paled. "They will want me to service them, like the others."

"No, Suki. You never have to service anyone again. You could choose a mate. I believe the Earth term is husband. The two of you could start a family."

"Husband," she repeated then looked up at him. "You could be my husband."

Tark felt his heart kick in his chest. "I'm too large for someone as small as you."

Her gaze fell to the front of his pants, and Tark felt his cheeks warm under her appraisal. That hadn't been what he'd meant, but that part of him was rather large too. And it was getting larger the longer she stared. He shifted, wanting to hide himself. No one had ever stared at him like that before. Tark was used to females fleeing in terror, not sizing up certain parts of his anatomy. She couldn't seriously be thinking of being with him, could she?

"I heard the master tell you that I was a favorite for princes, kings, and ministers. Did you know that he often took me Palua to service the princes? Sometimes all of them at once. Do you know what a naked Paluan prince looks like?" she asked.

He did. While they were not large males, they were rather well-endowed. And she'd had to service more than one at a time? That had to have been painful for her. If he could erase those memories for her, he would. She shouldn't have to live with any of it. But if she'd handled the Paluan princes, then maybe... No, she deserved someone better than him, someone smaller and gentler.

"What about Duadaderans?" she asked. "Their minister often requested me for his parties."

Bile rose in Tark's throat. How could she have been through all that and still seem sane? Most females would have lost their mind. The Duadaderans looked like monsters with their green and yellow scales, spikes along their arms, reptilian eyes, and claw-tipped fingers. He'd seen one naked before, and the thought of her being with one of those males sent a shiver down his spine. He didn't know how she was still here and in one piece.

"I want to stay with you," she said. "Unless…"

"Unless what?" he asked.

"I'm used. Damaged. I've been touched by many. I would understand if you didn't want me because of that. Or if you didn't find me attractive," Suki said. "I'm dirty, Tark. If you knew the things I've done…"

"I don't care about any of that," he assured her. "You're very beautiful, Suki. Any male would be lucky to claim you. I just don't want you to regret making this choice now. You should meet the other males on my world. Perhaps one of them would suit you better."

"Yoko trusted you to come and get me," Suki said. "She wouldn't have told you to come for me if she thought you would hurt me. She saw kindness in you, and so do I. I want to stay with you."

"I would be honored," Tark said.

"Do you want children?" Suki asked.

"I would never ask my mate to bear children if she did not want to," Tark said.

"But you want them?" she persisted.

He hesitated a moment, unsure if he should be truthful. He didn't want her to reverse the procedure just because he wanted children. It should be something she wanted as well. But he didn't like the idea of lying to her either.

"Yes."

"Then I will have the procedure reversed," Suki said, lying back again.

The lid closed once more on the med bay, and the robot pressed more buttons. Tark paced the room as the med bay did its job and repaired Suki, giving her the ability to have children again. The machine hummed and glowed as it worked on Suki, repairing her reproductive system. Tark didn't know enough about female anatomy to understand exactly what had been damaged to cause her to be barren, but he hoped being healed wouldn't cause her more pain.

Tark glanced her way several times, uncertain what to make of the small female. How could someone as beautiful as her, as fragile and… He shook his head. It didn't make sense. She should be quaking with fear just looking at him, much like she had when he'd first picked her up. He didn't understand any of it.

Once she was healed, he would find her clothing and take her to the *Wayfarer*. He would care for her, watch over her… but it would be best if he didn't claim her until she'd seen Xpashta and realized she had other options. Better males than him.

He wanted a mate, but Suki wasn't what he'd expected. He would be honored to claim her, to raise a family with her, but he wondered if it would be a disservice to her. After all that she'd suffered, she deserved a happy life, and Tark realized that he would give her anything he could to make that happen.

Even if it meant she wouldn't belong to him.

Chapter Two

Suki felt different after she'd been healed and had clothes, even if they were ill-fitting. She was still filthy but hadn't wanted to wash at the med clinic. Despite the fact the large cyborg was with her and had saved her, she felt too exposed and worried her previous owner would come for her. Tark had brought her onboard a ship called *Wayfarer*, and now they were closed in a small room. There were no personal items around, and Suki wasn't certain if she was staying in the room alone or sharing it with Tark. She'd agreed to be his, but he seemed reluctant. At first, she'd thought it was because of her, because of her past, but as she studied him she made a few observations.

Tark was large, probably the most massive male she'd ever seen. She'd been around large aliens before, but none that had both his height and muscle mass. If she had to guess, he was likely around six foot eight or so, and as broad as the American wrestlers she'd seen on TV back on Earth. And yet he seemed very insecure when it came to females. Or maybe it was just her. There was a longing in his eyes, but he kept away, only touching her when necessary. Suki had feared him at first, thinking he was like the others, but he'd taken her to a med clinic to be healed, had touched her with kindness, and Yoko had sent him. That was the most important part to Suki.

Her big sister had always watched out for her, and Suki was the reason Yoko had been taken to begin with. Knowing that Yoko had sent Tark was enough to make Suki trust him completely. Her sister had a gift that few knew about, a sense of knowing. She could look at someone and tell if they were good or evil, and Yoko would have never sent Tark after Suki if her big sister hadn't been certain the male was good. Despite everything that had happened, she knew her big sister would have taken care of her, even if it used her last breath. Yoko had showed no ill will toward Suki, even though it had been her fault they'd suffered.

Tears blurred Suki's vision and a great sense of loss filled her. Yoko had always watched over her. If Suki had only listened to her sister, then maybe they never would have been captured. But Suki never listened. She'd been selfish all her life, getting herself and Yoko into trouble again and again. Until the last time… when they'd been picked up by aliens and sold into slavery. If anyone had told her aliens existed before all this, she'd have laughed at them. And she'd have been wrong.

They weren't cute, they weren't friendly, and they'd only caused Suki and Yoko pain. She'd thought she'd never experience happiness again, would never know freedom. Suki had feared that she would die whoring herself out to aliens of all types, being drugged when she refused to obey and come out of the haze in extreme pain. It hadn't taken long before all the fight had drained from Suki. If she fought, she was drugged and the abuse was even worse. Part of her wanted the drugs, but when they wore off, it was always more dreadful, the pain more intense. When she'd seen what they'd done to Yoko, she'd been so damn scared, worried they were both about to die.

Then Tark had come for her, had taken her from the hell she'd been living in for who knew how long. Now she sat on his bed, onboard his ship, and she was free to make her own choices once more. This time, she'd choose wisely, and everything inside of her was screaming that she needed to stay with Tark. Perhaps she'd gained a bit of knowing herself. Her mother and grandmother had both had it, and even though Suki had never shown signs of it before, maybe she was growing into it.

"Are you hungry?" he asked. "Have you eaten recently?"

"Master fed us every other day," she said.

Tark growled. "Never call him that again. He's not your master."

"I'm sorry," she said softly, not wanting to anger him. "It's what we were supposed to call him. If we didn't, then we were punished."

She bit her lip, thinking he probably didn't want to know exactly how she'd been punished. Just because he didn't look down on her for the things she'd done, it didn't mean he wanted the details. He was a large male, and likely feared for his size alone, but he also seemed to be tenderhearted.

"Do you want to stay here while I get something from the galley? Or do you want to come with me?" Tark asked.

"I can leave the room?" she asked.

His gaze darkened and he paced for a moment. "I told you that you were free. How many times must I say that you aren't a slave before you believe me? Did you think I was going to lock you away? Keep you caged?"

"It's what master did," she said. "When we weren't being... used. He kept us in cages. We had to sit in our own refuse, and he only allowed us to wash before we were meeting clients. For me, that meant anytime someone special had reserved me. He starved us, beat us." Her hand rubbed over her belly. "Did things without our permission, changed us in ways we never wanted."

Tark's expression softened and he knelt at her

feet, taking her hands into his large one. "I'm sorry for everything you've been through. And I'm sorry for the way I snapped at you. It was uncalled for, but… you have me on edge. It's not an excuse, just an explanation."

"Why is it hard for you to believe I would want to be with you?" she asked.

"Females don't want me," he said after a few minutes. "They never have. Even whores have run from me in fear. I've never…"

He looked away, but Suki could tell he was embarrassed. Was he trying to say he was a virgin? She couldn't believe it. How could anyone turn him away? Tark was kind and protective. And he'd been gentle with her. Despite his mechanical arm, he hadn't harmed her, not once. He was always careful when he reached for her, or carried her. She didn't understand why women didn't beg for his attention. On Earth, she'd been independent for the most part, hadn't felt she needed a man for anything. She'd had boyfriends, but none that lasted longer than a month. But being a slave had taught her that out here in space, far from the world she'd called home, she did need a male, as long as it was the right one. She'd been too weak to fight them off, too weak to save herself and her sister. The thought of someone big and strong offering protection was tempting.

Suki stood and placed her hand on his bicep. He was so strong, so… He made her feel safe, and that was something she hadn't felt in a very long time. If she could do anything, she wanted to make him realize that not all females feared him. She didn't. If he claimed her as his mate, she would feel like the luckiest of women. She just didn't know how to make Tark see that.

"I'm not running," she said. "And I'm not afraid of you."

He looked at her, his gaze holding hers. If he'd never been with a female, had he ever been kissed? Suki leaned forward and lightly brushed her lips against his. Tark froze, every muscle in his body tense. Suki moved her mouth against his, giving him the softest of kisses, until he began to relax. She pulled back and stared into his eyes. Tark looked stunned as he reached up and touched his lips.

"Do you want to do it again?" she asked. "You could kiss me this time, if you want."

"Kiss you," he repeated, staring at her lips.

"Yes."

Tark's gaze flicked up to hers then lowered to her mouth again. Slowly, he leaned in and pressed his mouth to hers. Suki placed her hand on the back of his neck, her fingers tangling in his hair. Suki parted her lips and touched her tongue to his lips. Tark groaned and opened, letting her in. She kissed him slowly, deeply. And all too soon, he was pulling away. Suki clung to him, not ready for it to end just yet. It had been so long since she'd felt anything like that, and maybe she never had. Kissing Tark felt different, but in a very good way.

"You need to eat," he said, his voice deeper than before, gruffer. She knew he was aroused, could feel the tension in his body, see the need in his eyes. And yet he was choosing to take care of her and not take what he wanted.

Suki knew in that moment, that one day she would fall for Tark. Completely and fully, and the thought didn't terrify her like it might have once. She looked forward to it. Love had always scared her, but with Tark she knew she'd be safe, that her heart would be safe. And maybe one day, he'd come to love her as well. If he'd never been kissed, never been touched, then he likely hadn't been loved. Not romantically anyway. She wanted to be the one to give that gift to him. He'd freed her, given her life back to her, and that was something she could never repay. But maybe she could make him happy, and that would be enough.

Tark stood and led her from the room. Suki couldn't keep track of the twists and turns, but they eventually entered the galley. The ship was far bigger than it seemed from the outside. She sat at a long table and watched as Tark fixed a plate for each of them. When he joined her, he sat on the bench right beside her, their thighs pressing together.

A little thrill went through Suki. The big, powerful cyborg had the ability to crush her, to kill her with one blow, but he was the gentlest male she'd ever met. Nurturing. Caring. Suki had never known anyone like him before, not even on Earth, and while he was still a stranger, there was no disguising the goodness inside of him. It shone through his eyes.

"Why do you look different?" Tark asked. "I mean, different from other human females? The others on my world don't look like you."

"Like me?" she asked.

"Yes. Your eyes are different, your size. I've heard Earth is full of many different types of humans."

"I'm from a place called Japan. Perhaps the other humans you've met were from other places."

Tark nodded. The look on his face was one of fascination. She wondered how different his home was from her world. She'd seen many planets since being captured though she never had a chance to explore any of them. As a slave, a whore, she'd had one purpose and it had only involved spreading her legs or giving aliens access to whatever part of her they wished.

Suki ate slowly, even though she wanted to stuff her face as fast as possible. It had been so long since she'd eaten real food she knew she'd throw up if she didn't take it slow. Everything tasted so damn good! The master had fed her this nasty paste she'd been told was full of nutrients but had tasted like chalk. The food on her plate... it was heavenly. So many flavors and textures. It would be so easy to eat until she burst, but Suki was careful not to overdo it.

When she was finished, she pushed her plate away. Tark had been done for a while, nearly inhaling his food. He put their plates into the cleansing unit, then took her hand and led her back the way they'd come. Tark opened the door to their room and pulled her inside. As the door shut, he turned to face her, his chest heaving as if he'd run a marathon, and his eyes were dark with passion. There was no doubt he wanted her, but Suki didn't think he would act on it. Not unless she prodded him.

"You need to rest," Tark said. "You can have the bed."

"And where will you sleep?" she asked.

He shrugged. "The floor is fine."

Suki crawled onto the bed and pushed the covers aside. She inched over as far as she could, pressing her back to the wall, then motioned for Tark to come closer. He stopped at the edge of the bed and looked down at her.

"There's plenty of room, Tark."

"I shouldn't," he said, looking away, a muscle in his jaw tensing.

"Please," she said softly. "What if I have a nightmare? What if I need you?"

He glanced her way again, just staring for a

moment. Then he removed his boots and got into bed, pulling the covers over both of them. Suki smiled softly as she curled against his body, her hand on his chest and her head on his non-metal shoulder. It was a small victory, but she'd take it. His body was tense, and his chest barely moved, as if he were afraid to even breathe. Did he even have to breathe? He'd said his lungs weren't organic. She wasn't entirely sure what it meant for some of his organs to be mechanical. She'd never met a cyborg before, not that she knew of anyway. She found him rather fascinating, in more ways than one. After everything she'd been through, Suki never would have guessed she might be attracted to an alien, but then she'd never met one like Tark before.

"Will we travel to your world tomorrow?" she asked, curious about what would happen to her next.

"Once the crew finds out there's a female on board, they will want to return to Xpashta as soon as possible. Suki, I didn't see other humans in that tent, but you said you were kept in cages when you weren't..."

"Servicing customers?" she asked.

"Yes. Were there other humans, maybe held somewhere else?" Tark asked.

"Yoko and I were the only humans from our country, but there were two other humans there. We didn't get to speak to them much, but one said she was from India. I never found out anything about the other woman."

Tark tensed. The look on his face was one of panic, and something else. Something she couldn't quite determine.

"There are more humans? Where did the slaver keep you when you weren't in that tent?" he asked.

There was a bite to his tone, and she realized he was worried for the other women. She hadn't given them another thought, and it made her stomach ache that she'd failed them.

"The cages are on his ship. It looks much older than this one, and isn't as well maintained from what I could see. The outside had dents and the metal was tarnished."

"Suki, can you tell me exactly where that ship is located? Maybe my cyborg brothers can locate it and free those humans."

She shifted so she could look into his eyes. "Really? You could find them and bring them here? Take them to your world with us?"

He nodded. "They would be free too. All of you could find mates and have families. If they've been sterilized like you, they will be given the option of having it reversed."

She pressed a hand to her belly. "I can really have children now?"

Tark nodded. "Maybe not right away. Your body is healing. Even if you find your mate, it would be wise to refrain from…"

His cheeks flushed and she smiled a little. It was rather adorable that such a big guy could be embarrassed over something like being intimate.

"Refrain from sex?" she asked.

He nodded. "Any male would understand and wouldn't push you. At least, any cyborg male would be understanding."

Well, that put a kink in her plans. She'd have to find out exactly how long she needed to avoid sex, because as soon as she was able, she was getting the sexy cyborg lying beside her naked. And then she would show him exactly what he'd been missing all this time. On Earth, she'd never found someone she trusted to take her virginity, had never truly desired anyone, and since… She'd never looked forward to sex, had dreaded it, but with Tark… she was going to enjoy every minute of it.

"The ship, Suki. Where was the ship?" Tark asked.

"I can't read alien languages so I have no idea what the docking area said. It wasn't near here though. Close to the trading post, I think. I remember passing a lot of ships, and there were still about a half dozen more on the other side of it."

He nodded and closed his eyes. She wondered what he was doing, but he seemed to be concentrating and she didn't want to bother him. When he opened his eyes again, there was determination in their depths.

"What were you doing?" she asked.

"There are a few cyborgs close enough I could communicate with them. I told them about your sister and you, and that there were two other human females. They're going to search for them and take them by force if necessary."

"Are you going with them?" she asked.

"No. My duty is to protect you. I won't leave you alone on the ship with no way to keep yourself safe. What if the slaver came here? You'd be vulnerable."

"Is there any way to free all of them?" Suki asked.

"Two females won't be a problem for the crew, but all of them? That would be a bit more difficult. I know that slavery is horrible, but even if we freed those females the slaver would just get more. It's a never-ending cycle that won't stop until slavery is outlawed in the galaxies. Even then, the slavers would just operate off the grid, and then the slaves would be treated even worse."

Suki shivered. She couldn't imagine being treated worse than she'd been treated already. Or poor Yoko. Her eyes clouded with tears as she thought of her sister and all she'd suffered. The aliens had literally killed her with sex. Her sister had been so brave and fearless. Yoko had done anything asked of her, in order to make things better for Suki. And while Suki hated what she'd been through, it was nothing compared to Yoko. The slaves being whored out to anyone were treated far worse, and the slaver didn't seem to care if they contracted any diseases or died.

If Suki hadn't been a virgin when she'd been captured, she likely wouldn't have been singled out. Other than that, she couldn't imagine what was special about her. Yoko had that second sense, but Suki was ordinary. She was smaller than Yoko, and younger by five years, but there wasn't anything remarkable about her. It had never made any sense that she'd been chosen to service such important alien males, and she'd been too afraid to ask.

Tark gently cupped her cheek. "No one will ever hurt you again."

"If the other cyborgs can get the two slaves, what will happen next?" Suki asked.

"The females will be taken to the med clinic and then brought here. We'll likely leave immediately. It won't be safe to remain here, and the sooner we reach Xpashta, the safer the three of you will be."

"You should warn the others. The women they're going after will be filthy, scared, and might fight unless they're still drugged," Suki said.

Tark closed his eyes again. While he communicated with the other cyborgs, which she thought was incredibly cool, Suki laid back down and snuggled against him once more. Now that she was safe and fed, she was getting extremely tired. She hadn't slept well since she'd been captured. Every day, she'd been filled with fear, not knowing what would happen next. It was possible that Tark was lying, that he wasn't what he seemed, but deep inside she believed that he was a good male. When males had acted decent before, the kindness hadn't shone in their eyes the way it did with Tark. The evil inside of them had peeked out, regardless of how charming they tried to appear.

"They've been warned," Tark said. "They will treat the females with care and do their best not to scare them. Many fear us though, simply because we're cyborgs. While our enemies have every right to be afraid, we would never harm a female."

"They may be damaged. If not physically, then emotionally and mentally," Suki said. "I hope your friends won't take it personally if the women are afraid of them. I don't know what they've been through, but I can imagine. In some ways, I've been lucky. The women back in the tent, the master doesn't care what happens to them. Some have been severely abused, and not just sexually. The females your friends are going after are part of that group. Their minds may have fractured from all they've endured."

"Suki, you act like you haven't been through anything horrible, but I know better. I saw the bruises on your skin, before the med bay healed you. And being with those males…" He visibly swallowed. "Just because someone is in a position of power doesn't mean they aren't evil. I have no doubt that you've suffered greatly. But those days are over."

"You saved me," she said softly. "I'd thought I would die in that place, that I would never know freedom again. No one has touched me with kindness since I was captured on Earth. Yoko and I were kept separate from the time of our abduction, even though we were sold together. They kept us chained or caged where we couldn't reach one another."

"I'm only sorry I didn't get there in time to save Yoko. I would give her back to you if I could."

"You're a good male, Tark. Don't ever let anyone tell you differently. The females you've known, the ones who were scared of you, don't have any idea what they've passed up. And it may sound horrible, but I'm glad. If you'd been mated, you likely wouldn't have been anywhere near the brothel, and I'd still be there, waiting to face another day of spreading my legs for whoever paid enough."

His arms tightened around her. "I'm glad I was there too. Try to get some sleep, Suki. We'll begin traveling to Xpashta tomorrow. If the others are able to free those two females, you may be needed. Perhaps if they see you, if you can talk to them, they won't be as afraid."

"I'll do whatever I can to help," Suki said.

"Sleep. I'll wake you if you're needed."

She curled tighter against him and closed her eyes. And for the first time since she'd been snatched from Earth, Suki fell into a deep sleep, feeling completely safe.

Chapter Three

Tark eased out from under Suki, who had sprawled across his chest in her sleep, and answered the call from Haftyr.

Tark, we've found the other females. They were under guard and we had to kill a few of the males, but the females are safe now.

He listened to Haftyr as he pulled on his boots. The human females had been treated at the clinic and were now onboard -- but no one seemed to know what to do with them. They didn't have an extra room onboard at the moment, and no one knew where to put them. It would take days to reach Xpashta, and they would need a place to rest, somewhere they would feel safe.

Tark, you're needed on the bridge. Immediately.

He closed his eyes and exhaled deeply, wondering if he could just blow off Haftyr. The cyborg had a tendency to get on his nerves. Then again, Haftyr annoyed most people.

Tark considered giving up his quarters and placing two more cots in there, so all three females could share the space. But the way Suki had curled up next to him, the way she'd kissed him... He wasn't ready to let go of that just yet. She would probably pick another male for her mate once she'd met the others, but for now it was nice to be accepted by a female.

Tark slipped quietly from his quarters and made his way to the bridge. Haftyr stood in the command center, his arms folded over his chest, as he glowered at Vroxtin and Crisnar, who each held a human female in their arms. The females had their eyes closed and appeared to be sleeping, but Meriko, the medic for the *Wayfarer*, seemed concerned as he gazed at them.

"Why was I summoned?" Tark asked.

"You discovered the human females," Haftyr said. "You should be the one who decides where they'll sleep. These two seem to think they'll hang onto them. Hardly seems fair to everyone else."

Tark blinked then looked at his captain, Vroxtin, and had to admit the male did look a bit possessive over the female in his arms. The muscles in his arms bulged and he bared his teeth at Haftyr, making Tark question whether or not he should have gotten out of bed to deal with this mess. It wasn't like he had any say over what the captain did. If Vroxtin wanted to hold onto the female, Tark couldn't exactly tell him not to.

"You didn't see the fear in their eyes," Crisnar said. "You don't know what they've been through. We just want to protect them. Besides, there are no open quarters onboard. Are you volunteering to double up with someone so they can have your room?"

Haftyr's scowl deepened. That seemed like answer enough. The male was troublesome, and had he not caused problems on board the *Mystic7* when Lathim had found Maggie, then he probably wouldn't be here now. If Vroxtin had thought for one moment human females would be on board, Tark knew he would have asked to have Haftyr replaced. Everyone knew the male hadn't acted sane when Maggie had been found. Tark wondered if they were about to face something similar now.

"This is Navya," Vroxtin said, nodding at the darker-skinned female in his arms. "She was scared of me, but I was able to get her name before she passed out. The med clinic healed her, but she's going to need care. I asked why she looked different from the other human and she said she was from some place called

Mumbai. It seems that humans look different depending on where they live. It's rather fascinating, and a bit odd."

If travel to Earth was ever possible without scaring the little planet, Tark would love to visit sometime. It was so far away none of his people had ever been there, and they knew little about it. Other alien races had obviously found the place, since there were human slaves to be found throughout the galaxies, but it didn't mean the cyborgs would be welcomed with open arms. With more human females coming to live on Xpashta, he knew they would need to find as much information as possible about the planet that created such alluring females.

"This is Fenella," Crisnar said, nodding toward the redhead in his arms. She was curvier than any human female Tark had seen before, and so pale he feared she was dying. But the way Crisnar cradled her against his chest, Tark knew the male wanted to claim her. Perhaps she'd been awake long enough to agree.

"You're both keeping them in your quarters, aren't you?" Tark asked. "What if they bond with someone else?"

Vroxtin glared at him and Tark lifted his hands and took a step back.

"If Fenella wishes to be with another male, I won't stop her," Crisnar said. "But until then, I'd like to be the one to take care of her. She was badly damaged and needed a lot of healing. She passed out in the med bay."

"I will be happy to assist with either female if they need additional medical care," Meriko said. "I've been studying humans since Maggie, Jillian, and Shaylee arrived on our world, and I'm confident I could help if they need medical assistance."

Haftyr growled and stomped out of the room. Tark shared a look with the remaining males, and they all knew something would have to be done with the surly cyborg. Everyone on Xpashta wanted a mate, except for the few who already had one. For some reason, Haftyr seemed to think he deserved one more than anyone else, and it was turning him into a male no one wanted to deal with.

Tark wasn't sure if the females on board would be safe around Haftyr, but they couldn't exactly demand the cyborg remain behind. He'd keep a close eye on Suki, unless she wanted to be with the surly Haftyr. If that was the case, he would step back, even though he wished more than anything that he could keep her for himself. Suki was the only female to not shrink away from him in fear, or at least give him a wary look. She accepted him, trusted him, and it was a feeling he would cherish always. Even if she didn't want to stay, the feel of her pressed against him in his bunk would be with him for the rest of his life.

"If anyone needs me, I'll be in my quarters," he said. "It seems the two of you have everything under control."

"I'm sorry that Haftyr pulled you away from your female," Vroxtin said. "I think it would be best if he didn't go on future missions for a little while, not until he's mated."

"If anyone will mate him," Crisnar said.

Tark refrained from commenting. Even though Haftyr wasn't the most pleasant cyborg, at least his changes weren't on the outside of his body -- other than his stark white hair, which all Zelranian cyborgs had. He didn't have metal extremities that everyone could see, unlike Tark. Even though his mechanical arm gave him an edge in battle, there were times he wished he wasn't as different on the outside. When Wrylack had found a mate, he'd thought maybe there was hope, yet all females had still given Tark a wide berth. Until Suki. Was it wrong that he wanted to hold onto her? To make her his?

When he got back to his quarters, Suki was awake and looked fearful as she pressed against the wall, her knees bent and the covers wrapped tightly around her. The relief in her gaze as she saw him made him feel bad about leaving her without a word. He hadn't thought he would be gone long, and she'd been sleeping so peacefully. Next time, he'd know to wake her before he left.

"I didn't know where you were or if you were coming back," she said.

"I'm sorry if I scared you. It wasn't my intention. There was an issue that needed my attention."

"I thought… I thought maybe you didn't want to share your room with me."

"Suki." He moved closer and eased onto the bed. She immediately threw herself into his arms, and he cradled her close. "I'm sorry. Next time, I'll let you know when I'm leaving. You can stay with me as long as you wish."

"Forever?" she asked.

"You may not want forever when you meet the others."

She reached up and cupped his cheek. "Tark, I know you think that there's something wrong with you, that you're defective or something, but you're not. You're the kindest man I've ever met. Do you know that by now most men would have expected me to thank them for saving me? On my back? You haven't asked me for anything."

"Those males have no honor," he said.

"No, they don't," she said. "But you do. I don't need to meet the others to know that I want to stay with you, but if you don't want me as your mate then I'll understand. I'm tainted, dirty from my time in service, and you could do so much better."

"Suki, you're not dirty. I think..." He stopped and looked away a moment. "I think you're perfect. I'm the one who isn't worthy of you."

"Tark," she said softly.

He looked down at her.

"Tark, I want to be yours. In all ways. You are more than worthy, and I would be honored to belong to you."

"Suki, I..."

She shushed him by placing her lips against his. He groaned as her tongue flicked out. Opening, he kissed her the way he'd often seen Lathim kiss his mate. Suki tasted sweet, and feeling her mouth against his, her tongue stroking his, made his cock harden almost painfully. Despite her words, he knew he couldn't claim her right now. She had been damaged and needed time to heal. But this... kissing her was better than he could have ever imagined.

"Please," she said. "Don't make me pick someone else."

"Suki, being with you, being your mate, would be the greatest honor. If you're certain I'm the one you want, then I will gladly claim you."

She smiled and kissed him again, slower this time, and Tark savored the moment. He had a mate! A female had actually chosen him above all others. His heart felt as if it had grown three sizes, and he vowed that he would be the best mate Suki could ever want or need. She had given him a gift he'd thought he'd never have, and he would treasure her always.

She reached for his shirt, trying to pull it off him, and he grasped her hands in one of his and leaned away from her. Hurt flashed in her eyes, and he hated that he'd made her feel pain of any kind.

"Suki, we can't. Not yet. I want the medics on Xpashta to look at you once more, make sure you're completely healed, before we go further than kissing. While we have a medic on board, Wrylack has the ability to do an in-depth scan with his cybernetic eyes. I trust him. I won't take a chance on damaging you."

Her gaze softened and she leaned against him again. Tark held her close, and for the first time as far back as he could remember, he felt content. No, more than that. He felt… happy. Truly happy.

Suki kissed his cheek and then yawned widely. He released her and settled her back on the side of the bed along the wall, then stretched out beside her. She snuggled against him like she'd done before and it wasn't long before her breathing evened out and she was asleep again.

It took Tark a while to sleep, mostly because he was worried he'd wake up and discover it wasn't real, that Suki wasn't really his. He'd lived through a lot in his lifetime, but he didn't know that he would survive losing her. Tark would honestly prefer to go through the pain of the Cy-Con program again rather than watch Suki walk away.

Eventually, he fell asleep, his new mate curled against his side. It was the most peaceful sleep he'd had in a long time.

Chapter Four

Suki hated being trapped on the ship while they traveled to Xpashta. Not that the *Wayfarer* was a terrible place to be, but floating around in space reminded her too much of the life she'd been living since aliens had captured her on Earth. It would be nice to have solid ground beneath her feet, and to see her new home.

Excitement bubbled inside her when she thought about getting to live with Tark. Even though he'd claimed her, and let his friends know that she belonged to him, she felt like her newfound happiness could come crashing down at any moment. His crewmates seemed happy that Tark had claimed her, except for the angry-looking one he'd called Haftyr. What if the cyborgs on his world weren't happy with his choice of mate? He'd assured Suki that her past meant nothing to him, but would the leaders of his planet feel the same?

"We'll be landing any moment," Tark said, a broad smile on his face. "My home is rather plain, but there are rooms filled with items from your planet. You can add whatever you'd like to the house. Some of the human mates have chosen things like pictures and vases."

"You have things from my world, but you don't know how to return us to Earth?" Suki asked.

His expression fell. "I'm sorry you can't return to your home. We obtained those items through trading, or from taking over pirated vessels. If you truly wish to return, perhaps I can find a way to make it happen."

Suki reached for him, her hand curled around his bicep. "No, Tark. I don't want to go back to Earth. I was thinking of the others. Did you know that Navya is related to one of the royal families of her country?"

"Navya said that her family would not welcome her after what she's been through," Tark said. "While she misses her home, she said she was willing to travel to Xpashta. The same is true for Fenella."

"What if…" She swallowed hard. "What if the leaders of your world don't think I'm good enough for you? What if they say we can't be together?"

"Suki, no one will take you from me," he said. "The Commanders will be glad that I've found a mate. And the fact we're bringing home three females will be a blessing. It will also prove that perhaps Maggie and Shaylee were correct."

"What do you mean?" Suki asked.

"They are the human mates to two cyborgs, and they suggested that we could purchase human slaves and free them on Xpashta, give them another chance at life and at having a family. I never thought…" He looked away. "I never thought about the females at brothels being unwilling until it was brought to our attention by the other humans on our world. We'd always believed those females were willing. Perhaps instead of just searching the slave markets, we should also search the brothels for more human females."

"Why can't you get them through the Bride program?" she asked.

"What's a Bride program?"

Her mouth opened and shut as she stared at him in shock. "I just thought, since you look so much like the Terrans, that maybe you were related somehow. They're a race of aliens who have opened stations across Earth. They offer monetary compensation for females to go to their world and mate with their males."

He frowned. "Maggie mentioned something

about that. I'm not familiar with a race called Terrans, though. We've tried to search for information on them, and only get led back to archived information on your planet."

"Maybe they were called something else before," she mused. "If you don't know how to get to Earth, then maybe you're right to search the trading posts for females. Not all of them would be happy to go to your world though. Some will want to go home, and since you can't offer that to them…"

He nodded. "It could be a potential issue. We want the females on our world to be happy. We already have one human who wants to return home. I'm not sure how well it would be received to have several more as angry as Jillian is."

"Why is she angry?"

"She was unconscious when we found her, and badly damaged. One of the medics healed her, but a cyborg claimed her before she woke. She's been very angry and bitter."

"She was given no choice?" Suki asked.

"No." Tark grimaced. "I've suggested that perhaps Jillian would prefer a different cyborg, but Rorwick is adamant that she belongs to him."

"That's rather sad. Maybe if you bring more females to your world, he'll bond with one of them. Then Jillian will be free to choose someone else."

"Perhaps," he said.

The ship shuddered and pitched, making Suki gasp. Tark reached out to steady her, smiling once more.

"We're home," he said.

Her stomach clenched and she gripped his hand tight as he led her from the room they'd shared the past few days. Suki didn't know what to expect as they disembarked from the shuttle. There was a large wall that seemed to stretch for miles. There was grass and trees, a pretty sky, but none of it looked even a little bit like Earth. The colors and textures were all wrong, and yet they worked well together. It was beautiful.

"Welcome to your new home," Tark said as large gates opened.

A gathering of cyborgs greeted them, and Suki pressed closer to Tark. She didn't think they would cause her any harm, but they were an unknown. Until Tark, she hadn't had good experiences with aliens. They'd used and abused her, and hadn't shown her even the slightest bit of kindness. Maybe these cyborgs were like her sweet Tark, but with the way Haftyr acted, she doubted even on this world there were many males like her new mate.

Three imposing cyborgs came toward them. They weren't as tall or as broad as Tark, but they had a commanding air about them. Their gazes scanned over her and Suki shivered, feeling as if icy fingers had raked down her spine. The middle one smiled, but it didn't set her at ease even a little bit.

"Commanders, this is my mate, Suki," Tark said.

"Welcome to Xpashta, Suki. My name is Sorus. The two males next to me are Warver and Kiril. We make sure things run smoothly here. If you ever need anything and can't find Tark, seek out any of us. We'll be happy to assist you."

"You are aware that you could have mated anyone on Xpashta, correct?" Warver asked. "There are many unmated males here. Some who are…"

Kiril pushed Warver out of the way. "Ignore him, Suki. You chose wisely by accepting Tark as your mate. He's a fierce warrior, but I have no doubt he'll treat you very well. Warver tends to forget that not everyone makes their judgments based on looks."

Suki felt heat swirl in her belly and she stepped away from Tark, her hands clenched into fists. Her lips pressed tightly together as she stepped closer to the Commanders.

"There is nothing, and I mean *nothing* wrong with Tark, physically or otherwise. He's the handsomest man I've ever seen, and the kindest I've ever met on any world. I'm lucky that he claimed me, honored to be called his. And I won't let you stand there and disparage his looks or anything else about him, no matter who you are," Suki said.

Sorus grinned and looked from Warver and Kiril back to her.

"Very well said, Suki. I believe Tark found the perfect mate when he claimed you," Sorus said.

"My apologies, Suki," Warver said. "It was not my intention to upset you, or to make it sound like I found your mate to be less desirable than others. I just know that females have always feared him, and I wanted to assure you that you had other options if you were uncertain in your choice."

"No, I'm not uncertain," Suki said. "I want to be with Tark."

"Very well. Is there anything you need, Suki?" Warver asked.

"She'll need more clothes," Tark said. "And I'd like for her to access the storage rooms in case there are things she'd like for her new home."

"Of course," said Sorus. "Anything else?"

"She had a medical procedure before coming here," Tark said. "I want to take her to the med clinic."

"I believe Wrylack is on duty right now," Kiril said. "Suki, Wrylack is different from the rest of his. His cybernetics are…"

"His eyes glow," Tark said. "They're mechanical. I didn't think it would bother you since my arm doesn't."

"He's mated to a human," Kiril said. "He's learned a lot about your species and will be able to treat you. Did Tark explain to you about the injections we use to halt reproduction?"

Her eyes went wide and she shook her head. "No, he didn't say anything."

"Since he was just on a mission, he'll have taken -_"

"I didn't take the shot," Tark said. "Once I learned that all females, even the ones at the brothels, were scared of me, it didn't matter if I took one or not. I'm fully capable of having children, but if Suki would like to wait longer, then I will be glad to ask for the injection."

"Why don't we leave it in Fate's hands?" Suki asked.

"Excuse us, Commanders. The sooner I take her to the clinic, the faster I can get her home. Do we still have human clothing stocked?"

"Of course," Kiril said. "Lathim picked up another load not too long ago. He still hasn't figured out the different sizes so I'm not sure what's available. Hopefully, something will fit your Suki. If not, we have plenty of material so some garments could be made for her."

Tark led her through what seemed to be a city. They passed so many cyborgs, and not one single female. When he'd said there were only a few humans, she hadn't realized he meant that no one else was mated, not even to another species. Now she could understand why they wanted females so badly they would accept those who had even worked at brothels.

Suki knew if she'd gone home, no one would have wanted her. Not for a wife. They'd have used her the same way the aliens had, and she'd never have had a chance at a family of her own.

When they entered the medical clinic, a cyborg with glowing blue eyes smiled. "Tark, I see you didn't come back from your travels empty-handed."

"Wrylack, this is Suki. My mate. She had a procedure done at the space station and I need to know if she's completely healed."

Wrylack lost his smile as he came closer. His eyes lit up even brighter as he scanned her head to toe, his gaze coming back to lock on her lower abdomen. He made a humming noise and stepped across the room, coming back with two syringes filled with brightly colored liquid.

"Wh-what's that for?" Suki asked.

"One is a vitamin injection for you, and the other..." His gaze locked with Tark's before settling on hers again. "The other will give you a longer lifespan and keep you healthier than a typical human. I'm not sure what Tark has told you, but we've discovered that our species lives longer than yours. This will allow the two of you stay together longer."

Suki nodded and held out her arm. "Then go ahead. I want as much time with him as I can get."

Wrylack smiled once more, then injected both liquids into her arm. He nodded his head at Tark, but her cyborg seemed reluctant to move.

"I don't wish to keep secrets from Suki," Tark said.

"She's healed. I can see where a sterilization was reversed. From what I can tell, there's no reason she can't have children."

"What about..." Tark's cheeks flushed.

"Can we be intimate?" Suki asked. "Tark wanted to wait. He was worried it would hurt me."

"It should be fine. If you feel any discomfort or pain, let Tark know immediately."

"Perhaps you can come by for dinner later and bring Shaylee?" Tark asked. "I'd like for Suki to make a friend. Since Shaylee was once a slave, I thought she might be more sensitive to Suki's circumstances."

"You know Maggie welcomes everyone, and Jillian always has a smile for the human females. It's just Rorwick she can't seem to stand. I wish the Commanders would step in and remove her from his home. Everyone can tell that she's miserable with him and won't accept his mate claim. It's been a year!"

Tark nodded.

"Could I..." Suki paused. "Could I meet Jillian? Maybe she'd confide in a stranger what it is that she wants. I mean, I'm impartial and don't have anything vested in whether or not she stays with Rorwick."

Wrylack's eyebrow rose. "Not a bad idea."

"We're stopping for clothes, then I'm taking you home," Tark said. "You can meet with Jillian tomorrow if you feel up to it."

"Tark." She placed her hand on his arm. "What if she's miserable? Don't you want her to be happy, the way you make me happy?"

Wrylack coughed but looked amused. Tark sighed, giving me a lopsided smile then nodded.

"Very well. Let's stop and check for clothing, and then I'll take you to meet Jillian."

They left the clinic and took a few different walkways. Suki didn't understand any of the writing on the doors. Tark stopped in front of one and pushed it open. A light came on as they stepped inside and her eyes went wide at all the crates stacked inside. One was already open and clothing spilled out. Suki picked up several brightly colored silk dresses. They were on the plain side as far as style, but they felt so decadent in her hands. Tears gathered in her eyes as she looked into the crate and saw more dresses in different materials. She selected three in her size and looked up at Tark to let him know she was ready, but he was frowning at her.

"Did I do something wrong?" she asked.

"You need more clothing than that, Suki. This entire room is filled with clothes. You should get at least three or four times that many dresses. Or perhaps you want pants? I've seen Maggie wear them."

"I don't want to take too many," she said. "What if the others need them? Navya and Fenella need clothes too."

"Suki, there's more than enough, and the three of you don't seem to be the same size. Please take the items you like. If we need more, I'm sure Lathim can find them."

Suki chewed on her lower lip and dug through the crate. Tark broke another one open, and she found some leggings and tunic style shirts inside. She grabbed several of each. By the time they left, Tark was carrying at least ten outfits for her. Suki stared at everything as they walked through the town. There was a bazaar of some sort with tables and tents set up, wares and food of all types spread out. Tark paused by one that contained jewelry. He picked up a silver cuff bracelet and slipped it onto Suki's wrist.

"Tark, I don't need shiny things."

"Perhaps you don't need them, but it doesn't mean you shouldn't have them."

Tark nodded to the cyborg behind the table and pushed her further along. She looked over her shoulder and wondered why he hadn't paid for the bracelet. He stopped twice more, selecting the things he thought she might like, and again she didn't see him didn't pay for anything. She didn't understand this world or their society, but it seemed to be peaceful.

The homes were made of some sort of stone that was probably common on this planet. They walked a little further and Tark stopped in front of a home that looked like the others around it. He knocked on the door and a cyborg answered who looked like he'd last had a good night's sleep a few years ago. He glanced from Tark down to Suki, and a slight smile curved his lips.

"Tark, have you taken a mate?" the cyborg asked.

"Yes. Suki, this is Rorwick. Jillian is living with him."

Rorwick had a flash of pain in his eyes when her name was mentioned, and Suki wondered just how bad things were between the two. Rorwick motioned for them to enter, and he led the way back to a room that overlooked a patio of some sort. It would have been a spectacular spot for a garden, but there wasn't even a hint of dirt or grass back there.

A redhead sat on what looked to be an alien version of a sofa, and she scowled when she saw Rorwick. Her expression cleared when she noticed Suki and Tark.

"We have company," Rorwick said. "Tark has taken a mate."

"Did you get knocked over the head and dragged here caveman-style?" Jillian asked.

"Um, no. Tark saved my life."

She glanced at Tark and gave a slight nod. "Good for you. I hope you treat her well."

Rorwick made a sound like a wounded animal, though a big one, and then left the room. Tark kissed Suki's cheek and followed his friend. Jillian motioned for her to sit down, and Suki was pleasantly surprised at how comfortable the furniture was. It had looked like it might be a little stiff, but she sank onto the cushion.

"Tark said you've lived here a year," Suki said. "It seems like a nice place."

"Unless you live with a behemoth like Rorwick."

"He seemed... stressed. And tired."

Jillian shrugged. "I'm not making his life easy, but what would you have done if you'd woken on a strange planet, in a strange man's home, and he decided he was going to claim you like a piece of luggage?"

"I guess it would depend on the circumstances. It took us several days to reach Xpashta. Why were you asleep for the trip here?" Suki asked.

"I was sick and had been ejected into space in a rescue pod. According to the medic who tended me, I was nearly dead. Rorwick decided the second the pod was open that I belonged to him," Jillian said. "Didn't give me any say at all!"

"He doesn't seem like a bad guy, even though I don't really know him. There's no anger or hatred in his eyes, no evil. Why don't you want to be with him?"

"I'm not a piece of property! I should get to make my own choices."

Suki looked around the room a moment before settling her gaze on Jillian again. "If you could choose, who would you want to be with? Has another cyborg caught your attention?"

Jillian's cheeks flushed.

"So, there is someone?" Suki asked.

"There's a cyborg I've spoken to at the marketplace a few times. He's always smiling, always happy, and he's so polite. When I'm with him, even if it's just a few minutes, I feel a peace I haven't experienced since I left Earth. I tried with Rorwick. I did. Yes, I threw a tantrum at first and I was furious, then I understood his position and why he'd claimed me. It still didn't make it right, and I honestly don't feel a connection to him. It's like they're all forcing me to be with Rorwick, and I just..."

"You don't think you could ever love him?" Suki asked.

"No," Jillian said and sighed. "I really don't. I don't like it when he touches me, even though it's never inappropriate. I don't even like being in the same room as him. I'm sorry if that makes me a horrible bitch."

"Have you told anyone how you feel? Maybe told him about your connection to the other cyborg? Is it possible he returns your feelings?" Suki asked.

"I haven't because any time I've expressed my displeasure, I've been dismissed. The other cyborg... we don't discuss my situation with Rorwick, but I can tell by the way he looks at me that he cares. I feel safe with him. There's a kindness in his eyes that makes me feel warm. With Rorwick, I feel like he just wants me as a possession, like I'm his because he's the one who pulled me from the escape pod. I know he wants a mate, but I don't have feelings for him. Not like that."

Suki nodded. "All right. What's the other cyborg's name?"

"Balize."

"I know I'm new here, but maybe *because* I'm new I can get someone to listen. Would you be all right with me talking to Tark and maybe one of the

Commanders? I'm sure they would rather you be happy here than with someone who makes you miserable," Suki said.

"I make you miserable?"

Suki jerked her head toward the door and paled when she saw Rorwick and Tark. Rorwick looked ill and it seemed like a giant weight settled on his shoulders. She wished that she could ease his pain, that there was a way for both of them to win in this situation, but she didn't see that happening.

"I had thought maybe you would eventually…" Rorwick trailed off and shook his head. "I never meant to make you miserable. I liked your fire and didn't realize you truly hated being here. I thought you were playing hard to get. I've heard some human females do that. I thought I was supposed to chase you, to wait you out. It never occurred to me that you really didn't want to be with me. If you don't wish to remain here, I won't force you. You can have whatever you want from the house."

He turned and walked off and a look of guilt crossed Jillian's face. Suki reached for her hand and gave it a squeeze. Tark came closer and knelt in front of Suki.

"What do you need from me, mate?" he asked.

"Can you find Balize and bring him here?" she asked. "I think it's time he and Jillian talked about something more meaningful than whatever he has in the marketplace."

"Why don't we take Jillian to him?" Tark suggested. "Rorwick left, but he could return and seeing Belize with the woman he wanted to claim might be painful. He truly didn't understand that Jillian wanted her freedom to choose another. We have very little knowledge and understanding of human females, except for what we've learned since Lathim found Maggie. Rorwick never meant any harm."

Suki nodded.

She and Jillian stood and followed Tark out of Rorwick's house and to a home not far away. The cyborg who opened the door smiled at Tark, then it slowly slipped from his face as he saw Jillian. The intense look in his eyes told Suki everything she needed to know. He cared for Jillian as much as she seemed to like him.

"Why are you here?" Balize asked, his gaze landing on Tark.

"Jillian has let Rorwick know she doesn't wish to live with him." Tark looked at Jillian then Suki. "It was my mate's suggestion that perhaps she could find out what Jillian truly wanted. It seems she wants you."

Balize stepped out of the house and stopped in front of Jillian, his fingers twitched as if he wanted to reach for her.

"Is this true?" he asked. "You wish to be my mate?"

Jillian nodded but looked conflicted. "I didn't know if you wanted me though."

Balize reached up and cupped her cheek. "I would be honored to claim you as my mate."

Jillian gave him a hesitant smile. Suki reached for Tark's hand and led him away from the couple. They probably had a lot to discuss. And someone should check on Rorwick. The cyborg had looked completely gutted. Suki could only imagine how hard it must have been hearing Jillian was miserable when all Rorwick had wanted was to make her his and give her a good life. Even though he hadn't said as much, Suki knew that's what Tark wanted for her. If Tark called Rorwick his friend, then the cyborg couldn't be bad.

"Should we check on Rorwick?" she asked.

"He'll want some space," Tark said. "Possibly even off-world. If there's a ship leaving soon, I'd be willing to bet he'll be on it."

"I feel so bad for him, but I'm glad that Jillian can be with the cyborg she wants. Maybe the right female for him is still out there somewhere."

"I need to take you home," Tark said. "We'll put your clothes away, and you can see if there's anything you need or want for the house. It's rather plain right now."

"I'm all right with plain."

Honestly, just knowing she would have a home again was enough reason to celebrate. She didn't need pretty things. Tark had given her more than she'd thought she'd ever have again. And she was more than ready to expand his education on the other benefits of having a mate. It still baffled her that the sexy man hadn't ever been intimate with someone before. She only hoped she didn't disappoint him.

Chapter Five

Tark could admit that he was a bit anxious over Suki seeing her new home. He wanted her to like it, and hoped that she would do whatever it took to make the place feel like she belonged there. The fact he had a mate still seemed a little surreal. While he'd gone to that part of the station in hopes of perhaps purchasing a slave, he'd been worried that even a female he purchased would be terrified of him. Despite everything Suki had been through, she was strong and hadn't given up. And for some reason, she accepted him as her mate. Even seemed pleased with the idea.

She was more than he had ever hoped for, and Tark was worried he wouldn't live up to her expectations. It wasn't just his home, or the fact she was on a new planet with very few humans. He'd never been intimate with anyone before. Suki might not have chosen all of her sexual partners, but she knew more than he did. What if she found him lacking when it came to intimacy?

Suki wandered the house, touching things here and there, but he couldn't tell what she thought about the place. When she entered their bedroom, she ran her fingers across the blanket covering the bed. She turned and checked out the space, then focused on him. With a smile curving her lips, she crooked her finger and beckoned him closer. Tark swallowed the knot in his throat and moved nearer to his sweet mate, wondering what she wanted. Even though Wrylack had cleared her for intimacy, he'd thought she might want more time. They were still strangers, and she had so many things that were new in her life. Didn't females need an adjustment period?

"You liked kissing me, didn't you?" she asked.

"Very much." Was that his voice? He cleared his throat and looked around uneasily.

"Tark?"

He glanced down at Suki and saw that she was removing her clothes. His cock hardened immediately, but he took a hasty step back. He hadn't expected such a bold move from her and felt completely off balance, but then she'd made him feel that way from the moment she'd said she wanted to be his. Suki was different from anyone he'd met before, in a good way, but it sometimes made him feel like he was floundering.

"Suki, I... we don't have to do this right now. There's plenty of time," he said.

"Tark. Get undressed."

He slowly reached for the hem of his shirt and pulled it over his head. Her lips parted as she stared at his chest, but it was her light touch that nearly undid him. His body shuddered as she caressed him, her fingers stroking over every exposed inch of his skin. He held still, worrying that if he moved, he might frighten her. Just because she was instigating things didn't mean she wouldn't change her mind.

Suki reached for the fastening of his pants, then shoved them down his hips. Tark still had his boots on and stared at his feet a moment before leaning down and removing the boots and pants. Suki bit her lip as she walked around him, her fingers trailing along his skin. His cock was throbbing, and if she so much as touched his shaft, he worried he'd come before he could even get inside of her. Tark wanted to please her, to make the experience good for her, but he didn't know how. He was starting to wish he'd asked questions of the mated males.

He slowly reached for her, feeling how soft and

silky her skin was. His fingers slid across her nipple and she moaned, her eyes sliding shut. He wondered what other parts of her would elicit that response. Tark took his time, enjoying the feel of her. Her nipples were hard, and he discovered she liked it when he pinched them. The musk of her arousal filled the air, making him even harder. When Suki trembled and lay back on the bed, parting her legs, he groaned.

"So beautiful," he said. "Suki, I…"

She shushed him. "I know you're a virgin. You don't have to be embarrassed, Tark. There isn't a male out there who can last long his first time. I may not have had experience on Earth, but I heard the girls giggling at school."

She held her hands out to him and Tark climbed onto the bed, kneeling between her legs. He settled his body over hers, and the feel of her slick pussy was almost enough to make him come. He clenched his jaw as he sank into her. She felt like wet silk, her warmth wrapping around his shaft and welcoming him into her body. Tark looked down at Suki, holding her gaze as he thrust into her. There was tenderness looking back at him, and happiness. She ran her fingers along his jaw, her fingers rasping against the white scruff that wasn't quite a full beard, then wrapped her legs around his waist.

He slid deeper into her and knew he couldn't hold back for long. It only took another three strokes and he was coming. Suki kissed him, stroking his shoulder and back with her hand. He shuddered, still buried inside of her. Nothing could have prepared him for how good she'd feel. It wasn't like he'd never come before. He'd used his hand plenty of times, but it wasn't even a little bit like being inside of Suki.

"That was…" He didn't even have words for it.

"Perfect," she said.

"No." He frowned. "You didn't come. I may not know much about how this works, but I can tell you didn't experience what I did."

"Tark, the fact that it was you inside of me was what made it perfect. If you want to make me come, I can show you how."

His gaze traced what he could see of her body. "Show me."

She pushed at his shoulder a little and he lifted some, but kept their bodies joined. She reached for his hand and placed it at the top of her pussy, then parted the lips some more, showing him a little nub. It stood up and was slick from her need.

"Rub me here, and I'll come," she said.

Tark stroked her right where she'd shown him, and it didn't take long before he felt her getting even hotter and wetter. When she came, her pussy clenching tight on his cock, it was enough to make him rock hard again. He started thrusting as he rubbed the little spot and when she came a second time, he followed. Tark worried he would be too heavy if he collapsed on top of her, so he rolled them to their sides, his arm going around her waist as he held her close, careful not to squeeze too hard since it was his cybernetic arm.

"I'm sorry," he said. A male with more experience would have pleased her more. On the battlefield, he was legendary. But when it came to females? Tark had no experience and he couldn't help but feel as if he'd failed her.

"You have nothing to be sorry for," she said, snuggling closer. "You're the first guy to ever give me an orgasm. Instead of beating yourself up, you should be congratulating yourself."

"We'll have to disagree on that."

"Tark," she said softly.

He looked down and held her gaze.

"I meant what I said. The fact it was you making love to me made it special, perfect even. That you care about me, wanted to please me, makes this the best experience I've ever had. Please stop tearing yourself down. You're the most incredible man I've ever met."

His throat tightened with emotion. It amazed him that someone so small could have such an effect on him. Tark didn't know what he'd ever done to deserve a mate as sweet as Suki, but he wanted to give her the best life he could. If he needed to take fewer missions, then he'd ask for a job to do on Xpashta. Whatever she needed, he'd see that she had it.

"You should rest," he said, pressing a kiss to her forehead. "I know Wrylack said it was all right to be intimate, but you've been through a lot and may not be fully healed."

Suki sighed. "Tark, you heard him. He said everything was fine."

Maybe, but it didn't mean he couldn't worry about her. It seemed she'd been a long time without someone watching over her. From what he'd learned, her sister had tried, but they had been kept separate after they were sold to the brothel. It still pained him, his inability to save Yoko. Deep down, he knew he wasn't at fault, and it was a miracle he'd been able to get Suki out of there, and his brother cyborgs had retrieved the other two females, but it wasn't enough. The suffering they'd endured was beyond horrific.

"You know, there are lots of positions for us to try," she said.

"Positions?" he asked.

Suki smiled. "Oh, yeah. There are many different ways to have sex. Why don't I show you another one?"

When she pushed on his chest, Tark rolled to his back, taking Suki with him. She straddled his hips, placing her hands on his abdomen and sitting upright. As her hips shifted, he grew hard again. Suki had a wicked look in her eyes as she gazed down at him.

"What is it, mate?" he asked.

Suki reached for his hand, then placed it on her breast. "You can squeeze my breasts, as long as you don't do it too hard. My nipples are really sensitive. I like it when you pinch and pull on them. If you do anything that hurts, I'll let you know."

"And here?" he asked, rubbing the nub between her thighs again.

"Ohh, that feels good. I like when you rub me there, but you don't have to do it quite so gently. It's okay to put pressure on my clit. You can pinch or tug on it too, if you'd like, just not too rough."

Suki lifted her hips, then lowered herself on his cock. Tark watched her, mesmerized as her breasts bounced and swayed with her movements. Even though it felt amazing, having her ride him, he wanted her to feel just as good. He tugged on her nipples and gripped her hip with his cybernetic hand. As he pinched and pulled on the tips, he helped guide her movement. When she started coming, Tark didn't think he could handle much more. Using both hands, he held her hips firmly and slammed her down onto his cock as he thrust upward.

Suki's head tipped back, exposing the column of her throat, and she leaned back, bracing her hands on his thighs. The sexiest sounds came from her lips as she came twice more. Tark didn't know how he'd found his control when it came to having sex with his mate, but he felt a rush of pleasure at making her come so many times. Tark's cock jerked and he groaned as he filled her with his release, every hot spurt making his balls draw up tighter.

Suki collapsed on his chest, panting for breath, her hair clinging to her sweat soaked brow.

"I think you have the hang of it now," she said.

Tark smiled and ran his fingers through her long locks.

"Is there anything you'd like?" he asked. "A bath? A tour of Xpashta?"

She sighed. "I'd love to soak in a tub of hot water, but by bath, I'm going to assume you mean a shower like onboard your ship."

He frowned. He'd never thought of having one of those sunken pools of water in his home. The standing unit was fine for him, but a female might prefer one of the soaking pools. Now that he had a mate, he wanted to ensure she had everything she wanted or needed. Perhaps he could have one added, or ask to build a new home his mate might like better.

"How do humans bathe on your world?" he asked, wanting to know about Suki and where she came from. Until Maggie, he'd never met a human before, and Lathim didn't exactly encourage single males to have lengthy conversations with his mate. The few humans Tark had encountered hadn't wanted to speak with him either. Until his Suki, most females had tried to get out of his path as quickly as possible.

"Well, we have showers or tubs. The tubs sit on the floor and you can fill them with water, then let it drain through a hole that goes into the floor and runs through pipes under the house. How is it done here?"

"Some of my fellow cyborgs have homes with sunken pools, but I believe most are like mine with just the standing cleansing unit. If you would like one of the pools, I can find out if one can be added."

"I don't have to have one, Tark, but it's sweet of you to offer. This home is the best I've lived in for so very long. Even when I was on Earth, my home was smaller than this. You don't need to change anything," Suki said.

"This is your home now, not just mine," he said. "I want you to be happy with me, Suki. I don't want you to regret ever choosing me as your mate."

She smiled a little. "Tark, having a tub isn't going to change how I feel about being here with you. Would one be nice? Of course. But it isn't something I absolutely have to have."

"There's something else. My job is off world. There will be times I need to leave, and you may be alone for several of your Earth weeks or possibly even months. If you'd prefer that I stay nearby, I can ask for a job here on Xpashta."

She was silent, her teeth denting her lower lip. Her gaze met his. "As much as I would love to have you here all the time, I'm not going to ask you to change your job, or anything about you. I would imagine that every job is important to your people, and you were selected for yours for a reason. I'm not selfish enough to have you give it up."

Tark ran his fingers through her hair. She really was the perfect mate. As much as he hated all that she'd endured since leaving her planet, he was glad that she was here with him. If he hadn't found her sister lying in the alley, he would have never known about Suki, and he would have missed out on having the sweetest of mates.

"What will I do while you're gone?" she asked. "Is there some way I could help on Xpashta?"

"None of the females have a job. Shaylee is the closest, I suppose. She asked to create small gardens, and she's rather good at it. Maybe you could help her, if you like working with plants."

Suki nodded. "I don't really have any skills that would do much good here. Not unless you plan to open a brothel on your world."

He tightened his arm around her, then loosened his grip so he wouldn't harm her. "You will never do that again. You're free, Suki. It's why I wanted you to wait until we arrived before you chose your mate. You could have had anyone here, and now you're stuck with me, the least desirable cyborg on our world."

She leaned up and peered down at him. "I think you're sexy, and I like how big you are. Being with you makes me feel safe because I know that no one would ever get past you to hurt me ever again."

"Any who dared to try would die a slow and painful death," he vowed.

Tark narrowed his eyes, feeling another cyborg trying to communicate. He allowed the transmission to come through, surprised it was Querrill.

The Mystic7 *is landing soon. We need you and your new mate to come on board.*

Tark tried to contain his snort. Not likely. He wasn't about to put Suki in danger.

Why do you need my mate? And how did you even know I have one?

Querrill responded immediately. *Everyone knows. The Commanders notified everyone, including where and how you found her. There are others, Tark, other females suffering and in need of rescuing. We need your mate to convince them we mean no harm, and to come to Xpashta with us.*

Tark didn't like the idea of other females suffering as his Suki had, but he also didn't want to endanger his mate. He'd only just found her. What if something went horribly wrong on the mission? What if a slaver snatched her and he couldn't find her again? What if someone offered her a way back to Earth and she decided to take it, changing her mind about living with a beast such as him?

"What's wrong?" Suki asked.

"It's the medic on another ship, the *Mystic7*. They've found other females in a situation like yours. They want the both of us to board the ship and go with him in an effort to rescue the females and bring them here," Tark said.

"When do we leave?" she asked.

"We aren't. I'm not putting your life in jeopardy, Suki. That kind of mission is far too dangerous for you."

"Tark, please don't ask me to sit here where it's safe while other women are hurting and being used. I wouldn't be able to live with myself if I could have helped put a stop to it. They'll be scared, thinking your people are just as evil as the other aliens they've met. Please. Let me help," she begged.

He closed his eyes and tried to come up with reasons she should remain home. When his gaze locked with hers, he knew that he couldn't deny her request. If she wanted to help the other females, then he would let her, but he would remain by her side the entire time. No one would hurt his Suki, not ever again.

"Very well. I'll let Querrill know that we'll board the *Mystic7* when it arrives on Xpashta. You'll need to pack some clothes, and we should probably select some garments for any females we rescue. Since you all come in different shapes and sizes, stretchy things that would fit anyone would be best."

She nodded.

My mate has agreed to help. We'll be ready when the Mystic7 *arrives. We're bringing clothing for any females you take on board.*

He received a confirmation and landing time from Querrill, then rose from the bed to begin preparing. He and Suki rinsed off in the cleansing unit and dressed before gathering the items they needed for the trip. Querrill hadn't stated where they were going, and Tark could only hope it wasn't one of the more lawless outposts.

Suki added four of her outfits to what Tark had set aside. While he shoved everything into his bag, she braided her hair and tied it off with a leather strip. He remembered Lathim buying pretty hair things for his mate and wished he had something nice like that to give Suki. He'd have to look for more shiny things to gift her while they were at a trading post. Once he'd finished packing, they grabbed an empty bag and went back to the storage area, selecting half a dozen things for any women they might be able to rescue.

The *Mystic7* landed on schedule and Tark led Suki up the ramp, pausing in the cargo area when he saw eight bunks set up and only a small handful of crates. Normally, the vessel's cargo hold would be full to bursting with items for their world. It seemed they'd abandoned their mission at some point and begun searching for females, not that he couldn't understand. Finding females was crucial to their people.

Querrill met them in the corridor just outside the cargo area. He smiled when he saw Suki, but kept his distance.

"Welcome aboard the *Mystic7*," Querrill said.

"Suki, this is Querrill. He's the medic onboard," Tark said.

Suki gave the cyborg a bashful smile and a little

wave.

"I have quarters set up for you," Querrill said. "Lathim has opted to stay home with his mate for the past few missions, so Milore is the captain for this trip."

"Who else is on board?" Tark asked.

"Zorlok, Sanz, Pendrik, and Norkov. Warver will be joining us as well," Querrill said.

"And the beds in the cargo hold?" Tark asked. "Who are those for? Surely you aren't going to put the rescued females in there!"

"Only if an overflow area is required. We know of at least three human females at the floating brothel near Klaxion Prime. Zorlok and Sanz have agreed to share quarters, and we've placed two extra beds in Zorlok's quarters for the females. If there are more than that we can rescue, the overflow area will be needed. Pendrik and Norkov are also sharing a space so that you and Suki may have a room," Querrill said.

"Just how many rooms are there?" Suki asked.

"Six, which means we really don't have any to spare. When Lathim found Maggie, he claimed her immediately, but if he hadn't there wouldn't have been a place for her to stay unless someone gave up their quarters," Querrill said.

"This ship is far too large for only six rooms," Tark said, his eyebrow lifted.

"We have the med bay, the galley, command center, weapons hold, cargo hold, two supply rooms, and a few rooms that aren't in good enough shape to be turned into sleeping quarters. They're a work in progress," Querrill said. "Follow me and I'll show you to your quarters while you're onboard."

Tark grasped Suki's hand and they followed the medic down the corridor. Querrill pushed open a door, motioned them inside, then made himself scarce.

Tark put their things away before pulling Suki into his arms. She melted against him. If he lost her, if anything bad happened because she'd joined him on this mission, he would never forgive himself. The most precious thing to him was pressed against his body, and if he lost her, he knew he would lose his will to live.

"My mate," he said softly, tightening his hold on her. There was much he wanted to say to her, and yet he couldn't find the words. He only hoped she knew how much he needed her, wanted her, and how lucky he felt to have her in his life.

Since he didn't know how to tell her, he decided to show her. Tark stripped both himself and his mate quickly, then pinned her to the wall. The heat in her gaze was enough to tell him that she liked it. Her legs wound around his waist and his cock brushed against her slit. She was wet, but not wet enough for his liking. Tark reached between them and rubbed the little nub at the top of her pussy. Suki reached up and cupped her breasts, rolling her nipples between her fingers. Tark's cock jerked in response to the erotic sight and he pinched down on the little bud. Suki's body tensed and she made a keening sound as her pussy got incredibly wet.

Satisfied that he wouldn't hurt her, Tark adjusted his stance, lined up his cock, and sank into his mate. A groan tore from his throat and he fought to keep his eyes opened, his gaze locked on hers. Suki placed her hands on his shoulders and held on. Every drive of his cock made her cry out and beg for more.

"Don't stop," she begged. "Harder."

Tark felt his balls draw up and he gave her exactly what she'd asked for, slamming into her again and again. Her cries filled the air and made him feel downright primitive. He'd not liked the idea of fucking his mate, the term seeming too harsh, but that's exactly what he was doing. Fucking her. Giving her every inch of his cock, as hard and as deep as he could.

When she came, screaming out his name, Tark thrust a few more times, then filled his mate with his release. At first, he worried he might have hurt her, that he'd been too rough, but the smile she gave him said he'd done everything just right. Tark swelled with pride over pleasing his mate, and as she wiggled against him, other parts of him got bigger too. Before she'd even had a chance to come down from her orgasm high, he was taking her again. No matter how many times he buried his cock in her pussy, he'd never get enough of her.

Chapter Six

Suki wouldn't admit that she was nervous and more than a little scared. She might have been safer at home, but knowing there were other women out there, suffering and possibly having lost hope, she knew that she needed to help in any way possible. Before Tark had found her, Suki had thought she would die in that brothel. The only thing that had kept her going was knowing that Yoko was there too. She couldn't leave her sister.

Her heart still ached when she thought of Yoko. Her sister had used the last of her energy to ensure that Tark would come save her. Yoko hadn't deserved to die such a horrible death, no one did, and Suki still felt like it was her fault they'd been captured. Yoko had had had such a bright future, and now she was gone. Tears misted her eyes when she thought about never getting to hug her sister again, never getting to talk about boys or laugh over stupid things. After they'd been sold and put into service, she'd doubted they would ever see their home again, but some small part of her had hoped they would find a way to escape.

Now Suki was the only one free, and Yoko had died. Thankfully, Tark had been there and poor Yoko hadn't been alone at the end. She'd gotten to see the cyborg's kind eyes. If only Tark could have saved both of them! Suki knew that Yoko that would have loved Xpashta, and possibly even found a cyborg of her own. Maybe Rorwick would have liked Yoko. She still felt bad that Jillian had left, leaving the cyborg looking broken and defeated. If he was a friend of Tark's, then Suki had no doubt that he was honorable and would be kind to whatever female he claimed. Her mate wouldn't be friends with someone who would harm a female.

Suki stared at the door to their quarters, her hands trembling and her heart pounding. She'd been assured that it was safe to move freely on board, that she was protected. They'd been on board for two days and so far, she hadn't left their room without Tark by her side. No one had said or done anything to offend her, or that made her feel threatened. Tark had told her that his people were now her people. It had been so long since she'd had anyone other than Yoko, it felt strange to depend on other people and she found it hard to trust other aliens after all that had happened to her.

Squaring her shoulders, Suki approached the door and when it slid open, she stepped into the corridor. Looking one way then the other, she saw that she was completely alone. She made her way toward the front of the ship in hopes she'd find Tark along the way. He had left this morning before her, or what she assumed to be morning, and she had no idea where he would be. A few cyborgs smiled at her as she passed, but none made a move to get closer to her. Suki breathed a little easier and kept up her search for Tark.

"Good morning, Suki," Querrill said as she passed the med bay.

"Good morning," she said, then frowned. "But how do you know it's morning? You don't wear watches and all you can see outside is open space."

He smiled faintly. "Cyborg, remember? Consider it a perk. Besides, once you're used to being out in space, you become in tune with the cycle of a day, even when there aren't suns or moons."

She nodded. It had never happened for her, that attunement to the day, but then she wasn't a super soldier alien. She peered into the med bay, but still didn't see her mate.

"Looking for Tark?" Querrill asked.

"Yes. Have you seen him?"

The cyborg hesitated.

"What? Is something wrong with Tark?" she asked, feeling panic well inside her again.

"Not exactly, but he isn't on board right now," Querrill said.

"Not on…" She blinked. "Where is he?"

"They infiltrated the brothel. He's part of the crew searching for the human females. While it's not run by the same male who held you captive, the proprietor is just as nasty. The females aren't treated well. I've put out a call to a few other races in search of mates in hopes they may come rescue more of the workers."

"But Tark is fine, right? He'll be back?" she asked.

"Any mission is dangerous, Suki. Tark will do his best to come back to you safely, but I won't lie to you and guarantee that he'll come back."

She bit her lip and gave him a nod, then moved further down the corridor. She was nearing the bridge when alarms started blaring. Suki pressed herself to the wall and stared, wide-eyed, not knowing what it meant or where she should go. Booted steps ran toward her and she turned in time to see Norkov rushing in her direction. He didn't stop, didn't hesitate, just scooped her up as he ran. When they reached the command center, he deposited her onto a chair and sealed the room.

"What's going on?" she asked. "Norkov, why are the alarms going off?"

"Breach," he said. "The bastard who owns this place had security and we didn't detect them. Must have camouflaged their heat readouts somehow."

"And the men who went into the brothel?" she asked.

"I don't know, Suki. I lost communication with them seconds before the alarms went off. I'm glad I found you quickly. If you'd been in your quarters, it would have been much harder to reach you in time."

"Wh-what do you mean you lost communications? Are they..." She swallowed hard. "Are they dead?"

"No." He frowned. "I don't think so. It's probably a safety precaution. Or maybe the signal was scrambled by the owner of the brothel. If he has a security team, he likely has other measures in place. We underestimated him."

There was noise outside the door -- it sounded like blasts of some sort. Norkov grimaced and turned to the controls, tapping on the keys until a view of the area outside the sealed door appeared on the screen. Large orange aliens with multiple arms and bald heads were trying to open the door while one at the back fired on someone further down the hall.

"Can they get in here?" she asked.

"I'm not sure. They shouldn't be able to, but the doors have never been tested against a Terok before. They're typically muscle for hire, but I've never seen one on this sector before," Norkov said.

Another sound went off, making Suki tense as Norkov started cursing. "A ship is docking on our other side and coming aboard. We could possibly fight off the Teroks, but it looks like four more life-forms just came on board."

"How many Teroks are there? Just the ones we can see?"

"The four we can see plus three others. Wait."

Norkov narrowed his eyes as he stared at something she couldn't interpret. A bunch of dots moving on the screen made no sense to her, but the cyborg seemed to know what it meant. "The beings from the ship are attacking the Teroks. They're helping us."

He sounded a little dumbfounded, which didn't make Suki feel any better about the situation. Were they helping because they were good, or were they just wanting the ship to themselves? When one of them came into view on the large screen she gasped. He looked like the cyborgs except his hair was black and his skin was a deeper shade of purple, and she didn't see any cybernetic parts.

"A Zelthranite?" Norkov asked, his eyes going wide. "We were told they were extinct."

"What's a Zelthranite?" she asked.

"Our ancestors. Or part of them. My world, the one we came from before Xpashta, once held a life form that was pure white with blue hair. A ship of Zelthranites crash-landed there and mated with the natives. Zelranians, my people, today are a paler shade than the Zelthranites and have blue hair. Only those who were part of the Cy-Con program have white hair," Norkov said. "I've never studied the inside of a Zelthranite so I'm uncertain if we have the same internal organs. In looks, we're very similar aside from our coloring. For a while, we heard rumors of Zelthranites in another galaxy, then our government told us they were extinct. It seems they lied about yet another thing."

The Zelthranite was joined by another like him, and they took out the Teroks outside the door. Norkov paused a moment, then pressed the button to unlock the doors. He stepped out to greet the Zelthranites and Suki hovered in the doorway, wanting to see and hear everything without being in the middle of it. Unknown aliens, ancestors or not, still made her nervous. She was still adjusting to the cyborgs and she'd been with them for days.

The Zelthranite who seemed to be in charge, cocked his head as he studied Norkov, and then two more of his people joined them.

"I've heard rumors of cyborgs," the leader said. "Never met one."

"I was part of the Zelranian Cy-Con program," Norkov said, "as were all of my shipmates."

The leader's eyes narrowed as he studied Norkov more intensely.

"I'm Ryx. Are there others like you inside the brothel? We only detected three life-forms on board, aside from the Teroks. You and your female, and the med tech."

"Suki isn't mine," Norkov said. At the gleam in Ryx's eyes, he quickly amended his statement. "But she is mated to my crewmate, Tark, who is inside the brothel. We heard of human females inside and came to rescue them."

"And return them to Earth?" Ryx asked. "Or do you hold them hostage and force-mate them?"

Suki gasped and felt the blood drain from her face. "No! They would never force themselves on a woman! I don't care if you did save us. Don't you ever speak of them like that again!"

Ryx's lips twitched in amusement. "I see. Very well, fierce female. I apologize for offending you."

"We don't know how to reach Earth," Norkov admitted. "We were going to take the females to our planet. Only three of our males are mated and we hoped they might bond with someone. But we would never force them to choose a male. They would be free and their every need would be met."

"Every need but going home?" Ryx asked, his eyebrow raised. "Earth isn't difficult to find."

Suki blinked. "You're a Terran, aren't you? But Norkov called you a Zelthranite."

"To humans, we are Terrans. We hoped to appear less threatening if we used a term familiar to your people. Anyone who mates with us is told the truth," Ryx said.

"They're the Terrans you mentioned that had a Bride program on Earth?" Norkov asked, turning to face her. "You're certain?"

She nodded.

"Our people stopped birthing females," Ryx said. "We made an arrangement with Earth's government. We pay the females who consider mating with one of our kind. They're paid a fee, then travel to our world at no cost, and if they don't find a match within a certain amount of time, they're sent home. They keep the money. There's an application process."

"Could the cyborgs join the program?" Suki asked. "If they're part Zelthranite, it makes them your people too, doesn't it?"

Ryx didn't say anything for a moment. "It's something to discuss with the council. I'll bring it up to Chief Councilor Borgoz at the first opportunity. How would we reach your people?"

"We're on Xpashta," Norkov said. "One of our Commanders is in the brothel. He joined the mission, even though the Commanders typically stay on our world. You could always speak with him."

"Then let's get your cyborgs back to your ship," Ryx said, turning away.

Norkov looked down at Suki and she could tell he was about to tell her to stay behind. She shook her head and straightened her spine.

"I'm not staying here while you go after Tark," she said. "He's my mate and I should be there in case he's hurt. He saved me, and now it's my turn to help him."

Ryx snorted and muttered something about females not knowing their place. Suki narrowed her eyes at him.

"My name is Malin. I'm a crew member of the *Pryxus* and I would be honored to help keep an eye on your human female," said one of the Zelthranites, stepping forward. "My mate is no longer living, but I know she would want me to protect one of her fellow humans."

"You were mated to a human?" Suki asked, moving closer to him.

"Yes. She was one of the first in the Bride Program with Earth. Such a sweet female, but very headstrong. She insisted on accompanying me on a mission. It didn't end well and she perished," Malin said.

"I'm so sorry," Suki said, reaching a hand toward him.

He gripped her hand a moment before releasing her. "Thank you."

"This is Suki," Norkov said. "I'm Norkov, and the medic you saved is Querrill. We appreciate your assistance."

"Let's go save your mate," Malin said to Suki.

"If she gets captured, Tark will tear you apart," Norkov muttered. "She should remain on board."

"Not dealt with many human females, have you?" Malin asked in amusement. "Telling them what to do never works in your favor. I'll risk the wrath of your Tark if it gives her peace of mind to search for her mate. My Winnie was the same. So fierce and loyal."

Malin stuck by Suki's side as they left the *Mystic7* and entered the brothel. The first thing she noticed was blood, or what appeared to be blood. It was spattered across the walls and soaking into the carpeted floors, in a variety of colors. Her hand went to her mouth to fight back the bile. Malin helped her through the corridors and when they came to a downed cyborg, she openly sobbed. It wasn't Tark or the Commander.

"Sanz," Norkov said softly, kneeling beside him. "He's alive, but barely."

"Your Querrill was damaged and may not be able to heal him. There's a med pod on our ship, if you think it would work on a cyborg," Ryx said.

"I know Sanz would prefer the risk of it not working to dying," Norkov said.

"I'll take him," one of the Zelthranites said.

"Thank you, Zaryl," said Ryx.

The Zelthranite lifted the cyborg without issue and carried him back in the direction of the ship. The floating brothel shifted under their feet and Suki grabbed onto Malin for support. He kept her from falling into the gore on the floor and walls. Several doors opened and frightened females peered out. One was human, and Ryx quickly pulled her from the room, passing her to Malin. She gave Suki a fearful look, but she tried to assure the woman she was safe.

"They won't hurt you," Suki told her. "My name's Suki and I'm mated to one of the cyborgs."

"Rayne," she said.

"They're here to save you," Suki said.

Two more human females were found, and they hovered in the back near Suki and Malin. It would be smart to get them out of the brothel, but Suki refused to leave without Tark, and Malin refused to leave without Suki. They neared the back of the brothel where the whimpers and cries of women could be heard, along with a deeper voice that Suki instantly recognized.

"Tark!" she cried, trying to rush forward.

"No!" Norkov threw out an arm to hold her back. "We don't know the situation in that room, Suki. I can't permit you to enter and place yourself in danger."

Malin nodded. "He's right. Stay here while they secure the space."

The cyborgs and Zelthranites entered the room and Suki cried out as she heard the blasts of their weapons, fearing that her mate would die. She clung to Malin until Ryx stepped into the hall and motioned her forward.

"Your male is injured, but he's alive," Ryx said. "We've contained the owner of the brothel."

Suki rushed past him, running straight for Tark. She was nearly there, when a hiss at such a pitch that it deafened her filled the air. Suki froze, clamping her hands over her ears and slammed her eyes shut, willing the horrible sound to go away. Her eyes flew open as she was yanked off balance.

"Such a pretty female," the hissing voice said. "If you wish her to live, you won't follow."

Suki stared at Tark, saw the determination in his eyes and knew he would come for her. She glanced at the alien holding her captive and wished she hadn't. Slime dripped from his face, the bulbous shape a grotesque green. The rest of his body was nearly too slender and covered in black leather. The claw-tipped hand held her tightly as he dragged her from her mate and through a section of the brothel she hadn't yet seen.

"Deprive me of my livelihood, ruin my females, kill my guards. I'll keep you as payment," the alien said in his hissing voice. "Start a new brothel far from here."

Suki wanted to fight, to scream, to do something... but she worried if she broke free, the alien would try to kill her. If she were alive, then at least there was a chance Tark could save her. She'd deal with whatever happened, survive at any cost.

As long as Tark was alive, and so was she, then there was hope.

Chapter Seven

"You permitted my mate to enter the brothel," Tark said, trying to contain his fury. Suki would have been safe if she hadn't left the *Mystic7*. Instead, Norkov and the Zelthranites had allowed her to leave the ship, and now she'd been taken. He'd spent the past few hours in a med pod on board the *Pryxus*, his wounds too severe to heal on their own. Minor things healed quickly, but the slaver had gotten the drop on him and done his best to kill Tark. Now they'd lost valuable time in getting to Suki.

"'Permitted' isn't the correct word," Norkov said. "She was determined to find you. The med pod on board our vessel couldn't handle the severity of your injuries. Placing you in the one on the *Pryxus* was our only hope. It was my suggestion we wait until you were healed to pursue your Suki. Two ships remaining together while keeping up with the slaver might have proven difficult. The *Pryxus* and *Mystic7* are different class vessels."

"Human females are not to be underestimated," Malin said. The Zelthranite smiled sadly. "My mate was the same as your Suki. It got her killed in the end, but I couldn't have contained her if I'd tried. Not without breaking her spirit."

"That's supposed to be comforting?" Tark asked. "I refuse to lose my mate, to let her die because none of you could restrain her. There's no way that slaver is going to let her go. He'll keep her, use her, and kill her if she disobeys. Or sell her to someone who's even worse than him."

Malin placed a hand on Tark's shoulder. "Your Suki is strong-willed. I don't know the circumstances by which she came to be so far from Earth, but I'm going to guess she was captured and sold. I know she wanted to help you and refused to stay behind when she thought you needed her. She has a fighting spirit and will hold on until you can reach her."

"Any news yet on the slaver?" Tark asked Pendrik.

"Whatever ship he used to leave was moving fast. Or it was before it vanished. It left this sector," Penrik said pointing to the screen, "and if I had to guess, hit a black hole. We're approaching the area now where the vessel disappeared. Hopefully, we can find your Suki from there."

"Are the Zelthranites still with us?" Tark asked.

Malin snorted. "Ryx give up the chance to fight some slaver scum? Not likely. He'll be stuck to your ass unless you move too slow. Then he'll pull ahead and lead the way. My crew will be with you all the way, which is why they left me on board the *Mystic7*. To give you the reassurance that you had aid in retrieving your female."

"I can't believe we found five human females at the brothel," Norkov said.

"Don't get too excited. Ryx didn't seem all that thrilled over the females going home with us," Tark said. "Since the Zelthranites have an agreement with Earth, he may insist on returning them to their world."

"You're technically part Zelthranite," Malin said. "I don't see why they couldn't be considered potential brides for your people, if they agree. And if you compensate their families."

"I've already touched base with the other Commanders on Xpashta," Warver said. "They're arranging housing for females and some sort of... what did Shaylee call it? Orientation to alien living. Yes, those were her words."

The ship came to a halt and Tark stared at the oddly colored patch of space, like it didn't quite belong. It didn't look the same as a black hole, but was similar enough to give him pause. "What is that?"

Everyone in the command center moved closer to the screen. Whatever it was, it certainly wasn't a black hole, not with the way the light around it flickered now and then. Pendrik punched in some buttons and a readout popped up. Tark's eyebrows rose as he looked over the words on the screen, certain he must be seeing things. Such a thing wasn't possible. Was it?

"We're being pulled in," Pendrik said. "There's a magnetic force drawing us closer."

"Fuck," Malin said. "It's a MECO. I know of them, but haven't seen one. Similar to a black hole and yet not."

"Everyone hold on," Warver said. "The ship is picking up speed. It looks like the Zelthranites are being pulled along in our wake."

Tark braced his feet. The ship shook and vibrated around them before spinning. The gravitational field on board went out, leaving them floating in the command center as the *Mystic7* rocketed forward, gaining momentum. It was hard to tell how much time passed before they were spit out on the other end, Tark and the others crashing to the metal floor as the gravity reactivated.

"Well that was fun," Malin said, then groaned as he sat up.

"The *Pryxus* came through as well," Pendrik said.

Tark pointed to a ship in the distance. "Is that the slaver?"

Pendrik tapped on the controls and then nodded. "Yes, that's the vessel we were tracking. But there's only one life form on board. Systems show it's not human."

Tark's heart rate elevated, the chips in his brain unable to regulate the organ when his mate was missing. He gripped the nearest seat and nearly ripped it in half. Where was his Suki? How had the slaver disposed of her so quickly if he appeared so close? From what he could see from the screen, there wasn't a planet within reach of their current location. Not one the slaver could have landed on, dumped his sweet Suki, then gained enough speed to have this much distance between their ships.

"Scanning the sector for humans," Pendrik said.

They waited what felt like several solar cycles. Eventually a readout appeared, indicating there was not only one human in close proximity, but over a dozen. No. Not all human. Part human? But human mixed with what and how had they obtained the females? Assuming they were human females. Since they'd strictly searched for human genetics, the system had only given them the information they wanted.

"Tourmalane is nearby," Malin said. "I've heard they suffer a similar problem as my people. No females. I wonder if your Suki was taken there?"

"Set a course for --" Tark was cut off.

"I'm already on it," Norkov said.

When they neared Tourmalane, Warver reached out to their royal family. After receiving permission to land, the *Mystic7* and *Pryxus* set down on the small planet. A handful of guards, along with Prince Vandir, greeted them. As Tark's feet sank into the soil, he tried to contain his aggression. If any of them had harmed his Suki, then he didn't care if he started an intergalactic war. They would all pay in blood.

The prince smiled. "Welcome to Tourmalane. My

father says you're looking for a human called Suki."

"Yes," Tark said. "My mate. She was abducted. The slaver who snatched her came this direction, and your world was the only showing a human readout."

Prince Vandir nodded. "Of course. We do have a few new additions to our world, all human. Perhaps your Suki is one of them. Come to the palace and I'll arrange for the females to be gathered in a central location."

Think it's a trap? Tark asked Pendrik.

Might be. Only one way to find out.

Tark nodded. *If I don't make it, get Suki home. She's all that matters.*

They followed Prince Vandir and the guards through the city walls and into the palace. King Razyr and Prince Drexyl were waiting as they stepped through the palace doors. At Drexyl's side was a petite human female. Not his Suki, but it explained at least one of the humans that appeared on the scan.

"What's this about a missing human female?" King Razyr asked.

"My mate, Suki, was taken," Tark said. He told the king about her capture and how they'd followed the slaver through a MECO.

"What does your Suki look like?" the female asked.

Drexyl placed an arm around her waist and drew her closer, but she merely smiled up at him.

"Forgive my husband," she said. "He's very protective. My name is Lucie. You're safe here, and so is your mate if she's among the women recently dropped off."

"Dropped off?" Warver asked.

"We often buy human female slaves when they come through this area," King Razyr said. "It provides

Jessica Coulter Smith   Cy-Con

them a safe place where they'll receive any care necessary, and gives them the option of finding a mate among our people. We purchased several today off three different vessels."

I only saw the one ship, Norkov said. Tark nodded. He too had only seen the one, but that didn't mean the others hadn't been cloaked. For that matter, there was no guarantee the ship they'd seen was the same slaver who had taken Suki.

"My Suki is small like you but much slimmer," Tark said. "Her hair is dark and long. Her eyes are shaped differently than yours."

"She's young?" Lucie asked. "Maybe late teens or early twenties?"

Tark nodded, not liking the reminder of their age gap. He hadn't brought it up since Suki didn't seem to care, but he knew she had to be at least twenty years younger than him. He'd been more concerned over his cybernetics scaring her off. His sweet Suki accepted him though, no matter how he looked.

"I believe your mate is here," Lucie said. "But she was injured. Follow me. If the woman isn't your Suki, we can gather the others."

Drexyl growled and narrowed his eyes, but Lucie merely patted his arm. "He's mated, Drexyl. Nothing will happen to me. What would you do if your roles were reversed?"

Drexyl released her and Tark followed her through the palace. They entered a large room with multiple med bays. As Tark drew closer to the only pod with a closed lid, he saw his Suki through the glass. He reached out, running his fingers over the surface.

"Your mate?" Lucie asked.

"Yes. What's wrong with her?"

"Healer," Lucie called. An older Tourmalane came over. "This is Suki's mate. Could you please tell him what you've discovered?"

The male nodded. "Your human female sustained several lacerations, some contusions, head trauma, the bones in her right hand were broken."

Tark stared at his mate, his heart feeling heavy. He'd failed her.

"She's also pregnant," Healer said.

Tark jerked his gaze to the older man. "Pregnant?"

The male nodded. "If you'll provide me with a blood sample, I'll be able to tell you if the child is yours."

Tark held out his non-metal arm. He didn't doubt the child was his, but he wasn't going to argue with Healer. Giving a little blood was easier than getting angry over the assumption his mate could be pregnant by anyone else. Healer took a small sample of blood, then inserted it into the pod that held Suki. He pressed a few buttons and nodded as he read the screen. As Tark had never been anywhere near Tourmalane before, he didn't have the proper downloads to read the language, even though his translator worked well when speaking to them.

"The baby is yours," Healer said.

"Will she be all right?" Tark asked, pressing a palm to the med pod again.

"The pod has healed everything but the head trauma. That will take some time. I would advise that you not move her at this moment. Give her a few days."

"What sort of trauma?" Tark asked.

"There was bleeding on her brain. It also caused her brain to swell. She hasn't been here long enough to properly heal."

Tark frowned, not understanding how the slaver had gotten such a big lead on them. They'd gone into the MECO shortly after the other vessel. What had happened while they were in there? Was there a time lapse of some sort?

"Your Suki has been here for nearly half a day," Lucie said.

"That's impossible," Tark said. "We were right behind the slave vessel that took her. Followed him into a MECO that dropped us not far from your world."

Lucie looked at Healer, who only shrugged.

"I'm a physician, not that type of scientist," the male said. "It sounds like you were in the MECO longer than you thought. If it's similar to a black hole, it can be disorienting, from what I've heard. Never experienced it myself."

"We'll of course provide rooms for you and your crew," Lucie said. "You're welcome to stay until your Suki is well enough to travel."

"We have other females on board," Tark said. "Are they in danger of your males trying to take them? My world only has three mated pairs. Possibly four if the newest pairing decide to officially become mates. We're in desperate need of females and Earth seems to be the most compatible to our species."

Lucie pursed her lips and tipped her head to the side. "I can't make a promise that your women will want to return with you. Tourmalane is very beautiful and the males are extremely attentive. If they come to the palace, I can assure you that no harm will come to them, but if they wish to stay when it's time for you to return home, I don't believe my husband or his brothers will permit you to take them."

Tark glanced at Suki again. He knew she would return with him. Could he force the others to go as well? Would it be fair if they could truly be happy here? He knew his people were desperate for mates, but he never wanted to cause emotional or physical harm to a female. He couldn't say that his crew would agree, or that the Zelthranites wouldn't put up a fight.

"I won't force them to leave if they don't wish to, but I can't vouch for the others with me. I don't control their actions."

She nodded. "Fair enough."

He had a feeling he hadn't heard the last of it. No way she would agree so readily. If Lucie was half as compassionate as his Suki, then she'd never let those females leave if they preferred to remain here. There would be others, now that they knew how to find them, but it didn't mean the crew of the *Mystic7* or the Commander who had accompanied them would be so willing to let those females go.

"Commander Warver is in charge of my crew, and Ryx is in charge of the Zelthranites. You will need their promise," Tark said, not wanting any confusion later.

"My Drexyl will handle it," Lucie said with a broad smile.

"How many mated males do you have on Tourmalane?" he asked.

"You mean mated to humans?" she asked.

He nodded.

"Two, myself included, are in the royal family. We've managed to bring nearly one dozen human females here over the years. Most have paired with someone, but not all." She paused. "You know. Tourmalanes only have one true mate and can't have children with anyone else. Would you be willing to take the females who didn't bond with anyone here? Maybe in exchange for an equal number of females on your ship? They would have to agree, of course."

"It seems like a reasonable request," Tark said.

Lucie gave him another moment with his mate before leading him to a rather large chamber.

"This is in the royal wing," she said. "Your mate will need a quiet place to recover once she's able to leave the med pod. This particular hall is for my unmated brother-in-law, Vandir. The other two hallways have children and might be too noisy for Suki."

"Prince Vandir won't mind the intrusion?" he asked.

"No. I'll be sure to let him know you're here and why. The others will be placed in guest quarters on a different level. Same for the females. I will likely put them in rooms near the ones who arrived earlier today."

"Thank you for your generosity, Princess Lucie."

She smiled. "I'm just glad that you seem to care for your Suki as much as the Tourmalanes love their mates. If the others of your crew and the other ship are the same, then we shouldn't have any problems while you're here."

Tark couldn't vouch for the others, especially the Zelthranites, but he would do whatever was asked of him if Healer would make Suki well again. If she died, along with their unborn child, then Tark would no longer have a reason to live. Suki had been part of his life for such a short time, and yet she meant everything to him. He would rather Healer save her than the baby, if it came to that.

Lucie left him and Tark moved to the window, looking out over the palace grounds. Tourmalane was a beautiful place. While he had no doubt that Suki would want to remain with him, he did wonder if she would prefer to live somewhere like this. Xpashta had its own charms, but it wasn't quite as beautiful as this world. He scrubbed a hand down his face, his fingers rasping against the whiskers on his jaw. There was an ache in his chest in the vicinity of his heart. He rubbed at it, wondering if it was a mild version of the pain he would feel without her in his life. She had to live, her and the child.

Tark had never cared about a higher power, but right now he would beg every known god and goddess in all the universes for mercy if they would make Suki well again, and keep her by his side. She was his everything, and he was nothing without her.

Chapter Eight

Suki struggled to open her eyes. Every time her lids parted even a little, a bright light nearly blinded her and sent shards of pain through her head. It almost felt like someone had been pounding her brain with a sledgehammer. She lifted her arm to block the worst of it and groaned from the effort. What was wrong with her? It was like a ton of rocks were weighing her down, her movements sluggish and taking more effort than usual. Her lips were dry, her mouth having that cottony feeling people had with a hangover.

"You're awake," a male voice said. One she didn't recognize. Panic filled her, her heart rate spiking, and her entire body locking up tight. Who was that? Where was she?

Her mind scrambled, trying to remember. Everything started to come back to her. The brothel. The alien taking her as a hostage. Then being attacked by that same alien before being discarded on a strange world. She'd lost consciousness as her body had hit the ground, having been shoved from the ship without the vessel even fully landing. She didn't understand what had happened or why. Suki tried opening her eyes again, focusing on a blurry blue alien. No, the alien wasn't blurry. Her vision was. She blinked a few more times as everything sharpened.

"Where am I?" she asked.

"Tourmalane. I'm the Healer and serve the royal family, though most simply call me Healer. Princess Lucie has been quite worried about you. I'll notify her and your mate that you've woken."

Suki jolted. "Mate? Tark is here?"

Or had they mated her to someone else? Her stomach clenched and acid burned her throat at the thought of being given to some random male she'd never met before. Never seeing Tark again made her chest ache and she rubbed at the spot.

"Your Tark is here," Healer confirmed. "Please rest while I get Princess Lucie and your mate. You've suffered much trauma."

Suki attempted to lie back and relax, but it wasn't going to happen. Not until she saw for herself that Tark was really here. She didn't know how he'd found her, but she was grateful. When the alien had taken her, using her as his hostage, she'd feared she'd never see her sexy, sweet cyborg ever again. As the slaver had beaten her, her only thought had been *please let me live to be with Tark again*. If he was here, then someone had heard her prayers and answered them.

A human woman came into the room, smiling, and Suki studied her. She didn't remember seeing her at the brothel earlier. In fact, she didn't remember ever having seen the woman before. As if her thoughts had been heard, the woman held out a hand.

"I'm Lucie. Or Princess Lucie as they call me around here. I'm married to Prince Drexyl of Tourmalane."

Suki shook her hand hesitantly. "But you're human. Aren't you?"

Lucie nodded. "Yes. I was a slave on Keshpa. When my owner fled his planet, Drexyl boarded the ship and claimed me as his."

"And you're happy?" I asked.

"Very. He's amazing, and I love him so much. I didn't just gain a mate, but an entire family. Drexyl has a father and two brothers, who try to coddle me and I let them sometimes. We also have kids." Lucie's gaze dropped to Suki's belly.

Suki placed her hand on her abdomen and

looked down, wondering why Lucie was staring at her like that. Was something wrong? Had the slaver damaged her so much, he'd taken away her ability to have children? It hardly seemed fair, after Tark had given her the option of reversing her sterilization. What if the damage couldn't be undone this time? Would her cyborg still want her?

"Suki!"

Her head jerked up and she smiled as Tark ran into the room, not stopping until he knelt beside the pod she was lying inside. Suki couldn't stop the tears that slipped down her cheeks as she struggled to get out of the pod. Tark lifted her into his arms and held her tightly. She winced at the pain but wouldn't release him regardless of the discomfort. She fisted his hair and buried her face against his neck, breathing in his scent.

"You came for me," she said softly.

"Of course I did. I'm sorry you were injured, my sweet mate. I failed you."

She shook her head. "No, you didn't. I insisted on going, and when I thought you were hurt, I had to get to you. I'll never forget how you looked when I walked into that room." Tears gathered in her eyes. "It's no one's fault but mine."

"No," Lucie said. "It's the fault of the asshole who hurt you. Not yours. Not your mate's. Blame the alien responsible for this mess. The idiot demanded credits for you, which my mate gladly paid in order to free a human female, then just dumped you off his ship without landing. If Drexyl hadn't already transferred the credits, he never would have paid the asshole."

"She's correct," Healer said. "Were you injured, cyborg? You never mentioned that you needed to be healed."

"I'm fine," Tark said. "I was healed before I arrived here. It's why the slaver was able to get away from us so quickly. Myself and another cyborg had to be placed in med pods before we could track the slaver. My injuries took longer to heal and my cyborg brothers were hesitant to go after Suki while I was on board another vessel."

"Are the others here too? And the women we rescued?" Suki asked.

"Yes." Tark hesitated. "I'm not certain the females will be leaving with us. One bonded to a Tourmalane. Negotiations are in place for more human females to come to Xpashta, ones here who haven't bonded with anyone during their stay. And the Zelthranites are discussing the possibility of brides being offered to my people if they don't match with someone from their world. Since we're half-Zelthranite, their council feels it would be an easy enough agreement to make with your Earth."

Suki smiled. "It will be nice to have more women on Xpashta. When can we go home?"

"After you've rested more," Healer said. "You have more than yourself to consider right now."

Suki blinked at him. "What's that mean?"

Tark cleared his throat, looking pleased. "You're expecting our first child. I worried for a bit that you wouldn't survive, or the child wouldn't. If it came down to it, I wanted them to save you no matter the cost, but it seems you're both doing well."

"How long have I been out?" Suki asked.

"Nearly a week," Lucie said. "You had swelling and bleeding on your brain. The pod did as much as it could, but the rest had to heal over time."

"May I take my mate to our quarters?" Tark asked.

Healer nodded. "I recommend staying on Tourmalane another few days, just in case. I'll give her some vitamins to boost her system during your stay, and hopefully it will prepare her for the journey back to your world. I don't recommend going through the MECO again."

"What's a MECO?" Suki asked.

"You don't want to know," Lucie said. "But I've heard they're unpredictable at best."

"It would take years to reach our world without the MECO," Tark pointed out.

Lucie bit her lip and shifted from foot to foot. It was obvious she wanted to say something, but wasn't sure if she should. Suki was curious what was on the woman's mind. Was she about to suggest they *shouldn't* return to Xpashta? She'd only been there a short while before getting on a ship again, but Suki had liked the small planet and the home Tark had created.

"Perhaps discuss this later," Healer suggested. "Your mate will likely want food and some fresh air. I believe your quarters are in the royal hall and have a balcony that overlooks the grounds. I'll make sure furniture is placed out there so she can be comfortable."

Tark carried Suki out of the room, away from Healer and Lucie, and down many twisting hallways and up several staircases. She'd never been such a large place before. Even when she'd "visited" other royal families, they'd never lived in a place this grand. She was curious how large the family was that they needed so much space. Would she get to meet more of their mates? Were they human too?

The room Tark entered made Suki's jaw drop. It was the most beautiful suite she'd ever seen, and she could hardly believe it was theirs until they returned home. He eased her down onto the bed, the cover made of something soft and velvety. Suki ran her hands over the fabric and sighed in pleasure.

"You like it?" Tark asked, nodding to the cover.

"It's nice."

"I can ask about purchasing one before we leave, so you can have one at home."

Suki smiled and patted the bed. Tark hesitated only a moment before carefully joining her. She curled against his side, resting her head on his chest. Placing a hand over her belly, she marveled over the fact they'd created a life together. She'd be a mother, and that scared her beyond belief, but she had no doubt that Tark would be amazing. He was so kind and gentle with her that she knew he'd be the same with any children he might have.

Tark pressed a kiss to the top of her head and held her close. It was comforting, having his arm around her. If they could stay like this for a while, she'd be content. It didn't feel like they'd lost a week of time together, but the worry she'd seen in his eyes was enough proof. Not to mention, there wasn't so much as a bump or bruise on her. Although, the med pod at the clinic Tark had taken her to the night he'd saved her had healed her immediately. Her head injury must have been rather severe if the one here couldn't do the same. Or were the pods different depending on the planet? Different technology?

"How are the others?" Suki asked. "Are the women adjusting?"

"They're grateful to be free. Aside from the one who bonded to a Tourmalane warrior, the others seem content. I'm not certain if they'll want to stay here or move on. The Zelthranites have also offered to either take them to Zelthrane-3 or return them to Earth. They have a lot of options, and none seem overly taken with my cyborg brothers."

"Maybe they just need to get to know them better," Suki suggested.

"Perhaps. Norkov is rather taken with one of them, but he hasn't been obvious about it. I think he feels she'd be better off here, or back on Earth. He would never force her to go home with him."

"That's because you're all so wonderful," Suki said with a smile. "If she doesn't pick him, then she's an idiot. Norkov was really sweet and tried to keep me calm when you entered the brothel. I think he'd make a good mate to the right woman."

"After you've eaten and rested, would you like to meet the women?" Tark asked. "Perhaps you could reassure them more even though I know Lucie and the other human princess have done their best. Neither are familiar with my people, and I think we scare the females the most."

"I'd like that," Suki said.

There was a knock at the door and Tark bade them to enter. Tourmalanes dressed in some sort of uniform entered. Two were carrying trays of food, and the others brought plush looking chairs and carried them out onto the balcony, along with a small table. Tark helped Suki rise from the bed and led her out to the balcony. After she was situated on one of the soft chair cushions, he went inside to retrieve food and put a plate in her lap. He left and returned again with one for himself. It was peaceful here, and the scenery was breathtaking. Suki could see why some of the women might want to stay.

She ate until she thought she might pop, then set her plate on the little table. Tark had practically inhaled his food. A few strange looking birds swooped in front of the balcony, then dropped down to a pond. Suki stretched her legs out and pointed her toes while reaching her arms over her head. Even though she'd been unconscious during her stay in the med pod, her body was tight from not moving much.

"Would you like a hot bath or shower?" Tark asked.

"Only if you join me," she said, smiling a little. "I woke up scared because you weren't there, and I'm not ready to be apart just yet."

His lips tipped down at the corners and he knelt in front of her, reaching for her hand. "Suki, you know I would never leave you. Not willingly. I'm sorry it frightened you, but they assured me that I would be called the moment you showed signs of waking."

"I'm not blaming you or trying to make you feel guilty. I was just trying to explain why I'm not ready to be left alone," she said. Suki reached out and cupped his cheek, his whiskers rasping against her palm. "The thought that I might never see you again made my heart hurt."

His gaze softened and Tark turned his face, placing a kiss in the center of her palm. "My sweet mate, I was ready to die with you if they couldn't heal you. Life wouldn't be worth living without you, but now I not only have you back in my arms, but we're going to have a little one as well."

Suki pressed a hand to her belly. "What if I'm a bad mother?"

"You won't be," Tark assured her. "My mate, you are kind and have a good heart. Any child would be lucky to have you as a mother."

Suki smiled and leaned forward, pressing her lips to Tark's. He seemed to always say the right things. If anyone was lucky, it was her. He was almost too perfect, but she wasn't going to let anyone else have him. For whatever reason, Tark wanted her, and Suki wasn't stupid enough to let him go. Men like him didn't come along but once in a lifetime.

"I'll prepare a bath for you," he said, "and if you'd like me to join you, then I will."

"And after that, we can find out what Princess Lucie meant when you discussed going home. If we can't go through the… whatever it was called, there has to be another way. I haven't had a home in a long time, and I won't give up my new one without a fight."

Tark kissed her. "We'll find a way."

He rose and left her sitting on the balcony. Suki closed her eyes, lifting her face toward the rays of the suns. The air smelled fragrant, and there was a slight breeze that ruffled her hair. Callused fingers brushed against her cheek and she opened her eyes. Tark gazed down at her tenderly.

"The bath is ready, my sweet mate."

She nodded, and he helped her stand. It would have been easier for him to carry her, but Tark merely placed his arm around her waist and allowed her to walk into the bathroom. She didn't feel like she was at full strength, but each moment she was awake, she felt better than the last. Her sexy cyborg helped her undress before removing his own clothing. He lifted her into his arms then stepped down into the sunken pool of water. The heat of it lapped at her skin as he submerged them and Suki sighed in bliss. As the water closed over her, she felt as if all her worries were melting away.

There was a gasp from the doorway and Suki jerked her head in that direction, her eyes going wide when she saw Lucie, a hand clapped over her mouth and her eyes rounded with horror.

"You're pregnant!" Lucie screeched. "You can't be in that hot water!"

"What? Why?" Suki asked.

"Really hot water isn't good for the baby," Lucie said.

Her words shot panic through Suki. She struggled to get up, but Tark held her tight. He glowered at the other woman.

"The baby she carries isn't fully human. What makes you so certain it will be harmed? Zelranians are strong, and so is our child."

"Maybe we shouldn't take a chance?" Suki asked. She didn't want to anger her mate, or make it sound like she was siding against him, but she didn't want to harm the baby either.

Lucie turned her back to them. "I'll wait in the other room. I came to see if you would be willing to join my husband, his brother, and two of the Zelthranites for a meeting. One of the other cyborgs is joining them as well."

Tark stood with Suki in his arms. Air blew across their skin, drying them, and he used his shirt to cover her. After pulling his pants on, they went into the bedroom to speak with Lucie. Suki was curious why they were all meeting, and if it had anything to do with them leaving to go home, but she knew her mate would tell her anything important. Suki tuned out most of what Tark and Lucie discussed as she found a change of clothing, then scurried back into the bathroom to change. When she was finished and had braided her hair, Tark was fully dressed and Lucie was no longer in the room.

"Should I go with you?" Suki asked.

Tark nodded. "If this pertains to your future as well, then yes. I won't decide anything without your input. However, if I feel your suggestions will put you in danger, then I may overrule you."

It seemed reasonable enough. Suki took his hand. In the hallway, Lucie was waiting for them. They followed her down the winding staircase and down so many corridors that Suki was lost after the second turn. They stepped into a room with a table that could easily seat forty large males. Both Tourmalane princes were there, as well as two Zelthranites, and Norkov. Tark took a seat next to his brother cyborg and pulled Suki onto his lap. She went willingly and leaned against him.

"I think it's time we discussed your options, and the other human females," Prince Drexyl said.

Chapter Nine

Tark's arm tightened around his mate as he stared at Prince Drexyl. The thought of never returning to Xpashta made his chest ache, but he would do whatever was necessary to keep his mate and child safe. They were his priority now.

"As I've mentioned previously," Prince Drexyl said, "we have quite a few human females here who haven't bonded with any of my males. If they haven't by now, they aren't going to. Unfortunately, the only way for my people to have children is if they are paired with their true mates. One of the females you brought with you has bonded with a Tourmalane warrior already. I'd like to make a suggestion."

Tark and Norkov nodded, and the Zelthranite, Ryx, narrowed his eyes but waved a hand for the prince to continue.

"The females who aren't bonded, those who were already here, can return with your people. Either of you," he said looking at both the cyborgs and Zelthranites. "However, my sympathies lie with the cyborgs. The Zelthranites have a sure way of getting females to their world since they have an agreement with Earth. The cyborgs are like my people and will die out if something doesn't change soon."

"So all the human females should go home with the cyborgs?" Ryx asked.

"If that's what they want," Prince Drexyl said. "For those who wish to return to their world, I understand that you have a way to make that happen."

Ryx nodded.

"Then I see no reason the females who want to return to Earth can't go with the Zelthranites. As for Tark and his mate... The MECO is too dangerous for a pregnant female, according to Healer. They're welcome to remain here, but I don't think either would be happy with that scenario," Prince Drexyl said.

"I've discussed the issue with my council," Ryx said. "They found records of our people who did indeed leave and never return. We hadn't realized that they'd crashed on Zelran or that they'd bonded with those already living on the world. Since the cyborgs' ancestors are half-Zelthranite, and they carry our DNA, we see no reason that Tark and Suki can't make their home on our world."

Suki opened her mouth to respond, but Ryx held up a hand. Tark wasn't certain what to think just yet. Leave his home?

"In exchange, Tark can lend his expertise as a warrior, but he can also pave the way for human females to find mates among the cyborgs. It seems there is a Keshpan on this world who is an inventor. He's willing to discuss the creation of a portal from Zelthrane-3 to Xpashta, similar to the technology on their ships, but it would need to be stronger to cover a much larger distance."

"You mean teleport?" Tark asked.

"Yes," Ryx said. "It wouldn't necessarily be safe for a pregnant female to teleport such a great distance, but those who wish to pair with a cyborg could make the journey. Or perhaps the cyborgs could come to our world for the pairing."

"But if there's a portal to Xpashta, why couldn't we go home after the baby is born?" Suki asked.

The other Zelthranite, Malin, cleared his throat. "It isn't that you wouldn't be able to, but perhaps that it would be better if you didn't. If his people only have two or three other mated pairs, then there won't be a lot of children on that world, or an educational system in place for them. Your child would benefit greatly from remaining on our world. We've been mating with the humans for years now, and have children ranging from infants to those in their early teens. Your child would have others to play with, and you would have a larger support system from the other mates."

Suki twisted so she could look at Tark, and he glanced at her. He could see the hesitation there, but he wasn't sure if she hesitated over asking him to never return to Xpashta and his people, or if she wanted to go back to his world. It was a big decision to make, and not one that could be made overnight, nor made lightly. He would hate for his children to bond with those on Zelthrane-3, then uproot them to go back to Xpashta in the future.

"Our world has quite a few of the creature comforts of your Earth," Malin said. "The human females who live there now have brought many of their customs with them, as well as made requests for some of your technology such as movies and music. Zelthrane-3 is a good blend of how things used to be on our world, and how things are now on your Earth. I think you would enjoy your time there, Suki, and there are many human females you could befriend."

"The females willing to go to Xpashta won't be harmed from the MECO?" Norkov asked. "As much as I would love to take them home with us, I don't want to endanger them."

"They'll be fine since they aren't expecting," Prince Lyros said, speaking for the first time. "I understand this is a difficult decision for all of you. We not only need to consider what's best for the unmated males, but also for the females. And in Tark's case, his mate and unborn child. We know it's a lot to take in, and much to think over. You're welcome at the palace and on our world for however long you'd like to stay."

Norkov looked at Tark. *If you wish to go with the Zelthranites, it not only sounds like a good opportunity for your mate, but for our people as well. I know you feel like you'd be abandoning us, but you'd be helping. If the human females aren't afraid of you, then they won't fear the rest of us.*

Tark didn't take offense to the words, knowing they were true. He was the scariest-looking of the cyborgs. As much as he wanted to see his home again, raise his children alongside the others on Xpashta, Norkov was right. He could do much good for his people by living among the Zelthranites, and his Suki would have more opportunities to make friends and have access to things from her home. He didn't know what a movie was, but he'd heard music at the different outposts. Perhaps not the same kind, but his people didn't dance so music wasn't part of his world. Though, if humans liked things like that... He glanced at Ryx.

"The technology you use to offer the human females things from their home, like music and whatever a movie is -- can be it shared with my people? Is there a way to bring those things to Xpashta so the mates there will be as comfortable as the ones on your world?" Tark asked.

Ryx nodded. "There is much we can share with your people."

"Are you really thinking of going with them?" Suki asked. "Where would we live? All our things are on Xpashta. The home you built, your clothing and personal items."

Tark's lips twitched. "What personal items? You saw my home, mate. It was rather plain."

"I like our home," she grumbled.

"I will make sure a home is provided for you," Ryx said. "If there isn't one ready, you may stay in the tower, which I've been told is like a human apartment building. There are some larger suites there, but if you prefer having a yard or garden, a home would be better."

"No one is living in Syl's old quarters," Malin said. "The lab was dismantled and moved elsewhere, but it would give them space for a growing family and it has a great view."

Ryx nodded, and they looked at Tark expectantly.

"Any place would be fine," Tark said. "As long as there's room for my mate and our child when it arrives. There are vaccines my people use, serums that prolong life and some that are essential for those with cybernetics. We need access to those things."

"The council has assured me that they will do whatever is necessary to make you and your mate safe, comfortable, and happy." Ryx shrugged a shoulder. "Obtaining the formulas and creating the serums shouldn't be an issue as long as your people are willing to share those secrets."

"I won't frighten your women and children?" Tark asked softly. "Most people scream when they see me, or run in fear. Suki is the only female to ever come to me willingly."

"You and your family will be welcomed," Malin said. "No one will fear you. Or at least they won't once they meet you and see that you mean them no harm. Some people fear that which is different, until they realize that inside we're mostly the same."

Tark nodded, feeling a little relieved.

"Then it's settled," Prince Lyros said. "Tark and Suki will return with the Zelthranites. The females here on Tourmalane who haven't bonded will be given the option of returning to Earth or finding a mate among the cyborgs. I'd say this meeting is adjourned."

Prince Drexyl snorted. "You just want to get back to Roux."

Prince Lyros grinned. "Yes, I do. And don't act like you aren't just as anxious to return to Lucie."

Malin looked away, but not before Tark saw the sadness enter his eyes. He'd had that once. The male had had a mate and lost her. Tark wouldn't be able to keep going without his Suki. He didn't know how the male managed, but it proved he was a strong warrior. Tark hoped that one day the male would find another mate and find peace. It hardly seemed fair the male had been given someone to love and accept him, only for her to be taken away.

"Once the females are sorted," Ryx said, "we'll be leaving for Zelthrane-3. There's a room you may share on board the *Pryxus*. Malin has offered to pair up with another crewmember so you may have his quarters. The females will be housed in another room, if any choose to return to Earth."

Tark eased Suki off his lap and stood.

I'll miss you, brother. He looked at Norkov and the cyborg gave him a sad smile.

If they get the portal up and running, perhaps I can come visit. I'm not sure the female I like wants anything to do with me, or that I'm suited for her. I want her to be happy, even if it's with another male. One of the females mentioned something about me being in the friend-zone, whatever that is. I may need help finding a mate.

Tark nodded.

"You did that mind-talking thing again, didn't you?" Suki asked.

"Sorry, mate."

"Will you be lonely on Zelthrane-3 since you won't be able to communicate like that with anyone there?" she asked.

Tark hesitated. He hadn't thought about that aspect of leaving everything behind, but it was true. He enjoyed being able to reach out and hear his fellow cyborgs. Not having that option would almost be like having a limb severed.

"Then perhaps two of you should come to Zelthrane-3 and assist with the mating negotiations so you won't be the only cyborg on our world," Malin said. "Since Norkov is unmated, perhaps he'll find his mate while he's there. We have new human females arriving all the time."

Norkov smiled broadly and Tark knew his friend would not only consider it, but already seemed excited about the idea. It would be nice to have another cyborg present. While he might share genetic markers with the Zelthranites, they weren't truly family. Not like Norkov. He'd known the other cyborg since before the Cy-Con program was started. Having Norkov by his side would definitely ease the transition of living on another world.

"I accept," Norkov said.

Tark was glad that Norkov would be joining him. Not only so he'd have a familiar face, but things hadn't gone according to plan for his fellow cyborg. Norkov had joined many missions to attempt to save other human females and had hoped to gain a mate. Instead, most of the females had been dead when they arrived during his first mission, and the others were too badly damaged to ever be mated to someone. They'd been taken to a planet that was predominantly female and left in care of the people there. The female that Norkov seemed interested in out of those currently on Tourmalane didn't seem to return his favor.

"Suki, my mate and Lucie have both gathered some clothes for you. Whatever was placed in your room here at the palace, you may keep and take with you. I'm sure there will be more clothing options when you reach Zelthrane-3, but this way you won't be starting over completely," Prince Lyros said.

"Thank you," his mate said.

"I'm afraid we don't have anything in your size," the prince said with a smile in Tark's direction.

"I packed a small bag. It will be sufficient for now," Tark said. "There is also clothing on board the *Mystic7* for human females. We came prepared, not knowing if the females we rescued would have clothing."

"I'll gather the human females," Prince Drexyl said. "My mate will discuss their options with them and once we have them divided into groups, you're free to leave."

Tark led Suki out of the room and paused, waiting for Norkov. *Ready for a new adventure?*

Norkov grinned. *Always.*

I hope they treat my Suki well on Zelthrane-3; otherwise, I'm not sure I will be able to contain my temper. That won't do much for relations between the humans and our people.

Norkov patted his shoulder. *You will do fine, and everyone loves your Suki. You have nothing to fear.*

"Come, my sweet mate," Tark said, tugging on Suki's hand. "You should rest a bit more in case we leave soon. I'll make sure our things are packed and ready to go."

Back in their suite, Tark tucked Suki into bed, pressed a kiss to her brow, then made sure all of their things were ready. He wished he had Norkov's optimism over going to a new world, but past experience told Tark that the human females on Zelthrane-3 would likely fear him. He hated when that happened, since he would never hurt a female. They were precious and to be protected at all costs.

When he was finished, he noticed his sweet Suki was still awake, and was watching his every move. He smiled as he approached the bed, then removed his boots before stretching out next to her. She immediately curled into him, sighing in contentment. It still seemed impossible that such an amazing female would ask to be his, and yet she had. Regardless of where they lived, Tark would be thankful every day for the gift of his mate and their unborn child. They were both a treasure he'd thought would never be part of his life. If being on Zelthrane-3 made his Suki happy, then he would gladly remain there until the day he died. And perhaps it wouldn't be as bad as he feared. It sounded like a nice place to raise a family.

"You're thinking too hard," Suki said.

"Sorry, mate. I was thinking about our new home, and hoping that you'll be happy there."

She pressed a kiss over his heart. "I'll be happy as long as you're with me. I don't care where we live, Tark. I only need you."

He felt her fingers slide along the waistband of his pants before dipping inside. He grabbed her hand and stared at her. She'd nearly died, hadn't even been awake a full day. She needed rest, even if his cock had been hard since he'd joined her in the bath earlier. Suki's gaze lifted to his as she grew bolder. She pulled her hand free and unfastened his pants. Suki gripped his shaft, giving it a slight squeeze.

"Suki. Mate. We shouldn't."

"Please, Tark. I need you. I ache."

"You nearly died."

"It's not that kind of ache," she said. She released his cock, then grabbed his hand and put it between her thighs. "I hurt here. For you."

"My mate. I don't want to set back your recovery. What if I make things worse? You were unconscious for so long. You heard Healer. He said to rest."

Suki blinked at him, her eyes wide, and her lower lip protruded a little. He hated to deny her anything. Tark shifted so that Suki lay under him, and he slowly removed her clothes. Her nipples hardened and he groaned, staring at the tempting little buds. He licked his lips and leaned down, drawing one into his mouth. Suki cried out, her hands fisting his hair as he sucked on the tip. He toyed with her pussy. She was soft and slick, and getting wetter the more he touched and tasted her.

Tark switched to the other breast, giving her nipple a slight bite that had her gasping and arching into him. He lapped at the hard peak before tormenting the other side again. He worked his fingers into her tight channel, pumping them in and out, her cream coating the digits. Tark brushed his thumb over her clit and Suki's body went rigid before relaxing into the bed. She whimpered as her pussy gripped his fingers. Tark stroked her through her orgasm, and didn't stop playing with his sweet mate until she'd come twice more.

He withdrew his fingers and pressed a kiss to her forehead. "Now maybe you can rest."

"No! We're not done."

"Suki, please be reasonable."

"If you don't put your cock in me and fuck me

right now, I may never speak to you again." Her jaw tightened and she tipped her chin, glaring down her nose.

Tark tried not to smile and lost the battle.

Suki reached for him, working his pants down his hips enough that his cock and balls were free of the restrictive leather. She gripped his shaft and tugged until he shifted his hips and pressed the head of his cock against her wet slit.

"I need you, Tark. All of you."

Tark wrapped her hair around his fist and braced his weight on his forearm as he sank into her. He locked his gaze with hers as she stretched to accommodate him. Nothing felt as incredible as being inside his Suki. When he was balls deep, he held still a moment, just enjoying the feel of her wrapped around his shaft. He thrust, slow and steady, every stroke as deep as he could go.

It didn't feel right, taking his mate with his pants still on, but she didn't seem to mind. Her eyes darkened and her lips parted. The flush on her cheeks was enchanting. Tark wouldn't increase his pace, not even when she wrapped her legs around him and pressed her heels to his ass. He rocked into her, sweat slicking his skin from the effort not to take her harder, faster. Tark angled his pelvis on the next stroke and rubbed across her clit as he buried his cock in her pussy.

Suki bit her lip and grabbed his biceps, her nails digging into his skin. It only took a few more times of rubbing against her clit before she was coming. He closed his eyes a moment, breathing hard as he tried to gain control, but when she squeezed him tight with her pussy, he knew he'd lost the battle. His eyes flicked open and he growled as he pounded into her, unable to hold back another moment. Tark took her hard, fast, and so very deep. His hips snapped, his movements jerky as he came, filling her until his release ran out and soaked the bedding.

Tark remained buried inside her for a bit longer, kissing her sweetly. Suki twined her arms around his neck as her tongue brushed against his. The taste of her was enough to make him fully erect once more, but he wouldn't take her like a rutting beast. He started to withdraw, but Suki tightened her hold on him.

"No. Please."

"Suki." He kissed her tenderly. "I don't want to wear you out. Being with you is amazing, and I would take you all day and all night if I could, but I don't think it's in your best interest. You need to finish healing."

"Take your pants off, then kneel on the bed," she said.

He narrowed his eyes a moment, but slipped free of her body and did as she said. His mate gave him the sweetest smile before turning and showing him her back. He didn't understand what she wanted, until she backed toward him, and then sat down, his cock sliding inside her again.

"If you're worried I'll work too hard, you can put your arm around my waist and help. Or you can just grab a boob and enjoy the ride," she said.

"Suki, I don't think..." And then she started moving, and he really *couldn't* think. From this angle, he could go deeper than before. After she sank onto his shaft a fourth time, Tark's control snapped. He pressed forward, pushing her onto her knees, and he fucked her like a beast. The exact thing he hadn't wanted to do. He drove into her, his cock kissing the mouth of her womb with every stroke.

Tark reached for her breast and pinched her nipple, giving it a slight twist as he tried to maintain his balance and Suki screamed as her pussy clamped down tight and she came so hard she soaked him.

"Is this what you wanted?" he demanded. "To be fucked? To be taken hard?"

"Yes. Oh, yes. Please, Tark!"

He didn't stop driving into her until she came again, and then he spilled inside of her. His breathing was ragged and sawed in and out of his lungs. Shame filled him when he realized what he'd done. Withdrawing from his mate, he looked away. Pain filled him.

"Tark?" Suki pressed her palm to his cheek. "What's wrong?"

"I fucked you like… like you were a whore, and not my mate." Bile rose in his throat.

"No. No, Tark. I loved what you did, how it felt. The fact it was you and not some random male who paid for me? That makes all the difference in the world. It's okay for things to get out of control, to get a little wild. I loved that you lost control."

He glanced at her, trying to decide if she was telling the truth or merely trying to soothe him. Would she lie about something like that?

"Tark." She pressed a kiss to his lips. "I love you. You're mine, and I'm yours. Nothing we do together in bed is ever wrong. I like it when you're slow and tender, and I also like it when you're rough. My sweet, sexy cyborg… as long as it's you fucking me, then I'm going to love whatever you do. And if I don't, or something hurts, I'll tell you."

Tark gathered her in his arms and breathed in her scent. "I never want to do anything to hurt you."

"Then don't pull away from me, not even

emotionally."

"I love you," he murmured. "You're the best thing that ever happened to me, Suki."

"Let's get cleaned up and rest until it's time to leave."

Tark nodded his agreement and helped her off the bed before following her into the bathroom. As long as his Suki wasn't upset, then Tark was happy. He would do anything for her, even fuck her like a beast if that's what she needed.

Chapter Ten

One Month Later
Zelthrane-3

Suki stretched and reached for Tark, but his side of the bed was empty. She should have known he was gone, since she hadn't woken up wrapped in his arms. Light filtered through the window and she rolled out of bed. Padding across the room, she peered out at the world around her. The suite they'd taken as their home was spacious, and Malin had been correct, it had an incredible view. She could see most of the city.

It had originally belonged to one of the scientists who now lived on Earth. The entire floor was theirs, and the space had been renovated to accommodate a large family. If they had more than one child, they would have plenty of bedrooms. Even though Suki had been skeptical about coming here, she had to admit that she loved her new home. Not just the penthouse, but the city itself. She hadn't seen so many humans in a long time, at least not walking around freely.

While Suki still preferred to keep to herself for the most part, she'd made a few friends. The Chief Councilor's mate was really sweet, and Suki found it amazing that the woman didn't allow her lack of hearing to keep her from doing whatever she wanted. She'd been attempting to learn sign language so she could communicate with Charlotte and Borgoz's daughter, Arabella. Jacie had become a good friend as well, even though she stayed busy with her four children.

Suki washed and dressed. Pulling her hair back into a braid, she tied off the end and slipped on her shoes. A gorgeous day was too hard to pass up, especially for someone who had been locked up for so many years. As she exited the building, Suki closed her eyes and smiled, lifting her face to the suns. A warm breeze teased her hair and brought a sweet scent with it.

"Suki!"

She opened her eyes and smiled wider when she saw Jennifer and young Wareck heading toward her. She'd met Jennifer and Siril on her first day on Zelthrane-3, along with the other council members. It had surprised her to learn that Siril, a member of the council, was blind. She hadn't wanted to pry, but she'd been curious how it happened. During lunch with Jennifer one day, the woman had noticed Suki watching Siril and she'd explained that the councilman had lost his sight during a battle. He'd once been a revered warrior among his people and feared across the galaxies.

"Morning, Jennifer!" She waved. "And how are you today, Wareck?"

The little boy shyly looked up at her and smiled.

"We were going to the diner for breakfast and thought we'd see if you wanted to join us," Jennifer said. "Tark is with the council. I heard he left before you woke and thought you might be lonely."

"It was sweet of you to come by," Suki said.

"You keep to yourself too much. I promise we don't bite. Besides, there's someone I want you to meet."

Suki tried to contain her sigh. She knew Jennifer meant well, but sometimes being around so many people was a little overwhelming. Nodding, she fell in step next to her new friend.

The city was busy, but despite the ever-growing population, they didn't have issues like pollution, or litter. Terran Prime was the cleanest city Suki had ever seen, considering all the things around to do, and the vehicles that hovered over the city as they zipped from one place to another. Most of those in the city proper walked everywhere they went. Suki didn't mind. She liked to stretch her legs and enjoy the fresh air. Despite the greenery on the planet, it seemed to seldom rain.

Suki followed Jennifer and Wareck into the diner. A scarred warrior sat at a table with a woman who appeared to be just as damaged physically, and a very cute little girl sat beside her. The girl colored on a piece of paper and didn't even look up, but the way her head was tilted, Suki could see how beautiful she was.

"Beren. Rena. This is Suki. She's mated to one of the cyborgs assisting the council," Jennifer said.

"Hi," Suki said.

"I thought you might like to meet Rena, since she was also a slave," Jennifer said.

Suki was in the process of sitting and the shocking statement made her land hard on the bench seat. "What?"

Rena nodded. "My scars are from my old master. But Ryx came to make a trade and ended up taking me back to his ship, where I met Beren."

Suki glanced at the little girl and Wareck, knowing better than to ask the question on the tip of her tongue. *Were you a whore too?* Not that it was something she should ask anyway. Some things were better kept to herself.

"Tark, my mate, found me at a..." Her gaze shifted to the kids again. "A trading post."

Rena gave her a sympathetic smile and Suki knew she understood.

"While a lot of the mates here came through the Bridal program, you'd be surprised how many didn't.

Most weren't in our situation," Rena said, "but they suffered in their own way."

"I thought you and Rena might have enough in common that maybe you could be close friends," Jennifer said. "I know that being in a strange place can be unsettling, and your mate is very busy. You aren't alone here, Suki. You can visit with any of the mates anytime. We welcome drop-ins."

Rena nodded. "Definitely."

Were they right? Had she been hiding herself away too much? Suki had thought she was just overwhelmed, but maybe it was something more. Maybe she was just scared. Earth had been her home nearly all her life, and after that had been a nightmare. She hadn't been on Xpashta long enough to really call it her home, and while Zelthrane-3 was nice, it was almost too much at times.

"I guess I have been hiding," she admitted. "I'm not sure I remember how to act around people. I haven't had a friend in so long."

Jennifer reached out and placed her hand over Suki's. "Just be yourself. None of us bite. I was a single mom on Earth until Siril brought me here. Rena was sold when she was just a kid. Charlotte was given to Borgoz as part of a contract with a powerful politician on Earth. She was miserable before Borgoz fell in love with her. We all support one another. You don't have to be alone, Suki."

Suki's throat grew tight with unshed tears. "Thank you."

Rena smiled widely. "I think someone is looking for you."

Suki turned and saw Tark entering the diner. His gaze scanned the room until it locked on her. He moved with a warrior's grace as he drew nearer, then pulled up a chair and joined them. She reached for his hand, feeling the warmth of his palm seep into her.

"I was told I might find you here," he said.

"Are you done for the day?"

He nodded. "It was a productive council session. I think my people will be pleased."

"We haven't ordered yet if you'd like to join us," Beren said. "The females were too busy talking to look at the menu."

Tark chuckled. "I could eat."

The look he cast her way left Suki with no doubt he wasn't referring to food, and her cheeks warmed. Jennifer snickered and Rena looked like she was fighting a smile, neither missing the look. Beren smirked and turned his gaze away.

"Maybe you should get something to go," Jennifer suggested. "Enjoy your free afternoon and have a picnic in your home."

"Picnic?" Tark asked.

"You could spread a blanket on the floor, maybe near those lovely floor to ceiling windows in the living room, and enjoy your lunch in peace and quiet," Jennifer said.

"I think I like that idea," Tark said, rising. "I'll place an order and we can go."

As he walked off, Rena and Jennifer giggled.

"I don't think it's food he's interested in," Jennifer said.

Beren turned back toward them. "Really? As if any male would be thinking of food when his mate is so near, especially one who is expecting. Human females get even hotter and wetter inside when they're pregnant and turned on. Extra hormones."

Rena smacked him on the arm. "Not appropriate talk for lunch."

He shrugged, but Suki could see the humor lurking in his eyes.

When Tark returned to the table, he held a bag in his hand and reached for Suki with his other. She went with him willingly, and pressed close to his side as they walked through the streets back to their home. She pulled a blanket off the bed and spread it near the windows in the living room. Tark knelt on the edge of it, pulling the food from the bag and setting it out.

Suki went to their kitchen and got them each a drink before sitting next to her mate. They ate in silence, but there were more than a few heated looks exchanged between them. Suki had barely swallowed the last bite of her food before Tark had pinned her beneath him. She smiled up at her mate and ran her fingers through his hair. The weight of his body pressed against her, but he was careful not to hurt her. Tark was *always* careful when it came to Suki, and she loved him for it.

"Now that I've provided food to satisfy your belly, there's another part of you I'd like to…"

She giggled and covered his mouth. "Just get naked."

Tark winked and rolled off her, stripping off his clothes in record time. Suki pulled hers off as well, then held out her hands to her mate. Tark knelt between her splayed thighs and leaned down to kiss her, his lips nearly devouring hers. When he pulled away, she pulled her knees to her chest, slid her feet up his torso then draped her ankles over his shoulders.

Tark's gaze lowered to her pussy and heat flared in his eyes. He shifted his weight and she felt his cock brush against her slit. Without warning, he plunged deep and hard, filling her. Suki cried out and grabbed fistfuls of the blanket, her nipples tightening and need pulsing through her.

"Yes! Take me, Tark! Hard and deep. Fuck me."

He growled and narrowed his eyes. She'd learned he hated when she called it fucking, but sometimes that's exactly what a woman needed. He powered into her, his cock slamming into her wet pussy over and over. Suki tossed her head as she felt her orgasm drawing close. There were times she nearly came the moment he entered her. This would be one of the times she came quickly, but she knew Tark would never be satisfied giving her only one release. He always left her weak and sated.

"More," she begged.

Tark leaned back, spreading his knees and gripping her hips. His hips bucked, and every stroke of his cock made her gasp and plead for him to never stop. It amazed her that a man who had never been with a woman before her could turn her inside out so quickly. But he rocked her world every time they were together. He'd been a quick study, and she had no doubt that soon he would be the master and she'd be the student.

His body tensed and with every driving thrust, he pulled her hips toward him, not just fucking her with his cock but using her body to go even deeper. Suki screamed out her release and moments later felt the hot splash of Tark's release filling her.

His chest heaved and glistened with sweat. Suki smiled up at him and reached out to tweak his nipple. Tark growled, but there was affection in his gaze.

"You know, the doctor here said that pregnancy can make women want lots of sex," she said.

"Is that so?"

Suki grinned. "Lots and lots."

Her cyborg was still hard, even though his

release was leaking out around the shaft still buried in her pussy. He gave her a few strokes, then abruptly pulled out and flipped her over. Suki gave a squeak of surprise. Tark lifted her hips and slammed into her again.

"Oh, God. Tark, I... Oh, fuck."

He fisted her hair and took her like a man possessed. No matter how many times he made her come, she'd always want just one more. Even when her legs gave out, and she was seconds from passing out from exhaustion, she still craved his touch.

Tark grabbed her breast and played with her nipple, twisting and pinching, until she was screaming her way through another orgasm. When he came for the second time, he kept his body joined with hers, but lay on his side with her wrapped in his embrace. He kissed the top of her head and murmured words of love.

Suki might have thought her life was over the day aliens abducted her, but really it had just been beginning. If they hadn't sold her, she never would have met Tark, and he was perfect for her in every way. The longer they were together, the more confident he became in the bedroom and around her in general. The shy, unsure cyborg she'd met, the one who had feared she would reject him, was long gone. The warrior who proudly stood next to her, fucked her until she passed out, was the most incredible guy she'd ever met. And he was hers.

"I love you, my mate," he murmured.

"I love you too, Tark. So very much."

"Sleep, my Suki. After some rest, I'll make you beg for my cock some more."

Suki smiled and closed her eyes. Her life might not have been perfect, but it had given her a perfect guy. For a guy who had never touched a woman before, Tark knew exactly how to make Suki scream his name again and again. Although, she did wonder if there was such a thing as death by orgasm. Was it possible to come too much? Suki sighed and pressed a hand to her belly. An incredible man. New friends. And a baby on the way. Suki didn't think it was possible to be happier than she was now, and she couldn't wait to see what tomorrow would bring.

Jessica Coulter Smith

Award-winning author Jessica Coulter Smith has been in love with the written word since she was a child writing her first stories in crayon. Today she's a multi-published author of over seventy-five novellas and novels. Romance is an integral part of her world and she firmly believes that love will find you at the right time, even if Mr. Right is literally out of this world. Harley Wylde is the "wilder" side of award-winning author Jessica Coulter Smith.

Series in the Intergalactic Multiverse:
Intergalactic Affairs
Includes
- Vaaden Captives
- Vaaden Warriors
- Intergalactic Loyalties

Intergalactic Brides
Cy-Con

Jessica at Changeling: changelingpress.com/jessica-coulter-smith-a-144

Changeling Press E-Books

More Sci-Fi, Fantasy, Paranormal, and BDSM adventures available in e-book format for immediate download at ChangelingPress.com -- Werewolves, Vampires, Dragons, Shapeshifters and more -- Erotic Tales from the edge of your imagination.

What are E-Books?

E-books, or electronic books, are books designed to be read in digital format -- on your desktop or laptop computer, notebook, tablet, Smart Phone, or any electronic e-book reader.

Where can I get Changeling Press E-Books?

Changeling Press e-books are available at ChangelingPress.com, Amazon, Apple Books, Barnes & Noble, and Kobo/Walmart.

Changeling Press, LLC

ChangelingPress.com